THE AFTERLIFE
OF A DISASTER

A Novel

ARIA SKY

THE AFTERLIFE OF A DISASTER

Copyright © 2026 by Aria Sky

All rights reserved. No part of this book may be reproduced in any form or by any electronic or mechanical means, including information storage and retrieval systems, without permission in writing from the publisher, except by a reviewer who may quote brief passages in a review.

This is a work of fiction. While the narrative is inspired by the author's lived experiences, names, characters, places, and incidents are either the products of the author's imagination or are used in a fictionalized manner. Any resemblance to actual persons, living or dead, or actual events is entirely coincidental.

First Edition: January 2026

Cover Design by Aria Sky

ISBN: 9798244502541

Published in the United Kingdom.

For the disasters worth keeping.

Contents

Chapter 1 – The Rebuilding Phase 1

Chapter 2 – A Dance Number 11

Chapter 3 – The Great Blackout of 2012 20

Chapter 4 – Home Comforts 32

Chapter 5 – The Freezing Summer of 2012 42

Chapter 6 – Olden Handcuffs 54

Chapter 7 - 2004-2007: The Four-Year, Three-Ring Circus 68

Chapter 8 - Detox 79

Chapter 9 – The Uncovered Inventory of 2018 89

Chapter 10 – Indecent Exposure 98

Chapter 11 – The Fifteen-Year Itch of 2019 108

Chapter 12 – The Disney Princess.................117

Chapter 13 – The First Ending (2005)...........127

Chapter 14 – Legally Bland 136

Chapter 15 – The Widower..............................147

Chapter 16 – English Opening........................157

Chapter 17 – The Third Ending (2016) 167

Chapter 18 – The Black Dahlia 175

Chapter 19 – Modern Defence........................185

Chapter 20 – A Breakthrough.........................196

Chapter 21 – The Red Shoe Diaries 205

Chapter 22 – The Hangover...........................214

Chapter 23 – Passing The Torch 222

Chapter 24 – Quadratic Equation..................229

Chapter 25 - Icarus..247

Chapter 26 – The Red Wedding, 2022 262

Chapter 27 – Artificial Reality.......................277

Chapter 28 – The Second Ending (2016) 287

Chapter 29 – Croesi Ffiniau 300

Chapter 30 – Frankfurt, 2004 310

Chapter 31 – Fresh Eyes.................................323

Chapter 32 – Stockholm, 2008.......................337

Chapter 33 - Amsterdam 352

Chapter 34 – Budapest to Warsaw, 2009........370

Chapter 35 – Ebb and Flood 387
Chapter 36 – The Green Wedding, 2022 398
Chapter 37 – This Too Shall Pass 409
Chapter 38 – The Beginning 419
Acknowledgements 429
Resources and Support: The Map for Your Afterlife 431
A Letter from the Author 435
About The Author 447

Chapter 1 – The Rebuilding Phase

"All religion is a mental illness."

Daisy scrolled past the tweet, pausing mid-swipe. *And… we're off.*

The screen's blue light cast jagged shadows on the walls of her flat, where the paint had peeled into ghostly shapes, revealing the plaster beneath. The last time she'd bothered with a tin of paint, the walls in here hadn't even existed.

"You can't say things like that, you'll offend someone!"

The clock on her phone read 11:58 am. Far too early for this.

"It's true, though. I can prove it."

She exhaled smoke through her nose, watching the replies pile up like cars in a crash. *Predictable. Pathetic. Accurate.*

"It's a form of schizophrenia. Think about it – psychosis, delusions, hallucinations, disorganised thinking, disorganised behaviour. They want to control how women dress while forcing kids to read about rape and incest. It's textbook."

Daisy's mouth twitched. *Not wrong.* She took a drag, the cigarette burning down to her fingers.

"You're crazy."

Maybe they were all crazy, she thought, *and this was just the forum to prove it.*

"The DSM-V says I'm not."

"The DSM-IV says you are."

Christ, the pedantry. She could hear the keyboard warriors foaming at the mouth.

"Look, at best, religion is a mental illness, at worst it's a cult."

Daisy got distracted by sudden shouting. Somewhere outside, a pair of crackheads were arguing.

"You're going to get cancelled."

Hasn't everyone been cancelled already?

"So, the fuck what? I've got actual Nazis trying to exterminate me, but you think I'm worried about a cult that supports paedophiles?"

Daisy's thumb hovered over the reply box. *Almost.* Almost worth it to jump in and watch the meltdown. But then—

A cat jumped on the windowsill, long enough to distract Daisy from the online chaos. A black cat. Cute, but foreboding, if you believed in that kind of thing.

"You've got to stop calling everyone you don't like a Nazi."

"I don't. Sometimes I call them fascists."

That escalated into nonsense quickly. She chuckled to herself, flicking ash out of the window.

"What's the difference between a fascist and a Nazi?"

And there it was, the millionth iteration of the million-dollar question on the internet that hour.

"A fascist demands that everyone think and act like them. To be a Nazi, you have to actually join the Nazis."

She typed: *"Congrats, you played yourself."*

Deleted it. *Christ.*

Daisy dropped her phone on the bed, twitching as if she could feel the phantom vibrations of the debate. She had to stay online, of course. The last dregs of her career depended on it.

She'd never admit it publicly, but she was just about old enough to remember when people could have political differences without screaming at each other through a four-inch screen. She'd also never admit that her career was over.

When they say that 'life begins at 40,' they never tell you what that means for the people who've been internally dead for 20 years. Rebirth?

Looking for a distraction, Daisy headed for the bathroom. She needed to shave. Again.

Daisy had already sampled rebirth. Or, at least, transformation. Less a religious experience and more an attempt to quiet the voices in her head and seek some kind of psychological and spiritual absolution. Clarity. A chance to 'be her true self.'

She decided she couldn't let the stubble sit there and set about filling the sink. Her 'true self,' she thought, looking down at the £3 dress from Wish that barely fit, was more of a desperate, miserable misanthrope, with two degrees and two decades of employment, trying to find her place in a world that deemed her less than human.

As she shaved, she considered her plans for the day; she was supposed to be looking for work, but she'd given up all hope that anyone was going to hire her. All fun and games until they looked at her CV and figured out that she was either too qualified or too 'mature' for them to reasonably believe they could get away with paying her slave – sorry, minimum – wage.

Her ex had hated her clean-shaven. She'd hated herself stubbly. They'd had fights about it.

On the rare occasion she did get an interview, it usually took the interviewer less than a minute to figure out that Daisy had been born male and desperately start trying to find a way to get things over and done with without leaving them open to a discrimination suit.

At a loss for a plan for the day that didn't end in abject disappointment, she turned to AI for a solution – apparently, everyone's go-to for every problem under the sun; from using it as a therapist to doing creative projects to making up bullshit inspirational slop to make you sound productive on LinkedIn. *"I wake up at 3:11 am every day, and I don't eat breakfast, drink coffee, shower or shit. Rise and grind. Don't just do Taxidermy, BE TAXIDERMY."*

Fuck off.

"What do most 40-year-old women want from life?" she asked the omnipotent machine, getting up to make a coffee.

"Most 40-year-old women aren't a monolith," the robot began. Daisy snorted. *Here we go.*

"But around 40, priorities shift from chasing every possibility to focusing on what matters most."

This promised to be a treasure trove of cis privilege. Perhaps she should eat breakfast.

"They want fulfilment and purpose, a career or vocation that feels meaningful."

Well, that was something she could do.

She set about making breakfast. Well, toast.

What were her options?

OnlyFans account? It was hardly meaningful, but at least she'd be doing the internet's army of incels a favour by helping them get their first look at tits. That's charity work, right?

"Financial security, freedom from money stress."

What, in this economy? Are you having a laugh, love? She laughed sharply to herself, using the last of the butter on her toast.

"Deeper relationships; strong, supportive friendships that go beyond superficial chit-chat."

A forty-year-old with friends? That's how you know a robot has watched too much television.

She noticed the old family photo, fallen again – her ex, *him*, their kids – back when he was pretending. Her youngest had been gone from her life for years now, a shadow in her memory, after a venomous email about 'God's plan' and 'the love and kindness that came with it.'

The oldest was living halfway across the country.

She resurrected it whilst shoving a slice of toast into her mouth.

Happy families.

The glass was cracked.

"Romantic relationships built on mutual respect and emotional safety."

She found herself laughing out loud at the very notion that people still respected each other. *"Emotional safety"* had to be a joke at her expense, right?

"A good connection with family that nurtures, rather than drains."

Okay, one out of five. She had a family that called sometimes.

"Feeling physically strong and energetic enough to enjoy life."

She lit a cigarette – her third in the past half-hour – and tried to summon the energy to find the TV remote.

"Managing perimenopause symptoms and prioritising wellbeing without apology."

Shit, injection day.

Daisy fucking hated hormone injections, but because she knew she was going to die on a 50-year NHS waiting list, she had to buy DIY hormones, and that meant homebrew oestrogen injections or trying to con an online pharmacy into selling her oestrogen pills.

"Less focus on pleasing everyone else…"

How much more focus do you want? She turned on the TV.

Daisy tried to think of a single woman she'd ever met who actually had that option.

She drew a blank. If she did think of one, they certainly weren't a trans woman.

"Adventure and growth: travel, new hobbies, learning new skills. Embracing new chapters or changing careers; moving cities or starting fresh in unexpected ways."

She couldn't tell if this was AI or an influencer. The robot was about three sentences away from sending her a message on Facebook saying, '*Hey sis, haven't seen you since school. Want to hear about how I found financial freedom through owning my own business?*' followed by some bullshit about the pyramid scheme that she had bought into.

"At 40, many women are balancing the 'building' phase of life (career, family, finances) with a growing desire to make the next decades more intentional and joyful – and they often have both the experience and courage to go after it!"

Wait… Was Daisy supposed to have a 'building' phase of her life?

"Does having two kids, doing a stint in rehab and ending up unemployable at 40 count as a 'building' phase?" she asked the robot.

'Two kids' was generous. She'd fathered two, only one acknowledged her existence. He'd found religion and all the love and kindness that came with it.

"It can, but it's more of a rebuilding *phase than the typical "building" phase people mean in midlife discussions,"* said the robot, followed by more bullshit influencer positivity, then an offer: *"If you want, I can give you a realistic roadmap for a 'rebuilding at 40' phase that factors in kids, recovery and employment challenges. That might make it feel less abstract."*

Sure, why not? It wasn't like she had any other ideas.

Realistically, she was procrastinating. Half-unpacked boxes everywhere, a year later. She'd hoped it was temporary. Cute.

The robot returned with the plan. Stabilise finances, secure housing, maintain sobriety, take a skills inventory, retraining, prune toxic connections, find a 'team,' tap into resources, *'create the new normal.'*

Well, nobody said she had to come up with the entire system herself, I suppose. This AI-generated influencer bullshit beat watching yet another movie.

She'd switched to the Hallmark Channel, where a perky blonde cis girl was falling in love with a small-town baker who looked like he'd never known suffering.

Daisy played with her hair. It needed washing.

The baker's smile was *too white*, his life *too easy*. What would happen if he'd lost his kids, his home, his *name?* If he woke up one day and realised that he'd spent a decade pretending to be someone else just to survive?

"Must be nice," she muttered.

The laughter track from next door's sitcom grated like nails on a chalkboard.

She changed the channel. Contemplated asking more questions of the robot.

Then again, if she wanted to hear empty slogans and motivational nonsense, she could always go to an AA meeting. It had been a couple of weeks.

She should go to a meeting, shouldn't she? Even if it was going to be another painful admission of failure.

She saved the chat. Might as well try it out.

Fine, robot, rebuild me.

Wait, did that fucker call her '*mid-life*'?

Chapter 2 – A Dance Number

'Stabilising finances' sounds great in theory, but dreams and reality are often at odds when you put them into a spreadsheet.

Daisy had about £1,000 a month coming in; from that, she was expected to find £850 to rent her shitty one-bedroom flat in a forgotten town where the streets were lined with quiet houses, their windows like empty eyes. The paint on the storefronts was peeling away, revealing layers of what used to be, and the church bells, once a call to service, now only tolled like a tired, conclusive thought.

Then she had to find £100 for her credit card, £45 for broadband and phone, £200 for electricity and gas, £80 for water, £100 for meds and £150 for the council to pay themselves handsomely whilst neglecting the town she lived in.

She'd never pretended to be a mathematician, but it doesn't take Excel or Carol Vorderman to look at these figures and know that the sum of her situation could charitably be described as fucked.

What they didn't show was the reality of checking her bank balance before buying eggs and doing the mental bookkeeping: *If I spend £2.50 on food today, can I buy toothpaste tomorrow?* It was heating one room at a time – if any. It was wearing her coat indoors until March, and making a loaf of bread last four extra days by cutting the slices as thin as possible.

It was the shame of getting to checkouts and having the card fail, the shop assistant's look of pity mixed with mild irritation. It was rationing toilet rolls and evaluating whether she could afford to wash her hair this week, or if dry shampoo and a prayer would have to suffice until Friday.

Most humiliating of all, it was the Sunday phone calls to her mother, dancing around the subject of money like a diplomatic hostage negotiation. *"How are you managing?"* Always asked with enough concern to make the unspoken offer clear, and enough judgement to make accepting it feel like admitting failure as an adult human being.

She looked back at her youth; she was promised by the adults around her and the people in power that she only had to go to university and get a shiny degree, and she'd never have to worry about financial security in her life.

If she'd known that everybody is perpetually full of shit at 15, maybe she wouldn't be perpetually in the shit at 40.

The numbers were clear, though, as they often were. She was going to have to find another £700 a month to be able to live in poverty. Not fuck about with avocado toast – whatever that was – or buying a venti matcha caramel soy fifteen pump latte with extra pretension or whatever middle-class journalists in their seventies imagined her generation was doing with their money rather than paying to rent one of the 12 houses they bought for a fiver when Thatcher's government sold off all the council housing.

She turned to her computer to have a look at this week's mediocre offerings in the local job market and after realising that the same ten firms were offering the same ten jobs in her field of study – law – that they'd been advertising for months and never responded to her application for, she decided to once again let a dream die and see what was out there.

The application process was a ritual of self-flagellation. Open laptop. Browse Indeed. Feel the spark of initial hope at a job title that doesn't sound soul-destroying. Read requirements: *'5 years' experience preferred.'* Click apply anyway. Craft a cover letter explaining why her law degree and desperate enthusiasm should compensate for lacking exactly the tenure she needed this job to gain.

Each application was an exercise in creative writing, transforming her university dissertation on equalities' law into 'extensive research skills' and that year she'd spent working at a firm into 'proven legal administration background.' She'd perfected the art of making desperation sound like passion, and unemployment look like an exciting career pivot.

Whenever she hit 'send,' there'd be that treacherous moment of optimism. Maybe this time. Maybe they'd see past the CV gaps and the Google results. Maybe today would be the day her luck changed.

She refreshed her email obsessively, jumping at every notification. Even spam felt promising until she opened it.

She spent the afternoon sending out applications anyway. Bartending, shop work, anything that might pay the bills. Within days, the responses started coming in.

She'd begrudgingly sent applications to the usual suspects – paralegal work, admin roles, anything making use of her law degree. In return, identical form emails within hours: *"Thank you for your interest, but we've decided to pursue other candidates."*

Translation: *we Googled you.*

The rejections had their own cruel taxonomy. The instant, automated responses – at least they were honest about not considering her. And the special category of insult: rejections for jobs that she was wildly overqualified for, as if being desperate made her unemployable even for work she could do blindfolded.

Each email hit like a small slap. After the fifteenth '*we've decided to pursue other candidates,*' is there a template they shared, or had universe had run out of creative ways to say '*fuck off?*'

An interview at a pub lasted exactly four minutes. She'd prepared for this one, researched the venue, practised answers about her customer service philosophy and why she'd be passionate about working in hospitality. She'd chosen her outfit carefully – presentable but not intimidating, approachable but not desperate.

The manager – a sweaty man with arms like Popeye – looked her up and down twice before she'd even sat down. The interview was a masterclass in barely-disguised prejudice. He asked if she had any 'history of handling difficult customers' whilst his eyes lingered on her chest, clearly trying to imagine what kind of difficulties she might encounter. Then came the questions about whether she'd be 'comfortable' in their 'lively' environment, whether she could 'handle the banter' with the regulars.

She watched his face change when she mentioned her law degrees, watched him recalculate whether she was desperate enough to tolerate whatever he had planned, or threatening enough to know her rights. The interview ended when he abruptly remembered they'd already filled the position, though she'd been called about it that morning.

She watched through the window as he interviewed the next candidate – a young girl who looked *barely* eighteen, who giggled at everything he said and seemed genuinely excited about the opportunity to serve drinks to local alcoholics for minimum wage.

But the humiliation came at what they generously described as 'a cowboy-themed performance venue'.

They literally called it an audition, like it was a West End revival of *Phantom*.

Well, Daisy could sing, and she could dance – even if she didn't have an arse to shake – and she was desperate for money. A glorified strip club was a step above OnlyFans, she supposed. So, she went along with it.

The venue looked exactly like what it was: a regular pub with some hay bales scattered around and a 'Saloon' sign that had clearly been bought from Amazon. The smell of stale beer and broken dreams hung in the air, and the bar had been fitted with a small stage that looked structurally questionable.

All dressed up for the hoe down, hoping she wouldn't give the 'down' part a bad name, she showed up for the 'audition' and knew within ten seconds that this wasn't going to be her day.

The other two lucky auditionees were gorgeous, skinny cis girls half her age; it was obvious that she wasn't going to be in the running for a job where the target market is horny old blokes looking for permission to ogle and touch up the youngest girls that they could find without getting banned from living near a school.

She completed the paperwork next to a girl who looked like she'd been poured into her costume by a benevolent god in pure service of the male gaze. Another was doing vocal warm-ups that would've made Idina Menzel jealous.

Daisy looked down at her own outfit – a costume that had seemed adequately western in her bedroom mirror but now screamed fancy-dress party reject next to the competition. She'd spent an hour on her makeup, trying to channel 'sultry cowgirl' but achieved something closer to 'middle-aged man playing dress-up.'

But you only live once, so she tried to let her chosen personality of the day shine and got up on that bar and sang and danced like she was Shakira's overweight understudy.

The moment that she stepped onto the stage, she could feel the judgement radiating from the small audience of staff and owners. Not hostile, exactly, but a polite discomfort reserved for watching someone embarrass themselves in public. She launched into her routine anyway – a rendition of "These Boots Are Made For Walkin'" that she'd practised until her neighbours had started banging on the walls.

Halfway through, she caught sight of herself in the mirror behind the bar. A forty-year-old trans woman in cowboy boots, singing Nancy Sinatra in a fake saloon while two teenagers watched with the sympathetic cringe usually reserved for X Factor auditions. Her voice kept going on its own, a show she was no longer directing. The moment hung in the air, a slow-motion disaster as her brain charted the inevitable crash.

She finished strong anyway, because if you're going to humiliate yourself, you may as well commit to it.

Predictably, she was not chosen.

The feedback was delivered with an artificial kindness that somehow made it worse. "You have a lovely voice, really, but we're looking for a slightly different energy."

Otherwise, known as too old, too weird, and not desperate enough to pretend this place isn't what it really is.

Arriving home from the audition, she practically tore off her cowgirl outfit and launched it onto one of the many piles of disorganised belongings in her tiny flat.

She opened up her laptop, determined to hit record and make a video where she'd scream into the void on YouTube about how the world was unfair, and her life was a mess and talk at length about the discrimination and the bullshit that she was going through, to put Cowboy Hooters on blast and set light to the bridge, unleashing her inner emo teenager in a bout of explosive, dramatic rage.

"You think I can't perform? I'll fucking perform!" she thought, "You think I can't draw people's attention? Fuck you!"

And then it hit her. They were probably right. She had two YouTube channels. Each got maybe fifty viewers on a good day. Nobody cared.

Well, almost nobody.

She cared.

She cared too much.

Suddenly, OnlyFans wasn't sounding like the worst idea she'd ever had.

Great, she was fucking crying. Again.

And then it hit her.

Rock Bottom Part 2: Electric Fucking Boogaloo.

She allowed herself to wallow in the feeling, just for a moment. Then, reigning it back in, she remembered that she'd been here before. From the bottom, the only way is up. Back to the grind. She'd never been afraid of hard work.

Chapter 3 – The Great Blackout of 2012

It was a night like any other Friday. The regulars lined the bar, making small talk about the music of their childhood, analysing the latest ale offerings or unloading their work-week frustrations.

Elsewhere, a group of students were engaging in a cheap booze-infused revision that only Oxford students can, a Kafkaesque combination of textbooks, notepads, empty bottles, with vague reminiscence of Geneva Convention-affronting traditions from Eton or Harrow… or Hogwarts.

A stag do was building a tower of empty shot glasses in one corner, a hen party – apparently unrelated to the stags

– shrieked and waved around various forms of novelty toys shaped like penises, in case anyone was ever in doubt about how straight they were.

This was Daisy's life before she became Daisy. He'd always been good at playing roles. Bartender. Father. Drunk. But the one he'd been born into – man – was the hardest sell.

As your friendly neighbourhood bartender, he poured the drinks, cracked jokes, facilitated the conversation and always happily accepted one for himself, even when he was struggling to stand upright.

"Time at the bar", he shouted, eliciting a Greek chorus of resigned groans from the assembled cast of variously pickled patrons.

Closing was his favourite part of the night. After hours of constant noise had assaulted his undiagnosed autistic senses like they were sparring with Mike Tyson, the end was near. The crowd would slowly disperse, the lights could finally come on, silence. Peace.

Relief.

"Open mic night at the Cape tonight, you coming?"

Shane. Friend and colleague, once a reasonably famous musician and now a legend in his own lunchtime.

Daisy checked his watch.

"Ah, fuck it, why not?"

When they arrived, the pub was busy. A few friends had met them there, and this was fixing to be a great night out.

They'd start here, inevitably move on to the Irish bar next door and then see where the night took them.

Within minutes, they had two shots of Jager down their necks and a pint in each hand, as an attractive young blonde with a beautiful guitar took the stage and started to strum away her pain with her fingers.

Daisy, Shane and their usual crew of miscreants said "cheers" to another night behind the bar in the books and settled in.

The rest came back in scattered fragments.

There was the Irish bar, definitely. He remembered the sticky floor under his feet and the sound of Shane ordering another round in his atrocious "Irish" accent. There was karaoke – Christ, always karaoke – and a hazy vision of standing on a table singing something by The Smiths while the room spun slowly around him.

After that, snapshots. A taxi driver refusing to take them somewhere. Walking through the city centre at 3 am, stumbling over cobblestones that seemed designed by a sadist. Shane puking into a bin whilst he held his hair back like they were teenage girls at a house party. The taste of kebab and regret.

A girl with red hair laughing at something he'd said - or thought he'd said. The bouncer at some club telling them to fuck off home. Shane trying to chat up a woman old enough to be their mother while he held onto a lamppost for balance. Falling asleep standing up in a taxi queue, then waking up when someone shook his shoulder to tell him the queue had moved.

Then nothing. A black hole where Saturday should've been, twelve hours excised.

Next thing Daisy knew, it was Sunday morning.

Coming around slowly, like in a cartoon, he felt his head pounding like Woody Woodpecker had got loose with a jackhammer. He slowly rolled over and slid on his glasses… then it hit him in a wave.

First, the abdominal pain. A violent stabbing from somewhere deep within his very essence demanded as rapid a sprint to the bathroom as he could muster.

The journey to the bathroom was an odyssey of agony. Every step sent shockwaves through his skull, and his stomach felt like it was trying to digest a live grenade. He ricocheted off the door frame, nearly fell down the stairs, and barely made it to the bathroom before his body decided to stage a full-scale revolt.

Unsure of the direction of travel, he stripped off what few clothes he was wearing and jumped directly into the bathtub just in time for a full horror show.

The violence of it was breathtaking. His body expelled everything he'd consumed in the past month, retching until he thought he'd turn inside out. Between waves, he gasped for air like he was drowning, sweat pouring down his face and mixing with tears he didn't even remember starting to cry.

But it wasn't the explosive vomit or the uncontrollable colonic surge that caught his attention – as much as anything could, anyway – it was the never-ending stream of red piss that came flowing out.

Not pink. Not slightly discoloured. Bright fucking red, like he was pissing cherry Tango. The shade of red that makes your primitive brain start screaming danger signals even through the fog of the worst hangover in recorded history.

Daisy was not a doctor, but he knew enough to know that red piss is serious.

Slamming the power button on the shower, he felt the warm water stabbing at his body and tried to ignore the tapping on his shaven head – a perfectly ordinary sensation amplified by the hangover to feel as though it was a tap-dancing class for baby elephants.

He sat down in the bathtub, even among the remnants of the filth that had recently formed vital parts of his constitution and contemplated his current predicament.

He was 27 years old with no memory of the events that had led him to this exact moment.

In a moment of inspired panic, he began to check his abdomen for bruises. Perhaps he'd got in a fight?

Nothing. No marks, no evidence of external trauma. Just the internal carnage of a body that had said "enough".

Was he spiked? Who knows? It's not like he'd ever found a drug he wouldn't take voluntarily anyway.

This wasn't exactly his first rodeo.

He'd endured his first hangover at 14, the night of the Millennium. His parents had left him alone at home – he was, after all, too old and cool to be hanging out with his parents' friends – with permission to have a couple of beers from his father's collection.

When the smoke of the unfulfilled promise of technological apocalypse cleared, he woke up naked and cold from a sleep in a shopping trolley outside the local supermarket. Somehow, he found his way home, spending three days sick from what had been two cases of Belgian lager, not "a couple of beers."

Yes, he knew this feeling well.

He even knew the common thread.

It was no secret among his circle of friends that he had something of an affinity for alcohol. It had been politely suggested to him a couple of years previously that he might want to look into quitting drinking.

He attended his first 12-step meeting that night, in his mid-20s, in a church hall near the pub in which he worked.

He walked in slowly, full of trepidation. Fear, he supposed.

Until he looked around the room. Every other human being in the room was north of 60. The man speaking was in his eighties.

That was the answer he needed: he couldn't be an alcoholic – he wasn't old enough.

So, he left and went straight back to the pub.

This day, though? This day felt different. He'd never pissed blood before. That wasn't normal.

He thought back to a vaguely remembered school biology lesson. Something about the kidneys removing toxins from the blood – or was that the liver? – and turning it into urine and... blood bad, maybe?

Fuck. He couldn't think with this hangover.

A fistful of ibuprofen later, he was on the bus to a hospital to visit the emergency department.

The bus journey was its own special kind of hell. Every pothole a personal attack, every brake and acceleration a deliberate attempt to make him vomit on a bus full of Sunday morning churchgoers who all looked disgustingly healthy and put-together. He spent twenty minutes staring at his reflection in the window, cataloguing the damage: grey skin, bloodshot eyes, wrinkled clothes, the general aura of someone who had made a series of catastrophically poor life choices.

The hospital waiting room was a purgatory of too-bright lights and plastic chairs. He answered the admin questions as best he could – his name and address were just about doable. Allergies? *Making sensible decisions*, he thought.

When they asked what was wrong with him, he could've given a laundry list, but kept it immediate. "Pissing blood."

He hoped the administrator had heard worse. She probably had.

A friendly doctor confirmed that blood was, in fact, not good. The doctor looked young enough to be his younger sister, but spoke with the weary authority of someone who'd seen this exact scenario hundreds of times before.

"So," she said, "consulting his chart, "how much would you say you drink in a typical week?"

The question every drinker dreads. He did the mental arithmetic, the painstaking evaluation of which truths to tell and which to creatively reinterpret. A bottle of wine is really only two glasses if you have big glasses. Shots don't count if you're working. Beer is basically bread.

"Maybe… twenty units?" he ventured. Nobody really knew how many units they drank, but it sounded like it was above average, yet conservative enough to avoid further suspicion.

After running a few tests – blood work that made him queasy to watch, questions about his drinking that made him want to lie more creatively – she confirmed Daisy's biggest fear: if you drink more alcohol, you will be dead.

Not "you might die" or "it's not good for you." You will be dead. A full stop.

"Your liver enzymes are through the roof," she explained, showing him numbers on a screen that meant nothing to him but everything to his survival. "Your kidneys are struggling to cope. Your body is poisoning itself."

Dead was permanent. No more Friday nights at the pub, no more of Shane's terrible jokes, no more anything.

Dead was a problem you couldn't drink away, couldn't laugh off, couldn't pretend wasn't happening until it went away.

Now, the prospect of not drinking felt less terrifying than the prospect of continuing.

But knowing something and accepting it are different things entirely. He spent Sunday night lying awake, staring at the ceiling and trying to process the word "dead" in relation to himself. Whenever he closed his eyes, he saw that bright red stream, heard the doctor's matter-of-fact voice: "You will be dead."

Monday morning, Shane called. "Mate, you missed your shift yesterday. Manager's going mental. Where were you?"

How do you explain that you were in the hospital, being told your liver is failing? How do you tell your drinking buddy that the foundation of your friendship might literally be killing you?

"Hospital," he said finally. "Can't drink any more. Doctor's orders."

No one spoke. The quiet hung between them, growing more awkward with each passing second until Shane finally cleared his throat, a small sound that felt as loud as a shout. "Right. Well. That's... fuck, mate. Are you alright?"

"Ask me in a few months."

After hanging up, he sat in his kitchen and stared at the bottle of whisky on the counter. Yesterday, he would have poured himself a drink to deal with the stress of that conversation. Today, that drink would be a death sentence with a Jameson's label.

The choice wasn't really a choice at all.

Later that day, a couple of bags of saline and some self-reflection later, he found himself once again standing outside the doors of a church hall, nervously smoking a cigarette and peering in at the meeting that was happening inside.

Now it felt different. Maybe it was the doctor's blunt delivery of his potential death sentence. Maybe it was the way his hands shook slightly when he thought about that bright red stream in his bathtub. Maybe it was that he'd run out of other options.

The building was featureless, like every church hall. Through the window, he could see a circle of people sitting in those stackable plastic chairs that seemed to be standard issue for every institutional building in Britain. Someone was talking, gesturing with animated emphasis that suggested either passion or madness.

He'd been standing there for ten minutes, working up the courage to either go in or leave, when the decision was made for him.

As he watched, the door flew open, and a young man also lit a cigarette. Some grunts and small talk later, and a query: "Are you here for the meeting?"

The man looked his age, maybe younger. Not the octogenarian crowd he'd encountered before. Normal clothes, normal face, someone you'd serve a drink to without thinking twice about whether they should be having it.

Standing there in the evening air, as if he was about to jump off a cliff. Everything in his life up to this point had been cushioned by alcohol - every social interaction, every difficult emotion, every boring Tuesday evening. The idea of facing it all stone-cold sober became emotional nudity in a snowstorm.

"Sure," pre-Daisy responded.

"Come inside."

An hour of largely meaningless platitudes later, he left with a book, a pile of phone numbers from strangers and a suggestion to keep coming back.

The meeting itself had been a revelation in the most mundane possible way. The people were… ordinary. Disappointingly boring. A teacher, a mechanic, a guy his own age.

They talked about "powerlessness" and "surrender" and "higher powers" with the casual familiarity of people discussing the weather. They shared stories about waking up in strange places, losing jobs, disappointed families, and making promises they couldn't keep. Stories that sounded uncomfortably familiar.

The woman who spoke first after he entered talked about pissing herself at her daughter's wedding. The mechanic shared about drinking mouthwash when he'd run out of everything else. The teacher, soft-spoken and wearing a cardigan that looked like it came from Marks & Spencer, described waking up in a police cell with no idea of how she'd got there.

These people had been exactly where he was and somehow made it out alive.

The man who'd invited him in – Dave, he'd learned, though it felt weird to put a name to the face – had fifteen years sober. Fifteen years. That seemed impossible, like claiming to have lived on Mars or spoken to the Queen. How do you fill fifteen years without alcohol? What do you do with your evenings, your weekends, your celebrations, your commiserations?

"How do you do it?" he'd asked after the meeting, genuinely baffled.

Dave laughed, not unkindly. "One day at a time, mate. Some days, one hour at a time. Some days, one minute at a time. Today, I just had to not have a drink today."

Walking out into the fresh air, he had no idea what came next. Unfortunately, 'figure out how to adult while sober' wasn't covered in any of the leaflets.

Chapter 4 – Home Comforts

The robot was not a success so far.

One interview, one failure.

Daisy, however, was not really a one-step-at-a-time kind of girl, so she decided to throw out another pile of half-arsed job applications and try and tackle her financial situation from another angle. After all, she reasoned, she was overpaying to live in a shithole, right?

Maybe she could find a cheaper shithole and figure out the rest?

She loaded up a browser and navigated her way into the local housing market; the worst part of this was always setting up the filters.

One bedroom, minimum. No studios. Eww.

No sharing. Anybody who knew Daisy knew that she should not be living with other people.

No retirement homes. Despite what the robot said, Daisy was not old.

No student homes. Even if Daisy was still a student, that sounded like hell. She absolutely did not miss the thieving roommates, the endless forced socialising, the drama and the random parties.

Daisy was 40. Not old. Not a child.

She was usually at home. Always, some would say. Her home was her safe space. Her place to be herself, unapologetically.

A place where nobody could judge her, a place where she could sleep until noon and do whatever she wanted without the need to play Barbie and dress herself up for the world.

Okay, Daisy knew that people had this idea of her as… abrasive. Prickly, even.

What people didn't know is that the Daisy they saw and the Daisy inside her head were practically two entirely separate people.

When it came to a home, Daisy had strict specifications:

A bedroom with a built-in wardrobe. And lots of space for all her many, many drawers of clothes. A place for a TV, so she could use it as white noise to drown out the inner monologue of perpetual disappointment and sleep.

Room for a king-sized bed, because she liked having a massive bed.

The living room had to have room for her desk, specifically near (but not facing) a window for light whilst recording. Room for a sofa.

Room for her bookcases, and all the books that didn't fit in the bookcases.

The kitchen needed room to cook in. She'd lived in a flat once with a kitchen with no prep space, and she'd hated it for three years, even though almost everything else was perfect.

And the bathroom. The most important piece of her search. Call her old-fashioned – but never, ever fucking old, Mr. Robot – but a bathroom should contain a bath. She liked a bath.

Soothing bubbles for her back and far less risk of shredding herself to ribbons when attempting to shave her legs.

Daisy had uncompromising standards for everything these days. Homes, jobs, people. Easier to blame the world for not meeting her expectations than admit she might be the problem. Easier to control the criteria than risk the disappointment.

She closed her eyes for a moment, picturing bubbles and steam, before forcing herself back to the listings. The robot demanded it.

Entering her arbitrary, reduced-price range returned few results.

First, a maisonette in a pub conversion. Ground floor, reasonable location... but the kitchen/living combo (ugh) was basically a corridor. And the bathroom contained no bath.

Pass.

Someone trying to sell four flats in one ad. Three studios, one actual flat with a bedroom, pictures of all of them jumbled together in the advert.

Yeah, no, even with bills included, that was a hard no. Maybe.

Fuck it, she'd enquire. Bills included, in this economy? This was probably a scam anyway.

Next... Weird flat, no light, on a hill, shower, no bath... No.

OK, another house on a hill. Huge living room. Tiny bedroom, but she could maybe make that work. No floor plan (of course, why expect estate agents to make that much effort?) ... Bathtub. Fifty quid a month cheaper.

Details requested.

Daisy was a big believer in the rule of three. You apply for three, and at least one of the agents gets back to you. If three agents eventually get back to you, one might not look at you like a child molester.

She needed one more.

A garage conversion?

Bold. Quirky. Crazy.

Enormous kitchen with a breakfast bar… and an odd, closeable living room/bedroom combo on a second floor.

A *second floor?*

Daisy hadn't lived somewhere with two floors since she was… drinking.

And there it was, the catch. A "shower room". Ugh. Showers reminded her of IV drips and cheap hospital gowns anyway.

Slim pickings. Emailed.

The first viewing smelled of stale cigarettes and someone else's life. The converted pub's front door stuck, requiring the agent to shoulder it open with an apologetic grimace. Inside, the kitchen opened into what was generously called a living space – so narrow she had to turn sideways to pass the single sofa. The walls pressed in around her, painted magnolia over decades of cooking grease and disappointment.

"Cosy, isn't it?" the agent said, wiping his palms on his trousers.

The bathroom was a cupboard with a toilet and a shower tray that had seen better decades. No bath. Obviously.

Outside, she lit a cigarette and crossed the first address off her list.

The 4-in-1 situation made more sense once she was standing in what had been a family hallway. The carpet was threadbare in a path that led from the front door to where children had once thundered up and down stairs. Now those stairs led to four separate front doors, each with a different coloured number stuck on with Sellotape.

She could picture proud parents and screaming children running through the place. A simpler time. The walls held the outlines of family photos, lighter rectangles where happiness had once hung.

She wondered what decisions they'd made that had caused them to leave this place, to sell it to the current predatory landlord. She knew what kinds of decisions led to that – the same ones that had left Olivia visiting her dad in a series of desperate flats instead of having a proper home.

The agent unlocked flat two with a key that stuck in the lock. Inside, the hallway was barely wide enough for one person, let alone the wardrobe she'd need to cram in there.

Wherever the family who'd lived here were, she hoped they were happy, and that they'd never see what their presumably beloved former home had turned into.

Three tiny studios, one tiny flat, barely a kitchen and nary a bath in sight. The agent was nice enough, though.

The second flat reeked of damp and optimism. The agent – a middle-aged man who kept calling her "mate" in a way that made her skin crawl – gestured enthusiastically at the living room's high ceilings.

"Loads of space for entertaining!"

She nodded and made appropriate noises while mentally measuring whether she could fit her desk near the single window without blocking all the light. The bedroom was indeed tiny – she'd have to convert the hallway into storage to fit a proper bed.

She'd been folding herself into smaller and smaller spaces for years – first the drinking, then the recovery, then the bloody economy.

"Lovely area," the agent continued, though the sound of sirens outside suggested otherwise.

The huge living room was a plus, but the insistence of the agent on calling her "mate" made her feel uneasy, and the area it was in was easily the worst part of town. But it'd save eighty quid a month. Hmmm.

Outside, she ground her cigarette under her heel harder than necessary.

Okay, the garage conversion, though.

The garage conversion was different. She could feel the potential the moment she walked in – high ceilings, exposed brick, natural light flooding through skylights she hadn't expected. The kitchen was enormous, with a breakfast bar where she could eat comfortably instead of balancing plates on her knees.

"Previous tenant was a chef," the agent explained, running her hand along the granite worktop. "Hence all the space."

Upstairs, the open-plan bedroom-living room combo had clever sliding doors that meant she could separate the spaces when she needed to. She found herself walking the perimeter, mentally placing furniture, imagining morning coffee at the breakfast bar.

Everything about it was perfect. Everything. Except for the lack of a bath.

In the shower room, she stared at the gleaming white tiles and pristine shower head. *Do they still sell those old-timey baths you hang in a closet? How would you even attach the taps?*

Ugh, it didn't have a closet.

Why, after thirty years stuck in one, was she so obsessed with closets all of a sudden? Because a closet was safe. And she was done living in other people's spaces, done folding herself small to fit.

And why was it that whenever she thought about anything too much, it all turned to shit?

She left the viewing, lit a cigarette, and leant against the brick wall outside. The smoke curled upwards, and for a moment there was nothing – no estate agents, no bills, no robot, no future. Just the sound of her own breath and the distant rumble of traffic.

Then her phone rang. She glanced at the screen – "mum" – and automatically straightened her shoulders, running her free hand through her hair as if her mother could somehow see her through the phone.

"Yep?" she answered, taking another drag.

"How's the flat hunt?"

"Good. I've found the perfect overpriced casket to be buried in, only £800 a month." She flicked ash into the gutter, watching the flakes scatter in the wind.

"How's the job search?"

"Same old, same old. Wanted a chick, got a dick. They don't pay bonuses and don't accept them either." The familiar tightness crept into her chest. She pushed off from the wall and started walking, her free hand jammed deep in her jacket pocket.

"Have you tried being less cynical?"

"Yeah, wasn't for me." A bus rumbled past, and she had to step closer to the shelter to avoid the spray from a puddle. The plastic was cold against her back through her jacket.

"You're stressed."

"I'm poor." The words came out harder than she'd meant. She stopped walking entirely, her trainers scraping against the pavement. "I'm poor, mum."

"Have you been to a meeting?"

Daisy fucking hated being called out like that. She found herself pacing in tight circles on the pavement, the cigarette hanging limply in her hand, forgotten. A woman with a pushchair gave her a wide berth.

"No."

"Find one. Call me when you're feeling better."

The line went dead. Daisy stopped mid-pace and stared at the phone screen. She took a final drag from the cigarette, then dropped it and twisted her heel against it with more violence than the situation required. The paper and tobacco scattered across the wet pavement.

Her mother said it as though a meeting was a magic money tree; she'd never been in the rooms, but she occasionally sounded like those old-timers who had slogans and cheerily delivered empty platitudes.

And yet, somehow, she was right. Daisy always felt better after a meeting. Not because of the coffee or the digestives or even the familiar disappointment. It was the people. The recognition that everyone was as fucked up as she was, but they kept showing up anyway. They'd answer phones, jump to attention, and help without question.

All of them choosing connection over control, community over isolation. All of them in the gutter, looking up at stars.

Standing there on the pavement, watching her cigarette smoke disappear into the grey evening sky, she realised she'd spent the day looking for the perfect space to hide in while her mum was telling her to go find the one place where hiding wasn't allowed. Where you had to show up as you were, expectations be damned.

She pulled out her phone, checked the time, and started walking toward the bus stop. She knew where the next meeting was.

Chapter 5 – The Freezing Summer of 2012

It always amused Daisy that they tried to call these 12-step rooms "Anonymous." He saw the same faces day after day, night after night, week after week. He suspected he knew these people better than they knew themselves.

Tonight's venue had a reputation for being dark, dank and freezing cold, even in the height of summer, and it was living up to it. Wooden chairs in rows, American-style, a waft of cheap coffee filling the air and a serious lack of snack offerings. The radiators hadn't worked in years, and the dangling bulbs made the place feel less like a meeting and more like an interrogation.

The current speaker, Mary, for example. Mid-50s, four cats, three kids, no husband. He'd decided he couldn't handle her drinking anymore and ran off and left her for another woman because he didn't feel safe around Mary. Didn't take the kids, of course. Left her with the kids, the house and the drinking problem, took no responsibility.

Mary always spoke confidently, but laughed when recounting her most painful moments and fiddled with her cheap wedding ring whenever she mentioned the ex-husband. She said the word "gratitude" too often, too warmly. *Definitely hiding something.*

"…and I'm just so *grateful*," Mary was saying now, that familiar laugh punctuating her words as she twisted the ring around her finger, "because without hitting rock bottom, I would never have found my Higher Power. I'd never have learned to love myself." The laugh again, brittle as old plastic. "Even when I was drinking a bottle of wine for breakfast and the kids were eating cereal for dinner because I'd forgotten to shop again."

A few people nodded knowingly. Someone muttered, "Keep coming back." Daisy watched her hands – always moving, adjusting her sleeves, smoothing her hair, touching that ring. Her body knew something her mouth wasn't saying.

Next to Mary was Pete. Slightly older than her, used to be a policeman but drank himself off the beat and took a job at B&Q. He'd been married once, and the way he'd talked about the end of this relationship made it sound like he'd murdered her. He hadn't, of course, but he talked about her like the ghost of Christmas past.

Daisy vaguely remembered him mentioning he had a kid or two, but he never really talked about them. The blokes never did unless they were ranting or bragging.

Pete always spoke in a warm monotone when sharing. Not devoid of personality, he came to life when he wasn't telling his story, but there was something guarded about him when he did. He also had a slightly irritating habit of constantly adjusting his glasses, as if nobody had told him they could be fitted properly.

Tonight, Pete was sharing about his first week sober, how he'd thrown out all the bottles but kept finding hidden ones for months afterwards. "In the garage, behind the Christmas decorations. In the shed. Even one in the cistern." Push, push went the glasses. "Like I was playing hide and seek with myself, and I kept losing."

The room gave a collective hum of recognition. Everyone had their hidden bottle stories.

Three months of sobriety, and in the height of summer, Daisy was shivering in the corner of the room. "Rattling," they called it. Some called them "DTs" – detox tremors.

All he knew was that he felt like shit. Three months of no drinking, and he'd never wanted to chug down a bottle of vodka more in his life. Instead, he settled for a sip of green tea from the bright red mug.

Sipping tea, it turned out, was quite the challenge with your hands shaking like they were possessed. He hoped nobody noticed the drips down his shirt. *Never show weakness.* The tea was too hot anyway, scalding the tip of his tongue, but he kept sipping because it gave him something to do with his hands, something to focus on other than the crushing weight of being there, being sober, being present in his own skin without chemical intervention.

The shaking was getting worse. He could feel it in his legs now, too, a restless energy that made him want to bolt from the room, sprint to the nearest off-license, and drink until the world made sense again. Instead, he pressed his feet flat against the floor, trying to anchor himself to something solid.

Speaker after speaker, familiar tale after familiar tale. House burned down, dog ran off, car got repossessed, work sucked. If you could record one of these meetings, you'd have a pre-written country song.

The list was getting smaller. Two more people, then it would be his turn. His heart started hammering against his ribs like it was trying to break free. What was he going to say? What could he say that would sound authentic without being completely fucking honest?

One more person. Janet, who always cried when she shared, was always dabbing her eyes with a tissue that looked like it had seen better decades. "I just want to thank my Higher Power for getting me through another day," she sniffled. "Because I couldn't do it on my own. None of us can."

And then everyone was looking at him. The silence filling the room like beer into a pint glass.

Daisy's turn to speak; he hated this part of meetings. He really didn't want to talk about his shit, but the old timers would stare at you until you sensed your life depended on sharing. With the way most of them spoke about recovery, they probably believed that his life depended on sharing.

He pictured sitting there for long enough that he exploded. It amused him. Maybe that was the answer. Don't talk, bottle it up, explode, die.

But that'd prove the old-timers right, wouldn't it?

He took a breath – deeper than intended, which made it obvious that he was nervous. The intake of air seemed to echo in the quiet room. His throat like sandpaper. The weight of their expectation crushing, making it harder to breathe properly. His voice came out rougher than he wanted.

"I'm Daisy, and I'm an alcoholic."

"Hi Daisy," came the chorus, some voices stronger than others.

He always felt this was a bit hokey and defeated the purpose of anonymity once again, but it was tradition. Had to be, the average age in the room indicated that most members remembered the invention of the motor car.

"Three months sober today," he started. *Another line in the script.*

A few muttered, half-arsed "well dones" returned from the darkness of the room. He saw Pete nod once, definitively. Mary kept twisting her ring.

He was trapped in the quiet, the unspoken dialogue of the moment was a heavy weight. He was the one who needed to break, but the words were a long way from his mouth. It was dry, his tongue coated with the bitter aftertaste of the tea. He knew what he was supposed to say. What they wanted to hear.

"Honestly, I feel pretty good." The lie came out smooth, practised. "Haven't had a drink today, didn't have a drink yesterday, hopefully won't have one tomorrow."

You had to say that in meetings. Part of the script. Everyone said it. It's a programme of honesty.

The irony wasn't lost on him.

"But god knows I fucking want one," he thought, the words screaming so loud in his head that he almost worried he'd said them out loud. His need to confess something demanded more.

He looked around the room. Pete was nodding encouragingly. Janet had stopped crying and was leaning forward slightly. Even Mary had stopped fidgeting and was listening. They were waiting for something. Something that wasn't in the script. The floor seemed to grab at his feet as he shifted his weight, anchoring him to this moment, this choice.

"But three months ago, I almost died."

The words hung in the air like smoke. It wasn't in the script. It wasn't what you said in these rooms. But the words slipped out anyway. He swallowed hard, the sound audible to all.

The room seemed to shift slightly, the energy changing. Someone – he thought it was the old guy in the back, Jim maybe – made a small sound of recognition. But there was no going back now, was there? The words were out there, raw and hanging between him and these strangers who somehow weren't strangers.

"That's crazy, right? Like, I'm basically a zombie right now."

Another pause. But something about the way they were listening – really listening, not waiting for their turn to talk – made him want to keep going.

"I woke up today, no hangover…" He paused. That wasn't true, either, was it? Not the way he meant it. "Well, no hangover from drinking. But I woke up feeling like shit anyway. Went to work, finished work, came to this meeting, and I've survived this far."

He could hear his own breathing now, slightly laboured. The shaking in his hands was getting worse, so he clasped them together, trying to keep them still. Sweat was gathering at the base of his neck, despite the room's chill.

"And I keep thinking about my friends. Right now, they're out in a bar… They're having fun, getting drunk, laughing, partying, meeting people, living life. And I'm sitting here talking about how I'm not good enough to keep up with them and behave like a normal person."

The words were coming faster now, like water through a broken dam. His voice was getting stronger, steadier, as if the truth was giving it weight.

"They'll be in some noisy pub. Probably some terrible 80s cover band playing. And they invited me, you know? They always invite me. But I know that I wouldn't last ten minutes before I'd have a cold pint in my hand and…"

He stopped. The words had run out like air from a punctured tyre. The room was silent. He could hear his pulse louder than the creak of the lightbulbs overhead.

And then, because he'd already gone this far, because something demanded it, because Pete's steady gaze and Janet's forward lean told him it was safe:

"And I don't know if that makes me strong or pathetic. Coming here instead of going there. Drinking tea instead of beer. Sitting in this freezing room instead of living my life."

His voice cracked slightly on the last words. Shit. He hadn't meant for that to happen. The crack seemed to echo in his throat, a physical reminder of how close to breaking he was.

Janet was crying again, but quietly. Pete had stopped adjusting his glasses and was looking at him steadily. Mary's hands were calm. The room felt different now. Warmer somehow, despite the broken radiators.

"Anyway, yeah." He cleared his throat, the sound harsh in the quiet space, and tried to pull himself back together. "Good times. Very grateful. Thanks."

The reticence that followed felt different from the usual pause between speakers. Heavier. More real. Like something had shifted in the room's atmosphere, something that couldn't be taken back.

"Keep coming back," came the chorus, but it sounded more sincere than usual. Pete's voice was particularly clear.

There were, he'd learn, names for this in these programmes. 'White-knuckling' or 'chasing midnight' were the common ones. You were holding on, desperately trying to get to 12 o'clock without a drink so that you could count one more day on your tally chart.

He hadn't had a drink today. Or yesterday. That much was true. The truth was that he woke up feeling like shit, lost, alone and exhausted.

He went to work, putting on a brave face and trying to muster up the same jovial character he'd slipped into so easily after a couple of pints to get through the work day. He'd grind out menial tasks, watch the clock tick by, waiting to finish so that he could get away from the smells and the sights and the eternal temptation of the siren call of the liquor bottles on the back bar.

When his shift was over, he'd been invited out with his friends, but he knew he wouldn't have lasted ten minutes before having a cold pint in his hand and another forgotten adventure on the horizon, so he'd made his excuses and resolved to go to the meeting, taking the time to wander around the park beforehand, to grab a greasy fast-food burger and chain-smoke on the way to the meeting.

The fat from the burger dripped and made the cigarettes hard to hold, and he wondered for a moment if this was a fire risk. *"Local man spontaneously combusts in park"* would be one hell of an obituary. Might be more comfortable than sobriety, though.

The meeting continued around the room. Two more people shared after him, but he barely heard them. His words kept echoing in his own head. Had he said too much? Not enough? Was everyone looking at him differently now?

When the sharing closed, they did their usual ritual – the serenity prayer, the promises, the reminder that what was shared here stayed here. Then people started moving around, stacking chairs, making small talk about the weather and weekend plans.

Once everyone had shared, he collected a 90-day chip – the closest thing to an achievement certificate he'd ever get from sobriety, a little piece of faux-bronze plastic that he wasn't sure what you were supposed to do with – and started helping to clean up, making small talk along the way.

Pete appeared beside him as he stacked chairs. "Good share tonight," he said quietly, adjusting his glasses again. "That was real."

Real. Not the script, not the slogans. Just him. And somehow, that had landed better than all the lines he'd rehearsed.

Real. The word hit him harder than he'd expected. When was the last time anyone had called anything about him *real?* When was the last time he'd been real? Not the joking, deflecting, everything's-fine version of himself. Not the performer who kept everyone comfortable. Just… real.

"Yeah, well." Daisy shrugged, not sure how to respond. "Sometimes it comes out."

"That's when it matters most," Pete said, then moved away to help with the coffee things.

As he stacked chairs, the metal legs clanging together with each addition to the pile, he felt an arm placed gently on his shoulder. He didn't know this woman; he'd never seen her before.

"I heard what you said in there," she said quietly, her voice carrying something that might have been understanding. "Word of advice? It gets easier if you cut the bullshit."

She flashed a knowing smirk and turned on her heels, leaving as mysteriously and unexpectedly as she appeared.

He didn't remember asking for advice, and didn't enjoy the judgement that came with the words. *Bullshit?*

He wanted to shout at her, *"No, it's called survival, dickhead!"* but realised it probably wasn't healthy. Especially since she'd already left the room, and he'd end up looking like a lunatic. They'd definitely change their position on "keep coming back" if he did.

But even as he decided that he hated her, swallowing his resentment so he wouldn't cause a scene and returning to the task at hand, her words kept rattling in his head. Cut the bullshit. Like it was that simple. Like, he could decide to stop pretending everything was fine, and somehow that would make it fine.

Though, hadn't he done exactly that tonight? Cut some of the bullshit? Said he felt shitty instead of "pretty good." Admitted he wanted to drink instead of mouthing the script. Told them about feeling like a demon, about not knowing if he was strong or pathetic. And nobody had run screaming. Pete had called it real. Janet had stopped crying to listen.

Maybe that's what she meant. Maybe cutting the bullshit wasn't about making everything fine – maybe it was about making everything real.

He'd been assured that he'd eventually feel at home at these things, but for some reason, the room felt colder, heavier. But maybe, just maybe, it felt less lonely than it had ninety minutes ago.

Chapter 6 – Olden Handcuffs

She hated to admit it, but she'd started to think of these people as something of a second family over the last thirteen years. She'd somehow watched them simultaneously up close and from afar, seen them grow and change, almost studying them like a scientist peers into a Petri dish. Maybe that was why she was still travelling to her hometown for meetings more often than going to the local ones.

The local meetings felt different – uncomfortable – like wearing someone else's shoes. She didn't feel like someone who belonged there – she felt the judging eyes on her as the freak in the dress walked into the room; the standoffishness like she might be there to commit a crime.

The fear they had of her only fuelled the fear in her. It felt unsafe to attend, let alone to be honest.

The truth was, she knew these people better than they knew her, and possibly better than they knew themselves. She could predict who would share about what, based on the weather, their posture, and what they were drinking. Mary always got emotional around Christmas and the kids' birthdays. Pete shared about his ex-wife when the new guy's relationship stories triggered his own memories. Janet cried on the third Tuesday of every month like clockwork, even though Daisy never figured out why.

Thirteen years of the Tuesday night meeting. She'd watched Jim relapse three times and come back even quieter. Seen Janet lose her mother and gain ten kilos of grief. Witnessed the slow dissolution of marriages and the tentative rebuilding of relationships with estranged children. She knew who struggled in December, who got twitchy around their anniversary dates, who couldn't handle the smell of floral perfumes or the sound of ice clinking in a glass.

It was voyeurism dressed up as community, really. She absorbed their stories like a sponge, filing away details about lives she'd never be a part of. They shared their deepest shame and desperate hope twice a week, and she collected it all, this vast archive of people's stories that somehow felt more truthful than her own.

They were like characters in a soap opera that she'd been watching for over a decade, their storylines weaving in and out of focus whilst her own life remained frustratingly static. She collected their dramas, their victories, their setbacks, hoarding them like old newspapers. Other people's lives were so much more interesting than her own, so much more dynamic.

Sometimes she wondered if they knew they were characters in her private soap. If they'd be horrified to know how she catalogued them – Mary's laugh track, Pete's cop show intensity, Janet's monthly cry-scene. And, with an unforeseen jab of shame, wondered if they did the same with her. Maybe she wasn't invisible at all, just badly written.

And they barely saw her. Oh, they knew her – nodded when she walked in, said the right things when she shared – but she'd perfected the art of attending without being memorable. She was the audience, not the main character, and that suited her fine. Safer to live vicariously through their stories than to generate any story worth telling herself.

Mary was talking excitedly; she'd had quite a big few weeks, and she genuinely seemed happy – she'd recently become a grandmother again, by way of her youngest daughter. Listening to her talk about it was strange; she'd heard Mary discuss her daughters so much over the years that she felt as though she knew them, even though they'd likely never met.

But she knew her youngest through Mary's descriptions of her, in a way that was part-voyeuristic, part-literary. She was a character in Mary's autobiography, and she knew of the times when she'd made Mary everything from mad to sad to proud to happy and everything in between.

The daughter – Holly – was somewhere in her late twenties; Mary had given birth to her fairly late in life, such as these things go, and Daisy gathered she was a tall, curvy girl.

She knew this because when Daisy had come out, Mary had appeared at a meeting with a huge bag of clothes that Holly had been getting rid of, and they fit her perfectly. A genuinely warm, kind gesture, even if those clothes had probably been about twenty years too young for her. She'd also given her a few more things over the years, and these had been more age-appropriate. Perhaps they'd been Mary's once, or she'd spotted them in a charity shop. She hadn't asked. Supportive, accepting and helpful.

Holly had been a troubled teenager who worried her mother greatly. She drank, she smoked, she tried to hide her experimentation with drugs… standard teenage stuff. She sounded like a lot of fun, to be honest. Daisy imagined they could've become friends if they'd been closer in age.

The thing was, Holly's troubles sounded so… normal. Enviably normal. Sneaking out to go to parties, snogging inappropriate boys behind the bike sheds, coming home with pupils like pinpricks and thinking she was getting away with it. A rebellion that came from having something stable to rebel against, parents who cared enough to worry, a life solid enough that you could afford to shake the foundations a bit.

Daisy had never had that luxury. Her own teenage experimentation hadn't been about testing boundaries – it had been about survival, about numbing things that hurt too much to feel. Not because of a lack of parenting or boundaries at home, but because the boundaries outside of home felt far too close. Too restrictive.

So, when Mary talked about finding Holly's stash, or getting calls from school about her behaviour, or lying awake wondering where she was on Saturday nights, Daisy felt this strange mixture of envy and vicarious comfort. This was what normal family dysfunction looked like when it wasn't being complicated by an undercurrent of everyone desperately wondering what was wrong with you, including yourself.

They'd both been a mess, but Holly got to do it honestly – with an audience that worried instead of judged.

That bag of Holly's clothes had been a revelation. Daisy remembered the moment that Mary had hauled it into the meeting, awkwardly hefting it onto the coffee table like she was delivering evidence. "Holly's having a clear out," she'd announced with a mix of parental pride and bewilderment. "Says she's too old for all this stuff now. Thought you might like some of it, love."

And Daisy had taken it home like a treasure chest. Skinny jeans with strategic rips, band t-shirts for groups she'd never heard of, dresses that were probably meant to be worn over leggings, but she'd worn anyway. Each piece carried the echoes of Holly's life – a night out she'd never had, a concert she'd never attended, a version of young womanhood that had been foreign to her even when she'd been young.

The band tees smelled faintly of strawberry shampoo; a detail Daisy told herself she'd imagined. She wore them like costumes, like she was auditioning for a version of herself who'd had a normal adolescence, who knew the right lyrics to sing when the crowd shouted them back.

The strangest part was how perfectly they'd fit. She and Holly apparently shared the same measurements, the same proportions, as if they were variations on the same theme. Daisy had stood in her bedroom mirror wearing Holly's cast-off and wondered what it would have been like to live that life instead – to be someone's daughter who worried about normal things, to have friends who passed clothes around, to be reckless in ways that didn't end in hospital beds.

She still had some of those clothes hanging in her wardrobe like artefacts from a parallel universe. Sometimes she caught herself reaching for Holly's old band t-shirt on difficult mornings, as if borrowing her clothes might let her borrow some of her uncomplicated rebellion, too.

Mary was worried because Holly was with baby, without boyfriend or explanation and wasn't telling her mother anything else.

Daisy genuinely felt for the girl. She'd always had the impression that she was fun, not irresponsible.

Pete, meanwhile, was determined to find and kill the guy. He and Mary had only been married a few years; a romance in the rooms, right out of a Danielle Steel novel. But Pete was a good guy who treated Mary's kids like his own, as she did his. That police machismo never left him, even if his waistline expanded as his hair thinned in retirement.

You could see the copper in him, even after all these years. The way he positioned himself in meetings – never with his back fully to the room, always where he could see both entrances. How his eyes would sweep the space when someone new walked in, that quick threat assessment he probably didn't even notice himself making. When people shared about dangerous situations – abusive partners, dodgy living arrangements, threats from old using friends – Pete would lean forward slightly, and you could practically see him taking mental notes, filing away details for later follow-up.

If someone sneezed in the back row, Pete's head would snap around like he was about to demand their alibi.

Sometimes Daisy caught him studying people as they spoke, that interrogation room intensity flickering behind his glasses. Not unkindly, but with the focus of someone who wanted to spot inconsistencies, to read between the lines. Maybe that's what had drawn him to Mary, too: not just her warmth, but the mystery of what she didn't say.

And with Holly's situation, that protective instinct had shifted into overdrive. He'd probably already run through a dozen scenarios about tracking down this mystery father, had mentally plotted all the ways he could make the guy's life uncomfortable without technically breaking any laws. Retirement hadn't dulled him.

They'd had an adorable courtship, one that Daisy remembered well. It started with them always volunteering to wash up together, progressing to whispered chats at the post-meeting coffeehouse trip. They thought they were hiding, and no one believed it was "just a friendship" once people started to clock that Pete was appearing accompanied by a faint waft of tuna and a thin layer of cat hair.

That these two, both very much adults, had tried to hide their romance like an illicit modern-day Romeo and Juliet was genuinely cute. In recovery, people counted their chronological age – the "belly-button birthday" – and their sobriety age. They both had a few more miles on the clock, but they were sobriety teenagers and had acted like it. And they really were, in Daisy's mind, the perfect couple. The yin to the other's yang.

This, although she was publicly very happily and doggedly single, was the relationship she hoped to find.

She'd got so lost in her own wave of sentimentality that it dawned on her that the room fell into that aggressive, oppressive hush only a recovery meeting can produce.

She didn't even need to look up from the stim-bracelet she'd been playing with absent-mindedly to know what she'd see. The laser-focussed death stare daring her to speak.

"Daisy, alcoholic," she began. She'd noticed how the enthusiastic "Hi, I'm Joe, and I'm an alcoholic" always eroded to "name, alcoholic" – cliffs of hope worn down by the waves. She'd adopted the shorthand herself. Why fake it when you can cut the bullshit?

"I've been on a bit of a journey recently," she took a breath, let it land. Her flair for the dramatic kicking in. "I had a moment where I realised that life wasn't quite where I wanted it to be."

She twisted the beads of her stim-bracelet, felt the sharp edge bite into her skin. It kept her from fidgeting too much, gave her hands something to do while her words started slipping out faster than she could censor them.

"They told me that life would get better in this programme, in recovery. But after thirteen years, I'm broke, I'm terminally unemployable, heavily depressed and living in a shithole that I can't afford in a grassless town I can't stand."

Her voice came out too polished, like she'd rehearsed it, like she'd spat them out a hundred times in the mirror. Maybe she had.

A newcomer shifted in her chair, the scrape of plastic on tile like a wince. Daisy felt the shame coil in her gut – too far, too fast, again.

Mary's smile had flattened into something brittle. Pete's jaw set tighter, that old cop's instinct to fix problems sparking behind his glasses.

She exhaled, too loud in the dead air, and for a second wished she could swallow the words back down.

"I keep asking myself what's changed – asking myself if this sobriety shit is even worth it when I could just spend a few weeks partying and know it'd inevitably end when I sobered up."

She risked a glance around the room. Pete was staring at her, his usual fixed gaze sharpened. Mary's face was a mask of alarm, and Daisy hated it. Hated being pitied.

She knew she should've stopped there, but honesty always slid out of her sideways, too sharp to handle safely.

"Now that I'm sober, I see the world for the fucked-up system that it's built on; the oppression of the rich white cis man towards the poor, the women and the different. At least when I was drinking, I didn't see that and didn't care enough to try."

The thought burned like acid. This was it. The real stuff. The truth she usually whispered at 3 am, hands trembling.

A couple of heads nodded, slow and reluctant, like they knew exactly what she meant but didn't dare agree outside.

"Sometimes I wonder, you know? If ignorance is bliss, and alcohol causes ignorance, maybe alcohol is bliss. Maybe we're the ones failing, by making life hard for ourselves on purpose."

She paused, her heart pounding. The sentiment hung in the air, a kind of blasphemy. She expected someone to flinch, to break the void. No one did.

She rubbed her thumb raw against the bracelet, like she could erase the last sentence if she pressed hard enough.

It sounded harsher out loud. A couple of people blinked, unsure if they'd heard blasphemy or truth. Too late – she'd tugged the thread, and the whole jumper unravelled.

Her throat tightened. Maybe she'd gone too far. Maybe she always went too far.

She could almost hear the slogans now – *"don't quit before the miracle happens," "Just for today"* – the same old phrases a bad script she couldn't stop reading. One, maybe, she'd clung to them. Now they sounded like bad advertising for a product that she couldn't afford to return.

"But, I'm an optimist." She paused, inviting a reaction that never came. She'd swear she was funny once.

She tucked her feet up, trying to shrink herself. The hush washed over, drenching her. She wanted to vanish.

Mary's ring spun so fast she thought it might lead to an amputation. Pete's glasses pushed up his nose twice in ten seconds, his tell when he was uncomfortable. Someone in the back coughed, a deliberate sound that wasn't about clearing a throat. Daisy caught it all – the micro-reactions, the little betrayals of patience or unease. She watched them like a stand-up reading a crowd, except no one here was laughing.

"So… I've started a new thing; I asked an AI what I'm supposed to want. Then I asked the AI why I didn't have it, how I got it, and it gave me a plan. I literally asked a robot to fix my life."

She heard a low chuckle from the back of the room. A small victory. She almost smiled. Almost.

"It told me what to do, gave me its foolproof Skynet master plan. First step was to find a job. You know, because I hadn't been trying already?"

She spread her palms like a bad magician revealing empty palms. *Ta-da*. The punchline collapsed under its own weight.

"Anyway, I dropped some applications, found out that I'm not even good enough to be a stripper. Great for the self-esteem. Fantastic."

A chuckle escaped her, dry and humourless. Nobody joined in.

"Then it told me to sort my finances out. Obviously, in the absence of a job, that means cutting the living expenses. I looked at a few flats, and when I tell you it was the most depressing ordeal… You used to be able to buy a decent used car for £800, and now you can only rent a flat the size of a car."

She looked down at her hands, the familiar feeling of failure washing over her. Someone checked their watch; someone else coughed into their hand. The quiet said it for them: *here she goes again*.

Instead, she doubled down.

"So, anyway, looks like the robot revolution is a little while away yet. Unless this is part of the master plan to kill me off ahead of the inevitable takeover."

The words landed with a thud; nobody picked them up.

"But hey, at least I'm not drinking about it."

Stillness.

The meeting ended in the familiar way: empty platitudes, Serenity Prayer, and the clean-up. The chores done, Daisy made her way outside, a cigarette hanging from her scarlet lips as she fumbled in her bag looking for the latest runaway lighter.

The night slapped her across the face – air so cold that it made her teeth ache, emptiness broken only by the orange glow of a street light. For a second, she let herself breathe it in, like the world was reminding her that she was there.

The flame flared close enough to show a hand with neat nails, a wrist marked by a faint scar she couldn't place. Her pacifier came to life.

"Thanks."

Daisy followed the line up to a face that looked lit from within by some secret knowledge.

"Word of advice? It gets easier if you cut the bullshit."

Recognition lagged, like her brain buffering an old file. Daisy almost thanked her again on autopilot, but something stopped her. That same empty platitude, that voice. She knew them. It was that smug—

"Iris," she said. Daisy looked up to find a warm smile and an outstretched hand.

"Daisy," she responded, awkwardly returning the smile and accepting the handshake.

Something felt dangerous. Not loud, not obvious – the kind that ruins you before you register it. And for once,

Daisy wasn't sure if honesty would save her, or finish her off.

Chapter 7 - 2004-2007: The Four-Year, Three-Ring Circus

Daisy loved his job. Part clown, part stuntman, part action hero, performing the role of a live-action comic book villain in front of a pantomime crowd baying for blood, sweat and tears.

Most importantly, he was good at it. Loved, even revered, by his colleagues in some small way and truly hated on some levels by the audience. Every day, a new venue, a new cast, a new crowd and a new story. And yet, usually, everything was the same.

Usually.

Today, however... was not the same. Nothing ever would be again.

Before all this, there was Marisol. His Marisol. The girlfriend you could bring home to meet your parents, not that he ever had. A girl who'd send letters and e-mails instead of text messages, who laughed at his terrible jokes, who saw him for exactly who he was and loved him anyway. He'd known, for months now, that she was The One. His forever. He carried her picture as the wallpaper on his phone, a constant reminder of the life he intended to build, a life of stability and love and normalcy. This was what made his temporary escapes feel safe; he knew there'd eventually be a home to return to.

He made his way around the crowded makeshift dressing room in the back of the community centre that would be tonight's "arena," shaking hands with and hugging the boys he knew, introducing himself to the boys he didn't, as per tradition.

And then, in an instant, his life changed.

Appearing out of nowhere like an overgrown pixie with a warm, sudden hug and a smile that was as wide as it was mesmerising, accompanied by those fatal first words:

"Hi, I'm Faye."

And, underneath them, a gentle, yet commanding and unspoken "and I own you now."

Just as suddenly, another new face appeared; Martin threw his arm around Faye and introduced himself with a very subtle, silent "and I own her." It soon transpired that Daisy, Martin and Faye would be working together; a three-part package, a triple threat intended to incite anger from all who encountered them and, unexpectedly, an uneasy friendship would form.

Martin and Daisy, in truth, were very similar. They had a lot in common; Martin was slightly older, but slightly less wise, but they shared a love of football, music and their business. But this veneer of friendship masked an envy; each had something the other wanted – Daisy had the talent and the notoriety. Martin had Faye. He was, he thought, the better man. And her late-night text messages gave him the hint that she agreed. A secret within an industry built on secrets that everybody pretended they weren't in on.

But Daisy had another secret – Daisy had many secrets – but one that made this triangle a little trickier: Marisol, his long-distance fiancé. He was also aware that this sojourn was temporary; he was due to leave for university in a few months, onto pastures new both geographically and personally. Whatever spark was happening had no choice but to fizzle out; fate wouldn't allow any other option.

He wasn't cheating, he rationalised, because nothing was *actually* happening. Nothing could happen. In another time, another place, another lifetime, maybe, but the clock was ticking, and the books were calling. There are no lies and no deception if nobody is saying anything, right?

Summer ended, Daisy and Martin ended their feud with the fictional violence that the ever-turning calendar had prevented from becoming factual. The three parted ways with Daisy, prepared to ride off into the sunset, onwards and upwards.

A few months later, he settled into his student housing and, after a long web chat with Marisol, where they'd discussed their days, their lives, and their hopes and dreams – as well as planning some way to try and persuade Marisol's father to like him, at last, his phone rang.

Faye.

Unexpected, but he answered it. It wasn't uncommon to get a random call from a business acquaintance saying, "Hey, there's a job going with this guy, are you in?" And that was exactly what he expected when he answered the phone.

What he didn't expect were tears. It was hard to make out through the heavy sobbing, but he got the bullet points: Martin had hit her. She had left him. She was on a train. To Daisy.

Fuck.

Short of options, given her spontaneous 200-mile escape, he met her at the station. To say she'd packed would be an overstatement; she maybe had a change of underwear and a shirt in her bag. He took her back to his place, and he found himself wondering how the purple highlights in her blonde hair stayed in place in the driving rain. They ordered pizza, threw on a movie and talked.

It transpired that under their perfect public appearance, Martin and Faye had always had a troubled relationship. He was the perfect gentleman in public: Kind. Supportive. Affectionate, even. In private, when they were alone? Angry. Violent. Drunk. He listened as she talked; empathy didn't come easily to him. He knew how to act in this situation from years of obsessively devouring movies, TV and film. But it was mostly an "act" – it wasn't that he was incapable of feeling, just incapable of reading others.

Eventually, she tired herself out. Short of options, he offered her the bed and tried his best to make a comfortable space to sleep on the floor. She insisted that the bed was big enough for the both of them, and that she trusted him. He trusted himself. He was safe, responsible… taken. Why would this be an issue?

A few hours later, he stirred awake. He was confused – somewhere between crashing out and now, his brain had forgotten he wasn't alone. That unfamiliar feeling – the weight next to him, the warm breath on his neck, the fingers slowly tracing their way up his thigh.

Wait, the fingers tracing their way up his thigh?

He slowly turned to face her, opening his eyes. He was not dreaming, and neither was she. This wasn't some involuntary movement on her part, an inconvenient yet entirely innocent motor response to a dream. She was fully aware of what she was doing. And there it was. That smile.

Before he could process a thought – or even begin the process of processing thought – she was kissing him. He was kissing her, as if under her control. In a blur, she was on top of him, putting him inside her. Deflowering Daisy. The thought of Marisol flashed through his mind, searing hot and then gone in an instant. His brain captured the guilt and shame and deleted it. Repressed it. He wouldn't think of – let alone speak to – Marisol for another fifteen years.

After a few days of being actively bed-bound, Faye decided to head back to her father's house. It was reasonably safe from Martin and gave them both the space to unpack the events of the past few days. She looked uncomfortable as she peeled herself out of the bed, almost flinching as she dressed, in a manner that suggested that her body had forgotten what clothes, and that it didn't like it. He did the same, although with the benefit of clean clothes to choose from, and walked her to the station. They hugged, they kissed, he waved her off from the platform, and, as the train sped out of sight, he began to feel dazed; like he'd come around from a daydream, disoriented and deserted.

Their relationship became one of text messages and late-night calls, whispered sweet nothings and cautious expressions of emotions. They would, occasionally, visit each other as often as his academic schedule allowed. Their relationship remained, for all intents and purposes, a secret from everyone outside themselves and hearing range. To call it an academic schedule was charitable; he hadn't attended a class in months and was working almost full-time again. Something had changed; he'd slipped from motivated academic to feeling a desire to provide without ever really considering it. A priority shift that would've been nonsensical if anyone had analysed it.

She visited for his birthday, better prepared, even if their patterns remained the same. As usual, she left, returning to her real life. Their real life: calls, texts, work.

But one of these texts was not like the other: "I'm pregnant."

In the movies, the guy in this situation would do the right thing. You know, freak out and panic at first, then realise he had to marry her because that's what you did, wasn't it? Daisy and Faye didn't have a romcom romance, however. They lived in the chaos. They'd exchanged "I love yous" somewhere in the midst of that first night, and he'd proposed during the second. She'd said yes. Years of studying Austin and Bronte and Hanks and Ryan should've told him that this wasn't normal, but this was their normal. Their new normal. Their mutually-agreed-upon abnormal normal.

Within weeks, he'd formally dropped out of university – to the surprise of absolutely nobody – and moved in with her. They settled into a routine, newlyweds without the wedding, their families attempting whatever the opposite of a shotgun wedding was in the background, and in the new year, they welcomed a daughter. Daisy had always been adamant that he didn't want kids. Not at this age, anyway. He came from generations of young parents, and it had only seemed to end in generations of generational trauma. But, somehow, this felt… right? He'd saved the girl, like every pop culture hero he'd ever admired, and they'd built their happily ever after.

A few months later, Faye was pregnant again. A son. The whole set. Could this be more perfect? She'd gone back to work between the pregnancies, and she seemed as happy as he was. He had the family, she had the work, everything was ticking over perfectly. She went back to work after the second baby, but she didn't seem so happy now. Daisy assumed that she had just gotten used to the parenting thing. She missed her babies when she was on the road. That's probably normal, isn't it?

Except whenever she came home, she didn't grab the kids and smother them with affection... she retreated to their bedroom and picked fights whenever they were alone together. One day, after he'd returned from a weekend of working, he slipped into a hot bath to soothe his aching muscles and slowly drifted off to sleep.

Hours later, he woke up, freezing, to banging and shouting. The unexpected cold shocked him. He was shivering, teeth chattering uncontrollably. He opened his eyes to see the water, once hot, was now turning his skin a grey colour, covered in goosebumps. In a blink, the locked door flew open, and two burly police officers were dragging him out of the bath, ordering him to get dressed and handcuffing him. Refusing to answer the question of "What have I done?" with anything more than physical violence and "You know what you did!", he was resigned to spending the night in a police cell.

No answers, no contact, no help. He was awoken by cold coffee and a cold expression; a police officer waiting to take him to an appearance before a magistrate. In this moment he discovered what had happened. Faye had, whilst he slept in the bath, called the police to report that he'd been hitting her – something he had never, ever done. And now he faced a choice – he could plead guilty, go home to the kids and sort this out... or he could plead not guilty, and be banned from seeing anyone until trial. A "choice" in the most performative possible sense. He chose option one.

Upon release, he called Faye. No answer. He called her dad. Nothing. He called his parents. They knew. They were on their way. They were going to pick up his stuff.

"Why?" He asked.

Because she had already moved her new boyfriend in.

The world became muted. The sounds of a police station, the ringing of the phone in his ear – it all seemed to be happening underwater. He felt… empty. A profound nothingness where his life used to be.

He ended up moving in with his grandparents. Once he was done begging tearfully for forgiveness and second chances and some crumb of sanity, settling into acceptance of the end of his perfect life, he just felt numb. He ended up taking odd jobs, attempting to reinvent himself as a stand-up comic and an actor, but alcohol was calling him. He hadn't been much of a drinker when he was with Faye – he was as a teenager, but she'd somehow tamed him and made a point of keeping him healthy. Or, at least, she had when they were in proximity. But with her gone… the shackles were off and he was back out in the wild. He'd gravitate towards bar work eventually – it was flexible enough for his performing career, he reasoned, and paid well enough to support his liquid- and substance-fuelled emotional recovery whilst keeping the tools of his new trade close at hand.

As quickly as it started, it spiralled out of control. If only he'd realised that quickly. He'd been to exactly two meetings when he got the call from the unknown number. A social worker. The children had been taken into care.

Turns out that Faye and her new boyfriend hadn't handled the parenting duties – or, it eventually transpired, each other – very well, despite having had two more kids in the meantime. The social worker was calling to see if he was stable and could take care of them.

He was less than a week sober. He could barely take care of himself. But he had to do the right thing. He was reintroduced to his kids, and they assessed whether he could be a full-time parent. Despite their optimism, a newly dry alcoholic living with his grandparents was never going to win anyone over, and they and the courts read his still-undiagnosed autism as a risk to the children, so they were placed in foster care, and he was given supervised visitation with a 500-mile round trip every week to see them for two hours.

Throughout this custody drama, Faye and her boyfriend broke up, and she reached out to Daisy, full of apologies and attempts to recruit him as an ally in an attempt to secure custody of the children again. They would, when he went for a visitation with the kids, meet up. Sometimes for coffee, sometimes to talk, sometimes losing inhibitions and falling into bed together. Reconciliation on a romantic level was discussed and dismissed, and their attempts at proving themselves as parents were as fruitful as their attempts at reuniting as partners.

The pattern continued until Faye found herself in a new relationship with a genuinely lovely man whom Daisy became genuinely good friends with. No undertones of jealousy, just two people with someone in common. They seemed happy, and Daisy and Faye managed to function as best friends. It was, arguably, the most functional their relationship had ever been. Possibly even the most normal.

Nine years after their breakup, Daisy had resolved to go back to university, taking an access course to prove his worth. Faye was his biggest cheerleader, perhaps a sense of guilt at her involvement in his previous abandonment of education, perhaps out of care. Maybe both. After a year, in August, he had done well enough to move into a full-time degree and pursue an education. He'd called her that day, excited with the news.

"Yes, you did it!" she yelled into the phone, her voice bright with a pride he hadn't heard in years.

He felt, at last, that things were heading in the right direction. He was moving forward, and so was she. The phone call was a silent, beautiful peace treaty for all the chaos that had come before.

By October, Faye was dead.

Chapter 8 - Detox

"Okay, robot, what's next?"

Prune toxic connections and find a team.

Well, shit. Which toxic connections to start with?

Deleting social media? Cutting utilities? Burning down Parliament? If she were playing six degrees of separation, nobody would be safe. Instructions unclear, robot.

Find a team. Like, a football team? That was fair; the one she'd followed since childhood had been shit for thirty years. Valid enough. But she was being facetious.

She understood what the robot was saying: cut out the shitty people and find the good ones.

Good people.

She remembered good people. They used to exist. There was an old lady who used to sit in front of her at the football and gave her sweets. She never learned her name, but she was lovely. I mean, people on the internet would probably call her a "nonce" or something nowadays, but that used to be a thing nice people did.

She knew where to find bad people. She could look through her phone and call fifty of them if she wanted – she'd always been useless at keeping in touch.

Daisy scrolled past her father's name. An involuntary motion, a habit she'd never been able to break. Six months since they last spoke, always the same ending: her needing to "get her life together," her struggles framed as personal failure. She had a voice memo saved of him drunk, rambling about her being "a disappointment." She wasn't angry, only done. Cutting off the shitty people wasn't a choice; it was a way of life.

Another name – a drinking buddy. They hadn't spoken in years, but she could taste the cheap vodka on his breath whenever it lit up her screen. One call and he'd be outside with a bottle and a packet of cigarettes, both of them promising to behave and both knowing it was a lie.

Another – a friend who'd once been family, before the friendship curdled into silence. Not enemies, just… absent. Sometimes absence was a sharper knife than cruelty.

Every name was a reminder. Cutting people out wasn't some radical new AI hack for happiness – it was her biography.

And, to be fair, this was probably the easiest task the robot list had set so far. She made a mental note to get back to it later.

But finding good people... that intrigued her.

Cynical as she was, she did know good people. Like Mary and Pete, people from the rooms, as well as people in the various queer circles she occasionally interacted with.

She sort of had teams in that sense, right? She had the team that kept her sober, the team that normalised her queerness... but where do you find a team to make life itself less shit?

Is it possible to find a team of billionaire sugar daddies that don't want sex? That'd be fantastic. Smiling through social bollocks a few times a month in exchange for surgery money and shoes? That she could do.

Google says yes. Her instincts screamed "noooooooo!"

Look, she had no problem with sex workers. She *loved* sex workers. In her estimation, the most honest people alive, providing a valuable service to the community. They tamed incels, helped baby queers to experiment and trained them. They did God's work.

Daisy, however, was not going to become a sex worker. Even if she had the looks and the body (she didn't), and the death wish that she assumed must be a prerequisite, she didn't have the patience to deal with chasers or train anybody to do anything. Besides, she probably shouldn't be teaching anyone anything in her position, let alone in multiple positions.

So, where were these teams of good people that could help?

She supposed other people might think "church", but they'd be confusing good people for kind people. Church people were – aside from the extremists – generally very kind, in her experience. But she needed *good* people. People with their lives in order. People who didn't believe in fairytales.

Good people... she asked Google, "Where do good people hang out?"

Book clubs? Man, that involves being able to afford books, doesn't it?

Sports teams? She'd love to. She used to love playing sports.

Used to. Before she was banned from them.

Not for misconduct or cheating or even being shit at them. Just for existing. Can't play with the girls, it's unfair. Can't play with the boys, you'll get raped. To the girls, you're a boy... to the boys, you're a toy.

"Casual gatherings at coffee shops"?

She pictured people casually hanging around a coffee shop and somehow getting magnetically drawn to each other and becoming besties. It amused her.

She assumed people were probably organising themed meetups in coffee shops, and that was what this was referring to. But that'd mean finding those groups. The robot didn't say make extra effort, did it? Why would it?

Robot sets task; Daisy fails at task. This was their relationship. A perfect binary. The robot was the one; she was the zero.

Fuck, she hoped the robot wasn't "the one", but it was the most meaningful relationship in her life right now.

"Community centres and volunteer organisations" were on the list, too. Doing things for other people, for free? Like a slave? I mean, I guess there was the possibility of her doing something positive for someone, but it seemed so forced.

Her stomach rumbled. She'd been on a diet recently – she was *always* on a diet – but her levels of willpower were directly connected to the levels of contentment or resentment she felt at any given moment.

A trip to the kitchen revealed no bread and nothing to put in it. Cereal, no milk. She could cook something from the freezer, but that was effort.

She was going to have to go to the shops, and a quick look at her banking app revealed she was going yellow sticker hunting. If she were feeling positive, she'd refer to this as "loot box" shopping. You never knew what you'd find.

She wasn't feeling positive. She was feeling hungry. And poor.

The walk to the supermarket was a slog. The pavements felt damp with an invisible grime, and the air was heavy with the smell of exhaust fumes and damp rubbish.

The supermarket was, as it always is, hell. Bright, unforgiving fluorescent lights hummed a high-pitched song of manufactured cheer, and the loud music from the 90s – some pop song about a love she'd never had – drilled into her skull. Children running everywhere, their high-pitched screams a testament to the parents who were apparently incapable of shopping alone.

She found some milk, resigning herself to pay the hefty tax that was levied against her for requiring lactose-free, then grabbed the cheapest bread known to man. You know the kind – plain label, 50p a loaf, each slice the same thickness, consistency and flavour of a cereal box.

She grabbed a few processed red meats, some cheese, a pasty from the yellow sticker bin. Considered fruit, but remembered that she hated the consistency of it. That was probably why her dieting sucked. She was constitutionally incapable of eating rich people foods like fresh fruit.

She caught the eye of a man across the aisle – he glanced at her basket, at the budget bread, the reduced meat, the knock-off cheese – and then looked away quickly, like he'd seen something contagious. Poverty, apparently, was contagious.

At the self-checkout, the machine barked at her to "place item in the bagging area" in a tone that could have been invented purely to humiliate the poor. She fumbled to pay, aware of the queue forming behind her, people sighing, tutting. Nobody said anything directly – they never did – but the irritation hung in the air like static.

It wasn't the cost that hurt. It was the reminder that she was out of sync with everyone else, permanently fumbling, permanently behind. The world wanted her gone, but hadn't figured out how to say it yet. The robot would log it as enrichment. She logged it as humiliation.

Desperately shifting cash between apps to pay for it, she stuffed everything into her backpack and made her way home. Or, at least, planned to.

A coffee shop stopped her in her tracks, her eye caught by the green mermaid of the logo. Her curiosity got the better of her, and she really wanted to see what a casual gathering in a coffee shop looked like in action, in case it did match her roboballet fantasy.

She hesitated at the door. Her anxiety heightened. She felt a profound sense of self-consciousness, as if every person in the shop could see right through her – could see the hunger, the poverty, the loneliness she was trying to hide. She took a deep breath, telling herself it was a silly experiment, a little game to play with the robot. She pushed the door open, the bell above the door jangling a little too loudly in the quiet space.

She ordered from the barista and felt old, as the 12-year-old seemed confused that she didn't want anything extra in her tea. Milk, sugar, no foam, no matcha, pumped, faux-Italian bullshit.

She grabbed her drink and tried to avoid the judgemental gaze of the child, trying to decide if it was bigotry or a seething hatred of her denial of the "art" of steaming milk as pretentiously as possible.

Not so long ago, she'd have been certain that it was the latter, but you really couldn't tell with this generation.

They'd somehow morphed from edgelord to Brownshirt since she'd been a teenager herself.

As she turned from the counter, lost in thought, she came a hair from walking straight into someone, but stopped just in time.

Iris.

Right in front of her. What are the odds? Daisy caught the faintest trace of her perfume – sharp, clean, unmistakably her – and it hit harder than the sight of her face.

Daisy's heart stopped. She was so caught up in her own head, so consumed by her internal world, that the shock of a person in her path was jarring. She took an involuntary step back, clutching her tea like a lifeline. Iris' face, which had been turned away, looked up. Her expression was one of surprise, followed by a warm, familiar smile.

Daisy wanted to vanish into the wallpaper, but the wallpaper didn't move. It left her standing there.

"I was just thinking about you," she smiled. The warm smile, not the smug one.

"Why?" Daisy snapped back. She knew it came across as rude as soon as the words left her throat, but she truly was surprised that anyone was thinking about her. For any reason. Ever.

Her shoulders tensed. She waited for the inevitable lecture, the disappointed look, the condescension she was used to, but it didn't come.

"Sorry, I…" Iris started. Daisy took a breath, cut her off.

"No, I'm sorry. I'm having a bad… life?"

"You want to talk about it?"

She didn't. She really didn't.

Her brain screamed at her to lie, to say no, to make some ridiculous excuse about being late for a meeting with her imaginary sugar daddy. Her hands gripped the paper cup, and for a fleeting moment, she could hear the echo of a voice from a meeting: *"Just be honest."*

"Sure."

"Okay. I'll grab a drink, you cut the bullshit."

Somehow, that line hit Daisy like a bullet, as it had the last time. And the time before that. But this time, it didn't sting as much.

She watched Iris walk away and felt a weird mix of relief and terror. She absently traced the logo on the paper cup with her thumb, the mermaid's face an impossible, serene contrast to her own knotted stomach. Iris' life seemed a universe away from her own, and yet here they were. Daisy felt a strange, new curiosity. What was Iris' life like? How did she get her life in order? Was she truly happy? Daisy sat down at a small table near the window, her mind racing. She hadn't willingly engaged with another human being in so long. It felt both terrifying and, in a strange, small way, like a kind of surrender.

But they talked, and Daisy found herself opening up a little. Just enough to tempt the possibility.

Iris was a little older than Daisy, no kids, no failed marriages… she was a fellow traveller, with a job that had taken her out of the country regularly until very recently. Fifteen years in the rooms, she owned her own home. She loved art, she was a reader and dabbled in photography. She was…

Normal.

Normal. And nice. Genuinely nice, she wanted to be there for Daisy, to talk, to listen, to help.

She seemed… happy. Not fake happy. Not Instagram happy. No performance.

No bullshit.

As their conversation wove to a natural conclusion, Daisy couldn't help herself. She was having to be honest. Maybe too honest.

"You know, I can't believe I hated you for thirteen years."

Iris' jaw dropped.

"What?"

Fuck. Daisy wasn't ready to explain herself. But the words pressed against her teeth, sharp as glass, begging to cut their way out.

Fuck.

Chapter 9 – The Uncovered Inventory of 2018

He'd accidentally walked into a step 4 meeting, a hard lesson about not properly looking at the meeting schedule.

Step 4: making a searching and fearless moral inventory of ourselves.

He'd been making excuses to avoid engaging in this phase of recovery with sponsors for years, despite their nagging. It wasn't so much the fearless moral inventory that bothered him, he reasoned; it was the next step. He knew he'd have to share it with another person.

He knew who he was, what he'd done, why broadcast it? So that someone other than him and everyone he'd ever met could know that he was also a shitty human being?

"It's a programme of honesty," he was forever hearing.

Honesty. What a joke.

Honesty didn't get you sobriety, happiness or freedom. Honesty got you judgement, misery and, quite possibly, prison.

The room was a drab collection of fold-out chairs in a dusty church hall. The air smelled of body odour and a faint, institutional cleanser. As everyone proudly shared their dirty laundry – one woman confessed to shoplifting, a guy admitted he'd lied about having a degree – Daisy played it safe. He talked about his academic successes, his new job, the things nobody remembered and nobody cared about. As long as he finished with "but I haven't had a drink today," everybody was happy and nobody asked any questions.

He stared at the mauve walls, wondering if anyone put any thought into the colour scheme, or just made everything as bland as possible.

Another person spoke, a quiet man with kind eyes who admitted to stealing money from his sister's purse for a fix. He looked at the floor as he said it, and the woman next to him patted his knee. A simple gesture, but the kindness of it made Daisy's stomach churn. These people were baring their souls, offering up their ugliest moments for forgiveness, and he was sitting there, an apparition in a chair, a man who had nothing to hide.

He watched them, a profound sense of contempt bubbling inside him. He wasn't a saint, but he wasn't a thief or a liar in that way. He kept his hands clean. His secrets weren't about petty crime or a bad grade. They were about the very core of who he was. And that, he reasoned, was something you didn't casually throw out to a room full of strangers.

He felt a sharp, cutting envy. Their shame was so… manageable. Shoplifting. Lying about a degree. Stealing from a sister. These were things with clear beginnings and ends. Things you could confess, atone for, and then leave behind. His truth, the one that lay coiled deep inside him, had no such neat edges. It was a part of him, an ugly, screaming thing he had tried for a lifetime to bury. A lie so fundamental it had shaped every decision, every relationship, every single moment of his life. How could he ever admit that? How could he lay that out for a room full of strangers? The man with kind eyes had stolen money for a fix; Daisy believed he had stolen a whole life, and now he had to admit that he had no idea what to do with it.

That thought followed him out of the hall, clinging like smoke. Honesty. They all said it was the way out, but how could honesty touch something like this? At home, lying awake in the dark, he realised the envy in that church hall hadn't been about their sins at all. It was about the relief on their faces after they spoke. The unburdening. He wondered if he could unburden, too – not in a meeting, not to another person, but somewhere safer. A screen. A search box. A way of speaking the truth without anyone looking back at him.

He hadn't lied; uni was going well. He wasn't failing; he was socially active and living up to the promise that he'd made to Faye to really give it everything he had. He was working too much, precariously balancing the full-time education with the full-time bar work. It kept him busy, kept him out of trouble. Kept him from thinking about her being gone for a year.

As he lay on his bed that night, though, a voice was nagging him. That demand for honesty.

Daisy was used to keeping secrets: the secrets of the magic, the secrets of the drunken patrons, his circle of friends, and members of his family. Those secrets didn't bother him. His secrets, though… his secrets had been eating him alive for years.

He had first had that fleeting thought when he was about 11 or 12. *I wish I was a girl.*

He was sitting in front of his mother's dressing table, a bottle of her perfume in his hand. He'd sprayed it on his wrist, and for a fleeting moment, he had a sense of peace. He looked at his reflection, the short hair, the clothes he'd been forced to wear, and felt a profound sense of wrongness. The thought whispered in his ear: *I wish I was a girl.* He immediately pushed the feeling down, a frantic, internal shove that made his stomach knot. *Perfectly normal*, he told himself. I mean, sure, he'd also been the only boy on the school netball team, his circle of friends was entirely female, and he was stashing Cosmo when most of the other boys were stashing Playboys. But that was perfectly normal. Every boy did that. Right?

The thing is, that fleeting thought never went away. It was supposed to go away, wasn't it?

It was a very different era. You couldn't ask Google or an AI if something was normal and find out for yourself. And he wasn't about to go to the school librarian and ask if they had any books that might tell him if whatever this was in his head that he couldn't name was normal. What would he even ask for?

He'd asked a teacher once, and he'd laughed and said no.

So, Daisy kept the thoughts to himself.

Occasionally, he'd start seeing things on TV that might maybe make sense. Jerry Springer episodes titled "My Girlfriend Is A Man"; jokes on sitcoms about the snarky guy "kissing a dude". If what he was thinking led to whatever that was, he didn't want that.

Swallow the feelings waaaaaaayyy down.

So, he did his best to pretend. He played sports, dated girls, did manly things (and, occasionally, drama). He built things and broke things and did whatever else he could think of that was "manly."

But he'd never not had those thoughts in his head.

He had them as a child, he had them as a teenager. He had them when he met Marisol and when he met Faye. He had them when they lived together, even while they were having kids.

Despite all his hopes and prayers and best efforts, the voice never went away. "I wish I was a girl."

When he and Faye had broken up, he tried to drink the voices away. And it had worked. The more he drank, the quieter it got. The quieter she got.

He'd found a profound relief in the numbness. The drinking wasn't about the taste or the party; it was a way to be alone in his own head. To make her go away. To silence the screaming, the shame, the constant pressure of a public life. But then the drinking almost killed him. She almost killed him. His attempt to kill the voice in his head… maybe she'd turned it around and tried to kill him?

No, that was crazy. That's how crazy people think.

But now, in sobriety? She was back. And she was angry. She was screaming. She wanted out.

So, desperate for answers, he allowed himself to ask Google. He typed the words with a shaking hand: "I wish I was a girl. Is that normal?" Anxious as he hit enter, convinced he was inviting a verdict of madness. The good news was that it was normal; Reddit was full of people exploring that same thought. And the same thing came up in the replies. Every. Single. Time. "You might be trans."

He knew what that meant, but he didn't know what that meant.

He fell down the rabbit hole. Inching through it over days, weeks, months. His 12-step training kicked in: "Listen to the message, not the story. See if you can identify with anything. Hold on to that." He read stories of people who felt exactly as he did. The same sense of being absent in their own lives, the same feeling of wrongness, the same quiet, desperate wish. He could identify with things. He could identify with all of them.

Fuck.

So, what next? He looked it up. Buy things, try things. See how it feels. Does the pretty dress feel better? It did. It didn't fit, but it felt better. The make-up? The wigs? He tried it all out in his own room, never once expressing thoughts beyond that boundary. Not yet. Curtains closed to hide his shame.

The packages arrived on a Tuesday, unmarked and anonymous. He waited until the house was empty, the quiet of the afternoon thick and peaceful. His hands trembled as he opened the box and pulled out the dress, a simple black A-line that felt cheap and flimsy, but impossibly precious. He held it up to the light, the fabric catching the afternoon sun. He put it on, the material a strange, alien sensation against his skin. He put on the wig, a shiny, synthetic brown that felt too heavy, then clumsily applied the makeup. His reflection was a garbled mess of smeared eyeliner and smudged lipstick, but something in his eyes was different. They were wide, full of a terrifying hope. He walked to the mirror, holding his breath as he took in his reflection. The wig was a cheap thing, a little too shiny, but it framed his face in a way that felt... right.

He looked in the mirror. For a terrifying, silent moment, he didn't recognise the person staring back. The face was his, and yet it wasn't. It was someone else entirely. And then, slowly, a different person emerged from the reflection. A woman, a soft familiarity in her eyes and the curve of her jaw.

He felt the weight of it. Not the physical weight of the cheap wig, but the emotional weight of everything that had been buried. The years of pretending, the constant internal battle, the sheer exhaustion of it all. As the unfamiliar face in the mirror began to feel familiar, a quiet settled over his mind. The screaming stopped. The frantic questions about sanity, the shame, the constant pressure of the secret – all of it… ceased. Now, he wasn't a man trying to hide a girl. He was just a girl, looking at herself. The face was still his, but it was Daisy's, too. He didn't hate *her* anymore. He didn't have to.

She looked like his mother.

For a long moment, there was nothing in his head. The screaming voice, the frantic questions, the shame – it all went quiet. He didn't hate her anymore. She felt… real.

He slowly started coming out to the women outside of his family that he trusted in his life. Well… coming out was a stretch. More… half-heartedly asking if this was normal or if he was crazy.

Nobody thought he was crazy. Or, if they did. Nobody said it.

He was wary, though. He only ever mentioned it to women. Women are friendlier. Warmer… less likely to murder you.

He got comfortable.

He started playing with pronouns and choosing names... after he adopted Daisy – after his favourite superhero character – he used the anonymity of the internet to become Daisy online. To interact with the world as a woman in a way that nobody could see.

It began to feel... normal. But it didn't feel genuine.

He'd told his mum. "I always thought you were gay," she'd said, not unkindly. "But this... this makes sense." She was *technically* right, but she just hadn't guessed sapphic. She was okay with it. In fact, she was more than okay with it. She was supportive, offering to go shopping with her, offering to help her tell her father.

His dad... well, not unsupportive. "I don't get it," he'd said, his voice flat, his eyes fixed on some point over Daisy's shoulder. He didn't say it with a snarl or a sigh. A statement, as if he were discussing the weather. He was polite and distant, a man watching a play he didn't quite understand. "But if this makes you happy... fine." That was honestly the best he expected. He'd thought he'd leave in a pine box.

Eventually, he'd told his whole family how he was feeling and what he was thinking and once he was done, then everyone else around him. Everyone in his life regularly, bar the regulars in the pub and the people he wasn't close to at university.

He was dying... but she was living.

Chapter 10 – Indecent Exposure

Iris stared at her in silence. Stony silence.

Daisy was scrambling for words. Something to say to make this right. Something to make her or Iris or everything disappear – a Men In Black mind-eraser, a sinkhole or an apocalypse. Anything.

She scrunched her eyes shut, hoping that when she opened them, this would all go away, like she was waking up from one of those dreams about being naked at school or something, but when she opened them… Iris was still there.

Fuck.

The quiet wasn't an absence of noise; it was a physical weight that settled between them, heavy and suffocating. She could hear the murmur of other conversations in the café, the clatter of a coffee cup being set down, the soft hiss of the espresso machine. It was a soundtrack to her impending humiliation, each mundane sound a stark contrast to the earthquake happening inside her chest. Iris' expression was unreadable. Her eyes, a striking green, held no judgement, no pity –an unnerving, blank quiet. It was worse than anger. It was a void.

Daisy felt a cold sweat break out on her forehead. The air in the café, so recently a gentle thrum of background noise, now felt sharp and thin, difficult to draw into her lungs. She wanted to shrink, to fold in on herself until she was a tiny, imperceptible dot. This was it. The moment she'd been dreading since she first realised what she'd said. The universe was holding its breath, waiting for Iris to deliver the crushing blow. Daisy braced herself for the words: *You're a monster. You're insane. I don't want to be anywhere near you.* She'd rehearsed this moment, in her head, a hundred times, and she knew the script. Iris' reaction was a deviation, an act of mercy that made her panic even worse.

"What do you mean by 'you hated me for thirteen years?"

This wasn't going to end well, was it?

But Iris seemed intrigued. Passive. Kind, maybe? Interested? Probably not interested. That was too far. Although… Daisy supposed she'd be interested if a total stranger had declared that she'd hated her for over a decade. Maybe Iris thought she was a stalker or crazy or something. I mean, you would, wouldn't you?

Daisy swallowed, the knot in her throat making it hard to breathe. The words, once so neatly confined to the walls of her mind, were now a terrified, squirming thing trying to claw its way out. The thought of running, of sprinting out the door, ached. But she was rooted to the spot, trapped by her own confession.

"Daisy?"

She took a deep breath and info-dumped everything. About her drinking and Faye and her kids and her transition and… everything. As quickly as humanly possible, a runaway train. Iris already knew she was crazy, was already judging her. Why not scorch the earth so they could both escape this nightmare?

The words tumbled out of her like a dam breaking, a torrent of a decade's worth of pain and secrets. She didn't pause for breath, didn't stop to think. She spoke, and spoke, and spoke. The shame of waking up in a police cell, the heartbreak of losing Faye, the terrifying, exhilarating first moments of seeing Daisy in the mirror – she laid it all bare – a mangled mess of a life she'd spent so long hiding – like a passenger on a speeding train, watching the scenery of her life flash past, unable to stop it, unable to slow down. She ended on a gasp, the air burning in her lungs.

"So, we met thirteen years ago, at a meeting when you were still a guy… or pretending to be a guy… or… I have no idea how I'm supposed to phrase that, I'm sorry."

"I tell you that you've been my imaginary arch enemy for years and you're apologizing?"

Was this how normal people behaved? You could dump decades of self-loathing and hatred and confusion and pain on them and they just apologized? Venom met with forgiveness?

She waited for a rebuttal, a sharp word, a look of disgust. She locked eyes with Iris, who was silent. She tried to read her. She probably really, really screwed up this time, right? I mean, the meetings could be like schoolyards. Give it a week, and everyone in a fifty-mile radius would know the story of the chick with a dick who unleashed a nuclear explosion of crazy all over a Starbucks.

Daisy's hands, which had been clutching the edge of the table, curled into tight fists. She felt the sharp plastic digging into her palms, a small, painful anchor to keep herself from floating away in a sea of pure panic.

"Look, you don't have to say anything. I can see it. You tried to be nice and got confronted by this absolute mess of a fucked-up freak and now you want to run away as fast as possible. And I can't even blame you because it's exactly what I'd do and it's probably why I have no friends and no job and no life and no chance of ever having the perfect little life and—" she was aware that her voice was rising.

She felt a new kind of panic, hot and stinging, rise in her throat. The need to fill, to talk over the shame, was overwhelming. Her words grew louder, a desperate, frantic noise that had to be attracting attention. She could feel the stares. The people at the next table were looking, their conversation hushed. She could feel their judgement, cold and clinical, pinning her in place.

But Iris was smiling. She couldn't read the smile.

Iris leant forward, her elbows on the table, her body language a soft, gentle defiance of Daisy's rising hysteria.

"And now you're flashing that pretty smile to mask looking to get the fuck out of here and run away and change your name and address and never speak to me again."

Daisy began to cry. As she did, she became all too aware of her surroundings. In her tunnel vision, her spiral, it had been the two of them – she and Iris. But as Iris refused to speak and tears came rolling down, she was all too aware that she'd just said all of that – and yelled a sizeable portion of it – whilst sitting in the middle of a crowded café around other people. Normal people.

She closed her eyes again. The ground was failing to swallow her up, additional proof that she didn't need that there either wasn't a God or that God hated her as well. She supposed she'd deserve it; she'd been kind of a dick about the whole religion thing.

She felt a soft, warm touch on her arm. Iris' fingers were gentle, a soothing pressure that broke through the wall of her panic. Her grip was firm, but not tight. She took a breath, counted to ten, tried to calm herself and slowly opened her eyes.

"Congratulations, you finally cut the bullshit. How does it feel?"

"I fucking hate you."

Iris laughed.

"You said I was pretty."

"I said you had a pretty *smile*. Don't get cocky."

"I'm sorry. I love being right." She smiled again. Was that conscious? Was she teasing her now?

A flush of heat spread across Daisy's cheeks, a different kind of embarrassment. She had been a storm of messy emotion, and Iris had stood firm in the middle of it, unbothered, and now... amused. It was maddening. And yet, she felt the barest flicker of a smile touch her own lips, the first honest one she'd had in days. She found herself looking at Iris' face, not staring at it. Noticing the laugh lines around her eyes, the gentle curve of her mouth when she wasn't silent.

Was Iris actually fucking with Daisy right now? After she'd unleashed a torrent of her deepest, darkest thoughts and ripped herself open for the entire world to see. After she'd cried and told her she hated her.

"I didn't say you were right."

Daisy hated admitting people were right. Even by omission.

She was right though.

And she really was pretty.

Oh, fuck.

"Do you want to get out of here?" Iris asked, scanning the room.

Daisy looked up. There were people trying not to stare. It was a good idea.

Neither of them spoke. They just walked, each lost in their own thoughts. Daisy felt a constant, low-grade thrum of anxiety. Every step a new opportunity for disaster. She kept her eyes fixed on the pavement, the cracks in the concrete, the gum smudges – anything to avoid looking at Iris or, God forbid, the strangers they passed. Iris, by contrast, seemed at ease, her steps even and unhurried. The contrast between them was so stark, so obvious, that Daisy imagined herself a flashing neon sign advertising her own awkwardness. She could practically feel the silent, judgemental gazes of everyone they passed. *Look at that train wreck of a human being. And look at her, a beacon of cool, walking next to her.* She kept her hands shoved deep in her pockets, as if the fabric could somehow swallow her whole.

As they got closer to her flat, Daisy's anxiety ratcheted up another notch. She'd been so fixated on the café disaster that she hadn't considered the next stage of her public shaming. Now, the thought of Iris seeing her living space, her sanctuary of shame, was almost unbearable. Her mind raced, a frantic slide show of the unwashed dishes, the laundry pile that had taken on the shape of a small mammal, the general, inescapable filth. The shame was a hot, acid taste in the back of her throat.

They ended up back in Daisy's flat, as she tried to act normal and put shopping away to distract her from acknowledging that her living space was a shithole. And she was currently letting another person see it. A normal person, who probably lived in a mansion in a nice area or something. Probably had someone to keep things perfect for her, and another person to sustain her perfect hair and her perfect manicure and her perfect life.

Iris' presence seemed to make the chaos of the flat louder, more pronounced. Daisy's eyes darted from the pile of clean laundry on the sofa to the stack of unwashed dishes by the sink. Every piece of clutter an accusation. The half-eaten bag of crisps on the coffee table seemed to scream, 'Look at me, I'm a mess!' She felt a wave of profound shame, a gut-wrenching realization that she was a living cliché. The messy drunk, the hopeless slob. Iris, with her perfect, knowing smile, was seeing it all. Seeing her for what she really was.

Iris didn't say anything. She simply walked in, her gaze sweeping over the space with a calm neutrality that drove Daisy mad. She didn't gasp, didn't wrinkle her nose, didn't make a single comment. Daisy found herself chattering, a nervous, desperate attempt to fill the void. "It's... I know it's a bit of a mess. I've been really busy with... you know." She gestured vaguely at the disaster zone. She was aware of how pathetic she sounded. It was a lie, a flimsy excuse. She hadn't been busy; she had been hiding from her life. She stopped talking, the silence now even more terrifying than the cacophony of her own excuses.

"So, this is where you live? It's... exactly what I pictured."

Daisy felt her face flush red with embarrassment.

"I used to live like this. Some people hate the chaos, but I love it. Knowing where everything is because you can see it? Not keeping up appearances, or making unnecessary work for yourself. The added bonus of it driving away unwelcome company? Perfect."

Daisy's head snapped up. Iris wasn't looking at the clutter; she was looking directly at Daisy, a subtle dare in her eyes. The air between them crackled with unspoken meaning. It wasn't about the dishes or the laundry. It was about Daisy's life. The chaos wasn't the mess on the floor, it was the mess she'd confessed to in the café. And Iris wasn't running from it. She was daring Daisy to own it.

She let it hang. Daring Daisy to react. To try and pretend she hadn't heard it, or to respond. A test.

Daisy looked up. Iris smiled. She was caught.

She was used to being the games master, not the contestant.

Daisy felt her shoulders slump, an unlikely, weary surrender. "I don't... I don't get you," she said, her voice barely a whisper. "You should be a hundred miles away from me by now. I unloaded all of my baggage on you in a very public place, and you're here. In my messy flat. And you're... you're smiling."

"I see a lot of myself in you, Daisy," Iris said, her voice soft. She looked around the room, her gaze lingering for a moment on the pile of clothes, the remnant of a sad smile on her face before it was gone. "Not the exact same story, of course. But the shame. The hiding. The feeling like you're a mess that needs to be tidied up before anyone can see you."

"Do you want some help?" Iris asked, scanning the room.

Daisy looked at her. Her face was blotchy, her eyes stinging, and she felt a wave of profound fatigue wash over her. Not a tired fatigue, but a surrender. A giving up of the fight she had been fighting for so long. She looked at Iris, who was looking at her, waiting.

"Help with what?" Daisy responded; her voice full of despondent quiet. It wasn't a question of fact, but of possibility. Not *'what is it you want to help me with?'* but *'is it really possible to help me at all? After all this?'*

Iris *used* to live like this. Iris *used* to live in chaos.

Past tense.

But Iris *loves* chaos.

Chapter 11 – The Fifteen-Year Itch of 2019

Daisy was halfway through deleting another spam email when his phone vibrated.

A single notification. A name he hadn't seen in fifteen years.

A friend request.

From Marisol.

For a second, his thumb hovered over the screen, useless, like it belonged to someone else.

Some days the universe doesn't whisper. It grabs your face and forces you to look.

A friend request – a tiny, glowing portal to a past he had systematically destroyed. It had been fifteen years since they'd last spoken, a lifetime ago. This had to be a prank. A dream. A catfish scam. He pictured a bored kid in a basement, or a former friend of Faye's playing a cruel joke. He scrolled, heart pounding, to the profile picture: a smiling woman with the same kind eyes he remembered. The same laugh lines he once memorized. It was her. It was really, impossibly, her.

For a moment, he froze. Fear, guilt, trepidation.

Shame. And… curiosity?

He hadn't dared speak her name in years. She was a ghost, a beautiful, painful reminder that he had buried under layers of alcohol and bad decisions. He'd resisted the urge to look her up, to even vaguely mention her to those who knew she'd existed, but after the break-up with Faye, he'd be lying if he said he hadn't thought about her. Wondered if she was his *Sliding Doors* moment. The train pulling away from the station. The moment he'd had to choose between his old life and the promise of a new, glittering, chaotic one. The thought was a familiar, bitter pill. He had lived his life as a masterclass in choosing the wrong path.

Marisol was the train he'd missed and the adventure he'd craved.

Intrigue overcoming instinct, he accepted the request and allowed himself a moment to look, as if it could be snatched away at any moment. His thumb trembled slightly as he tapped the "Confirm" button. Like stepping into a cold river, a shock to the system he had kept so insulated from the past.

He let the screen load, a small, breathless moment of anticipation. Her page was a window into a life he hadn't known. He scrolled through her photographs. She hadn't aged a day; if she had, mother nature had been incredibly kind. He saw her on a beach, the wind whipping her hair, her face radiant with laughter. He remembered the exact way she'd laugh, a full-bellied sound that crinkled her eyes and made his whole world feel lighter. He could almost hear it, a phantom echo of a happiness he had once been a part of.

In another picture, she was holding a dog, her head thrown back in a fit of giggles. There were photos with friends, at family gatherings, and one with a tall, sandy-haired man he assumed was her husband. The man had a kind smile, his arm wrapped around her waist. He looked steady. Dependable. The exact opposite of everything Daisy had become. He saw pictures of them hiking, cooking together in a sunlit kitchen, and sitting on a porch swing, their hands clasped. The photos were a testament to a life built on small, meaningful moments. A life he had forfeited for the fleeting, toxic glitter of Faye and his public life.

Life had clearly been good to her. *Life after him*, he corrected himself.

The one-two punch landed, the messenger bubble of destiny. Her Face.

"Hi"

Brief. Suitably awkward.

They had always thought alike. Felt alike. Been able to simultaneously say what they and the other were thinking. A kind of synchronicity he had never found with anyone else, least of all Faye. Faye was a performance. With Marisol, there was an effortless flow, a shared language that didn't require words. The absence of that was something he hadn't fully appreciated until it was gone.

"Hi," he responded.

The exploratory opening jabs of a long-anticipated heavyweight contest.

After some tentative small talk, they slipped into a familiar rhythm. But it was polite, breezy, all the depth of a contact lens. Pleasantries. *How have you been? What are you up to? What's new?*

"I'm good, really," she typed. "Married now, to a wonderful guy named Ben. We've got a house, two dogs... the whole thing."

Daisy's gut twisted. "Married, huh? That's great. Congrats." He hoped it hadn't sounded disingenuous.

"And you?" she asked.

"Oh, you know," he typed, "the usual. Back at uni... uh... settled."

Marisol was married now. She worked an admin job at the same university that she'd graduated from, that she'd been so excited to go to when they'd last spoken. Her life seemed steady. Respectable. Enviable, even.

The casualness of her answers was a knife in his gut. She described her husband – a respectable, solid man named Ben – with an easy affection that made Daisy feel empty. She talked about their home, their shared hobbies, the quiet, predictable peace of their life. Everything he'd ever wanted and, in his self-destructive recklessness, everything he'd thrown away. The person who said that it was better to have loved and lost than never to have loved at all… hadn't met Faye or Marisol. And, had he met both of them, he'd have shut his fucking mouth.

It felt weird to Daisy; he was envying a life that could've been his. That he'd given up in favour of years of trauma, anger and misery.

That was the moment it hit Daisy: he owed her something. An apology. An explanation. The truth or, at least, a version of it that might provide closure.

He paused at the keyboard. Deleting. Retyping. The words felt pathetic. *"Sorry. I regret it."* They were too small to contain a decade-and-a-half's worth of damage. He knew he had to do it anyway. He owed her at least this.

There was a long, long pause before the ominous three dots appeared.

"I thought you were *fucking* dead."

Dead.

Not metaphorically dead. She *literally* assumed that Daisy was dead. What choice did she have? With the absence… it was so complete that it dawned on Daisy that she must've grieved for him once already.

The words hit him like a hammer. The air rushed out of his lungs, leaving him breathless. He felt dizzy, as if the room were tilting. Grieved for him. She had mourned him. The shame was a searing, physical pain. He could barely see the phone screen through the blur of his vision.

And then there was the subtext, a subtext that nobody but Daisy could've spotted. He wondered if her husband would've spotted it.

Marisol *never* swore. Not out of some holier-than-thou principle, she'd just been raised better.

For Daisy, an F-bomb was punctuation. For Marisol, it was a nuclear bomb.

Daisy had reappeared in her life somehow. A friend suggestion, perhaps some sense of curiosity on Marisol's part... to Marisol, Daisy was, in this moment, quite literally the undead. Without thinking, without realising, perhaps selfishly, he'd ripped open a wound and thrown salt in it.

Another pause.

"You broke my heart back then, and I thought I'd never recover, but I did," Marisol wrote, "and then I found you again, and I wanted to believe there was some good explanation and... you did it again."

Daisy stared at the screen, the weight of everything he had heard hitting him like a right hook to the gut. He felt sick. His hands were shaking. He hadn't just ruined the past, he'd shattered her present, too.

He scrambled to try and figure out a way to make this right. To fix this.

His mind raced, a frantic, desperate search for an escape route. He'd never been in a situation he couldn't charm or lie his way out of. But this was different. There was no performance to hide behind. Just the brutal, gut-wrenching consequence of his selfishness. He thought back to their conversation. Through their previous exchange, he'd learned that she was married, but not happy. Her strict Catholic upbringing dictated that she not take the most obvious step. She was stuck. Making the best of it.

An impulse burned in Daisy's chest; he had always wanted to be a hero, always sought ways to save people. Years of playing a villain for a crowd had taught him exactly what people wanted to see in a hero. He knew what the next step was – to save the girl.

Except… this wasn't a show. This wasn't bright lights and showbusiness. There was no safety net, no training, no paycheque here.

He was, very literally, the villain in this situation. And he had no idea how to become the hero.

He could feel the old scripts rising in his mind. The swaggering bravado, the charming, self-deprecating wit. He wanted to say, *don't worry, I'm here now. I'll make it better.* He wanted to be the knight in shining armour, the one who rode in and saved the princess from the miserable castle of her life. But the words tasted like ash. He was the one who had built the castle out of broken promises. Had fate brought them back together as a sign? Was he supposed to swoop in, rescue her, sweep her off her feet and give her safety? Was this his second chance, his redemption arc?

Even as the thought passed through his mind, he knew the truth – he couldn't say that saving Marisol was something he wanted to do for her benefit, or his own. It would be another selfish act disguised as a noble one.

"I..." he began to type, as another message appeared.

"Where *were* you?"

It came loaded with subtext; she didn't just want an account of his whereabouts, like a deadbeat dad who had returned from getting milk. The questions were stacked like a Russian nesting doll.

"Why did you disappear?"

"Why wasn't I good enough?"

"Why didn't you love me?"

He stared at the screen. The weight of the moment felt immense, a boulder pressing down on him. The moment of truth. The moment he had to finally, truly be honest. His chance to stop the cycle of bullshit and to be seen for who he was. All of it. The good, the bad, and the very, very ugly.

And so, he confessed everything. He typed until his thumbs ached, stopping only when his phone showed a low-battery warning that he ignored. The words came anyway – Faye, the kids, the drinking, the collapse – a list that refused to end. He held back the biggest secret, because he knew that would ruin everything.

He did love Marisol. He'd never *stopped* loving Marisol. But he'd never been good enough for Marisol, he'd always told her that, and he'd proven it.

He was more than aware that she was a believer in the cleansing power of confession, but he didn't feel absolved. He felt dirty. Toxic.

"Thank you for telling me the truth. I need to think about this." She eventually responded.

Confession didn't always cleanse. Sometimes it poisoned.

Daisy sat there, phone in hand, the bright screen a cruel, unforgiving light in the darkness of his room. He had laid it all out, a map of his ruin, and instead of feeling lighter, he felt a crushing weight. The truth hadn't set him free. It had simply left him alone with the consequences.

Chapter 12 – The Disney Princess

Daisy had rolled out of bed about an hour earlier, a couple of cigarettes, a coffee, a shower… and that was her mandatory daily checklist finished. It was almost noon. The apartment, a testament to her apathy, felt smaller and dustier than usual, the stale air thick with forgotten routines.

She sat down at her laptop to resume the ritual of seeing what torture the robot had for her. Just as she was about to type –

A sharp, persistent knock at the door.

She froze. People didn't knock on doors these days. A sound that belonged to a different life, a different time, a world where the outside could intrude without warning. Her mum would have called; her siblings wouldn't be able to get to her place without detailed instructions. She considered the possibilities. A delivery she hadn't ordered? The Jehovah's Witnesses? Whichever politician was campaigning for free money at the low-low price of yet more of her rights? A childish, rebellious urge to mess with them, to open the door and unleash her unique brand of withering sarcasm, bubbled up.

Taking a deep, preparatory breath, she opened the door.

Iris.

Her stomach dropped. It wasn't a sickening lurch, but a slow, heavy descent. Iris stood on the other side of the threshold, beaming, a large box of cleaning supplies held like a peace offering or a weapon. She was in a pristine, white t-shirt and perfectly-fitted jeans, a walking, breathing reproach. A part of Daisy wanted to shut the door and pretend she wasn't home.

"Hope you don't mind? I was in the neighbourhood, I was thinking about you, thought I'd stop in."

Daisy's eyes narrowed, scanning the surreal scene. "And where in this chain of events, dare I ask, did you encounter a box of cleaning supplies?"

"Great question, very observant, very insightful," Iris said, her smile not wavering. "Today is the first day of the rest of your life. Tidy house, tidy mind." She took a step inside, the scent of fresh lemon and disinfectant an aggressive invader in Daisy's stale, smoky flat.

"I'm sorry, did you swallow Mary Poppins?"

Iris' gaze landed on the laptop screen, her eyebrows raising. "Oh, look, you were about to talk to the AI life guru. How's that going?"

"Fuck off."

"Exactly what I thought," she threw Daisy some rubber gloves, that landed with a soft, humiliating slap at her feet. "You want to start rebuilding your life, or do you want to sit around in your underwear all day crying about how unfair the world is?"

Mean. *Fair*.

Fuck.

She was quite literally in her underwear. Not even the good underwear. The old, red ones, with the frayed elastic.

"At least let me get dressed first."

"If you insist. I'll be in the kitchen."

When Daisy had dressed, a task that took much longer than it should have – how exactly does one dress for the occasion of the girl she'd accidentally called pretty appearing in one's shithole flat unannounced to clean up the detritus of the lazy twat that lived there? – Iris was already elbow deep in the oven. The chaotic piles of Daisy's life, a landscape of takeaway boxes, empty bottles, and dusty clothes, were being systematically dismantled. Iris was surrounded by filled bin bags, a tiny island of order in an ocean of chaos.

She worked quickly, a controlled whirlwind of productive energy. "Bin bags are on the sofa, if you want to get started in there?"

Daisy did not want to get started in there. If she had wanted to get started in there, she'd have gotten started in there before it became a landfill. Before Iris came into her flat. Before Iris came into her life. A wave of intense, hot shame washed over her. Now, she didn't feel passive resentment for the mess; she actively hated it. But she didn't hate the results of it. If not cleaning it had kept the people she didn't want visiting out, why did she want to help? It was a stalemate, and the camera had flipped.

"Did you forget where the living room is? Because it's that room you're standing in. You know, with the sofa. And the bin bags."

Was that sarcasm? Bossiness? Was Iris mocking her, or giving her an order? Daisy did not like being mocked or given orders. She hated it. So, naturally, she plucked a bin bag from the roll and started stuffing it. She started with the pile of old bills, then the takeaway containers, each one a tiny monument to her failure.

Between them, they worked diligently and in just a few hours, most of the worst of it was stuffed into a stack of bin bags in the hallway. The smell of bleach and lemon started to replace the stale smoke, a small victory. As the place became cleaner, Daisy fought the childish urge to "accidentally" knock something over or split a bin bag. She wanted to disrupt the order, to piss Iris off. But a small, curious part of her wondered what Iris was like when she was angry. Was she capable of it? Or was she this eternally patient, Christ-like figure? Daisy had always had a thing for angry girls. Or maybe she had a knack for making them angry. She decided it was best not to risk it.

One room left: the bedroom. As Iris stepped towards it, Daisy found herself instinctively throwing her body across the door.

A bizarre, involuntary reaction. She'd never done that before.

Iris jumped back, a shocked look across her face. Then a smile. Not *that* smile, a small, smug smirk.

"Ohhhhhh," Iris laughed, the sound warm and full. "Okay, you've got secrets."

The word "secrets" had never had so much subtext.

"Fair warning," she continued, her eyes twinkling, "when I come back, that's where I'm heading first."

Come back? The thought of Iris willingly returning sent a jolt through Daisy.

"Let's get these bags out." Iris cheerfully started gathering as many as she could carry, whistling – *literally whistling* – "Whistle While You Work," from Mary Poppins to Snow White via Little Bo Peep.

After Iris left, Daisy got to work on the bedroom. It reminded her of being a child, when her parents would force her to tidy her room. She'd sweep her toys into a box, and fold clothes, but the dirty laundry would get stuffed into a washing machine for a quick wash, lest anyone see the shame of it.

She was awoken the next day at dawn by a banging at the door. The flat smelled different – clean, sharp, unfamiliar. She was alert enough to at least throw on a white vest and some green sweatpants before she answered it.

"Wow, you're hard to get out of bed!" Iris' voice was too loud, too cheerful for 7am, "I've been knocking for about ten minutes!"

How the fuck was anyone *this* cheerful at 7am?

"I need to, uhm…" Daisy pointed towards the bathroom.

"Oh, yeah, of course. I'll be waiting in the bedroom." There was a long, knowing pause. "Cleaning, obviously."

As Daisy headed for the bathroom, she felt a small thrill of triumph. She knew Iris was about to be very disappointed. She'd made very sure that there was nothing to clean.

When she emerged, she found Iris perched on the edge of the bed.

"Very impressive; I guess I underestimated you. You're not completely helpless."

Daisy let that one slide, a small smile playing on her lips. "So, what's next?"

"Next, we de-clutter. We get rid of everything you don't want, don't use or don't need. Bin it, donate it, sell it."

"Keep it is an option, too, right?"

"Sure, as long as you're not going to try and convince me you need all 30 of those empty deodorant cans."

Fuck, she forgot to throw those away. She felt a familiar burn of shame. The empty cans were a physical reminder of how long she'd let things slide.

"Let's start with the closet," said Iris, bouncing across the room and throwing it open. Fingering through all the newly-neatly-hung clothes, her eyes landed on a long-faded Nirvana t-shirt. "I used to have one just like this."

Cinderella had an edge. Or was she a poseur?

"Okay, awkward one: do you really *need* twelve suits?"

Okay, maybe Daisy had been hoarding. She hadn't worn a suit since *he* died. These weren't clothes; they were artifacts from a life she had systematically abandoned. The suits were a physical representation of the man she used to pretend to be – the one who cared about success, about impressing others, about fitting in.

"Yeah… they can go."

"Donate?"

"Sell! Those things cost a fortune!"

"Okay, sell."

Iris picked through the rest of her clothes like a tornado through a trailer park. Controlled, yet natural, chaos. When they were done, Daisy looked at the three piles. Most of them belonged to *him*. All she had left of *him* after the first round were a few t-shirts and *his* collection of football shirts.

Her collection. As much as she'd tried to divorce herself of *him* entirely, they obviously still had a few things in common.

"You weren't ready for this, were you?" Iris had read her mind, somehow.

"There's a big difference between the theoretical and the practical."

"We can stop if you want?" Iris offered.

"Do you want to stop?" Daisy fired back.

"I'm just getting started."

Iris' eyes turned to the mountain of cuddly toys on – and around – the bed. She reached for one – a purple punk-styled teddy bear with multicoloured hair.

"These next."

"No!" Daisy snatched the bear from Iris' hand, the force of her movement surprising them both. A small tear formed at the corner of her eye.

"There's a story here?"

Daisy clutched the bear to her chest, the soft fabric a painful comfort. "I bought this because it reminded me of Faye." She hadn't just loved her; she was addicted to her. Faye was a drug, a beautiful, toxic chaos that she couldn't live without, even as she destroyed her. She hadn't said the name aloud in years. She'd amassed most of the collection while they were together. The teddy bears were a lie she told herself, a soft, cuddly symbol of a relationship that was anything but.

"They all stay," she said, firmly.

Iris nodded; her expression softened with understanding. She didn't push, didn't prod, simply let the quiet hang in the air between them. Her eyes held Daisy's, a silent exchange passing between them: *Are you okay?* Daisy shook her head, a barely perceptible movement. A small, sad smile on Iris' face.

Daisy fought to hold back the tears. She grabbed her packet of cigarettes from the dresser. "I'll be back." She had to get out, had to breathe. The air in the room, once stale, now felt too clean, too real.

Once she returned, the rest of the de-cluttering process concluded without incident. Everything in neat boxes of things to be sold or donated, the things to be thrown out bagged and thrown in the communal bins. The things to be sold were listed on eBay – on Iris' account, because she correctly sensed that Daisy might be tempted to delist things – and they sat in the freshly-organised living room for a hard-earned cup of tea.

"About earlier," Iris offered, her voice quiet, "I'm sorry."

"For what?" Daisy was genuinely confused. Whether it was a trauma response or the product of pickling her own brain for years, she was not famed for her memory.

"For the clothes… and the bears," she responded, cautiously. "I didn't mean to stir up anything… uncomfortable."

"Oh, that! No, that's fine. That's perfectly fine. No problem." Deflection. That's how you avoid catching feelings.

"Okay," Iris responded, cautiously. "I just forget that you've got an awkward past and, to be honest, sometimes it feels like I'm cartwheeling through a minefield."

"It's okay, really. I get it. Don't tiptoe around it, ask. Ask me anything. I'm an open book."

"And a world-class bullshit artist," Iris laughed, but it was gentle. "But you've been a good girl, so you get your reward now."

Daisy responded with a raised eyebrow. *Reward?*

"I got you a job." The words were a simple statement, but they landed with the force of a lifeline, a promise, a challenge. Daisy stared at her, the mug trembling slightly in her hand. A job. The one thing she'd been circling for months, the one thing she'd been too afraid to truly go after. Now, it was… handed to her. The fear was a cold knot in her gut, but it was mixed with something else: a tiny flicker of hope. It was a terrifying possibility, but a possibility nonetheless.

Chapter 13 – The First Ending (2005)

Another day, another shitty community centre. But this one was different. This one had the weight of the world on its shoulders, and every square foot of its linoleum floor was a testament to Daisy's failures.

He had dropped out of university and moved in with Faye almost immediately after the plastic stick of destiny had changed both their lives. Somewhere along the line, she had gotten the bright idea to go from performer to promoter, and this was her debut show. Naturally, he had been left in charge of doing all of the heavy lifting. He was 19; he did not have the skills or training for this much responsibility, and the role involved keeping thousands of plates spinning even before they incrementally discovered that some of the plates weren't showing up.

On top of these responsibilities, he was also supposed to be performing that night, and his dance partner was one of those plates that wasn't appearing.

Because complications were piling up, Faye had somehow sweet-talked Martin into paying for the whole thing and he – understandably raw, given the circumstances – also hadn't shown up as planned.

To make matters worse, because they'd already had weeks of problems in the lead-up to this, a headliner had dropped out late-on, forcing Daisy to draft in Jason as the replacement.

Jason was a big star, but was also publicly known to be Daisy's biggest rival. As far as the fans were concerned, they legitimately hated each other. Not in a showbusiness sense; it was believed by all those who considered themselves to be in the know that they would be two cats in a bag if they were ever to be put in the same dressing room. The reality, as it often is, was much tamer than the fiction. They had a relationship, and they'd had problems in the past, but it had never been anywhere near the blood feud that the public believed. The closer you got to the top of the pyramid, the less room there was. Their relationship was cordial. They'd never be the best of friends, but there was an element of mutual respect. They could – and had – quite easily occupied the same space on numerous occasions.

Had.

Because Faye, eighteen at the time, had dropped the revelation – as if he needed any more stress having been burdened with the responsibility of handling *everything* else – that she had also had a relationship with Jason several years previously. One of the personal variety; less romantic, but something that had left her feeling used and discarded.

So, faced with the challenge of running someone else's business, financed by his fiancé's ex, featuring a man his fiancé had heavily intimated had a past that had left her with deep-seated trauma and faced with little choice but to break in a rookie as his "opponent" for the night, he'd done the only responsible thing that a 19-year-old could do in that situation, and started drinking. Early.

Daisy had been blessed with what the experts called "hollow legs". He could consume ungodly quantities of alcohol without anyone being any wiser.

All he had to do was get through tonight, pray that there were no disasters, that nobody got hurt, and avoid killing a guy.

Easy.

With an hour until showtime, as the doors opened to the audience, everything seemed to be running smoothly. He'd reshuffled the creative into something that could work, made sure everybody knew their places, their roles… even somehow kept things cordial and polite with Jason whilst trying to manage Faye's ever-accelerating emotional rollercoaster.

Maybe he had this. A quick, reassuring sip from his hip-flask – couldn't have the boys seeing him drinking, that was wildly unprofessional – and a deep breath. He'd done the backstage headcount; a quick peek through the curtain to do the one that mattered.

He parted the heavy, stained curtain a crack, the scent of mildew and pessimism in the air. Typically, you got used to doing this. You'd get the sense of a not only the size of the crowd, but the demographics of it. Little hints that, in his limited experience, could help you craft the difference between a good show and a great one.

What you didn't want to see was exactly what he was seeing. An audience that you could literally count the heads of. Twenty-six of them. They were dead in the water. The handful of faces in the front row looked bored, their expressions already a judgement.

The second Faye saw the empty seats, her face crumpled. "I'm fucked." The words were a quiet, exasperated sound.

Too late. The tears followed, as did the incoherent panic as he could see her processing the crumbling of her dreams. He opened his mouth to reassure her, and nothing came out. If he had been able to feel any sense of peace, success, achievement and even capability before whilst taking on far more responsibility than he'd bargained for, he had a realisation of his own: he now had one more problem, and he was totally on his own to deal with everything. He felt a sharp, cold knot of panic twist in his stomach, a feeling that no amount of alcohol could dull. He had to be the rock, the solution, the one who held it all together, and he was shattering.

He was out straight after the first match – Jason hadn't arrived in the building yet – for a simple segment, a set-up and teaser for later. He and his opponent would have a verbal back and forth, a little physical altercation. Simple. He'd done this a hundred times before.

Of course, sober, this was like breathing. He'd sleepwalk through this on any other night.

Tonight was not that night. The verbal went fine – he'd never lacked the ability to talk – but the physical should've been a foreshadowing of what was to come. It was clumsy, awkward... he assumed the kid was nervous.

It couldn't be him. It was the kid's debut, of course he was nervous.

When he returned to the back, Jason had arrived with his entourage in tow. He'd found a few extra bodies to help move pad the show and brought them with him. A genuinely smart, knowledgeable gesture that perfectly demonstrated the wisdom gradient between the two of them.

They exchanged pleasantries, and Daisy calmly laid out the scenario for Jason for the night. The scent of Jason's expensive cologne was a stark contrast to the stale sweat and dust of the community centre, a reminder of the chasm between their levels of success. It crossed his mind that he should explain the full extent of the chaos to his more senior colleague – Jason had run things elsewhere – and maybe ask him to help out. He was a seasoned pro, and he probably would've done it.

Unfortunately, Daisy also had the recent revelations running through his mind. The thought of entrusting this sinking ship to a man who had hurt Faye was a non-starter. How do you trust a man to save your arse when you know you can't trust him to be alone with the most important person in your life?

Besides, Jason was respected by the boys. He'd have taken a leadership role no matter what Daisy asked. Maybe they didn't need to have too much conversation? He felt a new kind of resentment bubbling inside him, an acrid mix of jealousy and personal fury.

Between then and his big moment, Daisy had to balance asking questions, bantering with the boys and keeping Faye calm. Given everything going on, it could've been much worse, but maybe he'd misjudged how bad things were.

Nothing happening in the ring was bad. Little of it was spectacular, but it wasn't unacceptably bad. Just another run-of-the-mill show in an industry that had seen millions of them.

More miraculously, no injuries – especially impressive given that one contest featured a real-life husband and wife facing off with weapons in play. The healthiest display of domestic violence ever seen.

And, finally, it was Daisy's turn to go back out in front of the crowd.

His entrance theme was long; he'd deliberately always used something with a long intro before he appeared on the other side of the curtain; he'd always got a touch of stage fright before showtime, and this gave him space to breathe, meditate and clear his mind. Usually, he'd be relaxed and focussed when the vocal hit.

Tonight, he felt sick. His head felt light and detached from his body, his stomach a tight, churning mess. The alcohol, which had promised him a warm escape, had betrayed him, turning into a sour, nauseating poison.

The contest itself was the worst fifteen-minutes of his career. Everything was sloppy, disjointed. The storytelling non-existent, everything mistimed. Even his tights refused to stay up. He felt tired, dizzy, confused, angry.

He was sure the kid really was the drizzling shits. In no way on his level. Sure, he worked hard, did everything he was told to do and did it well, but he clearly wasn't ready. He'd even delivered a stiff shot that he knew would lead to an angry purple bruise by morning.

When it was over – mercifully over – Daisy did what he was supposed to do. Thanked the kid for the work, told him he'd done everything he wanted, towelled himself off and got on with seeing through the rest of the night.

He checked a clock on the wall; only half an hour to get through, and he was finished.

Jason went out to close the show. He was, as always, outstanding. He carried a kid he'd never met to something that was almost art, found a level in the lad that even Daisy had doubted he had – he'd been a friend of Faye's that she insisted take the spot.

Daisy had a small part to play in it, helping Jason to victory in a tiny meta "fuck you" to the fans who insisted they'd kill each other – that'd get the internet talking.

And, when the bell rang, it was over. He breathed a sigh of relief.

As they packed up and the boys filtered out, Jason stopped to shake Daisy's hand, to thank him, to ask him to say thank you to Faye on his behalf.

"She told me what happened between you two," Daisy said, quietly, his voice a low, dangerous rumble. "I suggest you keep her name out of your mouth in future."

Jason laughed. A hearty laugh. A mocking laugh. A laugh that cut through the noise and landed with a vicious, personal blow. He slapped Daisy on the shoulder – hard – as if he'd heard the funniest joke ever, turned to his entourage, and left.

Just like that, the civil war had turned cold.

A few weeks later, the videographer that Faye had hired to record the event released the footage of the event. Daisy's scheme to get people talking by having that brief public alliance with Jason had got people talking, and people were buying it – although, unhelpfully, Faye would never see a penny of the proceeds.

What people would see, however, was the disaster that Daisy had been a part of. Now sober, lucid, he watched it back in horror. It wasn't the kid that sucked, it was him. He'd ruined everything.

Worse, the footage had been uploaded online and was going *viral*. Everybody was seeing this, and everybody would be seeing this forever. And those fans he'd been so confident of getting excited for the next instalment with his creative brilliance were now publicly mocking his ineptitude.

Panicking, he took to the internet to defend himself. He made every excuse he could short of telling the truth – that he was wasted. That he was incompetent. He doubled down and doubled down, digging the hole deeper and burying himself.

He felt himself sinking into a spiral of depression as the weeks went on, and Faye became keen on doing it again. She, like a gambler, was chasing her losses and he, emotionally-eviscerated, never wanted to do it again. Not for her, nor for anybody.

Luckily, he wasn't exactly being overwhelmed with offers to do it again. The community is small, and everybody *knew* he'd been drinking. *"Unfit to perform,"* as they would politely refer to it. He was done, and nobody did him the common courtesy of telling him.

Chapter 14 – Legally Bland

The first thing Daisy noticed about the office was the sterile, unforgiving monotony. Not a warm, earthy tone but a washed-out, lifeless colour that leached the light from the room and the energy from the people within it. The walls were beige, the desks were beige, and the people – a sea of them, all seemingly younger, all so effortlessly *normal* – were a uniform mix of beige, grey, and pale blue. She felt a familiar tickle of anxious energy, a need to pick at the hem of her trousers. She pressed her hands into her lap, a desperate attempt to still herself, to keep a spotlight from her. She looked down at her red shoes, the only splash of colour – a neon sign broadcasting that she did not belong.

Iris had called it "an opportunity," but she got the impression of being babysat. Parked. The job was something she was qualified for – a junior paralegal working for Iris' uncle. The idea of being "junior" at 40 amused her, but the stakes didn't.

It wasn't just the work, which was naturally putting her in a position to ruin other people's lives – her specialty – whilst somehow being entrusted not to. This felt less like a job and more like a secret trial. Iris had trusted her with an assessor, a trusted expert who would offer a second opinion.

She sat at her new desk and tried to make sense of everything; the caseload, much of which was already deep in-progress and required her to read diligently to catch herself up. The "case management system" – intricate databases and spreadsheets containing millions of pounds worth of other people's personal drama – was almost impossible to navigate. She was expected to handle not just caseloads, but communications. Being required to use a phone in 2025 had to be considered an act of torture, or perhaps a cruel joke of the universe to prevent her from her usual habit of avoiding outside contact.

On top of that, she was expected to keep track of the financial accounts related to those caseloads. Iris had, brilliantly, got her a job that required her to perform at least three separate tasks that she was *legendarily* awful at.

She looked around her; everyone seemed to know what they were doing. The other paralegals, some of them legitimately half her age, worked quietly – a headset for the phone calls, an AirPod drowning out the low, bland whir of the office. The air was thick with the faint smell of week-old fruit from an overfilled bin, sweet beneath the sharp bitterness of burnt coffee from the communal machine. The ringing of a phone a shrill demand, the clattering of keys an insistent drumbeat. She ran her tongue over her teeth, a small, repetitive tic, a habit she'd tried to break but that had resurfaced the moment she walked into this sterile box.

Her new boss – Iris' Uncle, whose name Daisy hadn't learnt, given that neither the job nor her relationship with Iris was ever going to last long enough for her to have any need to remember it – seemed nice enough.

He gave her the tour, the welcome speech. Mumbled something about punctuality – another thing Daisy was renowned for – about how they were all "one big family" whilst introducing her to fifty people who all looked identical to one another. A token "I'm here if you have questions, don't be afraid to ask."

She couldn't decide if it was kindness or the formalities of corporate bullshit. Corporate kindness, maybe?

She could feel the other paralegals watching her, whispering about her. Their polite smiles when she walked towards the bathroom felt thin.

Offers of help, coffee, information came easily – too easily. She knew better than to trust it.

They were probably all talking about her. Not just about her age or her looks, but about how she'd gotten the job. She'd be a running joke, the boss's bizarre favour to his niece.

They were trying to decipher who she was. The way her voice was too low, the way her hands trembled, the way her body looked like a hastily assembled collection of parts that didn't quite fit together. They were trying to figure out if she was a 'she' or a 'he,' or a 'they.' Or, worst of all, an 'it.' You always knew the stab in the back was coming; you just never knew what type of blade they'd be using.

The only person who seemed genuinely friendly was the receptionist – a woman about her own age with dark brown hair and an easy smile who introduced herself as Sophie. When Daisy stumbled through the lobby that morning, clearly lost and visibly panicking. Sophie had guided her to where she needed to be, with a warmth in her voice. "You'll be fine."

Not *"you'll do fine"* or *"it'll be fine"* – just *"you'll be fine."* Like she was talking to an actual person rather than a problem to be solved.

By lunchtime, she was already ready to quit. She wanted to text Iris, saying "You win. I lasted three hours. Now you know how big a screw-up I am. You get to have the full Daisy experience."

But she didn't.

Maybe it was pride, or stubbornness? Maybe it was the knowledge that this might be her last chance?

Maybe she didn't want to disappoint the one person who seemed to think well of her.

The highlight of the afternoon was when she spilt coffee all over a form. She had panicked, finding herself flapping around saying "fuck, fuck, fuck" under her breath – classy and feminine as always – until someone reassured her that she could print off another one.

"Happens all the time," they said, calmly, "relax."

Relax? Easy for them to say as her cheeks flushed pink with embarrassment. Daisy hadn't relaxed in about twenty years, and she'd been the least relaxed she'd ever been in her life since she arrived at 9am.

The second day started with three hours of sleep. Three. The rest of the night had been spent replaying every moment from Monday on a continuous loop, analysing every look, every pause in conversation, every polite smile that might have been masking contempt. She'd arrived twenty minutes early, partly because she couldn't bear to spend another moment alone with her thoughts, and partly because she was terrified of being late and giving them ammunition.

The environment felt even more oppressive on day two. Like a psychological experiment designed to break down human resistance through pure, soul-crushing blandness. She wondered if this was how laboratory rats felt.

Sophie waved at her from reception. "Morning! How was the first day?"

"Survived," Daisy said, surprised by herself. Most people asked how it went, not whether you survived. There was a difference.

"That's the main thing," Sophie said with a grin. "Coffee's free if you want some before the vultures get to it."

Daisy screwed up some filing, labelled something wrongly in the CMS under the wrong client and messed up the recording – she'd never understand the insistence on billing everything in six-minute increments, even when the task took ten seconds – and when someone needed to access that document later, she could feel them muttering about "the new girl", even if she couldn't hear it. Probably for the best, because there was a one-in-ten chance they'd be muttering about "the new guy" and meaning her, and that wasn't what she needed on top of everything else.

A paralegal called Leah – twenty-five, confident in a way that only came from never wondering whether you belonged somewhere – approached her desk around eleven.

"Hey, so you know, the CMS is a bit mental when you're starting out. I've got some notes that might help"?

She seemed genuine, but she'd learned not to trust genuine. Genuine was often the setup for the punchline. She took the notes anyway, mumbled thanks, waited for the catch. It never came. Leah just went back to her desk.

Maybe corporate kindness was... kindness?

No. Too risky to assume.

The third day brought a phone call that nearly broke her. A client, angry about delays in their case, shouting down the line about *"incompetent staff"* and *"what kind of operation are you running?"* She'd fumbled through an apology, promising to pass the message on, hung up with shaking hands.

She'd sat there for a full minute, staring at the phone like it might explode, when Sophie appeared beside her desk with a cup of tea.

"Rough call?" Sophie asked quietly.

"Is it that obvious?"

"Only to someone who's been there. First week phone calls are the worst. They smell the fear."

Daisy almost smiled. "Like sharks."

"Exactly like sharks. But you know what the difference is between you and the sharks?"

"I'm the one getting eaten?"

"You're the one who gives a shit. Half the people in this office could take a bollocking and forget about it by lunchtime. You're sat here looking like someone kicked your cat because you care about doing it right."

Daisy stared at her. "How do you know I'm not just afraid of being fired?"

"Because terrified and caring look different. Trust me, I've seen both."

Sophie disappeared back to reception, leaving Daisy with tea and something that felt dangerously close to hope. Which was stupid. Hope was what got you hurt. But the tea was good, and Sophie hadn't asked anything of her in return, and sometimes stupid was all you had.

By the fourth day, she'd developed a routine. Arrive early, nod to Sophie, make coffee before the machine got destroyed by the morning rush, sit at her desk and pretend she knew what she was doing until it almost came true.

She was getting better at the CMS, mainly through bloody-mindedness and Leah's notes. The phone still terrified her, but she'd navigated three calls without totally humiliating herself. Small victories.

The other paralegals were starting to treat her like furniture, which was oddly comforting. No one whispered when she walked past anymore. No one watched her eat lunch. She'd achieved her ultimate goal: invisibility.

Well, mostly invisibility.

There was the bathroom situation. The eternal trans woman dilemma of which door to walk through, the split-second, life or death decision. The women's bathroom meant potential confrontation, questioning, complaints to HR. The men's bathroom meant... Well, that was obviously not happening. So, she'd taken to timing her breaks around when both would be empty, or holding it until she got home, which was probably doing terrible things to her kidneys but seemed safer than the alternative.

Small compromises for survival. She'd made bigger ones.

At lunch, Sophie invited her to sit together in the break room instead of eating alone at her desk. They talked about nothing much – television, the weather, how the coffee machine had a personal vendetta against anyone who wasn't trained to use it properly. Normal conversation. The kind Daisy had forgotten how to have.

"So, what did you do before this?" Sophie asked, and Daisy tensed, waiting for the follow-up questions, the probing, the inevitable moment when she'd have to decide how much truth to reveal.

But Sophie listened to her abbreviated version – "bit of everything, really, took a career break, decided to get back into law" – and nodded like it made perfect sense. Like a "career break" at 40 was normal. Like everyone's career path was a straight line until it wasn't.

"Good for you," Sophie said. "Fresh starts are hard work."

Daisy studied her face for signs of sarcasm, condescension, pity. Found none. Just compassion from someone who seemed to mean what she said. It was unsettling.

When Friday arrived, she reached the end of her first week feeling like she'd survived some kind of endurance test. The office was still drab, the tasks were still endless, and being in a junior position at her age was still humiliating. But she was still there. Still employed. Still pretending to be a functional human being with reasonable success.

Leah had brought her coffee that morning without being asked. Two other paralegals had included her in a conversation about weekend plans. Sophie had complimented her earrings. Small things, but they added up to something that felt almost like belonging.

Which was dangerous thinking. Belonging was temporary. Belonging was conditional. Belonging was something that could be taken away the moment they figured out she didn't deserve it.

But for now, for today, for this week, she'd convinced them she was worth keeping around. That had to count for something.

At five o'clock, as the office emptied out around her, she pulled out her phone. She'd been avoiding it all week, ignoring messages from Iris asking how it was going, petrified of having to explain that she was failing, that she was about to be found out. That the whole thing was a mistake.

But she hadn't been found out. She hadn't failed. Not this week, anyway.

She drew out her phone again and decided to text Iris.

"Thank you."

Two words that covered everything she couldn't say. Thank you for believing I could do this. Thank you for not giving up on me. Thank you for seeing something in me that I can't see in myself. Thank you for the chance to remember that I'm not completely useless.

Thank you for Sophie, and Leah, and even the terrible coffee machine. Thank you for normal conversations and small kindnesses and the possibility that maybe, just maybe, I might be able to build something here.

She sent the message before she could second-guess herself, then sat back in her chair, looking around the beige office that had felt like a prison on Monday and now… Well, not home, but maybe not enemy territory, either.

Somewhere in between. Somewhere she could work with.

Chapter 15 – The Widower

The office hummed with the ghosts of two generations – the whirring of old copiers and the faint glow of new computers. She still couldn't figure out how she'd ended up behind this desk, surrounded by a stack of forms she was barely beginning to understand.

Iris had confidently told her that this job was a "good first step." Daisy suspected that it was more an act of charity. A job was a job, right?

Her client for the morning was a fresh widower. Young. Too young. He sat opposite her, his eyes red-rimmed and his voice raw, smelling faintly of old aftershave and something else Daisy couldn't place – stale grief, maybe. He signed off the estate papers with a shaky hand, tears welling in his eyes as they landed on the page. The rustle of the paper seemed deafeningly loud in the quiet room.

She'd headed back up with the stack of papers, checking with her supervisors to make sure everything was in order before they could take the next steps. With it confirmed that everything was exactly as it needed to be, she returned to the reception area.

He was leant over the desk; the tears Daisy had seen vanished as he whispered something to Sophie. He smiled, his whole body seeming to relax as she let out a soft giggle. Sophie played with her hair, a simple, unconscious gesture that Daisy's mind instantly labelled as coquettish. She watched as Sophie's hips angled slightly towards him, a subtle shift that was all the encouragement he seemed to need. He responded in kind, his own smile so sweet it made Daisy's stomach turn.

Jesus Christ, his wife was barely in the ground. Sure, grief's a bitch, but at least wait until you get over the cold body before looking for a warm one.

Daisy would never understand how people move on so fast.

And of course it was Sophie. They always went for a Sophie, didn't they?

Daisy felt her lip curl. She bit the inside of her cheek, the taste of blood a faint, sharp punctuation to the thought. "Classy. Real classy," she muttered under her breath, a quiet judgement she hoped no one would hear. At that moment, that Sophie looked up – her smile fixed in place – and directed the client's attention to her.

She reassured the client that everything was in order and that they'd be in touch to close up the case.

After he'd left, Daisy was so wound up that she could barely think coherently. Her mind span in dark circles, and she could feel herself spiralling. At how disgusting he was, how pathetic she was for even noticing, how desperate Sophie must be to be flirting so openly with a widower… she chided herself for even caring – it didn't affect her in the least – but part of her felt something else. Jealousy, maybe? Why didn't somebody look at her like that? Not that guy, of course – never that guy – but why was it the Sophies of the world who got all the attention?

Nobody plays with the broken toys.

The rage curdled into something heavier as the day dragged on. Her eyes scanned the legal documents, the dense black text a meaningless blur on the page. She found herself reading the same sentence three times, each word barely a sound in her mind. A phone rang and she jolted, making a terse note on her notepad before ignoring it. The inbox icon flashed, a tiny red dagger in the corner of her screen, but she only moved the urgent emails to a separate folder.

Her brain couldn't let go of this nagging feeling of resentment. It wasn't the widower's performance that had stuck with her, or even Sophie's casual flirtation. It was the easy way he had looked at her, the way she had received it without a thought. A silent, uncomplicated exchange she had never had. A recognition she would never get. This feeling was something deeper, something Daisy refused to name.

Leah, the paralegal from the previous week, approached her desk before lunch. She held a small, plastic container.

"My mum made too many of these," Leah said, her voice bright. "Fig rolls. You want one?"

Daisy's entire body tensed. She watched Leah's smile, searching for the crack, for the pity or the condescension that had to be lurking behind it. A trap. A small, sugary test to see if she would accept their charity, to confirm she was a charity case.

"No, thank you," Daisy said, her voice flat, the words feeling like bricks in her mouth.

Leah's smile didn't falter. "Suit yourself. They're good though, I'm telling you." She put the container back in her bag and walked away without a second glance.

Daisy stared after her, the small kindness now a resentment. The rage felt so heavy it was like her bones were made of lead. She spent the rest of the day hunched over her desk, a human knot of tension. The low purr of the office became a grating buzz in her ears, and the smell of stale coffee from the communal machine made her stomach churn.

When she'd reached her street, all sense of time and space and self-regulation had abandoned her. The rain had started, a cold drizzle like tiny needles on her skin. She didn't bother to open her umbrella. She pulled her coat tighter, the soaked fabric clinging to her body. She must've smoked half a pack of cigarettes on the way home, each drag a furious, burning release that left her lungs aching and her voice a little hoarse. The streetlights bled into soft, watery glows in the darkening evening, and she drifted like a lullaby in her own city.

On autopilot, reaching for her keys, something stopped her. Standing between her and the front door, magically appearing with two takeout cups in hand and looking the picture of serenity, was Iris.

"Did you have me microchipped or something?"

"I thought you might need a cup of tea and some company," she said. "You look like you do."

Daisy was very aware of the state of herself: her windswept hair, the faint smell of stale cigarettes on her coat, the wild look in her eyes reflected in the glass of the door. The sight of her own tired reflection was a shock.

Iris handed her a cup, the ceramic heat a faint shock, and snatched the keys from Daisy's hand. She let herself in, the door clicking shut behind her; the small, final sound of the end of the day and the beginning of something else. Daisy's throat tightened. *Who the fuck does she think she is?* She tried to convey the thought with a scowl, a tightening of her jaw that felt as flimsy as tissue paper. If Iris saw it, she didn't bite.

Iris parked herself on the sofa, making herself firmly at home. She took a slow, small sip from her own cup. The steam curled around her face, softening her expression as she gestured to the other cushion with a glance. Daisy stayed standing, clutching her takeout cup as if it were a weapon.

"What are you even doing here?" Daisy said, half a hair from snapping it.

Iris wasn't biting. "Sophie called me."

That stopped Daisy in her tracks.

"Sophie?"

"I know you're not the most observant, nor famed for your listening skills," Iris said, casually, "but she's my cousin."

Daisy did vaguely remember someone saying something about her being the boss' daughter. And not kindly.

"She told me what happened; she tells me some creep was hitting on her five minutes after crying to you over his dead wife, said it bothered you."

"Oh," Daisy blinked. She hadn't thought Sophie had noticed. Or cared.

"And, just to clear things up, she wasn't flirting back – if she was, I'd be having this conversation with her girlfriend right now – but she's got to keep up appearances. Part of the job. She was as disgusted as you."

Daisy felt lighter. Not relief, but something else. As soon as the weight was gone, she felt another replace it – Iris had got her a job with her uncle *and* cousin. Maybe she was keeping an eye on her?

"Look," said Iris, interrupting her train of thought before she could go full paranoia. She patted the cushion next to her. "Come and sit down. This isn't what you think it is."

Daisy hesitated, then relented. The fight had gone out of her, replaced by a deep, bone-weary exhaustion. She sank onto the sofa, the cushion a welcome softness.

"I know people think Sophie's not the sharpest tool in the shed," Iris continued, her voice lower now, more serious, "but what she lacks in academic qualifications, she makes up for in people skills. She can read people like a book. So, if she sees you're struggling with something, she's going to call me." Daisy made a mental note. "And don't think you're going to hide things from her. Take it from me, it's far more effort than it's worth." She sighed, and looked at Daisy's clenched hands. "It's not the job, is it? It's not just the creep. It's… everything."

Daisy let herself slump onto the sofa, curling her arms around her chest. The tea was untouched on the coffee table. "It was so disgusting."

Iris let that hang in the air for a moment, her fingers laced loosely around her cup. She didn't look at Daisy when she spoke. "And it got to you."

It wasn't a question.

"Of course it got to me." Daisy pulled at a loose thread on the hem of her skirt until it snapped, the small sound as loud as a gunshot in the quiet room. "He's a piece of shit."

Iris took a slow sip of her tea, the glow seeming to soften her face. "And?"

Daisy's head snapped up. She met Iris' steady gaze, a challenge in her own eyes that was a flimsy bluff.

"And?" she shot back.

"You're not this angry just because he's a creep," Iris said softly.

The words landed like a rabbit punch to the jaw. Daisy felt the pressure in her throat. "Fuck you."

Iris' calm façade cracked. She sat up straight, her eyes fixed on Daisy, and set her teacup down with a sharp clink on the coffee table. "No," Iris replied, her voice calm but firm, as if training an animal. She leant forward, closing the distance between them. "Fuck the part of you that thinks you're only worth something if somebody is looking at you like that. Fuck the part of you that thinks you're not good enough. Fuck the part of you that insists you persecute yourself for every little mistake."

Wow. Daisy *had* wondered what Iris was like when she was angry. Be careful what you wish for.

"Daisy, that's not who you are anymore."

Daisy smirked. "Clearly it is."

"It doesn't have to be."

Daisy felt her eyes welling up. She turned to look away, furious at herself for feeling anything. She wasn't going to let anyone see her.

"I think," Iris started, her voice a calm wave lapping at a rocky shore, "it's time we got you some help."

"I'm not crazy," Daisy responded, the words a thin, fragile shield.

"You're using AI for therapy. You can't carry on like that."

"I'M NOT CRAZY!" Daisy screamed, the words ripping from her throat like a physical tearing.

"And it's much more convincing at that volume." Iris said, patiently.

Daisy shot her a look and poked her tongue out at Iris.

Real mature, Daisy, she thought, catching it.

"I'm serious, Daze," she responded, "you need proper help."

Daisy laughed. A loud, sarcastic one. "What, a shrink?"

"A therapist," Iris corrected her, gently. "You need someone who can help you let go of this."

"What, so I should pay some dickhead seventy quid an hour to tell me that I'm broken? I already know that. Case closed, Sherlock."

"Or," Iris responded, her voice dropping to a low, quiet command, "I could pay a professional seventy quid an hour to stop you from breaking yourself anymore."

Daisy contemplated it awhile. Or contemplated a way to talk her way out of it. She glanced down at her knees, then at her hands, tightly balled into fists. She felt utterly drained, the fight leaving her.

"This therapist," Daisy finally asked, "isn't related to you, right?"

"You think I'd inflict this side of you on my family?" Iris responded, with a giggle.

Daisy hesitated. She attempted to take 'three calming breaths' – she'd read about that in *Cosmo*.

"Fine."

"Fine?"

"I'll go to a fucking therapist."

"It's cute that you thought you had a choice."

Daisy took a sip of the tea. It was cooler now, but the sweet ginger and lemon flavour was a faint comfort. Iris leant back against the cushions and watched her. She took her time, desperately seeking an escape route.

"What's her name?" Daisy asked, her voice quiet.

Iris' smile widened. "I'll text you the details. She's very good. She's seen it all before."

Daisy nodded, her hand trembling almost imperceptibly as she brought the cup to her lips. The thought of a stranger seeing "it all" was terrifying. She took another, longer drink of the tea, the warmth seeping into her cold, tired body. Daisy looked down at the mug in her hand, the paper softened and crinkled from her tight grip. *And what if she sees it all... and agrees?*

Chapter 16 – English Opening

She'd arrived late at the therapist's office, partially because the buses were shit, mostly because it had taken her forever to persuade herself to go.

The therapist's opener had been simple enough: "So, Daisy, tell me about yourself."

Daisy stared at her shoes, the scuffed leather a more interesting study than the woman across from her. She listened to the quiet whir of an air conditioner, the faint sound a metronome for the silence. *"Seventy quid for this,"* Daisy thought, *"I could've bought two bottles of vodka, a dozen packs of ibuprofen and saved everyone the trouble."*

Daisy felt her palms begin to sweat. She wanted the therapist to flinch, to shuffle papers, to do anything but sit there in perfect stillness. She glanced up, met the therapist's patient gaze, and felt a flare of pure, hot irritation. *Fuck, this therapist was good.*

"Okay, you win." Daisy scowled. "I like my mum, my dad disappeared when I was two weeks old and I have no interest in fucking either of them." She felt her jaw clench as she forced the next words out. "I have a son who hates me and a daughter who doesn't know how to relate to me, and that's probably because they blame me for killing their mother, or at least for not keeping her alive." She paused, the air feeling thick and heavy in her lungs. Her gaze drifted to a potted fern in the corner of the room, anything but the therapist's face. "I have no friends, because whenever I let anyone in, they disappear or die, and I don't know which of those choices is right."

She took a ragged breath and looked at the therapist, who seemed unmoved. Neither angered nor impressed.

Daisy leant forward in her chair, a challenge in her eyes. "I am, and this is no understatement, an awful human being. Possibly the worst you've ever met. I know you probably think you can fix me but, realistically, you're going to end up wanting to put me down."

She looked to the therapist for a reaction once again. The therapist's face remained neutral, but Daisy caught a small, almost imperceptible sigh. The therapist slowly removed her glasses, polished them on the hem of her cardigan, and put them back on.

"Daisy," the therapist began, her voice a little softer now, as if trying a new approach. "I've worked with... well, with all sorts of people. And... look, it's not a good look for a therapist to start killing their patients."

A therapist with jokes. And a bad delivery, at that. Excellent. She made a mental note to look for a clown that did surgery.

The therapist gave a small, weary smile. "So, now that we've established that I'm not going to be horrified by you, and I've got no intention of hurting you, what would you like to talk about?"

Daisy stared, her mind a blank. She wasn't used to someone refusing to back down.

"Okay, let me try again," the therapist said, a flicker of something in her eyes that wasn't quite irritation, but was close. "You've just spent a lot of energy trying to convince me that you're terrible, mocking my profession, and I'm still here. How about we try a different angle, and you tell me what the event that brought you to me was?"

Daisy kept staring. The therapist checked her watch.

"I swear to God," Daisy said, "if you say 'I'm afraid that's all we've got time for', I'll—"

"Sit and sulk?"

What?

"Daisy, you made an appointment to see me—"

"I didn't. Iris did."

"Ah, and Iris is...?"

"A pain in my arse."

The therapist's mouth twitched, a hint of a smile she quickly suppressed. "And clearly one who cares about you. Doesn't sound like she's planning on disappearing, does it?"

Daisy let out a harsh, humourless laugh. "So," responded Daisy, "I guess that means she'll die?"

"If she does, I'm sending the police your way."

"Funny." Daisy didn't laugh.

"So, why did Iris book the appointment?"

Daisy told her the story about the widower and the flirting, talking quickly, as if getting the words out would make them less real. "...and Iris' bullshit armchair psychoanalysis." She finished; her voice raw.

"How long ago did she die?"

"What?" Daisy asked, the abrupt shift catching her off guard.

"You mentioned that you think your children blame you for their mother's death. How long ago did she die?"

"About ten years ago?" Daisy wasn't sure. Try as she might, she could never recall the exact date, and always had to look it up.

"And why would they blame you for it? Were you there?"

"No."

"Did you say or do something that led to her death?"

"Not directly."

The therapist leant forward slightly in her chair; a subtle shift that made Daisy want to pull away. "How did she die?"

Daisy swallowed hard. Her gaze dropped to her hands, twisting a small loose thread on her skirt. "Overdose."

"On?"

The therapist's pen hovered over her notepad, waiting. "Painkillers."

"Did you buy the painkillers?"

"No, they were prescribed."

"Were you her doctor?"

"No."

"So… why would your kids think you were responsible?"

"I don't know, maybe if I'd—"

"Maybe, what? Maybe if you'd been there, you'd have stopped it? Maybe. Maybe if I'd bought a lottery ticket I'd be sat in the Bahamas. You weren't, I didn't." The therapist's voice was blunt, a hammer blow of logic.

Daisy's hands stopped. She felt a strange, irrational feeling spreading through her. "But I—"

"You need this to be your fault." The therapist interrupted. "Because if it's your fault, you can fix it?"

Daisy thought for a second, then nodded.

The therapist leant back in her chair, a sigh escaping her throat. A sound of professional exhaustion, not personal one. "You know, throughout recorded history, we've got thousands of claims in mythology, from all over the world, of people being able to raise the dead. Yet, nobody currently alive has ever seen it. Have you ever wondered why that is?"

Daisy shrugged.

"Because it never happened."

"You ever say that to a Christian?" Daisy asked.

"They don't tend to come to therapy."

"Figures."

"Let me ask you something," said the therapist, not pausing long enough for consent. "Is it your fault your dad left?"

"What?"

"You said he left. Was that your fault?"

"How the fuck would I know? I was a baby."

"You'd be amazed what lessons we learn as children, even if we can't remember them."

"Well, that's a new fear unlocked."

"And that's for your kids to deal with in therapy."

"So, this guy from the office. Maybe you saw something of yourself in him? Being that young, widowed father? Maybe you could relate?"

"What? No. People die. Sometimes people die young. It sucks, but it happens."

"How old was the guy?"

"I don't know. Thirty?"

"Interesting. And you said they had two kids?"

Daisy nodded.

"And that part didn't bother you?"

"Like I said, it sucks, but it happens."

"It's not common, though, is it?"

"Define 'common.'"

The therapist stood, the startling movement causing Daisy to jump a little. The therapist's shoes made no sound on the carpeted floor as she walked to a bookshelf, her touch gliding over the spines of books before pulling one out. She returned to her desk, not sitting, but leaning against the edge as she opened the dictionary.

"'Shared by, or done by, two or more people.'"

A fucking dictionary? Daisy stared at the book, a useless, frustrating prop in an already absurd situation.

"It seems to me that maybe you've been in that position?"

"I would never—"

"I didn't accuse you of doing something. What was he doing?"

"She's barely even dead and he's already trying to cheat—"

"But she *is* dead. And if she's dead, is he cheating?"

"It's spiritually cheating."

"Some people have different coping mechanisms."

"That doesn't make it okay!"

"In your opinion."

"You don't get over someone by getting under someone else."

"I'd bet I can find a hundred magazines that say otherwise."

"That's different."

"Because they're alive?"

"If they're alive, they have options."

"Is that what's really bothering you? The idea of cheating?"

"Why wouldn't it?"

"For someone who makes jokes about religion, you seem really keen on the idea of eternal life."

What a stupid idea, Daisy thought, *people didn't live forever.*

"Is it possible that you're feeling guilty?"

"I thought we'd established that."

"Not about the death," the therapist said. "About moving on." She paused, and changed tack, "do you feel like you're cheating?"

"With who? My vibrator?"

"No, with a human."

"There's no human right now."

"So, there *was* a human?"

"*She* was the human." Daisy's voice dropped, barely a whisper. She looked at the potted fern. Anywhere but the therapist's face. "My ex. She was the one I cheated with."

The therapist's pen, which had been still for a moment, began to move across the notepad in a steady, rhythmic scratch. "Mmm-hmm."

"What?"

"Look, it's not my job to tell you what you're feeling—"

"Then what is your fucking job?" Daisy spat back.

"My job is to help you figure things out for yourself."

"For seventy quid an hour, I'd say your job is to tell me what's wrong with me."

"Okay. You cheated, you felt bad. You stuck with it. She died. Now, you feel disloyal to her if you move on with your life. As if you have to punish yourself for both things. Sound familiar?"

Daisy sat, blinking. The fact that she had – quite literally – asked for it didn't make it easier.

She looked at her watch. The session was nearly up. "Okay," Daisy took a breath, "let's pretend you're right. How do I fix it? Medication?"

"Would you like medication?"

I'd fucking love about a litre of it, thought Daisy. She nodded.

"Well, you're out of luck. The only cure for this is talking about it."

Daisy took a moment to process the information. The therapist checked her watch.

"And, unfortunately, that is all we have time for."

Daisy laughed.

"Same time next week?"

Daisy nodded.

Chapter 17 – The Third Ending (2016)

He stood in front of his closet, his eyes scanning the rows of clothes. The black suit he'd worn to so many funerals before hung on its hanger, a ghost of an outfit for a ghost of a man. But he hadn't gone to Faye's funeral. Funerals were for families, for friends, for people who could show their faces without feeling like a fraud. He was none of those things anymore.

He pulled a black hoodie from the rail, then a pair of black jeans. His version of mourning clothes: functional, casual, and a clear statement that he was not an official part of this ceremony. He dressed quickly, the familiar fabric a comfort against his skin. There was a brief moment of hesitation as he walked past a framed photo on the wall – Faye smiling brightly with the kids, a moment frozen. He reached for his phone, a dozen numbers stored under a dozen names, but the two he wanted most were the ones he couldn't call. He couldn't talk to the children about this. He couldn't force a conversation about their mother, not when they had shut him out entirely after her death.

He left the house and got into the passenger seat of his mother's car. She didn't say anything; she gave him a single, knowing look that held a mountain of unspoken grief and concern. The long drive to the coast was a blur of silent miles, broken only by the drone of the engine and the quiet rhythm of the windscreen wipers. He didn't look out the window. He just stared at his hands, a man on a pilgrimage to a place he wasn't welcome, to a ceremony he wasn't a part of.

When they arrived, his mother parked the car and turned off the engine, but she didn't get out. She sat there, waiting for him. He met her gaze for a brief moment, then pushed open the door and stepped out into the cold night.

He stood staring at the waves as they crashed on the shore. The air was cold, damp with the coming tide, and the smell of salt was thick and sharp in his nose. He hadn't been invited to the funeral and, he learned, neither had the children.

They weren't here for the scattering of the ashes, either. The urn felt impossibly light in his hands, a cheap plastic container that seemed far too insignificant to hold her.

Fine, grey powder. A dust on his fingertips. A sharp gust of wind caught a plume, and for a fleeting second, it seemed to hang in the air, suspended, before being pulled by the ocean. He sobbed heavily as he did so. It felt so final.

Because it was.

He let the grief consume him for a moment before the thoughts drifted back to the day of the funeral. He hadn't been there. He hadn't had the right to be there. He had sat at home, the silence heavy on his shoulders, trying to imagine what it would be like. He'd pictured a sea of black, the faces of her family – some familiar, some he'd never met – all sharing a grief he was locked out of. He'd imagined the priest's words, the respectful eulogies, and the soft, shared sobs of people who had been there for her in a way he hadn't been. The world had gone on without him that day, marking a moment he had no right to be a part of. The children hadn't been allowed to be there, either. He wondered if that made it any easier. He pictured them in a distant house, sitting in a quiet as heavy as his own, mourning a mother and the goodbye she never got. A shared punishment for a private betrayal, an act of exclusion from a family that had never fully accepted him or their children.

The others slowly left, inviting him to join them at a nearby pub for a drink when he was ready.

Ready. As if anyone was ever ready for this.

He watched as the waves, tinted with the slight hint of wisteria in the moonlight, slowly drew her from the sand into the sea, taking her away as though cleansing the earth of her.

It didn't feel right. It would never feel right.

Once he was alone, he sat on the sand in the moonlight. The cold seeped through his trousers, but he didn't care. He was numb.

He wanted to talk to her. Just once. Just once more. Just tell her everything he was thinking, everything he'd ever hidden from her or even tell her he loved her one more time.

But he couldn't do that. They did that in movies, right? Stand at a headstone having a long, intimate conversation with a piece of rock.

What did they get from that? He wondered. A diagnosis? Some kind of mental illness, or apparition or imaginary friend?

He checked up and down the beach once again. He was alone. Nobody that could see him, hear him, or judge him.

Only one way to find out, right?

His voice came out a rusty whisper, ragged from the sobs. And so, quietly, he told Faye everything. The whole story of their relationship from his point of view.

He dug his fingers into the cold, wet sand, a small, anchor of pain. He told her about Marisol; he knew Faye would've been furious if she'd ever known whilst she was alive, even after they broke up. He could almost hear her voice now, sharp and cold as a shard of ice: *"Are you serious? You'd do that to me?"* He told her he was serious, that he hated that he'd done it. He remembered the feel of Faye's hand on his thigh that first night, the nauseating feeling of remorse as he'd discarded Marisol from memory. He could see the framed photo of Faye on the wall, her smiling face a silent accusation of failure. Perhaps the greatest irony of her life was that, despite being a prolific cheater herself, she never condoned it when others did it. When she was asked about that, she'd always make an excuse, blaming her own trauma.

He thought it was funny, in hindsight. The idea that being a victim of trauma gave you free reign to cause trauma to others. As if that was how it worked.

He told her about how their break-up had exacerbated his drinking. How he blamed her. How she destroyed him and it made him try and numb the pain. He'd spiralled so quickly after she left, turning to alcohol to fill the emptiness she'd created, only to end up in bar work, a paid drinker to support a liquid recovery. How much he'd hated her for what she did. How much he hated that he'd hated her. A wave rolled in, cold foam washing over his shoes, but he didn't flinch. How hard it was to hate someone that he was – and always would be – so deeply in love with.

He talked to her about how there hadn't been a single day since they broke up – despite all of the hatred and trouble that it caused him – that he hadn't hoped she'd call him to get back together. He felt a bitter taste on his tongue, a mix of salt and self-loathing. He hated how pathetic that sounded out loud.

He told her that he hated how much their troubles had affected their children, how scared he was that they'd ruined their lives after they had sworn themselves that they'd never turn into their own parents. He told her about the 500-mile round trips every week to see them for two hours, a brutal commute for a painfully brief taste of fatherhood.

The wind was starting to pick up – a sudden, icy chill that seemed to amplify the sound of the waves.

He told her about how the back and forth, the 'will they, won't they' of the many teased reconciliations had torn him apart. He remembered the phone call where she'd said, "Maybe one day, when we're both in a better place." He'd spent months living on that empty promise, clinging to it like a life raft, only to see her with another man a week later. That he wished he'd been strong enough to say no, or that he wished she'd been brave enough to say yes.

He told her how much he loved that she'd always been there for him, right until the very end, ready to encourage him to be a better person. And how much he hated how easily she found it to toss him aside every time a shiny new guy appeared on the scene.

He told her about their most recent reconciliation, the one that had been the most functional of their entire history. He remembered a quiet evening where they had sat together on the couch in her shitty flat, not fighting, not bickering, just watching a movie. He had felt a small, steady sense of peace that he hadn't felt in years, a momentary belief that they had actually, truly, found their way back to each other. It had been the most normal their lives had ever felt.

He told her how guilty he'd felt when, for a fleeting moment, he'd almost been glad she was dead, because it meant she'd never hurt him again. And how much he'd cried afterwards.

He apologized for his lack of empathy, for the emotional distance he'd created, and for the way his shame had made him lie and hide. He apologized for all the times he'd failed to be the man he should have been.

He apologized for her last moments, when he hadn't realised that something was seriously wrong during their last phone conversation, when he'd heard her talk about her new fitness regime. He remembered her voice on the phone that day, bright with a pride he hadn't heard in years, saying *"Yes, you did it!"*

And he told her, saying it out loud, how much she made him realise that he'd failed as a man. And how little it bothered him. He was past that.

He remembered the phone call he got from her, telling him she was pregnant. It wasn't a celebratory moment; it was a bombshell that landed with the finality of a death sentence. In an instant, his life shifted from being his own to being that of a father, and he hadn't been ready. He hadn't been a man, he had just been a boy, and she had been a terrified girl, and they had been forced to play at being adults without ever having a chance to grow up.

He remembered a night years ago when the kids were sick, and he'd been blackout drunk. Faye had taken care of everything, calmly. He had watched her from the couch, a worthless, useless observer to her strength. He had been filled with a shame so deep it had almost broken him. He could almost feel that shame now. And how much he wished that he could be half the woman that she was.

And then he cried. For an hour.

Eventually, the tears subsided, leaving behind grief; no longer a piercing wound, but a dull, heavy weight sitting on his heart.

His hand, trembling, fell to the sand and brushed against something solid. He dug it out, revealing a gnarled piece of driftwood. Worn smooth on one end, a beautiful, polished grey that seemed to whisper with the memories of a thousand tides. But the other end was a jagged, raw break, a splintered wound where it had clearly been torn from its larger body. He ran the rougher edge gently across his wrists, in dangerous contemplation. He thought about how some things can't be mended, only weathered, and how some breaks are too deep to ever truly heal. He looked at the waves, at the relentless, patient rhythm that had shaped the wood, and felt a cold, empty sort of peace.

And then…

He said goodbye. He stood, his legs stiff, and bent to pick up a smooth, grey stone from the wet sand. He held it tightly in his palm for a moment, then dropped it back into the sand and walked away, not looking back.

Chapter 18 – The Black Dahlia

Daisy awoke with a start, the vague, persistent gnawing in her chest an immediate companion. Her eyes burned, a reflex against the searing orange sunlight that sliced through the gap in her blinds. That nagging feeling she'd come to know so well, a whisper in her bones that told her something was wrong. It wasn't the kind of wrong that sent a searing bolt of panic through her veins – the hangover-wrong or what-did-I-do-in-a-blackout wrong of her old life. This was the softer, more insidious kind: the feeling of a forgotten appointment or a missed bill, the weight of a life she was still learning to manage.

She flicked through her phone. Nothing in her calendar. No texts. No obvious signs of – there it was. A Facebook notification: Marisol's birthday.

Her thumb hovered over the message app. The cursor blinked in the blank box, a silent, taunting invitation. She stared at it, the half-life of a thought, for a while. The seconds a slow, agonizing drag, a frantic drumming against her ribs. Finally, she tapped out a message, her fingers moving as if possessed. "Happy birthday, hope you have an amazing day!"

Short, safe. A wall of polite distance. Yet, her stomach twisted as she hit send, the familiar, stab of guilt. She stabbed the phone into the front pocket of her jeans as if it had bitten her, the sharp corner of the device pressing uncomfortably into her thigh. She tried not to contemplate having taken half an hour to compose eight words.

At that moment, a message flashed up; Iris had planned something. Of course she had, she always did. Daisy's presence was demanded.

She asked what the plan was, half expecting it to be yet more house cleaning or some brutal assault on her privacy or sanity. Instead, she was being dragged into town – a place Daisy generally avoided in the way one might avoid diving head-first into a wood chipper – with an ambiguous "trust me" as her only explanation.

Ah, yes. Trust. Famously one of Daisy's key identifying traits.

It started with coffee – of course – at a little independent place Daisy had never seen before. It smelled of freshly ground beans and a faint, sweet scent of warm pastries. The space was bright and clean, with the gentle murmur of conversation that she found both soothing and terrifying. Iris ordered for them both, a quiet assumption of intimacy that Daisy found simultaneously infuriating and comforting. Daisy drank the coffee black, its bitterness a familiar friend against the alien sweetness of her day.

From there, they began their brutal assault on her senses: a trip around some charity shops. Daisy *loved* shopping, but Daisy *hated* charity shops. She wanted Givenchy, not poverty. The first one they entered was a sensory overload. The air filled with the scent of a thousand different lives packed into one small space: old lady perfume, mothballs, musty books, and the unmistakable, lingering smell of something indefinable, like crushed dreams and forgotten memories.

Daisy groaned throughout, loudly, even declaring at one point that she didn't do charity shops; they smelt like "dead grandmothers and crushed dreams." The words came out with more bite than she intended, a reflection of how she felt about herself. Like a used, discarded thing, a piece of someone else's past.

She glanced at Iris after saying it, a defiant look on her face, expecting a sympathetic nod or a gentle rebuke. Instead, she saw a fleeting flicker in Iris's eyes, a sadness so profound and knowing that Daisy's shield of sarcasm faltered. Gone in an instant, replaced by Iris's usual calm demeanour, but it left Daisy with a disquieting thought: that Iris hadn't chosen this place on a whim, but for a reason Daisy wasn't yet ready to understand.

It was a complaint that probably would have landed better if she hadn't gone quiet for a moment too long whilst staring at a rack of scarves. She couldn't explain it. She hated scarves, almost never wore them – she found them itchy, uncomfortable, cumbersome, even.

But one had caught her eye; a deep green. She put her hand out to feel it – cautiously, like it was a live wire. Cashmere? She didn't know for sure – she'd never been able to afford cashmere, only heard stories – but it felt like she was told cashmere was supposed to. Just thick enough, perfectly soft, none of that scratchy texture that she – She gently brushed the fabric, the softness like a secret. She closed her eyes for a moment, inhaling a faint, clean scent of lavender that clung to the fibres.

In the corner of her eye, she clocked Iris watching her. Her eyebrow raised, completely silent.

"You're imagining it," Daisy muttered. Iris moved on, a small hint of a smug smile.

They wandered the stores for hours. Iris tried on shoes that were clearly *at least* two sizes too small. Daisy teased her for it, but secretly admired the confidence that took, even if she did find it amusing to watch a cis woman struggle to find shoes that fit for a change.

At one point, Iris had suggested they make a detour into a tiny used bookshop tucked between a vape shop and a nail bar. A dark, cool space that smelled of old paper and dust. The scent was a time machine, transporting Daisy back to her mother's bookshop. Did Iris know? She was sure she hadn't mentioned it.

Daisy could feel Iris watching as she got lost in the shelves, like a trip through the past. She brushed gently along the spines of the forgotten soldiers, their knowledge once trusted and beloved. The weight of each book, the slight roughness of the paper covers, the musty scent of pages yellowing with age – it was all so familiar.

She lingered on a copy of one of her favourites, James Ellroy's *The Black Dahlia*. She had loved that book from the moment she read it, marvelling at the mastery with which the author had taken a real-life crime that shocked the world – and turned it into the romantic tale of a wayward heroine, wronged by a cruel world.

She drew it from the shelf, turning the familiar cover to face her – that portrait of Elizabeth Short. *I see you, Liz.* She admired the woman's portrait on the cover, a quiet, almost heartbreaking act of communion. A feeling of kinship with a lost, broken woman who had never truly belonged.

"Thought you didn't do second-hand?" Iris said, sweetly.

Daisy rolled her eyes. "I don't. This is… archaeology."

Iris didn't argue. She didn't have to.

By late in the afternoon, Daisy's feet were aching, a dull throb that radiated up into her shins. As they walked, the city's sounds seemed to grow louder, the traffic a deafening roar, the shouts of people on the pavement a jarring cacophony. A wave of dizziness hit her, a sensation like the world had tilted on its axis. Her vision swam, the vibrant colours of the city blurring into a watercolour smudge. She stumbled, and without thinking, her hand shot out and grabbed Iris's arm, gripping her tightly. The panic was overwhelming, but so was Iris's solid, grounding presence. She didn't flinch.

She steadied Daisy with a gentle but firm hand on her back, her voice a calm anchor in the storm of noise. "You alright?" she asked, with an unspoken warmth.

Daisy didn't have to answer. Her silence was more than enough.

Her patience was thinning, but she realised – begrudgingly – that she hadn't hated herself for most of the day. Iris had that effect. Infuriating.

She even – although she very quickly hid it – allowed herself to smile. Just slightly.

As the shops began to close Daisy found herself almost disappointed. She couldn't explain it but, somehow, she'd enjoyed a whole day of doing things that she would never have voluntarily partaken in – except, maybe, the coffee.

A small part of her presumed that, surely, Iris would have been sick of her by now. She was exhausted by her own presence. It was a surprise when she suggested they find something to eat.

Daisy suggested something simple – a burger from a generic American chain, something with as red a logo as possible and as little green inside it as she could order; she felt bad suggesting this, because it was clearly beneath Iris, but this was comfortable for her. Besides, she wasn't about to admit that this was the limit – if not beyond – of her price range. Yes, Iris probably would've insisted on paying anyway – and even here, she tried – but it was the principle.

Iris had done so much for her already. Too much, really. Daisy had wondered often why anyone would go to such efforts to try and get involved in cleaning up the mess that was her life. But insisting on paying for her therapy, as well? Had she never heard that you can't polish a turd?

Eventually, Daisy was convinced, Iris would figure that out and flush her like everyone else did.

As they ate, Daisy picked at the bun of her burger, avoiding eye contact. Iris asked leisurely questions about therapy; nothing intrusive, of course. She was too well-mannered to pry, but she was keen to know if it was helping.

Truthfully, it was. It was helpful to be able to put a name on her issues – abandonment, anguish… and she was sure some kind of diagnosis of a personality disorder wouldn't be far behind.

"Too early to tell," she responded. She took a large, avoidant bite of her burger.

"Is the therapist nice, at least?" Iris leant forward slightly, her elbows on the plastic tabletop.

"She's… precise."

"Precise?"

"Loves a dictionary."

"I like a dictionary. You like a dictionary. You own six of them."

"She's pedantic."

"Did she call you out on your bullshit?"

Daisy paused. Her hand, holding a chip, froze in mid-air. The question was so on-the-nose it was like a gut punch, stripping away all her meticulous defences. Iris's smirk was gone, replaced by a quiet, knowing gaze. Daisy knew, in that moment, that Iris wasn't just asking a question; she was asking a question that Iris herself already knew the answer to. Daisy opened her mouth, but the words wouldn't come. What did she want? She'd never even allowed herself to think about it. The shame of that realization was worse than any insult.

"Yeah," she mumbled, her voice barely audible. "She did."

"And what did she say?" Iris asked, her voice quiet and gentle. "What's the end goal?"

Daisy took a shuddering breath. "I want to stop being an archaeology project for myself," she managed, the words a fragile whisper. "To not be a story about someone else's past."

Daisy, naturally, threw the chip at her. The chip sailed across the table and landed with a soft, greasy plop on Iris' cheek. Iris laughed, shaking her head as she gently brushed it off.

Arriving home, Daisy collapsed on her sofa with the bag containing her purchases. The book slipped from the bag as it landed, and Daisy fingered it for a moment, once again enjoying the soft feel of the well-loved pages.

Feeling the discomfort of it in her back pocket, she pulled out her phone for the first time in hours. She glanced at it, half-expecting – hoping? – to find a message from Marisol. Nothing.

She stared at the screen. At first, she felt that old sting of rejection, the familiar panic. Perhaps a small pang of disappointment. Then, slowly, something else. Maybe this was the message – she'd read Daisy's.

Maybe Marisol's hadn't meant to be cruel. Maybe it was… her choice.

Daisy thought about sending another message, a little nudge, in case Marisol had seen the message, got busy, forgotten to reply. And then she realised that she didn't need to keep knocking, to kick this door down. It was Marisol's decision on whether or not to open it. Maybe it was okay for her to be there if Marisol needed her, but not to need Marisol.

She set the phone down next to her – but not before checking that it wasn't on silent – and picked up the scarf instead. She didn't just rub it against her cheek. She brought it to her face and buried her nose in it, inhaling that clean, gentle scent of lavender. It was the softest thing she'd ever touched, a feeling that felt foreign and right all at once. A quiet, unassuming comfort that she was allowing herself to have, a small safe place to land. It might be the nicest thing she'd ever owned. And in that moment, she realised why she felt that way: it was the first thing she'd ever chosen to own that wasn't used, discarded, or worn out. Probably nicer than she ever deserved to own.

"Fine," she muttered to no one. "Maybe charity shops aren't shit."

Had Iris been in the room, she'd have smirked like she'd won a battle. Daisy, however, was not yet ready to lay down her arms.

Chapter 19 – Modern Defence

Daisy was late. Again. She rode the bus like a reluctant passenger on a funeral procession, each slow, jarring movement a physical manifestation of her dread. Rain lashed against the windows, a miserable drumbeat that echoed the drumming in her head. She offered all of the usual excuses. They were cheap, like the park bench cider she'd once subsisted on, and she was just as good at pouring too many of them.

The therapist didn't scold her, nor ask any questions. She just looked at the clock, and at Daisy, and said, "and yet you came."

Daisy folded her arms. Her jaw was set, and she stared at a point over the therapist's shoulder. "Yeah, well... I didn't have a choice, did I? Iris booked it, so I had to come."

The therapist nodded, her eyes tracking Daisy's defiance, slowly made a note. The scratch of her pen on the paper sounded impossibly loud in the small room. "Tell me about choices."

"What?"

The air in the room was thick, the quiet pressure almost as suffocating as a crowded bar. The therapist's pen hovered over the notepad expectantly.

Daisy had nothing; the therapist offered nothing. Daisy glanced at the clock. So did the therapist. Fifty more minutes of this.

Daisy could sit in silence all day. She wasn't going to play the therapist's mind games. Even if she hated them.

The therapist silently sipped her coffee. She offered a bottle of water. Daisy took it. The plastic was slick and cold in her hand. She opened it. Sipped it. *Fuck*.

Daisy shifted awkwardly in her seat. The worn fabric of the armchair felt scratchy against her skin. "Look, when someone pays for something, you show up. That's how the world works."

"Is it?"

"People don't help you unless they're getting something out of it. There are always strings attached. Always a price."

The therapist set down her pen. The click echoed the certainty in Daisy's voice. She leant forward slightly, her elbows resting on her knees. "Always?"

"Always." Daisy felt more confident now. This was familiar territory. "Take Mary. She gives me clothes. It's not generosity, though, is it? It's image. Ego. She gets to play the Good Samaritan, to be the hero. Faye gave me children, but the price of that was ownership of me. Another object to toss away when she got bored."

"Mmm-hmm." A noncommittal response. "And Marisol?"

"Marisol wanted honesty until it didn't suit her." Daisy found the edge of her scarf, rubbing the cashmere between thumb and forefinger. The rhythm of the rub was a familiar comfort. "Same pattern. Everybody has an agenda."

"Including you."

The words hung in the air like a challenge. Daisy blinked. Her hands tightened in her lap, clenching into small fists. "What's that supposed to mean?"

"What's your agenda in being here?"

"I don't have—" Daisy stopped. Catching herself just in time. "I'm here because Iris is paying you."

"That's her agenda. What's yours?"

Daisy could hear the tick of the clock, almost deafening. The radiator hummed softly. The sound was a low, constant vibration that made her teeth feel on edge. That bloody dictionary at a weird angle in the bookcase. She could feel the therapist's steady gaze. She touched the scarf again.

"I don't know what you want me to say."

"I don't want you to say anything specific." The therapist leant back, relaxing slightly. She gestured vaguely at the scarf. "But you keep touching that scarf when we talk about people's motives."

Daisy's hand froze. Shit. She pulled it away, like it had been bitten. Crossed her arms defensively. Her back pressed deeper into the worn cushions of the chair. "So?"

"Just an observation."

The therapist shifted, a subtle adjustment in her posture. "It's a form of grounding for you, isn't it?" she suggested, her voice soft but with a hint of intrigue. "A way to anchor yourself in the moment when you feel uncomfortable?"

Daisy scoffed, a quick, sharp intake of breath. "I don't know," she muttered, her eyes darting away. The interpretation felt too simple, too pat. Like something you read in a trashy magazine. It made her want to retreat even more. "It's just… soft."

Daisy hated this game. It was torture. The therapist was clearly waiting for something, but what? She tried a different approach.

"What about you, then?"

The therapist barely reacted.

"What do you get out of this, besides seventy quid an hour?"

"Interesting question." The therapist smiled slightly. "What do you think I get out of it?"

Daisy's knuckles were white from clenching her hands. "Don't do that. Don't answer a question with a question."

"Why not?"

"Because—" Daisy stopped. She realised that she was being toyed with. Tried to find a counter. "Because it's manipulative."

"Is it?"

"Yes! This whole thing you're doing, this game. You want me to say something specific, don't you? Have some breakthrough moment where I suddenly realise that Iris loves me and I should stop being such a miserable bitch?"

The therapist's expression was calm, unchanged. "Do you think Iris loves you?"

Daisy felt a swell in her cheeks. A flash of exposure, hot and uncomfortable. "That's not – I didn't say that."

"You mentioned it, though."

"I was giving you an example, obviously."

"Of what?"

A trap. Another one. Daisy could feel it closing in around her, but couldn't see the mechanism. "Of what you want me to think."

"What do I want you to think?"

"Stop it!" Daisy's voice was sharper now. She could feel it. A familiar sense of panic. Of loss. "Stop answering questions with questions. It's like talking to a fucking mirror!"

The therapist nodded slowly, her gaze never leaving Daisy's face. She made another note.

"I have a hypothesis," the therapist said, her voice a little softer. "Tell me if I'm wrong." She looked directly at Daisy, a subtle shift in her posture that made her seem more human, less of a monolith. "I think you're here because you're scared. Scared that this new version of you is legitimate, and terrified of what happens if you let yourself believe it."

Daisy stared at her. She sought the scarf again, rubbing it so hard that the soft fibres burned her. She looked away, toward the window, where the rain was streaming down the glass. The therapist had stumbled before, made wrong guesses. But this… this one was too close to the truth. She hated her for it.

The therapist waited; her pen poised. Daisy could almost hear the quiet expectation in the air. Daisy could no longer stand it. "Fine. You want to know what I think? I think Iris gets off on being Florence bloody Nightingale, Jesus Christ with better hair. She gets to feel important. Gets to play the saviour with the broken tranny."

The therapist put down her pen and took a moment to process this.

"And what do you get?"

"Migraines." The response came automatically, a dry, sharp retort.

"Coffee shops," the therapist continued, as if Daisy hadn't spoken. Her voice was calm and steady. "Charity shop adventures. McDonald's. The pleasure of listening to you complain for hours."

Daisy looked down; the green cashmere hung loosely around her neck.

"Quite an elaborate setup for an ego trip, isn't it?"

"Maybe she's very committed to her hobbies." Daisy's voice was flat, a shield of sarcasm back in place.

"Maybe," the therapist offered, reaching for her notebook again and looking at her intently, "it wasn't about her at all."

There it was, the trap sprang shut. Daisy felt her chest tighten, that familiar panic. She shifted in her seat, her body stiffening as if preparing for a blow. "That's ridiculous."

"Is it?"

"Yes! People don't just… they don't help people for no reason. That's not how the world works."

"How does the world work, Daisy?"

"It works—" She stopped. With every answer she was being dragged deeper into quicksand. "It works the way it's always worked. People leave. People get bored. People find better options."

"Always?"

The therapist's quiet tone was a relentless pressure. "Always."

"Including Iris?"

Daisy's hand went to the scarf again before she could stop it. The therapist's eyes silently followed the movement. Daisy squeezed the soft fabric in her fist, her knuckles pale.

"She will," Daisy said quietly. "Eventually."

"When?"

Her voice was a whisper, but it escaped like a shout. "When she realises that I'm not worth fixing."

The therapist set down the pen entirely now. She folded her hands in her lap, her full attention on Daisy. "Worth fixing. That's an interesting choice of words."

"It's accurate."

"Is it? If you're broken, what makes you think Iris is trying to fix you?"

Another trap. Daisy felt it. Saw it coming. In slow motion, even. But she couldn't avoid it. "Because why else would she—"

"Would she what, Daisy?"

"Care." The word caught in her throat, a fragile thing Daisy hadn't intended to say. It came out smaller than she intended.

"Ah." The therapist made a note. A gentle nod of her head acknowledged the admission. "So, if someone cares about you, it means you need fixing?"

"It means they want something."

"What does Iris want?"

Daisy opened her mouth to answer, then closed it. The quiet settled in, filling the room with an awkward weight. Daisy could feel the pulse in her ears, a frantic beat. The therapist waited.

"I don't know," Daisy admitted. Her shoulders slumped slightly.

"That bothers you."

Daisy nodded despite herself.

"Why?"

Because…" Daisy touched the scarf again, realised that she was doing it and forced her hands into her lap, squeezing her legs together tightly around them. "Because if I don't know what she wants, I don't know when she'll stop wanting it."

"Mm." The therapist made another note. And if you can't predict when she'll leave, you can't protect yourself from it."

"Exactly." Daisy breathed a small sigh of relief. Someone who understood.

"So, the real question," the therapist said, setting down her pen and meeting Daisy's eyes directly, "isn't what Iris wants from you. It's what you're so afraid she'll discover about you to make her want to leave."

Checkmate.

Daisy stared at her; mouth slightly open. The therapist waited, patient as ever.

"Seventy quid for that?" Daisy finally managed.

"Easy money, really."

That night, Daisy paced her flat anxiously. She tried to read, but couldn't focus. Tried to watch TV, but couldn't find anything to watch even with a million apps containing a billion options. Tried to eat, but couldn't face yet another Pot Noodle.

Instead, she ran a bath, lit a few candles, luxuriated among the bubbles. She shaved her legs, her arms, the rest of her body, seeking the peace that came from erasing the remaining traces of her masculinity. The ones that could be moved with a razor and not a scalpel, anyway.

Satisfied that she was as groomed as she'd ever be, she closed her eyes. She allowed herself to enjoy the warm embrace of the water, the feint smell of jasmine from the candles, the soft sound of the meditation video that she'd chosen to fill the silence of the room – even if she wasn't directly listening to it.

For a moment, she allowed herself to feel... nothing. Not her usual nothing. A new nothing. One that felt... calm?

Once the water began to cool, forcing her into movement, she dried herself off, meticulously brushing and even straighten her hair. She gently folded the scarf over the edge of the bed. She grabbed a glass of water and slid in between her faux-satin sheets.

Plugging in her phone, she felt an urge. She opened up her messaging app – ignoring a message from her sponsor – and found the thread with Iris.

She tapped out some words. Deleted them. She was going to regret this, wasn't she?

She tapped them out again. *"I think the therapy might be helping."*

No fluff, no flowers. No room for interpretation. She hit send before she could delete them again.

She pictured Iris smirking as she read those words. They'd sent. Been read. No reply, though. She tried to will a response.

Nothing.

Fuck.

Check.

She set the phone down on the nightstand, turned out the light, and allowed herself to sleep.

Chapter 20 – A Breakthrough

The following morning, Daisy arrived at work. The door was stiff on its hinges, and the smell of stale coffee and humid air hit her first. She shivered, pulling her collar tighter around her neck. Bright. Early. Exhausted. Her mind was a relentless loop of her therapist's voice and the blank glow of her monitor. *What are you afraid she'll discover?* It played on a loop, a quiet hum beneath the surface of her thoughts. Had Iris discovered something? Was she gone? Her stomach churned with the gnawing unease.

She felt a jolt of panic as she reached her desk, a small, cluttered island in a sea of identical MDF surfaces. Her anxiety manifested itself in a thousand tiny annoyances that morning. The copier jammed, its blinking red light mocking her. She slapped the side of it, the plastic rattling in protest, before giving up entirely. She'd misspelled half the words in a document, sent an e-mail half-finished. She'd even made coffee without boiling the kettle at all. The icy sip was a punishment for her distracted mind. It tasted like shit, and she winced as she swallowed it.

She needed a cigarette.

She made her way outside, pushing through the heavy glass door and letting it slam shut behind her. She cowered from the rain in the bike sheds outside, the metal rattling softly in the wind, somehow feeling like she was back at school.

She pulled out her phone. The screen lit up, a beacon of hope. One new message. She opened it. It was from her sponsor, a simple check-in. She dismissed it and opened the thread with Iris. Still no reply. She scrolled up, looking at the last message she sent, a brave, foolish thing floating in the digital ether. She held the phone tightly, her thumb hovering over the screen. A quick check of the status icon confirmed her phone was off. A small, pathetic relief washed over her. At least it wasn't a choice. Not yet.

She lit a cigarette and inhaled deeply. As she flicked the first load of ash away, she heard a sharp, metallic ping near her feet. A coin.

She startled, her head snapping up. "Penny for them?"

She looked up. Sophie.

"Dad jokes?"

"You've met my dad; he doesn't have jokes."

True. He was a fantastic solicitor, but nobody admired him for his cutting wit.

"Seriously, what's wrong?" Sophie's gaze was direct, her head cocked to the side. "You look like you're trying to solve a quadratic equation with a migraine."

"Nothing, trying to enjoy a cigarette." Daisy took a long drag, exhaling a thin cloud of smoke that dissipated in the damp air.

Sophie nodded, not pushing it. She gestured to Daisy's hand. "You've hardly smoked this past week. I just… noticed."

Daisy began to wish people would keep their observations to themselves.

"Well, you kicked the copier and drank ice cold coffee, even though you could've made a hot one."

Like a book. Iris was right. Again.

Back at her desk, the office felt louder than before. Daisy was met by an e-mail from the boss. A new case – to Daisy, at least – and a bit of a mystery to solve. A client who may or may not exist and whose dubious immigration status was dubious. Lost. The file – both digital and physical – was thick. Home Office files, photographs – she was young, pretty – a few scant personal documents, reams of letters from other firms who'd given up on this.

Daisy read the file with a jolt. This wasn't a case; this was a challenge. A client that everyone had given up on. A lost cause. She didn't print the file. Instead, she got up, her palms a little sweaty, and walked down the hall to the boss's office. The door was ajar, and she saw him at his desk, head buried in a document. "Mick?" she asked, her voice smaller than she intended.

He looked up, pushing his glasses up his nose. "Ah, Daisy. That file on my desk is for you. Don't worry about it if it's too much. I'll get one of the senior solicitors to take a look at it next week."

Daisy swallowed, her anxiety about Iris now channelling itself into a resolve. "I've already looked at it, sir. I'd like to take it on."

Mick raised an eyebrow, the universal symbol of "Are you sure?" "Daisy, this case is a mess. Half a dozen firms have already tried and failed. The client has no paper trail, no clear immigration status. It's a dead end."

"I don't think so," Daisy said, taking a step further into the room. "The other firms were looking for a clear path. I think we need to look for a different one."

Mick leant back, a low groan escaping his throat as the old leather of his chair protested. "A different path? There's no such thing in immigration law. There's only the right path, which nobody can find, and the wrong path, which leads to deportation. I'm telling you, it's not worth your time."

Daisy's hands clenched at her sides. "With respect, Mick, I think it is. This woman... she's been invisible for years. She's been discarded by the system, just like all the other firms have discarded her. I understand that. I'm not going to give up on her."

The words hung in the air, a raw, unintended admission. Mick stared at her for a long moment, his gaze sharp. Then, slowly, he nodded. "Alright, Daisy. The file's yours. But don't say I didn't warn you. It's a ghost chase."

She smiled cautiously. "I'm good with ghosts, sir."

Back at her desk, the weight of the physical file in her hands felt both heavy and satisfying. She made another coffee – being sure to boil the kettle – and settled in to read through it. Every file, every letter, every statement, every detail. She felt a connection with the client, and she felt entirely responsible for making sure she did everything she could for her.

She spent the next few hours in a deep, frantic dive. The photocopied pages blurred, the tiny text a maze of legal jargon and bureaucratic shorthand. Every few minutes, she'd hit a wall. A missing date, a footnote that led nowhere, a handwritten annotation that was totally illegible. The paper trail wasn't just thin; it was actively hostile. At one point, she found a picture of the client, a woman named Elena, looking far younger, her smile tentative as if she wasn't sure she was allowed to be happy. Daisy taped it to her monitor. As if she was looking at her own reflection, a lost cause staring back.

Her head began to pound. She knew the answer wasn't in this pile of paper, but the system demanded she go through the motions. She logged into the Home Office database, a clunky, outdated piece of software that seemed designed to frustrate. She typed in every possible variation of Elena's name, her date of birth, her flimsy reference numbers. Nothing. The server timed out, forcing her to start over. Again. And again.

As lunch came and went, her eyes were aching. She got up, her chair scraping against the floor, and walked to the kitchen, feeling a hot flash of frustration in her cheeks. Leah was there, stirring a mug of coffee. "Long day?" she asked, her face perfectly smooth.

"Something like that," Daisy mumbled.

"This place is full of them," Leah said, not bothering to lower her voice. She went back to typing, a rhythmic clatter that sounded like a countdown. "Nothing to be done about it, though."

The words landed like a blow. *Nothing to be done about it.* The mantra of the broken, the defeated. The thought made the anger inside her rise, a slow, steady burn. She was so tired of being defeated.

She took a deep breath. She wasn't an expert, but she was a hell of a lot more stubborn than she'd ever given herself credit for. The answer wasn't in the obvious places. It was buried, hidden. She logged back into the CMS, her fingers flying across the keyboard, retracing every step of the previous solicitors, not just looking at the facts but at the way they were filed. Every file, every letter, every statement. She found a reference to a specific government guidance memo, one that was outdated and officially superseded. It was cold and precise, but in the middle of a dense paragraph, her eyes landed on a clause, a single line she hadn't seen anywhere else. An exception.

She read the clause again and again. It was as if the words themselves were glowing on the page, the answer to a question she hadn't known how to ask. The language was precise, cold, but it felt… familiar. Like it was something she had to find, a truth that could only be uncovered by someone who was also a discarded case.

Suddenly, inspiration. She grabbed the pile of pages she'd already read and tore through them quickly. Her hands were shaking with adrenaline, pages fluttering as she flipped through them, her eyes scanning for a familiar phrase. And then… she found it. The line she'd been looking for, buried in the middle of a dense paragraph. She felt a shiver run down her spine that had nothing to do with the cold.

She highlighted it. Took it to the boss. Explained what she'd found.

He nodded approvingly. Suggested they pick it up tomorrow.

"Why?" she asked.

"6 o'clock, Home Office is closed." He gestured to the office around them, still brightly lit. "So is this one."

She tidied her desk, logged out, turned off the computer and grabbed her things.

As she passed the reception desk on her way out, Sophie chimed in "I don't know what you did, but that's dad's impressed face."

"Must be a low bar," she responded.

"You wish." Sophie grinned. "Honestly? Watching you handle that case today was pretty impressive, too. If it's the one I think it is, that's been bothering dad for weeks."

Daisy forced herself to meet Sophie's gaze. The positivity was uncomfortable, but she didn't deflect it entirely. "You're here late." She gestured to Sophie's laptop, open on the desk.

"Car broke down."

"I'd offer you a lift, but I don't drive."

"That's okay, dad'll drop me home. Eventually."

She ran a hand through her hair, the simple motion showing her exhaustion. "Does he ever go home?"

"Not nearly as early as mum would like him to. He's the only reason she owns a microwave."

Daisy laughed. A genuine sound, light and unexpected. She leant against the reception desk for a moment, a small sign of how tired she was. "You know, people don't give you nearly enough credit. You're funny."

"You don't give yourself enough credit. You're better than you think."

"Still a low bar, though."

"Talking of which, we should grab a drink sometime. You might actually be fun. That's rare around here."

A drink or… a drink? Daisy hedged her bets. "Sure," Daisy said, trying not to sound as if she was grabbing at the first lifeline she'd seen all day.

She walked to the bus stop, the cold evening air a sharp contrast to the warmth that had bloomed inside her. The case was hers. She'd fought for it, and she'd won. A small victory, but it was a victory she'd earned on her own terms. The anxiety hadn't disappeared, but it didn't own her. She felt, perhaps, not "worth fixing," but simply... worthy. She hadn't needed saving, not today. And as the bus pulled up, she didn't even think to check her phone.

She pulled her coat tighter, a low, cold shiver running down her spine that had nothing to do with the wind. The brief feeling of peace was gone, replaced by the unsettling feeling of being watched. She scanned the street, but saw no one. She had found a way to save someone who'd been written off, but she had no idea what kind of demons she had awakened.

Chapter 21 – The Red Shoe Diaries

Daisy's mind was a whirlwind of panic, a relentless loop of self-doubt. The red shoes cast a spotlight on her feet, the cashmere scarf a woollen security blanket. What if she said something stupid? What if Sophie realised that she was a fraud who didn't deserve nice things or attractive women?

Stop. Breathe. Sophie had asked her out. Sophie found her interesting. Maybe even attractive. This was happening.

She arrived at the pub fifteen minutes early, claiming a table by the window, back to the wall, facing the door, so she could see Sophie approaching and compose herself accordingly. The pub was a low-lit refuge, smelling faintly of stale ale and woodsmoke. Her palms were sweating, and she ordered a Diet Coke to give her hands something to do. She wanted a cigarette, but didn't want that to be her first impression. She regretted not ordering something stronger – even if thirteen years of sobriety had taught her that liquid courage was liquid cowardice in disguise.

Sophie was punctual, scanning the room with an easy confidence that Daisy envied. The bell on the door jingled as she entered, a small, jarring note in the low murmur of conversation. She looked… well, she looked like Sophie from work. Same casual style, same friendly smile. Maybe that was good? Maybe that meant she was comfortable around Daisy, that she didn't feel the need to dress up?

"Sorry I'm late," Sophie said, sliding into the opposite seat. "I had to drop Iris' phone at the repair shop first."

"Repair shop?"

"Dropped it down the toilet, didn't she? Absolute disaster. She's been phoneless for two days, driving the entire family mental by calling and texting them from random numbers."

Down the toilet. That explained the radio silence. Daisy felt a strange mix of relief and disappointment – relief that she hadn't been deliberately ignored, disappointment that she hadn't been deemed worthy of a text from a random number.

Sophie was already rising to head for the bar. "Right – what are you drinking? And don't say 'just a Diet Coke'."

"I don't drink," Daisy said. "But I'll have a Coke Zero if you're buying."

"Fair enough. I respect that."

Sophie returned with Daisy's Coke and a pint of cider for herself, settling in with that casual way she had of taking up space. The weight of the opposite chair. The smell of cider. Anchors, in the sea of her panic. Daisy took a grateful sip, using the straw so as to not ruin the lipstick she'd agonised over. She tried not to read too much into Sophie being so understanding about the sobriety thing.

"So," Sophie began, looking genuinely curious, "tell me about your type."

Daisy almost choked on her drink. Was Sophie really being this direct? She swallowed hard, the carbonated fizz a shock to her throat.

"My type?"

"You know, in women. What usually catches your eye?"

A sense of giddy vertigo spun through Daisy's head. She tried to play it cool, but she could feel her pulse racing. She leant forward, her elbows on the table.

"I like smart women. Independent. Someone that can hold their own in a conversation."

"What about looks? Blonde or brunette?"

Daisy glanced past Sophie's shoulder, at a group of students laughing at a joke she couldn't hear. If Daisy were answering honestly, she'd have said "redhead," but she glanced meaningfully at Sophie's brown hair. "Something darker."

Sophie smiled and made what Daisy assumed was a mental note. "Tall or short?"

Daisy picked up her Coke, using the chill of the glass to cool her warm hands. "I'm not fussy about height." Though Sophie was perfectly proportioned, not that Daisy was staring.

"Introvert or extrovert?" Sophie's questions came rapid-fire, almost like a game.

Daisy felt like she was at a job interview but, then, isn't that what a date is? An interview for the job of partner? She was warming to the questioning. Sophie was methodical, trying to figure out what made her tick.

"Depends, I suppose. I like complexity. Someone who surprises me."

"How so?"

"Someone who calls me on my bullshit, I guess. Who sees through my defences, doesn't let me use them."

Sophie took a slow sip from her drink, her gaze holding Daisy's across the rim of her glass. She lowered the pint, a single raised eyebrow her only response. "That's quite specific."

"I know what I want." Daisy hoped she sounded confident, not desperate.

"And what about age? Older, younger, your own age?"

The questions kept coming. Each one made Daisy feel more exposed, but also more hopeful. When was the last time someone had shown this much interest in her preferences, thoughts, or desires?

"I don't really think about age," Daisy said. "It's about connection. Chemistry."

Sophie nodded seriously, like she was filing this information away for future use.

"That makes sense. Iris was asking about you the other day."

Daisy's stomach tightened, a sharp, cold knot of dread.

Of course, Iris had to come up eventually. "Oh?"

"She's been wondering how you're doing. With the therapy and everything."

Right. So, Sophie and Iris had been talking about her. Whispering about her behind her back, dissecting her like a case file. Daisy tried to keep her voice neutral. "Well, you can tell her I'm fine."

"She really cares about you, you know? She thinks you two have a lot in common."

Was this... jealousy? Sophie trying to work out how Daisy felt about her cousin before making her own move? The thought sent a cheap thrill through her – the idea of two women potentially interested in her, and one of them concerned enough about competition to bring it up directly.

"Look, Sophie," Daisy said cautiously, "if you're worried about me and Iris—"

"Worried?" Sophie looked genuinely puzzled. "Why would I be worried?"

"I know you're close. Family and all. I wouldn't want to complicate things between you two if something happened between us." Daisy subtly gestured between them, hoping she was striking the right note of consideration.

Sophie's confusion visibly deepened. "Complicate things how?"

Was she being deliberately obtuse, or was Daisy not being clear enough?

"This," Daisy said, a little more boldly. "Us. If we… If this goes somewhere."

The awkwardness that followed lingered a beat too long. Sophie was staring at her with an expression Daisy couldn't read. Surprise? Concern? Dawning horror?

"Daisy," Sophie said, very gently, "do you think this is a date?"

It hit like a slap to the face. All the fastidious preparation, the outfit changes, the meaningful glances – it felt ridiculous, pathetic. The blood rushed to Daisy's cheeks so quickly she thought she might pass out.

"Isn't it?" she offered, meekly.

"Oh, babe, no. No. I have a girlfriend." Sophie's voice was kind, but firm. "Sarah. Five years together. Mortgage, dog, matching dressing gowns."

The humiliation was complete. Daisy wanted to sink through the floor, to disappear, to wake up and discover this had all been a nightmare. She'd spent well over an hour getting ready for a date that was never a date, had been attempting to flirt with a woman who was already taken, had been –

"I'm so sorry," Daisy croaked. "I utterly misunderstood—"

"Don't apologize," Sophie said quickly, stifling a laugh. "This is my fault; I should've been clearer about why I asked you here."

As she said the words, Sophie pulled her phone out and checked the time. The screen flashed with a photo of a woman in a matching dressing gown, dog nestled on her lap.

"Why did you ask me here?"

Sophie took a deep breath, clearly choosing her words forensically. "I was trying to figure out your feelings about someone else."

"Someone else?"

Sophie shot her a look. *Come on, catch up.*

"Iris?"

The name dropped between them like a stone. Daisy stared; her embarrassment momentarily overtaken by confusion.

"She's been worried about you," Sophie offered. "Ever since you started therapy, she's been asking how you're doing at work. If you seem okay. She didn't want to intrude – she knows you're going through a lot – so she asked me to check in now and again. And maybe…" Sophie hesitated, uncomfortable. "Maybe see if you feel the same way she does."

"The same way she…?"

"She likes you, Daisy. Likes you. Has done since you two reconnected. But she didn't want to push her luck, so, as always, she sent me in to do the recon." Sophie grimaced. "Though I don't think either of us saw this much confusion coming."

Daisy sat back in her chair, silent. The new information crashed over her in waves. Iris liked her. Had been thinking about her, worrying about her. And she was too scared to make a move herself? The girl who showed up at her door uninvited, who dragged her out of her pit, was now waiting nervously for a report?

Which meant Iris was open. Waiting. And Iris had no idea Daisy knew.

"She doesn't know you've told me," Daisy said slowly.

Sophie shook her head. "That's right."

Something shifted in Daisy. The humiliation ebbed. In its place, something else. Control.

"Are you going to tell her?" Sophie asked. "That you know?"

Daisy could feel Sophie studying her face, trying to catch something to relay back. Every flicker would be reported back to Iris. She needed to play it smart.

"I'm not sure," she said. "It's a lot to process."

Sophie looked like she wanted to push, but Daisy was already finishing her drink, gathering her things.

"Thanks for the drink, Sophie. And for… clearing things up."

"Daisy, wait—"

"I'll see you at work," Daisy said, standing before Sophie could probe further.

She walked to the bus stop with measured steps, her face composed even as her mind raced.

Yes, she'd humiliated herself. Yes, she'd practically proposed to a woman already in matching dressing gowns. But the game wasn't over. Now, she held all the cards, and as she imagined Iris waiting for news, she felt a small, almost imperceptible straightening in her spine. The evening air was cool against her flushed cheeks, and a thoughtful smile crossed her lips.

Chapter 22 – The Hangover

Daisy had never enjoyed going to work quite this much.

The lights now felt reassuring, not draining. She'd arrived bright and early, made herself a proper coffee, the bitter scent of the grounds a small, familiar comfort in the stark kitchen. The faint scent of cleaning products and day-old paper was no longer oppressive. She logged on, the quiet whir of the computer a sound of purpose that resonated with her own focus, and systematically checked her email, deleting the junk and flagging the important, a small act of control. When Sophie arrived – as usual, dead on half-past eight – she scanned the office like she was looking for something. Or someone.

Daisy, deliberately, didn't even glance up from her computer. She typed a few lines into a form, the quiet click of the keyboard a calming rhythm. Every tap was precise, unhurried. She knew Sophie's movements intimately – the distinct shuffle of her bag being dropped by her desk, the soft sigh as she sat down, the click and glow of her phone as she would check it before doing anything else. Daisy waited in a jungle of desks and pot plants; her senses finely tuned. This new feeling of power was an armour she hadn't known she was missing – or how heavy it was.

"Morning, Daisy. How are you feeling today?"

Loaded, like a shotgun. Daisy looked up, slowly, with the blandest expression she could muster. "Fine, thanks. You?"

Sophie lingered by her desk, her weight shifting from foot to foot, clearly fishing. "Good, yeah. Good weekend?"

"Quiet. Productive." Daisy turned back to her screen. "Yours?" She could feel Sophie waiting, poised.

Eventually, Sophie spoke again, a faint note of forced casualness in her tone. "Oh, you know. Family dinner yesterday. Iris was there. Asked how you were getting on."

There it was. Sophie, dutifully, reporting back. Probably instructed to gauge Daisy's mood. Her receptiveness. Any hint of how Thursday night's revelation had landed. Daisy felt a little thrill, not of anxiety, but of power. She was the subject of the conversation, the one being sought out, and Sophie was the messenger. The dynamic was totally reversed.

Daisy kept her expression neutral, but internally, she was figuring out her options. Every conversation now a test of information – what to reveal, what to hold back. The words chess pieces, each move calculated for its future impact.

"That's nice of her. I'm doing well."

Sophie waited, obviously hoping for more, but Daisy had learned the power of silence. Let other people fill the gaps. Let them show their distress whilst holding position. She deliberately sipped her coffee. A dare.

Just as she sensed Sophie was about to give up and retreat, Daisy looked up with a studied casualness.

"Oh, speaking of Iris – when's she getting her phone back? Must be driving her crazy, being cut off from the world like that."

Sophie's face brightened, clearly thinking she'd found an opening. She took a step forward, as though coming closer would allow her to read Daisy better. "Tomorrow, I think. Why?"

Daisy shrugged, turning back to her computer. "No reason. Just struck me how much she'd hate to be unreachable."

The pause that followed was *delicious*. Daisy could practically hear Sophie's mental gears turning, trying to decode whether that was significant, whether there was a message that she could pass along here. Daisy allowed a flicker of a smirk as she typed a meaningless line into her computer, the quiet clack-clack of the keys an act of perfect indifference. She didn't need to do anything. The game was being played for her. All she had to do was watch. Sophie was looking for tells, but Daisy wasn't giving any.

"I could... let her know you were asking?" Sophie offered, testing the waters.

"Was I asking?" Daisy's tone was perfectly innocent, with enough edge to let Sophie know that she could see right through her ruse. "I was just making conversation. But you can tell her I said hello, if you'd like."

As Sophie retreated to her own desk, looking faintly unsettled, Daisy allowed herself a small smile. This, she presumed, was like holding the strong position in a negotiation.

The morning passed in a quiet, satisfying rhythm. She felt a new sharpness, a clarity that had been missing for years. She worked with an efficiency that surprised her, clearing out her inbox and finishing a report that had been sitting on her to-do list for weeks. It was easy to be productive when your mind wasn't cluttered with worry about what other people thought of you.

Lunch was a new kind of victory, a public declaration of her newfound sovereignty. Daisy walked into the small, sterile breakroom, the air thick with the smell of microwaved curries and stale coffee that usually made her stomach clench. Instead of huddling in a corner with her plain turkey wraps, a familiar habit of self-effacement, she chose a seat in the middle of a large, shared table.

She unwrapped her lunch, the plastic crackling faintly, and opened her emails with an intentional focus, ignoring the low buzz of colleagues chatting. She wasn't avoiding eye contact; she simply wasn't looking for it. Her gaze swept over the screen with a calm, assured intensity. She ate slowly, savouring the simple meal, perfectly aware of Sophie's twice-caught glances from the other side of the room, like a nervous bird-watcher. Every mundane action was deliberately weighted with power – the power of being the one everyone else was trying to read, the silent, unyielding centre of attention.

Just as she was finishing up, wiping her mouth meticulously with a napkin, a colleague from a different department, Mark, approached the table. He was a lanky man with a perpetually rumpled shirt and a forced joviality.

"Working hard or hardly working, Daisy?" he said with a half-hearted laugh, leaning on the back of an empty chair, trying to catch her eye.

Daisy offered a small, polite smile, a barely perceptible curve of her lips. "The usual," she said, her voice even and calm, devoid of the usual self-deprecating addendum she might have offered a week ago.

Mark paused, his smile faltering slightly, clearly expecting more, a conversational hook to latch onto. But Daisy simply returned to her phone, her thumb gliding over the screen with a deliberate focus, dismissing him without a word.

Mark fidgeted for a moment, amplifying his awkwardness, then backed away, the conversation dying on the vine. Daisy felt a lightness in her chest, a freedom she hadn't known was possible. She wasn't desperate. She wasn't begging. She was the prize – or, at least, she told herself she was – and the game was to make the other person work to get it.

When she got home that evening, the town was painted in the soft orange glow of a setting sun. The usual exhaustion that followed a day at work was absent. She felt a restless, confident energy buzzing beneath her skin. She wasn't tired; she felt like a strategist who had completed the first phase of a successful operation. She was already thinking several moves ahead. Not the desperate, scattered hope of someone playing from behind, but the moves of someone who understood how the game worked.

She dropped her keys on the hall table with a precise clink and walked into the living room. The apartment felt different, not a refuge, but a command centre. She surveyed it, mentally reorganizing, as if the physical space mirrored the new order in her mind. She was mapping it all out, the board finally visible. Every misstep with Marisol, every wrong turn with Faye – they all made sense now. She'd been too quick, too eager, too willing to show her hand. This time would be different. This time, she would choose when to escalate. She would dictate when and how this played out, and on what terms. The power was seductive.

She went to the kitchen and made a cup of tea, the routine a grounding counterpoint to the wild calculations in her head. She sat down on the sofa, her mind replaying the conversation from the pub. Iris had sent Sophie to do the recon. She'd been too shy to make the move herself, too nervous to show her cards. That was the crucial piece of information. Iris wasn't the confident, unbothered woman Daisy had assumed. She was scared. More scared than Daisy had realised. And, for the first time, Daisy believed she might be the one holding the balance.

Daisy leant back into the cushions, letting the details of her scheme unfold. She could call Iris the second her phone was fixed, let her know the recon was successful, and make a grand gesture. That was the old Daisy. The desperate Daisy. The Daisy who moved too fast and ended up getting hurt. No. That would be a wasted advantage. The move would be hers, but it would come too soon. It would show her hand and forfeit her newfound power.

Better to wait. Let Iris wonder. Let it be unbearable. Let her ask Sophie again what she found out. Let her stew in her own anxiety. The longer she waited, the more delicious the eventual reveal would be. Daisy smiled to herself. She had a week. Seven days to let the tension build. Seven days to decide the perfect setting to make her move. Seven days to enjoy the feeling of being in control. Her mind a finely tuned instrument, every decision precise and cold.

She rose from the sofa and walked over to the bookshelf, pulling down a thin volume of poetry. One of Faye's old books, filled with notes in her distinctive, sprawling handwriting. Daisy opened it, not to read, but to feel the worn paper beneath her fingertips. She wistfully traced the faded ink of a margin note. Then, with a decisive move, she closed the book and placed it back on the shelf, a silent acknowledgment that this chapter of her life, while cherished, was now firmly in the past. She then went to her phone, scrolled through her contacts, and found Iris' number. Still there, even though the phone was sitting in a repair shop.

Tomorrow, Iris would have it back. Would probably check for messages she might have missed. But she wouldn't have anything from Daisy. Not yet.

Daisy locked her phone and placed it face down on the coffee table. She sipped her tea, the perfect contrast to the cold, hard reality in her gut. She could have Iris in a single phone call. But she was going to make her wait for it. And she told herself she was going to enjoy every single second of it.

Chapter 23 – Passing The Torch

The urge was a physical thing. It hummed as she sat on the sofa, a persistent whisper telling her to send a single word, a single gesture, and Iris would come. She could give Sophie the slightest hint, a casual "Tell Iris to give me a call when she gets her phone back," and she could almost guarantee it would be done. But that would be amateur hour. That would be ceding ground, showing her hand, and worst of all, showing her interest.

Her hand slid into her coat pocket, closing around her phone. She pulled it out, thumb hovering over the screen. A single tap, a few words, and she could get the answers she craved. The temptation was a sharp, physical jolt, but she resisted. Pressed the home button, not the call log. She had gained the upper hand, and she wasn't about to give it up for a moment of impatience.

Better to let the tension build. Iris had been thinking about her for weeks, apparently. A few more days wouldn't hurt. It might even strengthen her position. Let Iris wonder what Sophie had learned, what Daisy was thinking. When someone was already that invested in the outcome, you made them wait. Made them want it more.

She stood, her body humming with that restless energy, and decided to channel it into something practical. She made herself dinner – a proper meal that required focus and a methodical mind, not the hasty toast or cereal of her old, distracted life. She started with pancetta, the smell of it sizzling and rendering in the pan a rich, savoury scent that filled the kitchen.

She methodically whisked eggs, a precise movement that felt oddly calming, and grated a block of Parmesan cheese, the fine powder a testament to her efforts. As the pasta boiled, she mixed the egg and cheese with a touch of black pepper, a rich, golden paste that would coat every strand. She drained the pasta, tossed it into the still-warm pan, and added the egg mixture, stirring quickly and purposefully to create a rich, creamy sauce without scrambling the eggs. It required control and timing. It was a mirror for the game she was playing. The result was a rich, comforting, and perfect spaghetti carbonara.

She found herself mapping out different approaches as she ate. She could play it cool, almost disinterested. Let Sophie report back that she seemed fine, unbothered, maybe even a little distracted by other things. That would drive Iris crazy, wondering if she misread the entire situation.

Or, she could go for something more direct. Show up at Iris' place unannounced, the way Iris had done to her. Turn the situation on its head.

That was perfect. Ring the bell and lay it out simply: *"I know how you feel about me. I feel the same way. What do you want to do about it?"*

The directness would catch Iris completely off-guard. No preparation, no choreography, just honest reaction. And Daisy… Daisy would get to watch her composure crack, probably see her stumble over her words for once. Payback for all the times that Iris had wrong-footed her, had been one step ahead.

The more she thought about it, the more perfect it became. She wasn't responding to Iris' feelings – she was taking control of the entire situation. Making herself the one to decide when and how things happened.

At that moment, she wasn't the one desperately hoping for someone else to make the move.

A new kind of energy coursed through her, no longer desperate, but charged with a cool, confident purpose. She found herself pacing the living room, working through the psychology of it. This was about power dynamics, not attraction; about who got to set the pace and terms. And right now, incredibly, that might be her.

She found herself drawn to her bedroom, a place that, until recently, had become a refuge and a prison all at once. Her eyes swept across the familiar landscape, feeling a new kind of calm within its confines. The books lined the shelves – Faye's favourites mixed with her own, volumes of poetry and philosophy that had shaped both of their thinking. The football shirts hung in the wardrobe, preserved even if she rarely wore them outside of the house anymore. Those things weren't debris of a difficult past; they were part of who she was.

But scattered across the bed and the nightstand were the teddy bears. A rainbow of plush creatures that she'd collected over the years. Some of them connected to fond memories, many of them impulse purchases during periods of grief, or moments when she wished she could regress to a simpler time. They weren't stored away or hidden – they were very much a part of her daily life, witnesses to her sleep and her solitude, their soft, synthetic eyes staring out at the room.

She'd let go of his clothes eventually – those had been easy once she'd accepted that they belonged to someone who no longer existed. But everything else? The books, the football shirts, the bears? They weren't anchors to a dead past; they were the foundations of who she'd become.

Still, as she looked at them now, one bear seemed different from the rest. The purple punk bear with the multicoloured hair, sitting on her pillow where she'd placed it that morning after making the bed.

The one that made her cry when Iris tried to touch it.

The one she'd bought because it reminded her of Faye.

Daisy picked it up, the familiar plush softness giving way to a different, more complicated weight in her hands. She remembered the day she'd found it, out shopping with her own mother, a reluctant companion on a dreary Saturday. She'd spotted the flash of purple hair from across the store and smiled. A perfect reflection of Faye, her warmth and softness, and her spikier side that she hid from the world. A tiny, ridiculous symbol of a complicated person. In the moment, it wasn't a source of pain. The familiar plush toy was no longer a relic of grief, but a bridge.

Their daughter, though. Olivia was nineteen now, away at university. She probably thought teddy bears were ridiculous, but this wasn't just a teddy bear. Maybe she'd want to know the story behind this one. Maybe she'd appreciate knowing that her mum had loved punk music and colourful hair, that someone had thought she was worth remembering with a silly purple bear.

Maybe Olivia deserved to have this piece of her mother more than Daisy deserved to keep it.

The decision hit her with surprising clarity. This wasn't about letting go of Faye – it was about sharing her. About giving Olivia something that belonged to her story, too.

Daisy found some bubble wrap in her kitchen, the sharp, satisfying pop of the plastic a new soundtrack to her decision, wrapped the bear precisely, and addressed a padded envelope in her best handwriting. She even found a card – plain white, nothing overtly sentimental – and wrote a simple message: "This made me think of your mum. I thought you might like it. Love, Dad x."

She placed the envelope near her front door, a visual reminder to take it to the Post Office in the morning.

Even with it outside the bedroom, Daisy felt something settle back into place. Not the manic energy of a temporary high, nor the desperate optimism of someone hoping for the best, but something steadier. She was doing the right thing – not for herself, but for Olivia. For the memory of who Faye had been.

Back in her bedroom, the remaining bears looked somehow more at home spread across the bed and nightstand. They weren't reminders of loss anymore – they were just a part of her space, part of her comfort, part of who she was.

And tomorrow, after her visit to the post office, she'd continue playing this new game carefully. She'd stay patient, keep her expression neutral, let the anticipation build naturally. Sophie would be watching for cracks in her composure, but she wouldn't find any. Not yet.

Maybe Thursday, once the tension had really built. When Iris had spent an entire week wondering what Sophie had learned, when the moment was perfectly ripe – that's when she'd make her move.

Settling back into bed, Daisy closed her eyes, with a faint, confident smile. She didn't have a picture of Iris's home, but she had a vision of the type of place it would be. Iris lived in Daisy's old hometown, after all, a place Daisy worked in and secretly wished she could return to. She imagined a three-bedroom, detached house with a neat garden and a window box full of bright flowers. A place with one of those fancy taps that boiled water instantly, maybe even a built-in espresso machine. A warm, quiet place that was a sanctuary not from gossip, but from the messy, chaotic world outside. A place that felt as comforting and stable as the spaghetti carbonara she'd made. The life she had always wanted.

Daisy fell asleep feeling like she might deserve to win. But in the quiet sanctuary of the three-bedroom house she'd built for Iris in her mind, there were empty rooms she couldn't see into. She didn't know what was in them. She didn't know who was waiting inside.

Chapter 24 – Quadratic Equation

Tuesday morning brought a fresh clarity. Daisy found herself moving through her routine with precision – coffee made with scientific perfection, breakfast eaten sitting at the table, rather than laying in bed. Clothes chosen with care rather than plucked from whatever was clean.

The difference wasn't energy. It was focus.

When she reached the office, Sophie was already at her desk, but there was something different about her posture. A tension that suggested that she'd been waiting, watching the door. When Daisy walked in, Sophie's head snapped up with barely concealed eagerness.

"Morning, Daisy. Good night's sleep?"

Such a loaded opening. Daisy settled in at her desk, taking her time arranging papers that didn't need arranging. "Fine, thanks."

"Great. That's great." Sophie's voice carried a brightness that felt manufactured. "I was thinking: do you fancy grabbing lunch today? There's a new place around the corner, it's supposed to be quite good."

Interesting. Sophie had never suggested lunch before. Daisy looked up, letting her expression register mild surprise. "That's kind of you, but I've brought something today."

"Oh. Right. Of course." Sophie's disappointment was almost comical. "Maybe tomorrow?"

"Maybe."

The morning progressed with a series of increasingly transparent attempts. Sophie found reasons to walk past Daisy's desk, to ask questions about work she clearly already had the answers to, or had no interest in. To make casual observations about the weather, the weekend that had passed, the week ahead.

Around eleven, she tried a different approach.

"Oh, I meant to tell you – Iris finally got her phone fixed. You know what she's like with technology. Can't function without it."

Daisy made a noncommittal sound, not looking up from her computer. But internally, she was calculating. A fixed phone meant Iris was probably checking her messages regularly. Looking for something that wasn't there.

"I bet she was relieved," Daisy said, her tone rigidly neutral.

"Absolutely. She spent most of yesterday catching up on everything she'd missed. Reading every text about three times. You know how she gets."

There it was – Sophie fishing, trying to gauge whether Daisy might be planning to send any of those texts that Iris was supposedly anticipating.

"I'm sure she was busy," Daisy replied, turning her attention back to her screen.

Sophie waited another beat; clearly, she was hoping for more of a reaction. She hovered a little too long, then returned to her own desk with visible frustration.

By lunchtime, Sophie's efforts had taken on an almost desperate quality. She lingered by Daisy's desk when she returned from her break, clearly looking for an opening.

"Any interesting plans for the week?"

"Nothing special."

"That's nice. Sometimes quiet weeks are exactly what you need." Sophie paused, then seemed to decide to push harder. "Iris was saying she's got a really quiet week, too. Sounded a bit lonely, to be honest."

Daisy looked up, allowing the feintest flicker of something cross her expression – hoping to convey curiosity, perhaps, or mild dismay. Just enough to give Sophie hope.

"Oh?"

"Yeah, she's been a bit… I don't know? Reckless, maybe? Like, she's waiting for something to happen, but doesn't know what."

Perfect. Daisy filed the information away, then returned to her work with the same neutral expression.

"I hope she finds something to occupy her."

Sophie's face brightened at what she clearly interpreted as a positive response. At last, something to report back.

That evening, Daisy allowed herself to appreciate the elegant simplicity of her position. Sophie was doing exactly what she'd intended – growing more desperate, more obvious, more willing to reveal information in exchange for even the smallest hint of reciprocal interest.

And, meanwhile, somewhere across town, Iris was presumably checking her phone and finding nothing. Wondering what Sophie had learned, whether her orchestrated reconnaissance mission had yet yielded any useful intelligence.

Three more days. By Friday, the anticipation would be unbearable.

Daisy settled onto her sofa with a book and a cup of tea, feeling like she understood how to use patience to her advantage.

Wednesday brought an escalation in Sophie's despair what was almost painful to witness. Every conversation attempt felt more forced, more obviously premeditated.

"Sleep well?" Sophie asked, the moment Daisy walked through the office door.

"Fine, thanks."

"Good. That's good. I always think a good night's sleep makes a world of difference to your outlook, don't you?"

Daisy nodded noncommittally and settled at her desk, but she could feel Sophie hovering, clearly building up to something.

"I was wondering – do you ever get lonely? Living on your own, I mean. Not that there's anything wrong with it, obviously, but sometimes I think it must get a bit quiet."

Interesting angle. Daisy glanced up, letting her expression register mild curiosity at the unexpectedly personal question.

"Sometimes," she said. "But I quite like my own company."

"Of course, of course. It's just that Iris was saying the other day how nice it is when you have someone to talk to properly, you know? Someone who really gets you."

Sophie's voice had taken on an almost pleading quality, as if she were trying to will Daisy into understanding some deeper message. Daisy, of course, got the hint. That didn't mean she was going to take it.

"Sounds like Iris knows what she wants," Daisy replied, returning to her computer.

By mid-morning, Sophie had moved on to increasingly transparent attempts at intelligence-gathering.

"What do you usually do on Friday evenings? I'm always curious what people's routines are."

"Nothing, really. Read, usually. Sometimes watch television. Maybe even a trip to the cinema."

Oh." Sophie's disappointment was audible. "Don't you ever fancy going out? You know, somewhere more social? Meeting people?"

"Not particularly."

"There's this lovely pub near Iris' place – the Rose and Crown? Really cosy, nice atmosphere. Perfect for, you know, just sitting and having a proper conversation with someone."

Daisy looked up, letting the slightest flicker of interest cross her face. Enough to keep Sophie talking.

"I don't really go to pubs," she said.

"Right, of course. Sober. But they do lovely coffee, too. Italian stuff. And it's such a nice area for a walk afterwards, especially in the evening when it's all lit up."

The desperation was becoming almost comical. Sophie was practically drawing Daisy a map to where she might casually encounter Iris on a Friday night.

"Sounds pleasant," Daisy said, neutrally.

That afternoon, she left the office at five-thirty sharp and walked to the bus stop, already looking forward to her six o'clock appointment. These weekly sessions had become something of a lifeline over the past few months, a space where she could untangle the complexities of her recovery, her grief, her tentative steps forward to building a new life.

Today, though, she found herself anticipating the conversation differently. Not so much seeking guidance as… vindication, perhaps?

The therapist's office was in a converted Victorian house, all high ceilings and large windows that let in the golden light of early evening. Daisy settled in the familiar chair, noting how different this felt from previous weeks when she'd arrived carrying the burden of her past.

"How has your week been, Daisy?"

"Interesting, actually." Daisy found herself smiling. "I think I'm starting to see the patterns that have been confusing me."

She told the story slowly, watching her therapist's face for reactions. The drinks with Sophie, the gradual revelation of what was really happening, the delicious moment when all of the pieces fell into place.

"So now I know," Daisy concluded. "I know where I stand with someone. No guessing, no hoping, no desperate attempts to read signals that might not even be there."

Her therapist was quiet for a moment, fingers steepled, considering.

"And what are you planning on doing with this... knowledge?"

"I'm going to act on it. On Friday. I'm going to be direct, honest. Show up and simply say what needs to be said."

"That sounds like quite a bold approach."

Daisy felt a surge of satisfaction at the word 'bold.' "Sometimes boldness is what's required. I'm tired of waiting for other people to make the first move."

"Mmm." The therapist leant back slightly, and Daisy sensed a shift in the energy of the room. "I wonder about the need for a surprise. You've mentioned you're tired of games, but this scheme sounds... elaborate."

"It's not a game," Daisy said, a flicker of irritation crossing her face. "It's a strategy. A way to avoid repeating mistakes I've made before."

"And what happens if she's not where you expect her to be? What if you arrive and the moment isn't right?"

Daisy felt a flicker of irritation. This was exactly the overcautious thinking that had kept her trapped in limbo for years.

"I haven't misinterpreted anything. The evidence is quite clear."

"Evidence." The therapist repeated the word thoughtfully. "That's an interesting way to put it. It sounds almost... analytical."

"What's wrong with being analytical? At least it's better than stumbling around hoping that someone will take pity on you."

"Nothing wrong with analysis. It can be a very powerful way of protecting ourselves. Though I sometimes wonder whether a perfectly analytical approach is always the most effective one when it comes to human connections."

The session continued like this, a gentle but persistent questioning that felt increasingly like an attempt to talk her out of her plans. Every suggestion seemed designed to induce doubt, to make her second-guess the clarity she'd achieved.

But Daisy found herself resistant to each attempt. This felt different from her usual patterns of romantic disaster. She wasn't acting from distress or need or the fear of being alone. She was acting from a position of strength, with clear information about how the other person felt.

"I think," she said as the session wound toward its end, "that sometimes you have to be willing to take calculated risks. To trust your judgement rather than always defaulting to the safest possible option."

Her therapist nodded slowly, but Daisy caught something in her expression – a kind of resignation, as if she understood that her patient had made up her mind and wouldn't be dissuaded.

"Promise me that you'll think about what you really want from this situation. Not just the satisfaction of knowing, but what you hope to build afterward."

Daisy promised, but as she left the office and walked towards the bus stop, she found herself feeling more convinced than ever. Two more days, then one perfect, decisive conversation that would change everything.

She knew exactly what she was doing.

Thursday dawned grey and unremarkable, a morning that suggested autumn was settling in properly. Daisy found herself moving through her routine with the steady satisfaction of someone whose plans were falling perfectly into place.

Sophie's dejection had reached new heights overnight, apparently. She was already at her desk when Daisy arrived, practically vibrating with nervous energy.

"Morning! How are you feeling today?"

"Fine, thanks."

"Great, that's great. I was thinking – it's such a shame when people miss out on opportunities, isn't it?" Sophie's voice was too loud, too bright, her hands clenching and unclenching on her desk. "Like, when timing doesn't quite work out?"

Daisy glanced up, letting mild curiosity register on her face. "I suppose."

"It's just that sometimes people are ready for something, but they're waiting for the other person to... well, to show some sign that they're ready too. And, meanwhile, time's ticking by."

The subtext was so obvious that it was almost insulting.

"Timing can be tricky," Daisy agreed, neutrally.

"Exactly! And sometimes you just have to... create the right moment, don't you think?"

Daisy turned back to her computer, but she was making a mental note of this... infodump? Sophie's mounting agony suggested that Iris was getting impatient, too. Perfect. By tomorrow evening, the anticipation would be unbearable.

The day passed in a series of increasingly unsubtle hints. Sophie mentioned that Iris would be home alone on Friday night. That she'd been 'hoping to hear from someone.' That she'd seemed increasingly thoughtful lately, as if she were 'waiting for something to happen.'

All of it exactly as Daisy had predicted.

At five o'clock, she gathered her things with the quiet satisfaction of someone whose scheme was working flawlessly. A few more hours and she'd send the text that would set everything in motion.

"Have a lovely evening," Sophie called out as Daisy headed for the door. "Don't do anything that I wouldn't do!"

The journey home on the bus gave Daisy the opportunity to assess her approach. She'd keep it simple – something like 'I think we should talk. Are you free tomorrow evening?' Direct enough to signal serious intent, vague enough to create anticipation. Then, when Iris inevitably said yes, she'd suggest meeting at Iris' flat around eight. On familiar ground, where Iris would feel comfortable enough to have the conversation that they both knew was coming.

She stopped at the corner shop near her flat to buy milk, and found herself smiling at the mundane normality of it. Tomorrow night, everything would be different. But tonight was just another quiet evening in, the calm before she took control of her romantic life.

The flat felt peaceful as she let herself in, autumn twilight filtering through the windows in long golden hues. She made herself a proper dinner – pasta with the good tomato sauce, not something grabbed from the freezer and thrown in the oven – and settled at her kitchen table with some YouTube philosophy.

Around seven-thirty, she'd make her move. Not too early, because that might seem desperate, but early enough that Iris would have time to anticipate, to prepare, to work herself into exactly the right state of nervous excitement.

Daisy finished her dinner slowly, savouring both the food and the anticipation. This was confidence – not manic energy or desperate hope, she was convinced of the outcome.

She was loading the dishwasher when she heard footsteps on the landing outside her front door.

For a moment, she thought nothing of it. Probably someone visiting a neighbour or delivering a package to the flat upstairs.

Then came the knock.

Daisy froze, trying to process what she was hearing. No one knocked on her door unannounced. Not at seven-thirty on a Thursday evening. Not when she wasn't expecting someone.

The knock came again. More hesitant, as if whoever was out there was having second thoughts.

Daisy walked slowly to the front door. Unconsciously checking her hair and her outfit, her heart rate beginning to pick up despite herself. This wasn't how things were supposed to unfold.

She looked through the peephole and felt the world tilt sideways.

Iris.

Iris was standing on her doorstep, shifting from foot to foot, clearly nervous but determined. She was wearing the same deep red coat that Daisy remembered from their charity shop expedition, her hair slightly messy from the wind.

This couldn't be happening. Not tonight. Not before Daisy had planned.

Not before she'd had the chance to control the timing and the setting of their conversation.

But there Iris was, raising her hand to knock again.

Daisy took a deep breath and opened the door. The cold autumn air rushed in, carrying the scent of damp pavement and Iris's perfume, which was light and woody, and made her want to step closer.

"Hi," Iris said, her voice carrying a mixture of determination and caution that made Daisy pause.

"Hi." Daisy gripped the door handle, trying to steady herself. "This is… unexpected."

"I know. I'm sorry. I should've called, but…" Iris gestured helplessly. "I couldn't wait anymore."

The words hit Daisy like a physical blow. *'Couldn't wait anymore.'* The exact phrase she'd been planning to provoke with precisely-timed messages and crafted anticipation. Instead, Iris was… conceding. Standing on her doorstep and admitting that waiting had become unbearable.

Daisy felt a flash of vindication, a rush of triumph. Iris wasn't just ready for this conversation; she was desperate for it. This was an even greater victory than Daisy had expected.

"How long have you been waiting around?" Daisy asked, though what she really wanted to ask was 'how did you know to come tonight?' As if she didn't know: Sophie.

"About an hour. Waited for you to come home, realised it was creepy if I showed up immediately. So, I tried to wait around long enough for it to not be creepy. Then I had to work up the courage to knock."

Daisy nodded, acutely aware that they were standing in the doorway, that this conversation was happening in public view rather than the controlled environment she'd been planning.

"Come in," she said, stepping aside.

Iris moved past her into the living room, and Daisy caught the scent of her perfume – it was light and woody, and made her want to step closer rather than preserve the distance she'd been cultivating all week.

"Can I get you something? Tea?"

"Actually…" Iris turned to face her, and Daisy could see the resolve settling in her expression. "I came here to tell you something. And, if I don't say it now, I'm going to lose my nerve entirely."

"It's okay," Daisy said, trying to be reassuring. "I know."

"Of course," she said, nervously. "Sophie told you."

"She did." Daisy took a step closer to her. "The question is: what are you going to do about it now that you're here?"

Iris' breath caught, and Daisy could see her pulse jumping in her throat. They were standing close enough now that Daisy could count her eyelashes, could see the way her pupils had dilated.

"I don't know," Iris whispered. "I had this whole speech planned, but now…"

"Now?"

"Now that you're looking at me like that, I can't remember any of it."

Daisy smiled. This was more like it – Iris off-balance, unbalanced, clearly wanting something she wasn't brave enough to ask for.

"How am I looking at you?"

"Like you know exactly what I'm thinking."

"Maybe I do."

The air between them seemed to thicken, charged with an electric want and possibility. Daisy could see Iris' chest rising and falling rapidly, could see the way she was fighting the urge to step backward, to create distance and safety.

But she wasn't stepping back. She was holding her ground, meeting Daisy's gaze with a mixture of fear and desire that made Daisy's pulse race.

"Tell me what you're thinking," Daisy said, softly.

"I'm thinking…" Iris' voice trailed off. She took that step back, that retreat.

"Go on," Daisy said.

Iris gathered herself, standing up straight, purposefully. "This was a mistake."

She turned on her heels and headed for the door. Daisy followed. Iris reached the door, pulling it open. Daisy leant across her to close it.

"Daisy, I…" Iris started, her breathing shallow.

"Me too." Daisy leant in to close the narrow distance between them, her breath catching as she came close, and kissed her. Her hand caressed her face, tracing Iris' cheekbone with her thumb.

For a moment, it was perfect. Her lips were soft and warm, and tasted faintly of coffee. Iris' lips parted under hers, and Daisy could feel a shiver run through her body, could hear the tiny sound of pleasure that escaped from her throat.

Then, suddenly, Iris went rigid. A complete stop, like a door slamming shut. The hands that had been reaching for Daisy's back came up to push gently but firmly against her chest. The soft, warm pressure was gone, replaced by a cold, improbable resistance.

"Wait," Iris gasped, breaking the kiss and stepping backwards. "Wait, I can't… I'm not…"

She looked stricken, her face flushed and her breathing ragged. But her eyes were wide with something that looked almost like panic.

"I'm sorry," she said quickly, quietly. "I thought I was ready, but I'm not. I can't do this. Not yet."

Daisy stared at her, trying to figure out what happened. The kiss had been perfect – she was sure of that. Iris had wanted it. Had responded for those first few seconds like she was exactly where she wanted to be.

"Iris…"

"I have to go." Iris was already wriggling her way out, her movements jerky with adrenaline or embarrassment or fear. "I'm sorry, Daisy. I shouldn't have come here. I wasn't thinking clearly."

"Wait, please. We can talk about this—"

But Iris was already opening the door, moving quickly through it, and already fleeing into the gathering darkness.

And then she was gone, leaving Daisy standing alone in her living room, the door hanging slightly ajar behind her. The cold wind rushed in again, but this time, it was all Daisy could feel. The scent of Iris was gone, replaced by the mundane smell of her own pasta sauce lingering in the air. She closed the door, the click of the lock a final, deafening sound in the silence. She tingled from a kiss that had lasted maybe ten seconds… and somehow destroyed everything.

Chapter 25 - Icarus

Silence was worse than rage. Rage had edges. Silence was a void.

If Iris had yelled, if she'd cursed, if she'd sent even a text that said "don't ever talk to me again," Daisy could've worked with that. Anger was something that you could grab hold of, wrestle with, maybe even redeem yourself from. But silence? Silence left you dangling over a cliff, staring into a blank wall that never blinked back.

It had been a month since the kiss. Thirty days of compulsive phone-checking, thirty mornings of self-loathing for doing it again, thirty evenings rehearsing explanations and apologies that had nowhere to go. Daisy had abandoned Marisol; she told herself that this was karma. The wheel turning. The universe correcting itself. She thought of the tale of Icarus. *Iris was the sun. Of course I burned.*

She had thought she was ready. She had thought she had control. She had thought wrong.

The first week was the worst because hope still lived there, crouched in the corner of her consciousness like a mangy cat that refused to be evicted. Every morning started the same: hand to phone before her brain had even booted. No messages. Then the sweep – WhatsApp, Instagram, even bloody LinkedIn, in case Iris had decided to reach out through there. Because, obviously, Iris would choose a corporate networking site to deal with romantic trauma. By the end of that first week, she'd even started checking her spam folder.

Off-licences became churches. Every bottle, a chalice. One evening after work she drifted into one without realising that she'd crossed the threshold. Neon lights blared, painting everything in that unique 9pm shade of melancholy that only corner shops could manage.

She drifted through the aisles like a sleepwalker, fingers grazing bottles of wine, vodka, whisky. The glass gleamed. A siren song in B-flat minor.

She picked up a bottle of gin. Hendrick's. Cold. Heavy, but not too heavy. Goldilocks' gin – just right for obliterating thirteen years of sobriety in one fell swoop. Her mouth watered. Just the thought of that first mouthful made her knees buckle.

Then she set it down. Hard. The clink echoed like a gunshot.

She left without buying anything, heart pounding, breathing shallow. No one in the shop even looked at her, but she felt branded by shame. The teenage clerk didn't even glance up from his phone. The security camera in the corner probably hadn't even registered her presence. But she walked out feeling like she'd performed her near-relapse for an audience of thousands.

She told herself that was strength. Then she told herself that it was weakness. She told herself both at once until her head spun like she was Linda Blair in *The Exorcist*.

By the second week, the ritual had become routine. Her phone-checking moved from hopeful to compulsive. The off-licence visits were regular, almost a form of masochistic pilgrimage.

But the real torture was work.

Sophie buzzed around like a bee with an agenda, and that agenda was transparently obvious to everyone except Sophie herself. She didn't know where Iris was – that much became increasingly clear – but she wanted to. Needed to. And somehow, in Sophie's mind, Daisy held the key to this mystery.

The morning after – that first Friday – had started innocently enough.

"How was last night?" Sophie had asked, casual, with all the subtlety of a flashing neon sign.

"Disastrous," Daisy replied, because honesty was the only luxury that she could afford.

"Oh?" Genuine surprise flickered across Sophie's features. This wasn't the script that she'd been expecting.

"You haven't heard from Iris?"

"I assumed you'd both be… well, happier."

"Me too."

Sophie's face cycled through confusion, concern, and something that may even have been panic. Her fairytale romantic intervention had apparently blown up in spectacular fashion, and she was only now realising that she might be in the blast radius.

The following week, the probing had begun in earnest. Sophie's questions started out subtle and, by the end of the month, had become an almost comical ritual in sorrow.

"Did you sleep well, Daisy?" Sophie chirped, the brightness in her voice cranked up to eleven.

"Like the dead," Daisy said, flatly.

"Oh. That's… nice." A pause, heavy with the weight of unasked questions. "Iris always says she needs at least eight hours or she's useless the next day. Well. Never mind."

"Always says." Present tense. Not "used to." Sophie thought she was still in touch. Daisy's first crumb of intel in days.

"How is Iris?" Daisy asked, flatly.

"Fine, I think? We haven't... I mean, I've been busy. You know how it is."

Liar. Sophie was many things, but she wasn't a natural deceiver. The hesitation, the way her eyes darted left – tells that even a mediocre poker player would spot. Sophie hadn't heard from Iris either. The revelation should've been satisfying. Instead, it was terrifying. If even Sophie – Iris' cousin, her closest confidant – didn't know where she was or what she was doing, then Iris hadn't only ghosted Daisy. She'd vanished from everyone.

Daisy caught herself narrating Sophie's manoeuvres in her head like David Attenborough.

Here we observe the desperate cousin, prodding again for a response from the emotionally-distant female. See how she dangles conversational bait. No bite. Will she try again next week? Naturally, it's all she knows.

The internal commentary should have made Daisy laugh. Sometimes it did. But usually, it made her ache. Sophie was circling an absence, pecking at the hole that Iris had left behind, and Daisy hated how much she wanted those scraps of attention to keep coming.

The cynicism grew back like scar tissue. She found herself sharper, meaner in her head than she'd been in months. Everything annoyed her – the way people chewed, the way buses always smelled faintly of damp, the way happy couples held hands like they owned the pavement.

It was regression, and she knew it. But there was comfort in it, too. Cynicism was a shield; one she had broken in well. She needed armour. At night, she'd lie awake, composing one-liners she'd never say out loud. It didn't matter if the audience was imaginary. It mattered that she still had teeth.

By the third week, it was unbearable. She went to a meeting out of sheer hopelessness, half-hoping that Iris might appear, half-hoping that she wouldn't.

The church basement smelled of coffee, old chairs, and the depressing brand of hope that comes from people who've learned to measure progress in days rather than years. The lights somehow too bright and too dim. She slipped in late, trying not to be noticed, but Mary spotted her instantly. Of course she did.

"Daisy," Mary whispered as she slipped into the seat beside her. "Didn't think we'd see you tonight."

"Neither did I," Daisy muttered.

Pete wasn't there – Mary offered some vague "family reasons" that Daisy didn't press. She didn't care. She didn't want to care.

The secretary invited Mary to share. Of course, Mary accepted. Daisy sat rigid, her arms crossed, listening to the woman talk about gratitude, about faith, about family. Every word made Daisy want to crawl out of her own skin.

She hated the way Mary's voice carried calm authority, hated the way people nodded along like disciples. But, most of all, she hated that Mary kept sneaking little glances at her, like she was tailoring it for Daisy.

"I'm learning to stop trying to force things into place," Mary said, her voice gentle and even. "I had this idea of how things were supposed to go, you know? How a relationship was supposed to work. And when it didn't, I kept trying to hammer it into a shape it wasn't meant to be. But all that did was break my hammer, and it didn't even make a dent in the stone."

The room murmured with agreement. Daisy ached. Mary wasn't talking to her, but her words struck a direct hit. She had spent the last month trying to hammer a solution into existence, trying to force a shape that wasn't there.

After the meeting, Mary touched her arm. "I'm glad you came."

Daisy jerked away. "Don't make it into something it's not."

Mary didn't flinch. "Okay. But I'm glad anyway."

That was almost worse. The gentle acceptance, the refusal to be pushed away. It made Daisy want to scream or cry or both.

By the fourth week, work had become its own special kind of torture. The job Iris had found her – had that been honest help, or a way to keep tabs on her from a safe distance? It gnawed at her like a splinter under her skin.

She sat at her desk, reconciling accounts and handling client communications, and wondered if every task was being monitored. Was there a report somewhere detailing

Daisy's productivity, her attendance, her social interactions? Was Sophie filing updates about her emotional state?

The office felt smaller with each passing day. The walls seemed to be contracting, squeezing her into an increasingly narrow space. She found herself taking longer lunch breaks, sneaking in an extra cigarette, to escape the atmosphere of forced normalcy.

One afternoon, she walked past the Starbucks where she'd met Iris for their charity shop expedition. The memory hit her like a lightning bolt: Iris laughing at something Daisy had said, the easy way they'd fallen into step together, the comfort between conversations.

She'd ruined that. All of it. In pursuit of what? Control? Strategic advantage? The satisfaction of being the one with power in a romantic situation?

She'd taken something beautiful and twisted it into a game. No wonder Iris had run.

The nights stretched longest. She tried books. She tried films. She tried podcasts about obscure philosophy, the kind of thing that used to soothe her. Nothing worked. Her brain played only one film: the kiss. Over and over. The way Iris had leant in, the way her breath had hitched, the way her lips had parted. And then… the way she'd pulled away. The way her eyes had grown wide with panic. The way she'd fled. Every replay ended the same, but Daisy couldn't stop watching. It was masochism, and she was fluent in it.

The off-licence visits became a routine. She never bought anything, but she visited anyway, seeking something. Never finding it. Seeking it again.

One evening, she made it as far as the checkout queue. An ice-cold bottle of white in her hands – nothing fancy, something reliable. A bottle of wine that she might have bought in her drinking days when she was trying to convince herself that she was being sophisticated.

The queue crawled. Cigarettes, lottery tickets, sacraments of self-destruction. Daisy clutched the sweating wine bottle and tried to remember when she'd last wanted anything so badly.

That was a lie; she could remember: it was wanting Iris to kiss her back. Look how that had worked out.

She set the bottle on the shelf next to the checkout and walked out. The teenage clerk didn't bat an eyelid. The security cameras might have caught it, but security cameras weren't in the business of judging people's abandoned purchases.

Outside, she stood in the evening air and realised that her hands were shaking. Not with craving – with relief. She'd walked right up to the edge and stepped back. Again.

It should've felt like victory. Instead, it felt like a postponement. In the rooms, they called it recovery, but it wasn't recovery. It was remission.

Because the want remained, patient and persistent. Waiting for the next moment of weakness, the next time her defences were down. The next time that she remembered that thirteen years of sobriety hadn't stopped her from becoming a person that others needed to disappear from.

One night, she sat on her kitchen floor with an empty glass. Just the glass. She turned it in her palm, imagining weight, juniper, ice. Her body remembered. Her body begged.

The glass caught the light from the street lamp outside her window. Crystal clear, perfectly ordinary. She'd bought it years ago, part of a set that had seemed vital. Adult glasses for an adult life. She'd drunk water from it, juice, tea when she was out of mugs. Normal things. Sober things.

It was an artifact from another life.

She set the glass down on the tiles and stared at it until dawn. She didn't drink. She didn't not drink. She endured the temptation, holding her hand above the flame to see how much she could take.

The sun came up slowly, painting her kitchen in shades of grey and gold. She was still sitting on the floor, staring at the empty glass. Her back ached. Her neck was stiff. As if she'd aged a decade in the space of six hours.

But she hadn't taken a drink. That had to count for something.

She stood up, joints creaking, and put the glass in the dishwasher. Normal morning routine for a normal morning. Except nothing felt normal anymore.

By the end of the month, she'd lost weight. Not intentionally – she kept forgetting to eat, or eating had become too much effort, or food tasted like ash and regret. Her clothes hung looser. Her face looked sharper in the mirror; angles more pronounced.

People started noticing.

"Are you feeling alright?" Sophie asked one morning and, for once, seemed authentic rather than probing.

"I'm fine."

"It's just… you look a bit peaky."

Peaky. Such a gentle word for what she was becoming. Drained. Worn down. Like a photograph left too long in sunlight.

She caught herself in bathroom mirrors and shop windows, startled each time by her own reflection. When had her eyes gotten so dark? When had her cheekbones become so prominent? She looked like someone convalescing from a long illness.

Which, in a way, she was.

Sleep came in fragments. She'd lie in bed, exhausted but wired, mind spinning through the same circuits: what she should have done differently, what she might say if Iris ever came back, what she'd lost by trying to control something that should've been left to its own devices.

Coffee became a food group. She drank it constantly, chasing the caffeine high that never quite arrived. Her hands developed a perpetual tremor – not enough to be obvious, but enough that she noticed whenever she tried to write or type.

Sophie stopped asking personal questions. Started bringing extra sandwiches to work, leaving them casually on Daisy's desk without comment. Small kindnesses that made Daisy want to cry.

Her cynicism hardened to steel. She annotated life with vicious footnotes that no one else would ever read.

A client complained about how long their case was taking to complete: *Yes, I'll get right on that. Let me just force the government to move faster at gunpoint.*

A colleague discussing weekend plans: *Ah, yes, the weekly ritual of pretending to have a life. How delightfully staged – we both know you're going to end up drinking alone with your cats, Sandra.*

Her own reflection in the ladies' room mirror: *Looking good, Daisy. Really nailing that prisoner-of-war camp survivor aesthetic.*

It was exhausting, but it was also survival. Every observation sharpened into a weapon. Every interaction filtered through layers of protective sarcasm. If she could mock everything first, perhaps it wouldn't hurt her.

The armour wasn't perfect. Sometimes, something would slip through – a song on the radio that reminded her of Iris, a woman in a red coat walking ahead of her on the street, the smell of the perfume Iris had worn that night. Each of these moments hitting like a knee to the gut, leaving her gasping for air.

But, most of the time, the defence held. She moved through her days encased in wit and bitterness, untouchable and untouching.

By the end of the month, she'd come full circle: the raw, earnest exposure of the past few months scraped away, leaving behind the old Daisy – snarky, cynical, sharp as broken glass. It wasn't progress, but it was familiar.

She told herself that she was safer this way. You couldn't get burned if you never touched the sun.

Whenever her phone buzzed with a spam email or a calendar reminder, her heart leapt before it fell. If she saw the colour red in a crowd, she half-expected to see Iris' coat. When she caught herself making a joke in her head, she wished Iris were there to hear it.

And that was the worst part. The armour didn't stop the longing. It only made the longing lonelier.

Sophie had stopped probing entirely by now. Their interactions had settled into a pattern of courtesy punctured by small acts of kindness that went unacknowledged. Sophie would leave tea bags by the kettle when Daisy's favourite brand ran out. Daisy would handle the more difficult clients when Sophie seemed overwhelmed. They orbited each other carefully, two women bound together by a shared absence.

The meetings became something Daisy attended sporadically, when home became too much to bear. She'd slip in late, sit at the back and let the familiar words wash over her without really listening. Sometimes, Mary would catch her eye and nod. Sometimes, Daisy would nod back. Not recovery, but maintenance. Keeping the engine running while the car sat in neutral.

One evening, walking home from yet another unproductive day, she found herself pausing outside the off-licence again. The familiar yellow storefront, the hand-written signs advertising deals on wine. A life she'd walked away from thirteen years ago, waiting patiently for her to return like a loyal dog.

She didn't go in, but she stood there for a long time, hands in her pockets, watching other people emerge with their purchases. Wine for dinner parties. Beer for football matches. Spirits for celebrations or commiserations. All the normal reasons that people bought alcohol, reasons that had nothing to do with the systematic destruction of brain cells in pursuit of emotional numbness.

She envied their simplicity. Their ability to have one drink, to use alcohol as punctuation rather than paragraphs. They made it look so easy, so casual. Like it was another grocery item, instead of liquid dynamite.

A woman emerged carrying the same bottle of gin that Daisy had picked up that first night. Hendrick's. The good stuff. The woman was roughly her age, well-dressed, probably heading home to cook dinner and share the bottle with a partner or friends. Normal evening rituals for normal people living normal lives.

Daisy watched her disappear down the street and felt the weight of all the normal evenings she'd never have. All the casual drinks, the celebrations, the simple pleasures that were forever off-limits. Not because she couldn't have them – she could walk into that shop right now and buy whatever she wanted – but because, for her, there was no such thing as casual. There was only all or nothing, and she'd been forced to choose nothing thirteen years ago.

Most days, that choice felt right. But tonight, watching that woman disappear into the evening with her bottle of gin and her presumably uncomplicated relationship with alcohol, Daisy felt the sharp edge of loss.

She turned away from the shop and continued home, to her empty flat and her empty evening and her empty phone that never rang with the voice she wanted to hear.

Tomorrow would be day thirty-one. The day after, day thirty-two. And so on, stretching into an indefinite future of counting days without Iris the way she'd once counted days without alcohol.

The only difference was that she'd chosen sobriety. This exile had been chosen for her.

And that, she realised, was the cruellest cut of all.

Chapter 26 – The Red Wedding, 2022

The church smelled of lilies and expectations. Daisy slipped into a pew near the back, watching the orchestrated chaos of pre-ceremony preparations unfold. A flower girl practised her walk, scattering imaginary petals with the deft flutter of fantasy. Ushers directed traffic with military precision. Someone's aunt was already crying, and the bride hadn't even arrived yet.

Weddings were theatre. Everyone knew their roles: the weeping relatives, the nervous groom, the photographer catching "candid" moments on cue. The whole production designed to transform two people signing a legal contract into something that looked like destiny.

She'd attended enough of these performances over the years to recognise the beats. The processional music would swell, Mary would appear in white – well, cream, probably, given her age – and everyone would pretend they believed in forever, even though the happy couple were each on their second marriage.

The organ wheezed to life, and the congregation rose like a synchronised swimming team. *Here we go,* Daisy thought, settling back to observe the ritual.

Mary looked radiant, which was what you were supposed to say about brides, but in this case happened to be true. Her dress was simple, elegant, and she moved down the aisle with the confidence of a woman who'd waited long enough to know what she wanted. Behind her came the bridesmaids: three younger women who looked like Mary, but slightly fuller, carrying themselves with the same quiet confidence. Pete stood at the altar looking genuinely moved rather than terrified, which put him ahead of about sixty percent of the grooms that Daisy had observed over the years.

The vicar launched into the familiar liturgy. Dearly beloved, we are gathered here today… Daisy let the words wash over her without really listening. She'd heard variations of this speech dozens of times. The promises were always the same: love, honour, cherish, until death do us part. The audacity of it never failed to amaze her – two people standing before "God" and everyone they knew, promising to feel the same way about each other until one of them died.

It wasn't bitterness, exactly. More like a pre-emptive flinch. Pete and Mary were good people. They deserved happiness. But promises made with such certainty always struck her as tempting fate. As if the universe appreciated being challenged.

The vows were personal, which meant that Daisy tuned out even more thoroughly. She found herself studying the stained-glass windows instead, the way afternoon light filtered through the blues and golds to paint rainbow patterns on the stone floor. Pretty. Peaceful. More honest than the promises being exchanged at the altar, somehow.

When the couple kissed and the congregation erupted in applause, Daisy clapped along dutifully. The first act was complete. Now for the after-party.

The reception was held at a hotel that had clearly been chosen for its function rooms rather than its charm. Vanilla carpet, magnolia walls, a bland elegance that offended no one and inspired no one either. Daisy followed the crowd towards the bar, checking her phone for the table assignment Mary had texted her that morning.

Table seven. She wandered through the maze of round tables draped in white cloth; each one decorated with centrepieces that looked expensive but forgettable. Table five, table six... ah. Table seven, tucked near the back corner. Not quite social Siberia, but definitely not the prime real estate near the head table.

Two people were already seated, drinks in hand, looking as slightly awkward as she felt. The man was probably her age, maybe younger, with an outdoorsy tan that suggested he spend weekends climbing things or cycling long distances. He wore his suit like armour – technically correct but clearly uncomfortable. The woman was younger, early thirties maybe, with short dark hair and sensible shoes that suggested she walked to work.

"Daisy?" The man stood as she approached, extending a hand. "I'm James, Mary's cousin's husband's brother, I think? The family tree gets a bit complicated."

"Alice," the woman added, not standing but offering a warm smile. "I work with Mary. Well, I used to work with Mary. We keep in touch."

Daisy shook James' hand and settled into the chair between them. "Daisy. I'm from the meetings."

"Meetings?" Alice asked.

"AA," Daisy clarified. "Mary's my sponsor."

"Ah." Alice nodded, and Daisy braced herself for the awkward pause that usually followed this revelation. "That's nice. She talks about you sometimes. Says you keep her on her toes."

"Someone has to," Daisy replied, and was surprised to find herself almost smiling.

James flagged down a passing waiter. "What are you drinking?"

"Diet Coke, thanks." The response was automatic now, delivered without embarrassment or explanation. James ordered a beer for himself, wine for Alice and Daisy found herself relaxing slightly. No awkward questions about why she wasn't drinking, no well-meaning offers to "just have one." Either these people were unusually tactful or they just took it in their stride.

The hour before dinner dragged on, filled with the polite but strained chitchat of people who had nothing in common.

Daisy excused herself to visit the ladies' room and took a detour past the bar on her way back, partly for the walk and partly to observe other guests.

Mary had assembled quite the crowd. Extended family clustered near the head table, Pete's work colleagues dominated the bar, and scattered throughout were what Daisy presumed were the strays – single friends, distant relatives, people who didn't quite fit the neat categories of "his side" and "her side."

She was scanning the room idly when she caught sight of a woman in dark green, red hair catching the light as she laughed at something her companion was saying. Pretty, Daisy noted absently – then frowned, irritated at herself for noticing, and promptly forgot as someone bumped into her reaching for the bar.

The crowd was beginning to thin as people found their seats, and Daisy spotted a brunette woman spinning around with her girlfriend near the dance floor, both of them laughing and clearly having more fun than anyone else in the room. *Good for them*, Daisy thought. At least someone was enjoying themselves.

She made her way back to table seven, where James and Alice had been joined by three more people: an elderly man who'd introduced himself as Pete's uncle, a woman roughly Daisy's age who radiated the energy of someone recently-divorced, and a young man who looked like he'd rather be anywhere else.

"So," Alice said as Daisy sat down, "I think we're the miscellaneous table."

"The what?" James asked.

"You know. The people who don't fit anywhere else. Singles, strays, random plus-ones." Alice gestured around the table with her wine glass. "The miscellaneous table."

Daisy felt a laugh bubble up despite herself. "Oh god, we're the singles table, aren't we?"

"The what now?" James looked genuinely confused.

"The singles table," the recently-divorced woman – Sharon, Daisy thought her name was – explained with the weary authority of someone who'd attended a lot of weddings alone. "Every wedding has one. They put all the unattached people together and hope we'll pair off."

James' expression shifted from confusion to something approaching horror. "Oh. Oh no."

"What?" Alice asked.

"I'm gay," James said flatly. "I've got a boyfriend. Mary knows I've got a boyfriend. She met him at Christmas."

Alice stared at him. "She thinks I'm gay, too."

"Are you?" Sharon asked with the directness of someone who'd clearly had several glasses of wine already.

"No! I mean, not that there's anything wrong with – I just – no. I'm straight. Very straight. Boringly straight."

Daisy felt the laugh escape properly. "Oh, Mary, you beautiful, well-meaning disaster."

James turned to her. "What about you?"

"What about me what?"

"Are you… I mean, what was Mary thinking putting you between us?"

Daisy knew the answer. "Honestly? I think Mary's working from a very outdated idea of how sexuality works. She probably thinks that trans equals either lesbian or gay man in drag, or that gay men need the right woman, and that anyone who works in environmental science must be gay."

"I work in renewable energy." Alice protested.

"Close enough for Mary's purposes," Daisy said, "but she means well."

"She really does," James agreed. "But Christ, this is awkward."

"It doesn't have to be," the elderly uncle said unexpectedly. Everyone turned to look at him. He'd been so quiet they'd almost forgotten he was there. "I'm eighty-three years old. My wife died two years ago. Mary put me here because she thinks I need 'encouragement to get back out there.'" He made air quotes with gnarled fingers.

"But you know what? You're all lovely people. We can just have dinner and ignore her matchmaking entirely."

"Hear, hear," Sharon raised her glass. "To ignoring Mary's matchmaking."

They toasted with varying degrees of enthusiasm, and Daisy found herself genuinely smiling for the first time all day. These were good people. Slightly mortified people, but good people nonetheless.

The meal arrived in waves: starter, main course, speeches, dessert. The food was fine – hotel catering at its most inoffensive – but the company turned out to be surprisingly entertaining. James had stories from his work as a tree surgeon, Alice was passionate about solar panels in ways that were oddly compelling, and Sharon had a dry wit that only came from surviving a spectacular divorce.

The speeches happened somewhere between the main course and dessert, a blur of best man anecdotes and heartfelt words from Mary's daughter that Daisy half-listened to while finishing her chicken. The usual wedding speech themes – worth the wait, best thing that ever happened, love conquering all.

She found herself thinking about Faye during the speeches, which was dangerous territory but seemed unavoidable at weddings. They'd talked about marriage, in the abstract way that couples do when they're comfortable but not quite ready for legal commitments. Someday, maybe. When Olivia was older. When they had more money. When the world felt more stable.

Someday had never come. Love hadn't conquered anything except Daisy's ability to trust promises.

But Mary and Pete looked happy. Genuinely, properly happy in a way that made Daisy want to believe they might be the exception to the rule. They deserved to be the exception.

The speeches ended with the traditional toasts, and the DJ started the music that would transform the function room into a dance floor. Most of their table dispersed – James to call his boyfriend, Alice to chat with Mary's work colleagues, Sharon to the bar for what she announced would be "one more, then I'm calling a taxi."

Daisy found herself alone at the table, watching couples take tentative first steps onto the dance floor. Mary and Pete moved together with the obvious choreography of people who'd taken lessons, while their relatives and friends joined in with only varying degrees of skill and sobriety.

It was a nice scene. Warm and human and tangible in a way that all the formal ceremony wasn't. People celebrating something good, however temporary it might prove to be.

She was thinking about heading home when a shadow fell across her table.

"Excuse me, love, but you look lonely sitting here all by yourself."

Daisy looked up to find Pete's uncle – not the sweet elderly one from their table, but a different uncle – this one probably in his sixties with the red nose and unsteady posture of someone who'd been sampling the open bar extensively.

"I'm fine, thanks," she said politely.

"Oh, come on. A beautiful woman like you shouldn't be sitting alone at a wedding. How about a dance?"

"That's very kind, but I don't really dance."

He leant closer, bringing with him a wave of whisky and aftershave. "I bet I could change your mind about that."

Before Daisy could formulate a response that was both firm and polite, James appeared at her shoulder.

"Sorry, mate, but I think Daisy promised me this dance." He offered her his arm with the gallantry of a knight rescuing a damsel, and she took it gratefully.

"Oh," the uncle said, deflating slightly. "Right. Of course."

James led her to the edge of the dance floor, not onto it but close enough to uphold the fiction that they might be about to dance.

"Thank you," Daisy said.

"No problem. Uncle Derek has been working his way around the room all evening. I think you were victim number four."

"You really know how to make a girl feel special."

"Family weddings," James shrugged. "Bring out the best in everyone."

Alice appeared beside them, slightly breathless. "Was that Uncle Derek trying to chat you up?"

"James rescued me."

"My hero," Alice said, batting her eyelashes at James with theatrical exaggeration. "Protecting innocent women from lecherous relatives."

"Someone has to," James said with mock gravity. "It's a dangerous world out there for unaccompanied females at wedding receptions."

They were all laughing now, the amusement that comes from shared absurdity. Daisy realised that she was having fun, which hadn't been on the agenda. She'd come here to fulfil her social obligations to Mary, endure a few hours of wedding theatre, and go home. She hadn't expected to enjoy herself.

But these people were good company. James was funny in a self-deprecating way that reminded her of the better sort of man she occasionally encountered in meetings; perhaps the one she'd once tried to pretend to be. Alice was smart and passionate about things that mattered. Even Sharon, now holding court at the bar with a group of Pete's work friends, had turned out to be excellent company.

Mary's matchmaking had failed spectacularly in its intended purpose, but it had succeeded in something else: putting together a group of people who might not have found each other otherwise, but who genuinely liked each other's company.

"I should probably head home," Daisy said, though she found herself reluctant to leave.

"Already?" Alice checked her watch. "It's not even ten."

"I know, but I'm not much for late nights these days."

"Fair enough. How are you getting home?"

"Taxi," Daisy said. "I don't drive."

"Sensible," James said. "I should probably think about leaving soon, too. I promised David that I'd call him before midnight."

"The boyfriend?" Alice asked.

"The boyfriend. He's working tonight – he's a nurse – but he wants a full report on Mary's dress and whether Pete cried."

"Did he?" Alice asked.

"A bit. Very sweet, actually."

They stood together watching the dance floor, where music had shifted from classic wedding fare to something more contemporary. The red-haired woman in the green dress was dancing with someone – a man, though Daisy couldn't see his face from this angle. They moved well together, comfortable and familiar.

"I'm glad Mary's happy," Daisy said, surprising herself with the sentiment.

"She deserves it," Alice agreed. "She's good people."

"Terrible matchmaker, though," James added.

"The worst," Daisy confirmed. "But good people."

She said her goodbyes, collected her coat from the cloakroom, and waited in the hotel lobby for the taxi. Through the windows, she could see the reception continuing – people dancing, drinking, celebrating the optimistic fiction that love could last.

The taxi driver was mercifully quiet, leaving Daisy to watch the countryside slide past the windows under the amber glow of the scant streetlights. She felt oddly peaceful, which wasn't what she'd expected from the evening. Weddings usually left her feeling melancholy, remembering what she'd lost and couldn't have again. Tonight, she felt... settled.

Mary's matchmaking had been a disaster, but the evening itself had been surprisingly pleasant. James and Alice were good people, the kind she might stay in touch with if their paths crossed again. The food had been fine, the music tolerable, and she'd avoided most of the usual wedding awkwardness by ending up at a table full of people who were all equally baffled by their placement.

Most importantly, she'd gotten through the entire evening without feeling bitter. She'd watched Mary and Pete promise each other forever, listened to speeches about love conquering all, observed couples dancing and families celebrating and she'd felt... not cynical, exactly. Cautious, maybe. Realistic.

They were good people making impossible promises. She hoped they got lucky.

The taxi pulled up outside her building, and Daisy made sure to give the driver a generous tip. The evening air was crisp, spring giving way to early summer, and she stood for a moment on the pavement breathing it in.

Her phone buzzed with a text from Mary: *"Thank you for coming tonight, it meant the world to have you there. Hope you had a good time! xx"*

Daisy typed back: *"Beautiful wedding. You looked radiant. Very happy for you both! xx"*

It was true, all of it. Mary had looked radiant, it had been a beautiful wedding, and Daisy was genuinely happy for them. She was also genuinely convinced that most marriages ended badly, but those weren't mutually-exclusive positions.

She climbed the stairs to her flat, kicked off her heels, and put the kettle on. The evening completed; a social obligation fulfilled without damage to anyone involved. She'd done her duty as Mary's sponsee, made polite conversation with strangers, and escaped without incident.

Tomorrow she'd be back to her normal routine: work, meetings, the quiet rhythms of a life built around recovery and solitude. But tonight had been a reminder that she could function in social situations when required. She could find people amusing, enjoy conversation, laugh at the absurdities of human behaviour without becoming cruel about it.

It was progress of a sort. Not toward anything in particular – she wasn't planning to start dating or seeking out new friendships or making dramatic changes to her deliberately-curated life. But it was good to know she could access those parts of herself when needed.

She made her tea and settled into her chair with a book, the sounds of the wedding reception fading. Mary and Pete were probably still dancing, surrounded by family and friends and all the optimistic chaos of celebration. Tomorrow, they'd wake up married, officially committed to their impossible promise.

Daisy hoped they'd prove her wrong about forever. Someone should.

But she wouldn't bet on it.

Chapter 27 – Artificial Reality

The cursor blinked at Daisy from the laptop screen, a patient, digital eye. She typed: *"I've been obsessing over someone who won't return my calls. How do I make them contact me?"*

The AI's response appeared after a brief pause: *I understand this situation can be very frustrating and emotionally difficult. However, I can't provide advice on how to make someone contact you, as this could potentially involve manipulation or boundary violations. Instead, I'd suggest focusing on your own wellbeing during this difficult time.*

Daisy stared at the screen. That wasn't what she'd wanted to hear, though she supposed it was probably the right answer.

"What if I've been investigating through mutual contacts? Is that normal when someone disappears?"

That kind of behaviour could be concerning and might indicate that professional support would be helpful. Investigating someone through their contacts or monitoring their activities without their knowledge can cross important boundaries.

There it was. The machine had called her a stalker. Maybe she was.

Daisy closed the laptop with more force than necessary. The silence in her flat felt different from the AI's diplomatic responses – at least it wasn't pretending to offer wisdom whilst refusing to help. She'd been coming here – to this digital confessional – for weeks because it was safe. She could type out sanitised versions of her problems and get gentle, meaningless responses that never challenged her to change anything.

She realised, with a small jolt, that she was trying to control even her therapy.

The realisation stung: recognising her own bullshit. She'd been treating the AI like a practice therapist – somewhere she could rehearse being weak without risking anything, receiving algorithmic concern for carefully censored versions of her problems.

The laptop sat closed on her kitchen table, as useless as everything else she'd tried over the past month and a half. She thought about the real therapist that she'd been avoiding, the one that cost money that Daisy didn't have and asked questions that Daisy didn't want to answer. The one who might be able to help, precisely because she couldn't be controlled.

The receptionist at the therapist's office sounded surprised when Daisy called the next morning.

"Daisy? It's been... let me check... nearly two months since your last appointment. How are you doing?"

"Not great," Daisy said, which was probably the most honest thing she'd said to anyone in weeks. "I need an appointment as soon as possible."

"Let me see what she has available. Are you in crisis? Because if you need immediate support—"

"I'm not going to hurt myself," Daisy said quickly, though as the words came out, she realised they weren't entirely accurate. She was hurting herself, just not in ways that would cause concern for her physical safety. "But I think I'm about to make some very bad decisions if I don't get help soon."

There was a pause, the sound of computer keys clacking. "She has a cancellation on Thursday at 2pm. Will that work?"

Thursday. Daisy could hold on for three days. Probably.

The three days passed with the slow-motion quality of waiting for something you both wanted and dreaded. She found herself practicing conversations in her head, trying out different ways to explain what had happened with Iris, different framings that might make her sound less pathetic. By Wednesday evening, she realised that she was doing it again – strategizing her way through powerlessness, trying to manage even her surrender.

The therapist looked exactly as Daisy remembered – kind eyes behind wire-rimmed glasses, greying hair pulled back in a way that suggested competence without severity. Her office still smelled faintly of lavender, still had that chair that Daisy had spent so many hours in, trying to pick her way through the rubble of her past.

"It's good to see you, Daisy," the therapist said, as Daisy settled into the familiar seat. "Though I'm sorry you felt the need to come back."

"I've been avoiding this place," Daisy said, surprising herself with her own honesty. "I couldn't afford regular sessions, and I knew you'd probably be right about things I didn't want to hear."

The therapist's eyebrows rose slightly. "That's quite an opening. What's changed that brought you back?"

"I tried to replace you with an AI." The admission felt both ridiculous and necessary. "Spent weeks feeding my problems into a chatbot and getting bland, noncommittal responses. It was pathetic."

"It sounds like you were looking for support without the risk of being challenged."

"Exactly. And I realise now that I was doing the same thing with…" Daisy paused, unsure how to best frame things. "With Iris. I've been obsessing over her."

The therapist leant forward slightly. "What does that tell you?"

"That I've got very good at accepting care from people while never letting them close enough to matter. Even when I want them to."

"You mentioned 'obsessing'?"

And, like that, Daisy found herself telling the whole story. No omission of the parts that made her look desperate or deceptive. The entire Iris saga, from the beginning.

"I turned her into a project," Daisy said finally. "This fascinating problem I could solve through the right combination of timing and tactical moves. And, when I made my move, I realised I'd been acting alone whilst she was trying to connect with a human being."

"What happened when you made your move?"

"We kissed. It was… more intense than I was prepared for. And then she panicked and ran, and I haven't heard from her. That was almost two months ago."

"How has that affected you?"

"I came closer to drinking than I have since Faye died," she said quietly. "I've been going to off-licences, standing in the alcohol aisles reading labels like they might contain some kind of answer. Just… testing myself, I suppose."

"I've been checking my phone compulsively," Daisy continued. "Scrolling through social media looking for any trace of her."

"You've transferred your addictive patterns to this relationship," the therapist said.

Daisy exhaled. "Yes. I became an Iris-oholic. And the worst part was, I used all of my recovery knowledge to torture myself with it. I could analyse my own obsessive behaviour perfectly, could see exactly what I was doing wrong, but I couldn't stop doing it."

"What stopped you?"

Daisy thought about it. "Muscle memory, maybe? Cult programming? But also…" She paused, trying to articulate something she hadn't fully understood until this moment. "I realised that drinking wouldn't bring her back. It would confirm everything that I was afraid of her thinking about me."

"Which was?"

"That I'm too much. Too intense. Too fucked-up to be worth the risk of getting involved with."

They sat with that for a moment. Outside, Daisy could hear the ordinary sounds of a Thursday afternoon – traffic, a dog barking somewhere, people going about their lives with manageable problems and reasonable solutions.

"This pattern of keeping people at a safe distance," the therapist said eventually. "When do you remember first developing it?"

Daisy felt the familiar urge to deflect, to turn this into a discussion of general relationship psychology rather than specific personal history. It was a game. Even now, she was plotting moves.

"After Faye died," she said, "But honestly, I think I was doing it before that too. I used her as... proof, I suppose? Proof that I could connect with people when I wanted to. As long as I had that one deep relationship, I could keep everyone else at arm's length."

"Can you think of a specific example?"

"There was Mary and Pete's wedding," Daisy said. "They put me at what was clearly the singles table with some lovely people they obviously hoped I'd connect with. And I... performed my way through the entire evening. Charming, entertaining, hollow."

"What did performing give you?"

"Control," she admitted. "If I kept it light and funny, I could enjoy their company without risking wanting something from them."

"What were you afraid of wanting?"

And there it was – checkmate. Daisy could see exactly where this was heading.

"That I'd be at risk of caring about someone who might leave," she said, and felt something loosen as she said it.

The therapist nodded, "Connection requires vulnerability," the therapist said. "And vulnerability always carries risk."

"And I'd already lost the most important people in my life. I couldn't afford to set myself up for that kind of devastation again."

"So, you've been protecting yourself from connection for so long that you do it even when you don't want to."

"Yes." Daisy found herself almost smiling despite the weight of the admission. "You're very good at this, you know. I can see exactly what you're doing, and I'm walking right into it."

"And with Iris?"

"With Iris, I tried a different approach entirely." Daisy could feel herself being manipulated into deeper territory. "Instead of avoiding connection through performance and deflection, I tried to control it. Map out all the variables, orchestrate the optimal moves, engineer the outcome through superior tactics."

She paused, recognising the pattern even as she named it.

"But it was the same impulse, really. A more sophisticated way of protecting myself from the full risk of caring about someone."

The therapist leant back slightly in her chair, "When did you first learn that loving someone meant losing them?"

That landed like a cricket bat to the face. Daisy felt tears forming in her eyes. When had she last cried?

"When Faye died," she whispered. "And I nearly destroyed myself because of it."

"We need to talk about that, don't we?"

Daisy nodded, not trusting her voice.

"I can't afford to come here every week," she said after a moment, "But I can't afford not to do this work, either."

"What would work for you?"

"Maybe… every other week? I need to stop managing this on my own."

The therapist smiled, "What would surrendering control look like in this context?"

Daisy considered the proposition, aware that even her consideration was being observed and analysed. The therapist would be watching for signs that she was still trying to give the "right" answer rather than the honest one. It was fascinating, really – even her surrender was being regulated by someone else's superior tactics.

"No more editing my problems to make them more manageable," she said slowly, "No more AI therapy where I can control the level of challenge. No more trying to solve my emotional issues through bloody roadmaps."

The therapist waited, and Daisy recognised the space she was being given to go deeper.

"Just… showing up, I suppose. Trusting that the work itself has value even when I can't predict or control the outcome. Even when I can see exactly what you're doing and know I'm going to lose whatever game we're playing."

"That's a significant commitment. Are you ready for that?"

Daisy took a breath.

"I have to be ready," she said. "Everything I've tried on my own has made things worse."

The therapist made another note. "I think our next session should focus on the period after Faye died. The loss that taught you that connection meant devastation. The incident that made protecting yourself feel like the only rational choice. Are you willing to go there?"

The old Daisy would have asked for a break. The Daisy who was trying to surrender control just nodded.

"Yes. It's time."

As she left the office forty-five minutes later, Daisy felt something she hadn't in weeks – not the absurd satisfaction of having successfully negotiated a difficult situation, but the frail hope of having committed to a process that she couldn't control. Terrifying. Necessary. Unfamiliar.

It was going to cost her everything that she thought that she knew about staying safe.

Maybe that was exactly what she needed to lose.

Chapter 28 – The Second Ending (2016)

The call came on an otherwise unremarkable Tuesday evening. Daisy had been scrolling numbly through his inbox, deleting messages without reading them, when his phone buzzed on the desk beside him. Unknown number. He almost didn't answer – but, despite his instincts, he did answer.

"Hello?"

The voice on the other end was strange in its flatness, like it had been ironed out of all colour. A man's voice, older, slow. It took him a moment to place it.

"Daisy?"

"Yes."

A pause. Not hesitation – more like preparation. The pause of someone who had had to practice the sentence before speaking.

"It's John. Faye's dad."

The name snapped the air like a whip. His mouth went dry. They'd once got on well, but they hadn't spoken in several years, and their most recent conversations hadn't been warm. To hear him now felt wrong in a way he couldn't yet articulate.

"She's gone."

Two words, stripped bare. No ceremony. No preamble.

"What?" Daisy asked, though he'd heard him perfectly.

"She collapsed this afternoon. An overdose. Something about a prescription mix-up. She didn't suffer, it was quick."

Daisy stared at the wall, as though meaning might be written on the wallpaper. *Overdose*. The word sounded almost fictional. It belonged to medical dramas, not to Faye – not to someone who'd called him a few hours earlier excited about her latest workout routine.

"I… I don't understand," Daisy said.

"I'm sorry," John said. His voice cracked a little on the second word. "We thought you should know."

We. Her parents. The family. The people who'd tolerated Daisy as a half-stray animal at their home for years. And now he was the one they had to call.

He held the phone to her ear, caught in a quiet that wasn't a pause – it was an empty space. It was only then that he noticed the line had gone dead.

He stood up, because sitting now felt impossible. His legs carried him out of the house without his brain's permission, through the front door and out into the street. The crisp evening air felt indecently ordinary, filled with traffic noise from the nearby bypass and the screams of children from the park next door.

The word *overdose* clanged around his skull like loose change. It was obscene, the way something so avoidable could erase a person entirely. No car crash, no drama, no chance for goodbyes.

His feet dragged him through the streets, and everything he saw turned into an accusation. The dog barking at his ankles faded into arguments he'd picked until love cowered, small and yapping. The pigeons that scattered when he walked past the bench looked like the promises he'd made and never kept – startled, flapping, vanishing. The world was continuing, and it was a personal insult.

Faye's voice kept resurfacing in fragments. Her laugh when he'd told her about his latest disastrous booking – high and delighted, like she was surprised by her own amusement. The way she'd hummed tunelessly whilst cooking, always slightly off-key but utterly unselfconscious. This morning's call – Christ, this morning – when she'd been excited about some new exercise class, something about core strength and flexibility. Her voice bright with the enthusiasm she got about taking care of herself, as though her body was a project she was constantly improving.

"I think I might be getting stronger," she'd said. "Like, properly strong, not just skinnier."

He'd been distracted, half-listening while scrolling through emails. Had probably made some noncommittal sound. The last conversation they'd ever have, and he'd been multitasking.

The memory was like swallowing glass. At least he'd told her he loved her.

A bus rumbled past with an advertisement for life insurance plastered across its side. The irony wasn't lost on him. Nothing was lost on him right now – his brain was cataloguing every detail with the mania of someone whose world had become unreliable.

Every shop window reflected his face and none of them looked like him. He tried to imagine telling someone – anyone – but the thought of saying the words out loud made his stomach clench. To tell others would make it real.

His body stopped before his mind realised where he was. The off-licence.

Inside, the lights flickered. He hadn't been here in months, maybe longer, but the layout was unchanged, serendipity guiding him down the aisle to the shelves that glittered with glass. Bottles stood like soldiers waiting to be chosen.

His hand hovered. He traced labels with his eyes the way other people read gravestones. Gin, vodka, whisky. His old language, waiting for him to speak it again.

The brands were familiar, almost friendly. Smirnoff – his old reliable, the one that had seen him through his first attempt at university and the early years of pretending to be an adult. Gordon's – Faye had drunk that once, mixed with tonic and too much lime, and spent the night being sick whilst he held her hair back. A Macallan 30 – the fancy stuff, for special occasions and celebrations that now felt prehistoric.

He could taste them already. The first burn, harsh and necessary. The second swallow, easier. The third, when warmth would start spreading through his chest like forgiveness. By the fourth, his thoughts would begin to soften at the edges. By the tenth, the word *overdose* might stop clanging around his skull.

He knew the progression. Knew exactly how much it would take to blur the sharp edges of this day, how much more to erase it entirely. His body remembered the ritual – the twist of the cap, the smell of ethanol and grain, the blessed numbness that would follow.

The man behind the counter glanced at him, then away, uninterested. Just another punter contemplating the shelves. But to Daisy, this aisle was everything: the edge of oblivion and the promise of relief.

He picked up a bottle. Heavy. Comfortingly heavy. The glass cool against his palm. He turned it over, read the back label as though it might tell him what to do.

His hand clenched into a fist. If he bought it, he knew how this would end. Not tonight, maybe not tomorrow, but eventually – the spiral would complete itself.

He set the bottle down. Too gently, as though afraid it might break and force the decision for him.

He didn't remember the walk home. One minute he was in the off-licence, the next he was on the kitchen floor, the bottle upright in front of him like a priest awaiting confession. He couldn't remember paying for it. Maybe he had. Maybe he hadn't. Time had become jump cuts, whole frames missing.

The tiled floor was cold through his clothes. His breath fogged faintly in the half-dark. He stared at the bottle until the words began lining up in his head, unbidden, like accusations scratched into the glass.

You promised forever. Forever lasted until breakfast.

I don't know how to exist without you.

I turned you into proof that I wasn't broken.

I made you hold all my need until your arms shook.

The thoughts weren't orderly, not neat lists – fragments circling him like vultures. Each one carried the taste of confession but none of the relief.

The memories came in flashes, uncontrolled. Faye sleeping, her face slack and peaceful, hair spread across the pillow like spilt ink. The way she looked when she was concentrating – tongue poking slightly out of the corner of her mouth, eyebrows drawn together. Her terrible habit of leaving coffee cups everywhere, rings of brown staining every surface of the house. How she'd steal his clothes and somehow make them look better on her than they ever had on him.

The last fight they'd had, years ago now, before everything fell apart. Money, always money. The bills were piling up, the bookings weren't coming through, and they'd been living on credit for months. Faye wanted to talk about practical solutions – one or both of them picking up a normal job, maybe they could ask her parents for help – but Daisy had been too proud. Too stubborn.

"We'll figure it out," he'd kept saying, without offering a solution.

"How?" she'd asked, and her voice had been more tired than angry, like she'd already given up before the conversation started. "How exactly are we going to figure it out?"

He'd been defensive, accused her of not trusting him to provide, made it about his failures as a partner when it was really about mathematics. Figures on a page that didn't add up, no matter how much he wanted them to.

She'd gone quiet after that, something between them had shifted irreparably. He'd kept pretending everything was fine anyway, kept making promises he couldn't keep.

It was evidence of some fundamental failure on his part. He'd been stubborn when she needed solutions, prideful when she needed partnership.

He felt empty, like someone had reached inside and scooped out everything vital.

The bottle sat there, patient and terrible. One twist and all of this would fade to background noise. One swallow and the senseless feeling would fill with warm numbness. One night of oblivion and maybe, somehow, he'd wake up in a world where this hadn't happened.

But he knew better. He'd wake up hungover and ashamed, and Faye would still be dead, and he'd have thrown away years of sobriety for nothing.

The temptation sat there like gravity.

The kids. The thought of them hit him sharply. Fuck. Seven and eight years old, in care, placed there after his drinking and her instability had spiralled beyond any pretence of functional parenting. Some social worker would have to tell them. Would have to sit down with children who barely understood why their parents couldn't take care of them and explain that now their mother was gone entirely.

Would they use the word *overdose*? Would they try and explain it to kids that age, or would they say "very sick" and hope that was enough? Would the kids blame themselves somehow, the way children did when adults disappeared from their lives?

He thought of their faces the last time he'd seen them – confused and trying to be brave during a supervised visit, asking when they could come home while he struggled to meet their eyes. Now they'd never have a chance to come home to Faye. Would never have those tentative conversations about whether mummy and daddy were better now, whether the grown-ups had figured out how to take care of them properly.

The weight of his failures felt crushing. He'd lost the right to comfort his own children years ago. Some stranger would hold them while they cried for a mother who'd died while they were living with strangers.

His phone lay face down beside him. He imagined picking it up, calling Mary, or Pete. But what would he even say? *I've been upgraded to widower. Send condolences in bulk.* He could already hear their pity, soft and unbearable.

The AA slogans became mockery now. *One day at a time* – except what do you do when one day contains a lifetime's worth of loss? *Easy does it* – except nothing about this was easy. *Let go and let God* – except what kind of God lets overdoses happen to people who'd finally figured out how to be happy?

He touched the cap. Just one twist and he could drown them in amber oblivion. One swallow and the indictments would dissolve.

So, he stayed where he was. The bottle a sentinel, his body a stone. Hours blurred past. His legs tingled, his back ached, his throat stayed desert-dry. The accusations kept circling:

You took her for granted.

You thought you had time.

You wasted years being afraid of losing her instead of just loving her.

You made her carry all your insecurities like luggage.

She deserved better than your damaged heart.

His own home felt different now, like the air had changed density. Every object seemed to mock him with its ordinariness. The takeaway containers from last night. The stack of unpaid bills on the counter. His guitar leaning against the wall, covered in dust from weeks of neglect. A life that had seemed barely manageable this morning now felt pointless.

The silence was different, too. Not the comfortable quiet of solitude, but the absence of possibility. No chance that his phone would ring and it would be her voice, telling him about her day or asking if he wanted to do something with her. No more of those awful conversations where they pretended their history didn't complicate every word.

Everything in his world remained exactly as it had been twelve hours ago, but none of it would ever mean the same thing again.

The thought was so large that it couldn't fit inside his head. It kept trying to make itself known and bouncing off his comprehension like a ball thrown at a wall.

Dead. Faye was dead. The person who knew him best, who'd seen him at his worst and decided to love him anyway, who'd made him believe that he might be worth saving – gone. Erased. Reduced to phone calls and funeral arrangements and memories that would fade at the edges until even they abandoned him.

The physical pain was startling. Grief, it turned out, wasn't just emotional – it was a full-body experience. His stomach churned with a nausea that had nothing to do with alcohol and everything to do with loss. His skin felt too tight, like his body couldn't contain the enormity of what he was feeling.

He didn't drink. He didn't throw it away either. He just… existed.

Sleepless, he watched the minutes crawl by. The beams of passing headlights were the only movement, a reminder that the world was still turning outside while his own night stood perfectly still. Yet, he knew the morning would come, whether he was ready or not.

At dawn, the first thin light came through the blinds. He was still on the kitchen floor. The bottle was unopened.

His body felt destroyed, his mind scraped raw, but he was alive. More failure than triumph.

The world looked different in daylight. Colours seemed too bright and too muted simultaneously, like someone had adjusted the settings on reality and gotten them slightly wrong. The familiar kitchen felt alien – the same objects in the same places, but arranged in a universe where Faye no longer existed.

He tried to imagine making coffee, brushing his teeth, the mundane tasks that comprised normal mornings. They felt impossible, like trying to perform surgery with boxing gloves. How did people function in a world that could erase someone in an instant?

He stood on shaking legs and picked up the bottle. Carried it to the bin outside. It landed with a dull thud among coffee grounds and packaging, as though he'd thrown part of himself away.

Not the part that wanted to drink – that would probably always be there, lurking at the edges in difficult moments. But the part that believed drinking would fix anything. The part that thought obliteration was the same as healing.

Back inside, he collapsed onto the bed without undressing. He stared at the ceiling until his eyes blurred. Survival was supposed to feel noble. It didn't. It was the absence of choice.

The bed smelled like fabric softener and his own unwashed clothes. The pillow held no impression but his own. On his bedside table sat a glass of water he'd poured for himself the night before, half-empty, waiting for a morning that felt impossible to face.

Somewhere, in the home she'd made for herself, Faye's things sat there waiting for her to return. Her coffee cup in her sink. Her book opened to a page she'd never finish. Her bloody tarot cards that had somehow failed to see this coming.

He would never see that space, never know how she'd arranged her life in the years since they'd parted. But he knew it existed, or had existed until this afternoon, and now it was another set of empty rooms where someone's future had been cancelled abruptly.

He squeezed his eyes shut. The word *"overdose"* reverberated in his head; a single, devastating note followed by the deafening emptiness on the phone.

Love meant loss. Always had. Always would.

And Daisy catalogued every reason why he'd never risk it again.

Chapter 29 – Croesi Ffiniau

Daisy's phone rang as she was walking towards the train station, the screen lighting up with her mother's name. Conversations with her mum required a very specific kind of emotional energy – a guarded calibration of tone and patience – and some mornings she simply didn't have it to give. She was already drained from the week, from the previous workday, from the constant crawl of unspoken thoughts that had been chasing her for months.

"Hello, mum."

"Daisy!" she chirped, and she could hear the surprised smile in her voice. The tone of someone who'd half-expected to be sent to voicemail. "Well, this is a treat, how are you?"

It came wrapped in motherly concern, the sort that carried three subtexts at once: *I hope you're okay, I suspect you're not,* and *please don't make me worry more than I already do.*

Daisy adjusted the cashmere scarf around her neck, fingertips running along the weave as though the softness could buffer the call. The morning chill bit at her cheeks, sharp enough to remind her that she was alive.

"I'm okay. Working, keeping busy. How are you?"

"I'm fine. I've got myself back in that vegetable garden again. Honestly, it's producing more tomatoes than I know what to do with. I keep telling myself I'm not feeding an army, but you know how I am with projects."

She smiled despite herself. Her mother's voice had that buoyant note it always found when she talked about growing things. A sharp contrast to the stilted, defensive tone that she sometimes had when conversations strayed too close to her transition, or her sobriety or anything she feared might upset her. Gardens were safe ground.

They moved easily through the ordinary choreography of family talk: her neighbour's yapping dog, a new TV drama she thought Daisy might like, the unpredictable weather. Daisy found herself surprised by how much relief there was in simply keeping it light. No landmines, no barbs, tomatoes and weather.

Twenty minutes later, when they hung up, she felt lighter. Not transformed, but… steadied. Like someone had tied down the corners of a tent.

The train to Cardiff was half-empty. Business types with laptops open, a pair of teenage boys in football kits sprawled across seats, an elderly couple sharing a crossword. Daisy claimed a window seat, set her bag by her feet, and watched the familiar suburbs give way to countryside. Fields flashed by in blurred greens and browns, hedgerows stitched into the landscape like scars.

She opened her contacts list. Scrolled. Hovered. Stopped. Pressed.

Olivia answered on the second ring, sounding breathless.

"Dad! Sorry, I was at the gym. What's up?"

Her voice came bright, fizzing with the energy of someone who'd found a rhythm in life. Pride surged in her, chased by regret. Olivia had built her stability mostly without her – and yet she still called her *dad*. That was the word that tethered them, fragile and solid all at once.

"Nothing urgent," she said. "Just wanted to check in. How's uni treating you?"

"It's good. Stressful, but good stressful, if that makes sense? I've got this massive assignment due next week on behavioural psychology, and I keep getting distracted by how applicable it is to basically every human interaction I've ever had."

Daisy chuckled. She could picture her, flushed from exercise, words tumbling fast as she walked home with headphones in.

They talked for a while: about coursework, flatmates, weekend plans. Olivia mentioned a boy that she'd been seeing, casually, without the weight that Daisy remembered attaching to every romance at her age. The sound of her daughter's laughter, free of the brittleness she associated with her own younger years, loosened something in Daisy.

When they wound down, Daisy sat with the phone warm in her hand, smiling faintly at her own reflection in the train window. Two conversations. Two pieces of normality. Two reminders that connection didn't have to be procedural.

Outside, the Welsh hills rose up, rolling and generous. Her hand went to the scarf again, tugging at it like it was protection.

The meeting was in Cathays, in a squat brick community centre that looked like it had been hosting recovery groups since the seventies. Painted cinderblock walls. Plastic chairs. A noticeboard layered with flyers for yoga classes and debt counselling and lost-cat appeals.

Daisy had looked up meetings in Wales the night before, with the logic of the desperate. Wales was technically another country. Another country meant another set of people, different dynamics, no chance of bumping into Mary's watchful eye, or Pete's nervous fidgeting. Distance felt safer.

She arrived early, choosing a seat in the back row where she could half-vanish. Slowly, the room filled: fifteen people or so, a cross-section of lives and losses. The construction worker with plaster dust on his hands. The middle-aged woman gripping a takeaway coffee like it was oxygen. The young guy in the expensive suit, scrolling his phone like he was trying to prove he was in control.

Not one familiar face. Perfect.

The secretary did the usual opening. When Daisy's turn came, fifteen minutes in, she felt her pulse hitch. She touched her scarf, steadied herself.

"My name's Daisy, and I'm an alcoholic."

"Hi, Daisy," the room murmured.

She'd practised this part in her head during the train journey, the opening that would give her permission to dive deeper. "I've been sober for thirteen years, and I've never been closer to throwing it all away over something that has nothing to do with alcohol."

A few nods. Understanding eyes. They'd been here too – the sideways derailments, the obsessions that weren't about drink but threatened to lead back there anyway.

"I got obsessed with someone I met in the programme." The words felt strange in her mouth, spoken aloud to strangers. Her hand found her scarf again, working the fabric unconsciously. "At first, I convinced myself that I was being clever about it. When I found out that they were interested in me, I started planning every interaction like it was a chess game. Every conversation was charted a few moves ahead. Every text message was analysed for subtext and opportunity."

The coffee-cup woman nodded, her gaze steady.

"I treated flirtation like poker – reading tells, managing my own expression, waiting for the perfect moment to play my hand. I'd analyse every conversation afterwards, looking for clues about their interests or preferences. Every casual comment got filed away as potential conversation material. Getting to know them felt less like a connection and more like market research."

She could feel the attention in the room sharpen. These people understood obsession, even if the object was different.

"But then they came to me. Made themselves defenceless, tried to tell me how they felt… And I kissed them, and they panicked and ran. Just disappeared, no explanation, no contact. Nothing for almost three months now."

Daisy's voice was gaining strength as she continued. This felt different from her usual presentations of problems – this was raw, much more necessary.

"And that's when the obsessions started. I found myself checking their social media constantly, refreshing their profiles multiple times a day looking for any sign of where they'd gone or what they were thinking. I'd analyse their posts from months ago, looking for clues about their state of mind. I started checking flight tracking websites, trying to figure out their work schedule. The rational part of my brain knew it was unhealthy, but I couldn't stop myself."

The young guy in the expensive suit had gone very still. The construction worker was shaking his head slowly.

"I spent hours standing in off-licences, staring at bottles, trying to decide if destroying thirteen years of sobriety was worth stopping the noise in my head. Because that's what happens when someone you've turned into your bishop does a runner. Your entire strategy collapses."

She felt the cashmere again. "The worst part is that this person had tried to help me before everything went wrong. Got me a job when I was struggling. And I've spent the last three months convincing myself their kindness was a way to manipulate me from a distance while they figured out how to deal with the mess I'd become."

Her voice cracked slightly. "I was going to quit my job today, hand in my notice and disappear. Make sure they never had to see me again. A last move: you can't abandon me if I abandon you first."

She looked around the circle, meeting eyes for the first time since she'd started speaking. "But sitting on that train this morning, building up my list of grievances, I realised something. I actually like the job. I'm good at it. It's given me stability and purpose and a reason to get up in the morning. And I was going to throw it away out of spite."

The familiar words weren't there anymore. The guarded explanations about how she'd been wronged, how she deserved better communication, how she'd been treated unfairly – none of it felt true when spoken in this room to people who had no investment in her being right.

"I turned someone who cared about me into a problem to be solved," she said. "And when they needed space to figure out their own feelings, I made that about me too. Made their fear into my abandonment."

The meeting continued around the circle, other people sharing their own struggles and victories. Daisy found herself listening instead of rehearsing what she might say next, present in the room instead of managing her performance in it.

When it ended an hour later, an older woman with short grey hair approached her as people were stacking chairs. She had a direct gaze that suggested she'd heard enough bullshit in her lifetime to spot it from across a room.

"That took courage," she said simply. "What you shared in there. It takes guts to admit when you've been telling yourself stories."

"I keep talking about being managed and manipulated," Daisy said, "but from what I just told you all, this person came to me honestly, I responded, and then they got scared and ran. That's not manipulation – that's someone who wasn't ready for what they thought they wanted.

The older woman nodded. "And your response to them needing space was to turn their earlier kindness into evidence that they were controlling you. That's quite a story you built there."

Daisy felt her hand reaching for the scarf again. "You're right. I think I needed someone to call me on my own bullshit."

"We all do, love. That's what these rooms are for. You said you were planning chess moves, but chess is a game where one person wins and the other loses. Is that really how you want a relationship to work?"

"No," Daisy said quietly. "I just… I didn't know how else to approach it. I thought it was safer than being honest about wanting something."

"And now?"

"Now… I think maybe I need to let them have their space without making it a referendum on my worth."

A man in his fifties who'd been listening nearby stepped closer. "Sounds like you're ready to stop punishing yourself for someone else's choices."

"Or maybe stop punishing them for mine," Daisy said, and felt something change. Not relief, not forgiveness, but the surprising awareness of how long she'd been carrying the weight.

The train back was more crowded, with people heading home from day trips to Cardiff. Daisy found a seat and settled in for the journey, pulling out her phone to scroll through messages she'd been avoiding.

Halfway through reading a work email, she realised that she was sweating. The scarf around her neck, which had been a comfort all day, now felt suffocating. She unwound it, neatly folded it, and tucked it into her bag without ceremony. Just another piece of clothing – useful when needed, easy enough to put away when it wasn't.

Through the window, the Welsh countryside was giving way to familiar territory again. The same landscape she'd travelled through that morning, but somehow it looked different now. Less like terrain she was escaping, and more like a journey she'd completed.

Her phone buzzed with a message from Olivia *"Hope your day went well, whatever you were up to. Love you."*

Daisy typed back *"Love you too. Just figuring some things out."*

She put the phone away and watched the world blur past the window. Tomorrow, she'd go to work, do her job well, and stop resenting the circumstances that had led her there. She'd show up to her life without turning every interaction into a chess game she needed to win.

And maybe, eventually, she'd stop checking her phone every few minutes for messages that would tell her nothing useful. Stop constructing elaborate narratives about other people's motivations when the simple truth was usually enough.

The train pulled into the station as the sun was setting, and Daisy gathered her things with the satisfaction of someone who'd accomplished what they'd set out to do. Not the meaningless victory of having outmanoeuvred an opponent, but the quieter triumph of having stopped fighting a war that existed almost entirely in her own head.

She walked out into the evening feeling lighter than she had in months, her bag weighted with nothing more significant than a folded scarf and the ordinary debris of a day well spent.

Chapter 30 – Frankfurt, 2004

Daisy hated airports. Still, he was determined to savour this trip, knowing it might be his last for a while.

The departure lounge at Heathrow was the usual chaos of delayed flights and overpriced coffee, but he found himself taking it in with unusual attention to detail. In two weeks, he'd be starting university, and international wrestling bookings would be a luxury that he couldn't afford – not if he wanted to take his studies seriously. This weekend's triple-header in Germany represented the end of an era, even if it was an ending of his own choosing.

He'd turned down three overseas bookings for September and October, including one in Japan that would've paid better than anything he'd done before. The promoter had been understanding but disappointed. "Call me when you graduate," he'd said. "If you're still in the game."

He made his way through security – ever more intrusive post 9/11 – and weaved through the brightly-lit capitalist dystopia of the duty-free shop. He had never understood the appeal of stocking up on perfume and overpriced chocolates, but could appreciate the desire for cheaper, tax-free alcohol and cigarettes. He'd be sure to pick some up on the way back.

Near the magazine rack, he spotted a familiar figure – Tommy Morrison, a veteran from the northern circuit who'd helped him learn the ropes during his first year. Tommy was flipping through a wrestling magazine, probably checking if any of his recent matches had made the photo spreads.

"Alright, Daisy?" Tommy looked up with a grin. "Off anywhere exciting?"

"Frankfurt. You?"

"Amsterdam, then Berlin. Busy month." Tommy's expression shifted slightly as he seemed to remember something. "Heard you're starting university. That true?"

"Yeah. Forensics degree."

Tommy nodded slowly, the way wrestlers did when someone announced they were getting out of the business, even temporarily. It was a look that held equal parts respect and pity – respect for having dreams beyond taking bumps until your body gave out, pity for walking away from something that most of them couldn't imagine leaving behind.

"Smart move, that," Tommy said, though his tone suggested he wasn't entirely convinced. "Always good to have options."

They talked for a few more minutes about the German wrestling scene, mutual acquaintances, upcoming shows that Daisy would have to watch from university rather than participate in. When Tommy headed off for his gate, Daisy felt a fear that had nothing to do with his usual pre-flight anxiety.

This was what the next few years would look like – watching from the sidelines while other people built the careers and connections he was choosing to put on hold. He told himself that it was the right decision, that a forensics degree would give him security that professional wrestling never could. But, standing in an airport duty-free shop, holding a magazine with photos of wrestlers he knew personally, it felt less solid than it had when he'd made the choice.

He found a quiet corner near his gate and pulled out his phone. A text from Marisol asking how the flight was going, a message that acknowledged the difference between them without pretending it didn't exist. They'd been engaged for a couple of months now, but university would put even more miles between them than there already were. She'd been supportive of his decision to focus on the degree, though he suspected she'd be happier if he gave up wrestling entirely. She saw it as a hobby that was getting out of hand rather than a legitimate career path, which was probably fair given how little money he'd made from it so far.

He typed back a quick response and considered putting the phone away. Instead, he found himself scrolling through the latest wrestling news, checking results from shows that he'd considered taking before deciding that his university preparation was more important. He wondered if he was making the biggest mistake of his life, walking away as things were starting to pick up.

The boarding announcement for a flight to Berlin echoed through the departure lounge, and Daisy watched a group of passengers gather their belongings. He recognised the rhythm of it – business travellers who did this every week, families heading off on holiday, people like him caught between one life and another.

For now, though, his usual pre-flight ritual. To the nearest bar to his gate to fuel up on beer; for all he should be used to it by now, he hated to fly and had a routine that involved consuming enough alcohol to feel sleepy before the plane left the tarmac, to drift off before the flight was in the air. But – and this was crucial – never so much that he was visibly intoxicated and refused passage onto the aircraft.

The airport bar was exactly what he expected – overpriced beer and a generic atmosphere designed not to offend anyone. He claimed a stool with a view of the departure boards and ordered his first pint, watching the gate information update with soft clicks.

The beer was cold and unremarkable, but it served its purpose. He could feel the familiar loosening in his shoulders, the way alcohol smoothed the sharp edges of anxiety. By the third pint, the conundrum about university and wrestling had eased into something more manageable. By the fifth, he was ready to face the flight without the crushing awareness of being suspended in a metal tube thousands of feet above the earth.

The boarding announcement came as he was finishing the last of his beer. He made his way to the gate with the deliberation of someone who'd learned to micromanage their alcohol intake in public spaces, nodding to the gate agent as she checked his boarding pass.

As he boarded, he smiled politely at the flight attendants, looking pristine in their green uniforms as he desperately prayed that none of them would detect the whiff of the red IPA on his breath and ask too many questions. He stowed his bag – enough gear to get him through the weekend – and settled into his window seat, getting as comfortable as he could in the hope of quickly experiencing the lull and the darkness.

Then the screaming started.

He'd chosen the late flight to avoid this; what responsible parent would bring a baby out, onto a flight at this hour? For as much as he loved kids, the idea of spending two and a half hours trapped at 30,000 feet in a small metal tube with one was something he'd long considered a missing chapter of Dante's *Inferno*.

He hoped the alcohol would quickly overpower his brain, force it to shut out the noise somewhere on the ever-darkening taxiway, but as he felt the plane come to a stop at what had to be the end of their runway, he knew it was too late.

The engines whined, the thrust kicked in, and then came that gut-wrenching pull – his lest favourite feeling in the world – as tons of metal defied gravity and lifted into the sky. Calming himself with the knowledge that his life was no longer in his hands – not a lot you can do once you're in the air – he observed the scene out of his window. The sun was setting, a golden hue overshadowed by the lilac tones of the evening clouds.

The view reminded him of something, though he couldn't place what. Something about the way the light caught the edges of the clouds, turning them purple around the margins. He'd seen that colour recently, somewhere significant, but the memory remained frustratingly out of reach. The alcohol was doing its job too well, blurring the lines of recent events into a comfortable haze.

As the pressurisation system kicked in, the baby's screams grew louder. He hated the feeling as an adult – and, at nineteen, he was supposed to be an adult – but at least he understood what was happening. The poor kid had no way of comprehending this.

He was drinking to cope, and the thought that he was annoyed at a baby for doing the same thing made him feel stupid. The thought wasn't lost on him. University would probably teach him to articulate thoughts like that more clearly, assuming he could sustain the discipline to attend lectures, rather than taking wrestling bookings.

Eventually, the plane hit a cruising altitude and he watched as the light of the seatbelt sign faded with the accompanying ping.

Predictably, an immediate rush to the toilets by his fellow passengers, an almost Pavlovian response. With the failed attempt at using beers as a sleep aid, he would undoubtedly need to tread that path in the near future.

He pulled out the in-flight magazine, more out of habit than interest, and found himself reading an article about career changes in your twenties. The timing was accusatory, as if the universe was determined to keep reminding him of the choice he'd made. The article was full of generic advice that applied to everyone and no one – "follow your passion", "don't be afraid to take risks," "consider your long-term goals."

What it didn't mention was what to do when your passion was something that most people considered a joke, or when taking risks meant potentially wasting a university education that your parents had always hoped you'd get. He closed the magazine abruptly and stuffed it back into its holder.

Eventually, the announcement of the refreshment service. He'd already decided that he was going to ask for ear plugs, headphones, whatever option was available, and top it with as much alcohol as possible in the hopes of drowning out the baby and getting the sleep he so desperately craved – as much as he hated the liftoff, the landing was a close second.

As the flight attendant arrived with the trolley, he was pleased to find that ear plugs were an option. He admired her; not just for her beauty or for being one of the few people who could genuinely pull off a green uniform with style, but for the calmness and poise she portrayed whilst surrounded by this unholy noise and the demands of people that he knew were likely less polite than he.

There was something about her demeanour that reminded him of the best wrestlers he'd worked with – people who could hold their composure under pressure whilst making everyone around them feel more confident. She had that same quality of controlled skill that separated experts from amateurs in any field.

Ready as always to show his ID he asked her, almost conspiratorially, how much alcohol he was allowed to buy and was told that he could buy two of whatever he chose. "I'll take the strongest thing you have."

"Bad flier?" she asked, and there was something in her tone that suggested that she was genuinely asking, not making polite conversation.

"You could say that."

She tilted her head slightly, studying his face with an attention that made him self-conscious. "Anything else bothering you? You look like you've got more than flight nerves on your mind."

He was surprised by the observation, and even more surprised by his impulse to answer honestly. "Just… big life changes, I guess. Sometimes it's hard to know if you're making the right choices."

"What kind of changes?"

"Starting university in a couple of weeks. Having to step back from work I love to focus on something that's probably more sensible, but definitely less fun."

She nodded as if this made perfect sense. "What kind of work?"

"Professional wrestling." He said it with the slight defensiveness that had become automatic whenever he mentioned his career to strangers, especially strangers who looked like they'd never set foot in a wrestling venue.

But, instead of the polite scepticism he usually encountered, her expression remained neutral. "I see. And you're stepping back from that for university?"

"Forensics degree," he said, trying to read her reaction. "Probably more practical in the long run."

He felt his guarded posture relax slightly. "Most people think it's all fake."

"Most people think a lot of things," she said with a slight shrug, deftly reaching for the miniatures. "Doesn't make them right or wrong, just makes them people with opinions."

She handed him three miniature bottles of whisky, a can of Coke and one of those tiny plastic cups with the practised deftness of someone conducting a drug deal. "Our secret," she whispered with a smile. "And, for what it's worth, stepping back from something doesn't mean giving it up. Sometimes you need different skills before you can succeed at what you really want to do."

He thanked her and paid, and admired her as she continued down the aisle with the same grace that she'd shown throughout their conversation. As her vivid green uniform faded into a soft mint pastel with the distance, the rows of bulbs between them making the red of her hair glow, he found himself feeling oddly reassured by their brief exchange.

Cracking a couple of the bottles, he poured them into the glass, enjoying the sharp pop and soft fizz of the Coke before he poured it on top, and stashed the third in a pocket for later.

He downed it, greedily, then reconsidered her words. Maybe she was right about different skills. Maybe his forensics degree wasn't a retreat from wrestling, but preparation for a different kind of future entirely. Having options might make him more confident in whatever path he chose.

He made his way to the bathroom, reset, and returned to his seat to drift off into sleep.

Sleep wouldn't come, even with the aid of the third bottle diluted in the scant remains of the can and once again thrown back like medicine.

He was doomed to endure the inevitable.

The baby had finally quieted, leaving the plane in relative peace broken only by the steady whirr of engines and the occasional cough from other passengers. Through the window, he could see lights scattered across the landscape below – cities and towns full of people going about their evening routines while he flew overhead towards whatever the weekend would bring.

This was the part of travel he enjoyed, when the anxiety of take-off had passed and the fear of landing was hours away. Suspended between destinations, between decisions, between the life he was leaving behind and the one he was choosing to build.

As the flight continued, the attendant returned during her rounds. "How are you feeling?"

"Like there's not enough alcohol in the world to get me through this flight."

She slipped him another bottle with the same conspiratorial discreetness as before. "Just in case?"

He took it with a smile. "I think I could drink all night and not sleep at this point."

"Overthinking tends to do that," she said, glancing around to make sure that none of her colleagues were watching their extended conversation. "What conclusion are you reaching about those big life changes?"

"That I'm probably making the right choice for the wrong reasons or the wrong choice for the right reasons. Either way, it's too late to change course now."

She considered this for a moment. "You know what I've learned working up here? People regret the chances they didn't take more than the ones they did. University will always be there if wrestling doesn't work out. But you're only nineteen once."

"Is that advice?"

"That's observation. The advice would be…" She paused, seeming to weigh her words. "Sometimes the best way forward isn't choosing between two things you want. Sometimes it's figuring out how to have both."

"And if both isn't possible?"

"Then you make the choice that lets you sleep at night. Literally, not metaphorically." She gestured towards the bottle in his hand with a slight smile.

"Well, if you don't want to drink alone, I know a great little hotel bar in Frankfurt. You're welcome to join me."

He thought about it. A pretty girl, a hotel bar, and someone who seemed to understand the complexity of his situation better than most people he'd tried to explain it to. The road could be lonely at times, especially when you were travelling between versions of yourself.

He agreed, and next time she passed she handed him a piece of paper with the name of the hotel on it. "I'll be there by eleven," she added.

As the plane began its descent, he found himself looking forward to the conversation more than he'd anticipated. Refreshingly, he might be able to talk through his decision with someone who wouldn't try to push him in either direction – someone who understood that sometimes the best choices were the ones that felt slightly wrong in the moment, but opened up possibilities that you couldn't see yet.

As the wheels screeched against the tarmac, It surprised him to realise that the thing he was looking forward to most about the weekend wasn't being in the ring or the degree waiting for him at home. It was a drink in a bar with a stranger who'd spoken to him like he was more than the sum of his indecision.

Chapter 31 – Fresh Eyes

The alarm was definitely broken. Had to be. Because there was no way it was already five fifty-five when she'd only closed her eyes five minutes earlier. Iris fumbled for her phone, slapping at the bedside table until she brushed the cold glass. The glow seared her retinas, cruel against the gap in the hotel curtains where the streetlight had been drilling into her skull all night despite her best efforts with the inadequate blackout fabric.

Five fifty-five.

Bollocks.

She'd requested a six-thirty pickup, which meant she had exactly thirty-five minutes to transform from whatever this was – hair apparently attempting to achieve independent flight status, yesterday's makeup creating interesting abstract patterns around her eyes – into something resembling a seasoned member of aircrew.

The bathroom light was merciless. The lighting was unkind, turning her skin the colour of old parchment. A mirror that no one had bothered to wipe clean properly stared back at her, haloed with toothpaste spatter and streaks of old polish.

Right. Shower. That would fix at least some of this.

The water pressure was pathetic, dribbling out with the weary resignation of an elderly man losing his train of thought. Yet, it was hot, and she let the steam fog the edges of the mirror, lingering under it longer than she should have. The air smelled faintly metallic, like old pipes. She pressed her forehead against the tiles and told herself the knot between her shoulder blades was only physical, not everything else crowding at the edges.

Too many nights in unfamiliar beds. Too many hours. Nothing more complicated than that.

The hotel soap smelled like industrial disinfectant with a thin veneer of artificial wormwood. She'd stopped bringing her own toiletries months ago – what was the point when you were never anywhere long enough to use them properly? Everything in her life had become disposable, temporary, designed for easy abandonment.

When she emerged, wrapped in a towel that had the texture of cardboard and half the absorbency, she had twenty-eight minutes left. Her uniform was somewhere in the chaos of this room, scattered across surfaces like she was some kind of rookie who'd never done this before. Jacket on the back of the chair, skirt draped over the radiator, tights... where the hell were her tights?

Under the bed, apparently. Because that's where a rational person would put hosiery.

She caught herself in the mirror whilst pulling them on and paused. When had she started looking so tired? Not just morning tired, but a bone-deep exhaustion that sleep didn't seem to touch anymore. There were lines around her eyes that hadn't been there six months ago, a tightness to her mouth that suggested someone permanently braced for bad news.

Four months ago, she'd looked different. Softer, somehow. There had been moments – sitting in that coffee shop, cleaning that chaotic flat, even during the night of the kiss – when she'd caught herself in mirrors and liked what she saw. Someone who looked engaged with the world rather than just half-decent at navigating it.

Now, she looked like someone who'd spent four months avoiding her own reflection.

Her phone buzzed. The taxi, probably, though she still had twelve minutes.

Instead, it was a notification from some app she'd forgotten she'd downloaded. She dismissed it with irritation and was about to put her phone away when she caught sight of her recent calls list. Her thumb hovered over a contact that she'd been avoiding for four months, though not successfully. She'd come close to calling maybe a dozen times, usually late at night in hotel rooms like this one, when the loneliness felt less like an inconvenience and more like a personal failure.

She'd drafted messages, too. Deleted every single one.

What would she even say?

Sorry I disappeared after you kissed me?

Sorry, I panicked?

Sorry, I've been thinking about you every day and I can't seem to figure out how to have a normal conversation with another human being because everything reminds me of something she said or the way she looked at me like I might be worth the risk of genuine vulnerability?

Her thoughts clattered like broken glass, loud, chaotic, impossible to arrange into anything resembling coherent communication.

She remembered the exact moment that it had all gone wrong. Not the kiss, but the moment afterwards when Daisy had looked at her with such naked hope, such willingness to be hurt, and all Iris could think was: *I'm going to destroy this. I destroy everything.*

So, she'd left. Not just that night, but properly left. Packed her bags, called scheduling, requested international rotations exclusively. Put hundreds of miles and multiple time zones between herself the possibility of hurting someone who'd already been hurt enough.

Very mature. Very professional.

She put the phone away and focussed on the more manageable crisis of her appearance. Foundation to cover the evidence of chronic insomnia, though it seemed to be requiring increasingly heavy application these days. Mascara to create the illusion that her eyes hadn't forgotten how to sparkle – a losing battle, but one she fought daily out of obligation. Lipstick because regulations required it and because upholding standards was something she could rely on, even when everything else was sliding sideways.

The uniform helped. It always did. There was something reassuring about the ritual of putting it on, the way it transformed her from whatever emotional mess she might be into someone who could handle emergencies at thirty thousand feet, who could smile reassuringly at nervous passengers and stay graceful under pressure, even when the pressure was mostly internal and had nothing to do with cabin altitude.

Passenger having a heart attack? She could talk them through their breathing exercises whilst simultaneously gauging oxygen requirements and identifying the nearest medical doctor on board. Turbulence bad enough to have crew members gripping their seats? She'd move through the cabin with a steady smile, checking on elderly passengers and nervous flyers, projecting calm capability even when her own stomach was performing acrobatics.

But lately, the compartments seemed to be developing leaks. She'd catch herself mid-conversation with a passenger, explaining safety procedures, and abruptly remember the way Daisy had talked about her own years on the road. The wrestling circuit, the hotel rooms, the way you could be surrounded by people and feel alone. They'd compared notes about the specific loneliness of travel – not the romantic solitude that people imagined, but the bone-deep isolation of being always between places, never quite belonging anywhere.

Most people don't understand that distinction. They assumed that someone who travelled for work must love being alone, must be naturally independent. They didn't grasp the difference between choosing solitude and being chronically displaced, always in transit, always temporary.

But Daisy had lived it. She knew what it meant to wake up in generic hotel rooms, to have vacant conversations with people whose names you'd forget, to construct a persona while your personal life slowly atrophied from neglect. She understood without explanation because she'd been there herself.

Her phone rang properly this time. She answered before checking the number, already knowing it would be the taxi company.

"Five minutes," the driver said in accented English, and she confirmed she'd be right down.

She made one last sweep of the room, a habit so ingrained that it happened on autopilot. Passport, Crew ID, phone charger, the small collection of toiletries that constituted her mobile life. Everything else was disposable – the hotel shampoo she'd leave behind, the complimentary coffee she'd never drink, the information folder about local attractions she'd never visit.

The lift took forever, as hotel lifts always did when you were already running late, and she mentally reviewed her schedule: London, then Amsterdam, back to London, then another European rotation that would help to keep her away from anything resembling a settled life for another few days. It was a good schedule, busy enough to keep her mind occupied, but not so chaotic that she'd be useless by the end of it.

The hotel lobby was deserted except for a lone desk clerk who looked like he'd rather be anywhere else. The coffee station had been set up for the breakfast service that wouldn't start for another hour, the smell of industrial brewing mixing with the generic air freshener that all these places seemed to use. It was supposed to be "fresh linen" according to the label she'd spotted yesterday, but it smelled more like someone's idea of what fresh linen should smell like after being filtered through a focus group and a chemical plant.

The taxi was waiting outside, engine running, exhaust visible in the morning air. The driver nodded politely as she got in and pulled away from the hotel without much conversation, which suited her fine. She wasn't in the mood for small talk, and he seemed to sense that, focusing on navigating the early morning traffic whilst she watched the city wake up outside the window.

The streets were beginning to fill with the early shift – cleaners finishing their night work, delivery drivers starting their routes, the first wave of commuters heading to jobs that required them to be present rather than perpetually in transit. She used to envy people with regular schedules, predictable routines, the same route to work every day. Now, she wasn't sure she'd remember how to live that way.

They turned onto Kaiserstraße, joining the steady stream of early commuters, and she found herself studying the people on the pavements. Office workers with their purposeful strides and takeaway coffee cups, shop employees preparing for another day of customer service, early tourists consulting maps and looking slightly bewildered by the efficiency of public transport.

All these people going about their lives, dealing with their own complicated relationships and work lives and personal dramas. It should have been comforting, this reminder that everyone was struggling with something, but instead it made her feel oddly isolated. As if she were watching life happen from inside a protective bubble that kept her safe while sealing her off from the messiness of connection.

"You work for an airline?" the driver said, glancing at her uniform in the rear-view mirror.

"Yes, flight attendant."

"Interesting. Travel a lot, yes?"

"Yes, quite a lot."

His accent was Eastern European, maybe Polish or Lithuanian, speaking precise English that suggested effort. He seemed genuinely curious rather than making conversation.

He asked about favourite destinations and whether she enjoyed the work, and she found herself giving the standard responses that she'd perfected over the years. Yes, she loved travelling. Yes, the passengers were usually lovely. No, it never got boring because every flight was different.

All true, in their way, though they didn't capture the more complicated reality of what it meant to live perpetually in transit. Always between one place and another, never quite settling anywhere long enough to plant roots that other people took for granted. She'd become expert at the inane interactions – the friendly chat with taxi drivers, the camaraderie with crew members, the banter with passengers. But underneath all that was a growing awareness that she'd traded depth for breadth, stability for freedom, and wasn't entirely sure it had been a fair exchange.

The conversation lapsed into comfortable silence as they continued through the traffic, and her mind drifted back to the phone call she hadn't made. What was Daisy doing right now? Probably getting ready for work herself, assuming she'd kept the paralegal job. Iris had no way of knowing – she'd made sure of that when she'd chosen to disappear.

It would be good to know that Daisy was managing, that her disappearing act hadn't completely derailed someone who was already dealing with enough challenges. But finding out would require reaching out, and reaching out would mean admitting she'd been wrong to run, and admitting she'd been wrong would require examining why she'd run in the first place.

And Iris' immediate, overwhelming response had been terror. Not of Daisy, but of her own capacity for destruction. She'd spent years perfecting the art of inconsequential connection precisely because it was safe. Friendly, but not intimate, helpful but not invested, caring but not committed. She could be genuinely kind to passengers she'd never see again, supportive to colleagues she barely knew outside of work, charming to taxi drivers whose names she'd forget before the journey ended.

But the real connection – the messy, complicated, unguarded kind that Daisy had been offering – felt like standing at the edge of a cliff and being asked to jump without knowing if there was water below or just rocks.

"Here's good," she said as they approached the terminal, though he was already indicating to pull over at the crew entrance.

She paid the fare, adding a generous tip because he'd been kind and because good relationships with the local taxi drivers made her job easier. He wished her a good flight and she thanked him before heading into the terminal building.

The crew area was already buzzing with activity despite the early hour. The familiar dance of aviation – pilots reviewing weather reports, cabin crew checking their assignments and discussing passenger loads, ground staff coordinating the endless logistics that kept planes in the air and passengers moving between destinations. A world that she understood, where she knew exactly what was expected of her and could deliver it consistently.

She checked in at crew scheduling, confirmed her rota for the day with Amber, a scheduler she'd worked with for months without learning anything about beyond her tendency to drink too much coffee. A passive relationship that Iris had become an expert at preserving – friendly, but disposable.

"Morning, Iris," Amber said, handing over the flight documents. "London, Amsterdam, back to London, then you're on the Vienna rotation tomorrow. Busy few days."

"Perfect," Iris replied, meaning it. Busy was good. Busy meant less time to think, fewer opportunities for her mind to wander into dangerous territory.

She made her way to the briefing room where her colleagues were already gathering. Fake smiles, small talk about route changes, the comfortable rhythm of people who worked well together without needing to know anything about each other's personal lives. Not knowing was both preferable and encouraged.

"Morning, Iris," called Zuzanna, the senior flight attendant for their first sector. She was Polish, mid-thirties, a warmth that made passengers trust her implicitly. They'd worked together dozens of times, shared meals on layovers, complained about difficult passengers and irregular schedules, but Iris couldn't have said what Zuzanna did during her days off or whether she had family or what made her laugh when she wasn't at work.

"Ready for another glamorous day of airborne customer service?"

"Always," Iris replied, matching her colleague's cheerful tone. "Though I suspect the glamour might be slightly oversold in our recruitment materials."

Zuzanna laughed. "Just slightly. Right, let's get this briefing started so we can get in the air and sell overpriced sandwiches and perfume to our captive audience."

The briefing followed its familiar pattern. Emergency procedures they could all recite in their sleep, passenger manifest review, weather conditions for their route, crew assignments for each sector. Concrete information that required exact responses. No ambiguity, no emotional complexity, just procedures applied to well-worn potential scenarios.

This was what she was good at. Crisis management, customer service, technical problem-solving. She could handle a medical emergency whilst facilitating cabin service, calm nervous flyers through severe turbulence, mediate between difficult passengers without losing her composure. She'd once talked a passenger down from a panic attack whilst coordinating with the flight deck about a potential diversion and ensuring that the rest of the cabin remained unaware of any problem.

As they settled in for the detailed safety briefing, Iris felt some of the tension in her shoulders ease. This was familiar territory; systematic preparation that left no room for improvisation or indecision. Every possible scenario had been considered; every response rehearsed until it became automatic.

She could do this job in her sleep. The briefing concluded, and they made their way through security toward the aircraft. The early morning sun was streaming through the terminal windows now, illuminating the controlled chaos of airport operations. Baggage handlers loading cargo with ease, ground crew performing thorough safety checks, passengers beginning to queue at the gates for the first departures of the day.

But now she walked past them without making eye contact, not because she didn't care, but because caring had become dangerous, a mess she was still running from.

As they walked towards their aircraft – a tidy Airbus A320 that would carry them back to London in a couple of hours – Iris felt the familiar satisfaction of having a clear purpose. The pre-flight checks, passenger boarding, safety demonstrations, service routine – all of it mapped out in advance, and carefully rehearsed.

She straightened her uniform jacket and followed her colleagues aboard, running through her mental checklist of responsibilities. Check emergency equipment, review passenger manifest for any special requirements, prepare cabin for boarding. Totally within her control.

As she moved through the cabin, testing overhead lights and checking that safety cards were properly positioned, she caught herself wondering what Daisy was doing at this exact moment. Getting ready for work, probably. Maybe having breakfast – although she was terrible at eating properly, much like Iris, who'd been living primarily on airline food and whatever she could grab from hotel breakfast buffets.

The thought came with a sharp pang of something that might have been regret, or loneliness, or the recognition that she'd voluntarily exiled herself from the one relationship in years that had felt real.

But that way lay trouble, and she had passengers to serve. In forty minutes, she'd be demonstrating how to inflate a life vest to a cabin full of strangers, keeping her smile whilst explaining how to survive a crisis.

She checked her watch – fifteen minutes until boarding began. Just enough to get her game face on, to transform whatever complicated mess of emotions she was carrying into the care that passengers expected to see.

She unclipped her crew ID from her jacket and clipped it back again, the familiar click and snap a small comfort. It was a good system. It worked. But as she clipped it for the final time, she noticed the photo. The smile in the picture was too wide, too vacant. A shadow of the person she used to be. A reminder of the person Daisy had looked at and seen something worth the risk.

Chapter 32 – Stockholm, 2008

The Marriott's bar was exactly what she'd expected – all dark wood and brass fixtures, with soft jazz and lighting chosen to make travelling businessmen feel significant whilst they drank away their per diems. A place where a decent whisky cost more than most people spent on groceries, where the bartender wore a waistcoat and called everyone "sir" or "ma'am" with almost saccharine deference.

Perfect.

Iris perched on a barstool near the window, positioning herself where the harbour lights would catch her profile just right. She'd changed out of her uniform into the black dress that had never failed her – fitted enough to be interesting, conservative enough to suggest that she wasn't trying too hard. The fabric was expensive, or at least looked it, which mattered more than the reality when you were working a room full of men who equated cost with quality.

She'd been nursing the same gin and tonic for twenty minutes, letting the ice melt until it was mostly water, when he approached. Mid-fifties, decent suit, wedding ring that he wasn't bothering to hide. Sales executive, probably, or middle-management. He travelled frequently enough to know the best bars, but not often enough to develop any true sophistication.

"Excuse me," he said, settling onto the adjacent stool without invitation. "I hope you don't mind, but I couldn't help noticing that you're drinking alone."

She looked up from her phone with fake surprise, as if she hadn't been tracking his approach in her peripheral vision for the past five minutes. "Oh. Hello."

"Neil," he said, extending a hand. "I'm here on business; Stockholm's a lovely city, isn't it?"

"It is," she agreed, accepting the handshake with the right amount of zeal. Firm enough to suggest confidence, brief enough to build mystery. "Iris. I'm here for work as well."

The setup was textbook. He'd identified her as alone, approachable based on her body language. She'd given him her own name because lies were harder to support, but volunteered nothing else. Now he'd feel compelled to fill the void with information about himself, giving her everything she needed to calibrate an approach.

"What line of work are you in?" he asked, signalling the barman with the practised gesture of someone comfortable spending money in expensive places.

"Airlines," she said, which was true and usefully vague. "You?"

"Medical services. Surgical equipment, mainly." He ordered a Macallan 18, then paused, studying her face. "Though I suspect that's less interesting than aviation. You must encounter all sorts of people in your line of work."

The comment was a probe rather than small talk. "You do," she agreed. "What about you? I imagine hospitals can be... challenging environments to work in."

"They are." He accepted his scotch from the barman, who'd delivered her a fresh G&T alongside it without asking. "Lots of politics. Everyone thinks they know best, even when they don't have the full picture."

Something in his tone suggested he wasn't just talking about hospitals. She adjusted her assessment accordingly – Neil might be more perceptive than she'd initially deduced. The wedding ring wasn't hidden, but it wasn't prominently displayed either, suggesting history with situations that required discretion.

"That sounds familiar," she said, letting a hint of understanding warm her voice. "People often think they understand your job better than you do."

"Exactly." He leant back slightly, watching her reaction. "Though I find the smart ones usually know when they're out of their depth."

The comment hung between them, weighted with meaning that she couldn't quite decode. Was he talking about himself? About her? Testing whether she recognised the subtext of their interaction?

She took a small sip of her gin, buying time to recalibrate by deliberately squeezing the accompanying lime into it. Neil had torn up her script, reshuffled the deck – he wasn't another lonely businessman grateful for attractive company; he was observing her responses, looking for something specific that she hadn't identified yet.

"So, airlines," he said, settling back with his scotch. "That must be exciting. All that travel."

She gently tilted her head, letting her hair catch the light from the harbour. "It has its moments. Though, I suspect people imagine that it's more glamorous than it is."

"Oh, I'm sure. Everything looks easier from the outside, doesn't it?"

The phrase tugged at something in her memory. A fleeting impression of a crowded flight, the gentle hum of the engines, and the earnest gaze of a young man talking about his future. A wrestler she'd flown with a few years ago, flying to Germany for what he thought might be his final tour.

She'd ended up talking to him throughout the flight, which was unusual. Passengers were usually problems to be solved or obstacles to be negotiated, not people you had extended conversations with about life choices and courage.

But he'd been different somehow. Listening to her thoughts about stepping back from things you were good at, about how transitions didn't have to be permanent abandonments. Absorbing what she was saying rather than waiting for his turn to speak.

"You look like you're remembering something pleasant," Neil observed, his tone casual but his eyes sharper than before.

She refocussed on him, deploying her most apologetic smile. "Sorry. Long day. You were saying?"

"Just that travel can be isolating, even when it's exciting." He paused, watching her reaction. "I find myself having the same conversations in different cities with different people who all want to hear the same stories."

There was something about the way he'd phrased it, like he was testing whether she'd recognise herself in the description. She kept her expression neutral, interested.

"That does sound wearing," she said, letting sympathy colour her voice. "Do you ever meet anyone who wants to hear different stories?"

"Occasionally." His smile was practised. "Though I've learned to spot the ones who are just being polite. Experience teaches you to read people, doesn't it?"

The challenge was subtle, but unmistakeable. He wasn't making conversation – he was letting her know he understood the game they were playing. Her estimation had been wrong. Neil wasn't a lonely businessman grateful for any attention, he was someone who'd played this game before, possibly better than she had ever realised.

"It does," she agreed, taking a sip of her gin. "What have you learned to read?"

"Oh, the usual things. Body language, timing, what people really want versus what they say they want." He leant forward slightly, lowering his voice. "For instance, I can usually tell when someone's genuinely interested in conversation versus when they're working the room."

The words landed like pieces on a board. He'd identified her airline background, recognised her people skills as potentially businesslike rather than personal, and was now testing whether her attention was genuine or performed.

She should have deflected, redirected back to his concerns, safeguarded the blueprint that had been working. Instead, she found herself genuinely curious about this assessment.

"And which category do I fall into?"

Neil didn't smile. He put down his glass, the sound sharp and final on the polished wood. "You're the first person I've met in months who hasn't insisted they're here to 'see the sights.' You're very good at this, whatever this is."

The direct acknowledgement wasn't a compliment; it was a challenge. He was sizing her up, and she felt suddenly uneasy. This wasn't a lonely businessman looking for company. He wasn't here for company. He was here to win.

"Most passengers are focussed on getting where they're going," she said, which was diplomatic and true. "Though occasionally you can meet someone who's... I don't know. Present, I suppose."

The Frankfurt wrestler had been present. Not anxious about his destination or impatient with delays. Just genuinely engaged with the moment, with the conversation, with whatever insight she might offer about making difficult career choices.

"Present is rare," Neil agreed, then paused, studying her face over his scotch. "Especially in places like this. Most people in here are likely running from something, wouldn't you say?"

The observation was uncomfortably accurate. She kept her expression neutral, though something in his tone suggested he wasn't making casual conversation.

"Are you running from something?" she asked, turning the spotlight back on him.

"Aren't we all?" He smiled, but it didn't reach his eyes. "The question is whether we're honest about it."

She could sense the careful way his words were being chosen, a deliberate construction that was creating a pressure she couldn't understand. Neil wasn't a lonely businessman anymore – he was someone who understood the dynamics of these encounters, who might have his own background with the safe distance she was asserting.

"Honesty can be complicated when you're travelling," she ventured.

"It can be. Though I find dishonesty usually requires more effort." He took a thoughtful sip of his Macallan. "All that diligent handling of information, making sure your story stays consistent. Exhausting work."

The comment landed with uncomfortable precision, a test to see how she'd respond to a direct acknowledgment of their little game.

She could retreat, deploy her early flight excuse and abandon the evening before it became more complicated. Or she could engage with the challenge, match his level of intricacy and see who proved more skilled at the game they were both clearly playing.

The past flickered through her mind again – that simple conversation about stepping back from something you were good at in order to become someone you could live with. But right now, she was discovering exactly how good she'd become at something that probably wasn't worth being good at.

Neil nodded enthusiastically, clearly pleased to have found someone who understood the burden of subterfuge. He launched into a detailed explanation of his current sales campaign, the politics of hospital procurement, the challenge of affirming relationships with clients who changed positions every few years.

She listened with the appropriate level of attention, asked the right questions, made the right noises when he paused for validation. But part of her mind was in Germany, trying to understand what had been different about that conversation.

No manipulation. She hadn't wanted anything from the wrestler except perhaps to be helpful, to offer useful advice to someone who seemed genuinely unclear about his next steps. And he hadn't wanted anything from her except perhaps to understand his options better, to get a different perspective on choices he was trying to make.

Revolutionary concept, apparently.

"...which is why I think the German market is really the key to everything," Neil was saying, though his attention seemed more focussed on her responses than his own words. "But relationships take time to develop properly, don't they?"

The shift in subject felt considered, like he was preparing for a different kind of conversation. She nodded appropriately, but found herself analysing his technique rather than simply managing it.

"They do," she agreed. "Though some people are better at shortcuts than others."

"Shortcuts can be useful," he said, his tone suggesting that he understood exactly what kind of shortcuts she meant. "Though I've found the people who are really good at them often end up somewhere they didn't intend to go."

The observation hit closer to home than she wanted to acknowledge. When had her life become entirely about shortcuts? Emotional detachment which delivered outcomes without requiring investment.

The wrestler hadn't taken shortcuts with their conversation, he'd walked the long way round. He'd been willing to explore complicated questions about career transitions and personal identity, to sit with the questions rather than rushing towards easy answers. She'd respected that patience, that willingness to think things through properly.

"Where do you think I intended to go?" she asked Neil.

He paused, studying her face. "Where *did* you intend to go?"

The reversal caught her off-guard. She'd meant it rhetorically, a deflection that would let him expound on his theories about her motivations. But he'd turned it back on her, requesting insight rather than philosophical speculation.

"I'm not sure I understand."

"When you decided to become very good at manipulating conversations with strangers in hotel bars, what outcome were you hoping for?"

The directness was both impressive and uncomfortable. It cut right to the core of her life, and for a split second, she felt her composure shatter. She forced her glass to her lips, but her hand trembled, a tiny, visible tremor that Neil's eyes caught and held.

She could lie, claim confusion about his implications, retreat back to safety. But something about his approach – the respect for her intelligence, the acknowledgement of her skill without questioning its purpose – made dishonesty feel like a waste of both of their time.

"Free drinks," she said. "Company without complications. The ability to be social without connecting to anyone."

"Ah," he said, approvingly. "Though I suspect the efficacy might be costing you something."

"Such as?"

"The possibility of enjoying the company you're keeping."

Another direct hit. She couldn't remember when she'd enjoyed a conversation rather than indulging it. Even now, engaging with Neil's unexpected complexity felt more like problem-solving than pleasure.

Except for Frankfurt. That conversation had been genuinely enjoyable, stimulating in a way that had nothing to do with achieving specific outcomes. Just the satisfaction of useful exchange with someone who'd made her feel like her thoughts might matter.

"Tell me something," Neil said, leaning forward with what appeared to be genuine curiosity. "This person you mentioned earlier, the one who was different. What made that conversation work when these ones don't?"

That was too perceptive, too close to thoughts she'd been trying to avoid examining. But Neil was watching her with an attention to detail that suggested that he might be interested in her answer rather than positioning his next move.

"No agenda," she said. "Neither of us wanted anything from the other except honest conversation."

"And that was enough?"

"It was everything."

The admission surprised her with its intensity. She'd meant to be diplomatic, to give a thoughtful answer that would maintain their newly-honest equilibrium. But the words had carried more weight than intended, revealing feelings she hadn't fully acknowledged even to herself.

Neil nodded slowly, his expression shifting from purported interest to something that might have been sympathy.

"That does sound different," he said, "And probably impossible to recreate deliberately."

"Probably."

"Which explains why you're here instead of looking for him."

The observation was gentle but accurate. She could have tried to find the him, could have made some effort to reconnect with the one person who'd made conversation feel natural. But that would have required admitting that the encounter had mattered, that she was capable of wanting something beyond the isolation that she'd constructed.

"Looking would imply that it matters," she said.

"And mattering would be dangerous."

"Exactly."

A peaceful quiet settled between them, a silent admission that everything had been said. Neil finished his second Macallan and didn't signal for another, suggesting he'd reached his own conclusions about how the evening would proceed.

"Well," he said eventually, "this has been unexpectedly illuminating."

"It has," she agreed, meaning it more than she'd expected to.

"Thank you for your honesty. And the skilful deflection that preceded it." His smile was genuinely amused rather than disappointed. "I don't think I've had a conversation this authentic before."

Authentic. The word echoed strangely, acknowledging that neither person was actively steering the conversation.

"Thank you for making it interesting," she said, gathering her bag. "And for calling me on my technique. Most people don't."

"Most people aren't paying attention." He stood as she prepared to leave, the gesture automatic and courteous. "Safe travels tomorrow."

"And to you."

She left him at the bar, probably settling his bill and returning to whatever story he'd arrived with. The lift arrived instantly, carrying her towards the seventh floor and the anonymous comfort of her room. Her reflection in the polished steel doors showed someone who looked exactly like what she was: a working woman concluding a successful evening. Hair still perfect, makeup intact, lipstick a flawless crimson line. But as the lift carried her upward, she felt an exhaustion far deeper than physical tiredness – the kind that came from the relentless need for awareness, from a life of constantly monitoring other people's responses to calibrate your own.

Frankfurt hadn't required any of that. She'd just talked to him, offered thoughts that occurred to her naturally, listened to his responses without analysing them for useful information. An effortless interaction she'd forgotten was possible.

Her room was exactly like every other business hotel room she'd stayed in over the past few years – cheap carpet, abstract artwork that meant nothing, a bed that was comfortable enough for sleeping but too sterile for anything resembling rest. She hung up the black dress, washed off her makeup, and set her alarm for another early morning.

Tomorrow, she'd fly back to London, smile blankly at passengers who were travelling for reasons she'd never know, serve people whose stories she'd never hear. All of it perfectly executed and meaningless.

The vision lingered as she settled into bed. Not the details – she couldn't remember what he looked like, exactly, or what he'd said that had made such an impression. Just the feeling of being genuinely useful to someone, of having a conversation that mattered beyond its entertainment value.

Why did that conversation feel more substantial than years of subsequent interactions with colleagues, passengers, and men who had bought her drinks in exchange for temporary company?

Was it because he'd expressed an optimism; a desire for a home, a future, a family, all the things she'd always run from? Or was it just because he asked and expected nothing more of her than humanity?

The questions circled as alcohol and exhaustion began to take hold. But tonight, falling asleep in another generic hotel, she carried with her the image of someone who'd looked at her like she might be worth knowing rather than worth managing.

It was probably nothing.

But in a life increasingly defined by emptiness, even nothing was something worth remembering.

Chapter 33 - Amsterdam

The long layover stopped being a problem and became an unexpected pocket of found time; a chance to pause and breathe. Twenty-four hours between her inbound from Tbilisi and the following evening's departure to Heathrow. Long enough to leave Schiphol properly, to take the train into Amsterdam rather than spending another day in airport limbo, drifting between gate lounges while pretending she wasn't avoiding the phone in her bag.

The crew shuttle delivered her to the Novotel, where she checked into room 417 with the near-automatic routine of someone who'd done this hundreds of times before. She showered off the Tbilisi flight, changed into civilian clothes, and caught the train back into the city with nothing but her shoulder bag and the freedom of having nowhere she needed to be.

The tourist crowds moved with purposeful urgency around Centraal Station – people with maps and guidebooks, couples photographing each other beside canal bridges, families navigating the tram system with the determined cheerfulness of people making memories.

She was five months into the routine that began after the kiss. Five months of accepting every international rotation, volunteering for the longest routes, anything that kept her away from England and the possibility of accidentally encountering someone she wasn't ready to face.

She could've returned to the airport after her shower, found a quiet corner to read or catch up on paperwork. Could have slept away the hours until her next shift began. Instead, she found herself deliberately walking away from the station, following the canal paths toward the museum quarter with the methodical thoroughness she usually reserved for pre-flight checks.

The afternoon carried the scent of autumn leaves and canal water, mingling with coffee from the low-lit cafés and sweetness of stroopwafels from street vendors. The city felt crisp without being bitter, the last warmth of summer clinging to stone buildings that had weathered centuries of seasonal transitions. She'd walked these streets before on brief layovers, but always with destinations in mind; always moving between planned stops before returning to crew schedules.

Today felt different. Free time spreading ahead of her like an invitation to wander without purpose, to let the city reveal itself rather than ticking off mandatory tourist spots. And still, she found herself doing just that.

The Anne Frank House queue stretched around the corner, solemn families and teenagers looking appropriately grave whilst checking their phones. The juxtaposition felt jarring against the backdrop of a past that didn't tolerate inattention.

As she moved through the cramped, quiet rooms, a strange, suffocating familiarity settled over her. The space was smaller than any photograph could convey, more claustrophobic. She paused in Anne's bedroom, looking at the collection of film star photographs and postcards still taped to the walls. It could've been any teenage girl's room, a simple collection of ordinary adolescent dreams – except for the context that transformed it all into evidence of extraordinary courage.

In the next room, the famous quote was printed in Anne's own words: *"In spite of everything, I still believe that people are really good at heart."* The faith required to keep that perspective whilst living in constant fear felt almost incomprehensible. She, too, had built an elaborate deception, but hers was designed to protect her not from persecution, but from the simple frailty of human connection. Her hiding had nothing to do with courage.

She stepped back into the street as though surfacing from underwater, the weight of the Annex pressing against the chatter of tourists. She didn't want to go back to the hotel yet, but she couldn't go straight into another monument either. What she needed was something smaller, less monumental, something that reminded her survival could also mean curiosity, play, even indulgence.

Rather than rushing to her next destination, she found herself wandering through the museum quarter's quieter streets, past galleries displaying contemporary art that spoke to the city's thriving creative community. One gallery window showcased paintings that reminded her of illustrations she'd seen in books wealthy hotel guests sometimes read — not the bestsellers or the business trades, but art books, poetry collections, books that whispered instead of shouted.

She'd absorbed more cultural knowledge than she'd realised during those years. It was less about art and more about performance, and she'd become very good at hearing the difference. A small bookshop caught her attention. She browsed the poetry section, recognising names she'd picked up from overheard conversations in hotel bars. The bookseller noticed her lingering over a collection of contemporary Dutch poets.

"Wonderful choice," she said. "These writers understand the city beyond the clichés."

Iris bought the book impulsively, drawn by the bookseller's obvious passion for literature that challenged rather than confirmed expectations. She tucked it into her bag, looking forward to reading voices that might offer perspectives on the city she was experiencing beyond guidebook descriptions.

The Sex Museum occupied a narrow building near the red-light district, its pink neon sign competing with coffee shop advertisements and the cheerful tackiness of tourist trap souvenir stands.

Ancient fertility symbols sat alongside medieval chastity belts and contemporary erotic art. She had heard enough whispered conversations to develop an extensive education in human sexual behaviour, most of it depressingly transactional. But what struck her here wasn't the explicit content; ithe museum's straightforwardness.

Same-sex relationships were displayed without commentary, gender fluidity explored as natural variation, all without anyone wringing their hands about what was normal. Here was a world that wasn't about categorisation, but about acceptance.

It made her think of Daisy – of the effort it took to keep explaining yourself to people determined not to understand.

Iris, by contrast, had simply learned to play a part, and the effortless way she'd performed heterosexual interest in hotel bars made sense. Maybe it wasn't a lack of attraction, but simply a lack of expectation that she should feel anything at all.

Like managing difficult passengers or navigating workplace politics – situations that required responses without emotion.

But what did emotion look like when it came to attraction? She'd spent so many years cultivating unassailable distance that she'd lost the ability to distinguish between self-preservation and disinterest.

The museum's last room exhibited sexuality as spectrum instead of boxes, attraction as personal fingerprint instead of universal category. Reading about demisexuality, grey-asexuality, romantic orientation separate from sexual preference, she felt something settle into place without quite forming words yet.

Maybe it wasn't supposed to hit like lightning. Maybe some people needed deeper connection before physical interest developed, needed to understand someone's mind before wanting their body. Maybe the labels mattered less than recognising your own patterns, accepting them instead of forcing yourself into shapes that didn't quite fit.

The evening was crisp as she left the museum. Instead of rushing toward her next destination, she let herself wander through the city's transformation as daylight faded – less polite, more honest. People moved with a different energy, pursuing pleasure instead of cultural improvement.

She passed a small gallery displaying black and white photographs of working life – images that captured the beauty in ordinary moments: window cleaners silhouetted against canal houses, market vendors arranging flowers, cyclists navigating morning traffic with unconscious grace. The art required observation instead of expensive equipment.

A wine bar occupied the ground floor of a narrow house, its windows glowing warmly against the chill. Not tourist-focussed, but clearly welcoming to outsiders, serving good wine without ceremony whilst encouraging conversation between strangers who might discover unexpected compatibility.

She ordered coffee and asked about the wine selection, curious about the curation instead of planning to drink. The bartender recognised her interest and began describing his favourites with infectious enthusiasm – small producers, traditional methods, wines chosen for character instead of impressive labels.

"You work in wine?" he asked, noting her familiarity with his descriptions.

"Airlines," she said. "But I've spent enough time in pretentious bars to learn the difference between expensive and good."

He laughed, bringing her a second coffee without being asked. "Ah, where wine becomes theatre instead of pleasure."

The observation was so accurate that she found herself telling him about the worst wine selections that she'd encountered on layovers – prestigious labels chosen for price point instead of drinkability, sommelier recommendations based on profit margin instead of guest enjoyment. He shared similar stories from restaurant work before he'd opened his own place, both of them finding humour in the gap between wine industry theatre and true appreciation.

It was the first conversation she'd had in months that didn't feel forced. She caught herself laughing – properly – and the surprise of it warmed her throat. Just two people who happened to know something about wine, sharing observations that amused them both.

When he mentioned his partner's struggle to understand his enthusiasm for natural wines, she found herself asking questions that rose out of real curiosity about how two people navigated different interests whilst sustaining a connection.

The bar filled with late-night customers as they talked. At the corner table, two women were deep in conversation, their body language suggesting a long friendship. One was explaining something complicated, gesturing expressively while her companion listened with a focussed attention that indicated real interest. When the listener laughed, reaching across to touch her friend's hand, the simple ease between the two women caught Iris' attention. Their gestures belonged to a language she didn't speak – a familiarity that let conversation flow without hesitation.

She didn't envy their intimacy so much as the effortlessness of it, the way being together seemed to require no coordination at all. Not sexual attraction, exactly. Something more fundamental: the desire to be known well enough by another person that casual physical affection became natural instead of contrived.

She thought of Daisy and the single, purposeful kiss that had terrified her. She had spent a lifetime perfecting the art of a perfect handshake, a polite touch on the arm, but the thought of simply reaching out to Daisy, of being close to her without pretense, felt foreign. To trust someone enough that touching them required no consideration of boundaries or potential misinterpretation.

She tried to remember when last she'd touched another person. Work handshakes or the brief physical contact required for passenger assistance. But casual affection that came from fondness instead of positioning?

It had been years. Possibly decades.

The realisation should have been depressing, but the city's atmosphere of acceptance made it feel more like useful information than personal failure. Recognition of something missing instead of evidence of fundamental inadequacy.

By midnight, the red-light district was fully alive, neon reflecting off wet cobblestones, music spilling from open doorways. The energy was electric, but what struck her most wasn't the commercial energy – it was the absence of shame. The scene felt surprisingly adult, honest about what was being sought and what was being offered. Sex workers conducted their business calmly, clients made choices without apparent embarrassment, tourists observed without prurient secrecy.

She found herself studying the working women with curiosity instead of judgement, noting how they owned their surroundings. Some chatted between clients, others read or worked on phones, a few engaged in animated conversation with colleagues across the narrow alleys. Their control was obvious – they set their space, their pricing, their boundaries.

One woman roughly her own age caught her attention, reading what appeared to be a serious novel between assessing potential clients. When she looked up and noticed Iris watching, she smiled with amusement instead of sales interest. Not a commercial gesture, just recognition of shared understanding between women who both worked in service industries that required managing other people's expectations whilst maintaining personal boundaries.

Iris smiled back, surprised by how natural the exchange felt.

The neon alone might have been enough, but something tugged at her curiosity. If the streets showed the façade of the trade, she wanted to understand the mechanics beneath it – the rules, the protections, the realities hidden behind the glass. That curiosity carried her to the Museum of Prostitution, where intrigue gave way to explanation.

The Museum of Prostitution was not a spectacle; it was an education, filled with the stories of former workers. Their narratives, told without judgement or apology, spoke of an industry the city regulated instead of criminalised.

A recreation of a working room was direct instead of titillating – clean sheets, good lighting, safety equipment discreetly positioned. Everything was designed for the worker's protection, a detail that resonated with Iris more than she expected. One section examined the emotional boundaries required to uphold a private self while inhabiting a public persona – work touch separated from personal connection. She had practiced this same psychology for years, perfecting the art of being "on" without being present. But here, the women spoke of it with a clear, matter-of-fact dignity that felt foreign. They were honest about what was being sought and what was being offered. More honest than her own encounters had ever been.

She thought of Daisy again – of her openness, of the way she wore her identity as a simple truth. The women in the museum and Daisy seemed to understand a truth that Iris was beginning to grasp:

that the greatest dignity came not from hiding, but from being unapologetic about who you are and what you do, even if it carries a risk of judgement. Daisy's worldview, her bluntness, it wasn't about pushing people away, it was about refusing to accept fear.

She emerged feeling different, as if the night had shifted her perspective without her realizing it. Instead of heading back to her hotel, she found herself drawn toward the quieter canals where ordinary life continued beyond the famous entertainment districts. Past houses with bicycles chained to railings, past windows where people were beginning their Saturday mornings with coffee and newspapers as dawn broke, past the thousand small details that made the city feel lived-in instead of performed.

She paused on a bridge, watching the water reflect lights in wavering lines. A couple passed behind her, speaking Dutch in quiet voices, their conversation intimate without being secretive. She caught fragments — something about work tomorrow, weekend plans, the ordinary negotiations of people who'd chosen to build a life together. A casual domestic exchange that she'd observed from the outside for years without quite understanding what she was missing.

Listening to the couple behind her discuss groceries and work shifts, she realised it wasn't passion she envied, but ordinariness. A domestic shorthand built over years – complaints about tomorrow, laughter about nothing. Intimacy not as drama but as continuity, the steady rhythm of being known day after day.

She'd had glimpses of that possibility. Brief moments when work charm relaxed into something more. Early in her career, when she'd been young enough to believe that helping strangers was reward enough for the effort required.

But those moments had become increasingly rare as she'd perfected the art of manipulation.

It was effective at achieving what she needed without risking what she couldn't afford to lose. The problem was that she'd become too good at it. Good enough that even when she wanted connection, the well-worn habits engaged automatically, transforming potential intimacy before she'd decided to protect herself.

Like with Daisy. Five months ago, when real attraction had terrified her so much that she'd fled instead of risking discovery of whether it might be mutual.

But what was real attraction, exactly? She'd learned to perform interest convincingly, but she'd never examined what desire might feel like when it wasn't being deployed as a tool. Physical chemistry was obvious enough, but what about the deeper compatibility that seemed necessary before she could imagine wanting someone instead of successfully managing them?

With Daisy, the attraction felt different from anything she'd encountered while scheming. Not based on appearance or convenience or advantage, but on something more fundamental. The way Daisy's mind worked, perhaps. The combination of cynical intelligence and underlying jeopardy that made every conversation feel like discovering something new about how another person processed the world.

She'd found herself curious about Daisy's thoughts, interested in her responses to situations they encountered together. Not information-gathering for future use, but engagement she'd forgotten was possible between adults who'd just met.

The water continued its gentle movement beneath the bridge, carrying reflected lights along the canal. A group of late-night cyclists passed, their voices cheerful despite the hour, heading home from whatever entertainment had kept them out past midnight. The city accommodated all of it – tourism and local life, work and pleasure, conventional relationships and unconventional desires – with acceptance that made hiding seem pointless instead of necessary.

She hadn't eaten properly since Tbilisi; only airport food and airline meals, fuel that kept her functional without providing any pleasure. A small Indonesian restaurant caught her attention – not the tourist-focussed places near Centraal Station, but a family-run establishment where the scents escaping from the kitchen promised preparation instead of European adaptations designed for timid palates.

The owner's wife seated her at a small table near the kitchen, where she could watch the preparation that went into each dish. Years of listening to wealthy travellers discuss their culinary discoveries had taught her to appreciate technique, the difference between ethnic cuisine and tourist approximations. She ordered rijsttafel, a spread of small dishes that arrived in waves: glossy rendang, sharp pickles, coconut rice, heat threaded through everything. Each element had been prepared with obvious care. The food demanded attention to fully appreciate, revealing new aspects as she worked through the meal. Nourishment that reached further than the body; an act of care that reminded her meals could be more than transactions, more than calories slipped between obligations.

She looked at the couple at the next table, their heads close together as one passed the other a serving spoon of rendang. They were discussing which dishes they wanted to try making at home, their conversation revealing a familiarity with the food – and each other – that went beyond simple appreciation. Their easy intimacy made her think of Daisy – not with the ache of longing that had been her constant companion for five months, but with a new curiosity about what it might feel like to share a meal with someone whose company she enjoyed instead of tolerated.

Afterwards, she walked for a while, letting the warmth of the meal settle.

The city's architecture offered a final, quiet lesson: medieval foundations supported contemporary interiors; historic facades protected modern purposes. Amsterdam had preserved its character while accommodating change, growing without abandoning what made it distinctive. She, too, had erected a kind of survival by constantly adapting, but it was a lonely existence.

She returned to her room at the Novotel, which felt identical to a hundred others she'd stayed in over the years. The international assignments that were her salvation five months ago now seemed more like an elaborate postponement of a conversation she wasn't ready to have. But tonight, settling into bed, she carried with her something that felt close to possibility. She felt a shift – not monumental, but real. Running was no longer protecting her from anything except the possibility of discovering whether the connection she'd been avoiding might be worth the risk of disappointment. Too soon, perhaps. But waiting carried more danger than trying and failing. For the first time in months, she understood that silence itself was the greater risk.

She pulled out her phone. The battery was almost dead, the screen faint in the dark. She skimmed her contact list until she found the name – the one she had deliberately avoided for five months. Her thumb hovered over the number, the possibility of a different future a single tap away. But hovering was a game – the luxury of imagining a different life without doing any of the frightening work. She wasn't ready to call. But she was ready to stop running.

Not running didn't mean going back. It meant choosing, finally, to be the one who acted.

With a deep, shaking breath, she pressed firmly and held Daisy's name on the screen. A prompt appeared: Delete Contact? She closed her eyes and hit confirm.

Chapter 34 – Budapest to Warsaw, 2009

The wine had turned the uniform jacket slick under Iris' hands. She smoothed it against the hotel bed, its sharp smell of aircraft disinfectant clinging as stubbornly as the tang of recycled air. The jacket felt alien, more to the sky than to her. Her hands trembled. Not just with the drink. A deeper kind of tremor had taken root; some part of her body had decided that tranquillity wasn't safe. The empty glass glinted on the nightstand, its rim crusted with lipstick – a dried crescent. She lifted it anyway, hoping, tilting. Nothing. Just the cloy of sugar and stale grapes.

The bottle loomed across the room, its ruby liquid thick enough to make the glass heavy again. She raised it to the light. The whole world turned red. Her stomach lurched in warning, already sour and heavy, but she ignored it. That was the point: to ignore the body. To drown it before it could think.

Budapest had been golden from the taxi – postcard moments she was already determined to drink away. Beauty made her angry, sharpened the outline of her absence. It was better to stay in anonymous rooms where curtains closed and nothing demanded her attention. Downstairs, she had performed the solo dinner, moving from the first glass to the second, pretending it was sophistication and not sedation. Back upstairs, she had carried the bottle with her like a trophy, half-emptied by the time she noticed. Now it was fading too quickly, another glass disappearing into her.

Her suitcase lay gutted on the floor, contents spilling. Neatness had deserted her months ago. Knots of tights, twisted underwear, lace scratching against her raw fingertips when she pawed through for distraction. She wasn't looking for anything. Just moving, moving, moving, like stillness might expose her. The cardigan surfaced, navy wool creased and tired, holding faint airport perfume and chemical vanilla. Dublin, three months ago. She'd bought it while ignoring her mother's call, phone buzzing hot against her pocket. Third missed that week. The memory lodged sharp. She pressed the wool to her face and drank them away.

Time bent sideways. Glasses emptied and refilled. The laptop blurred; rota meaningless. She couldn't tell how many hours had passed, only that the wine was thinning out and the room was filled with chaos and the bustle of the street below. Sirens, laughter, music rising from the Budapest night. She pressed her palm against the cold windowpane and thought, absurdly, of how far away she was from anything that mattered.

Her phone vibrated against the pillow. She ignored it. Again. Then rang. The sound ripped the hush to pieces. She froze. Calls at this hour rarely meant anything good. She forced her throat clear, rehearsed sobriety.

"Hello?"

"Iris? It's Dad."

She sat hard on the bed, the cardigan slipping against her bare ankles. "Hi." Her voice came out trained, crisp. "Everything alright?"

Static. Then the words.

"I need to tell you something about your mum."

The glass went slack in her hand. "What?"

"She's dead."

The syllables fell like lead. He pushed through, voice cracked and fractured: "Half past five. She was using the saw in the garage. We argued about shelves. She said she'd do it herself. I went for a drive. When I came back—" His voice collapsed. "She was on the floor."

The room tilted violently. Iris clutched the duvet with white knuckles. Her throat scraped out: "When?"

"Just after six. I was gone maybe two hours. Driving like a sulking teenager while she—" He broke off. His breath hissed sharp through the line.

Five hours. While Iris had been beneath chandeliers, asking for another pour. Five hours while her mother bled into sawdust and she sat here ordering dessert wine to impress a waiter.

Her father's voice came again, smaller. "I don't know what happens next. I don't know what I'm supposed to do."

"I'll come home." It snapped out, unplanned.

"You're busy—"

"Dad." Her voice sliced, sharper than she meant. "I'm coming."

The air held unsaid words in a delicate, fragile quiet. Then: "She loved you, Iris. Worried about you. Said you were thin in those pictures. Said you didn't eat. Said you weren't happy."

Her chest convulsed. Her mother's voice lived in those words: You look tired. You never call. Are you eating? Criticism disguised as love. Love disguised as criticism. She couldn't tell anymore.

"What were the shelves for?" she whispered.

"Her cookbooks. You remember – she kept buying them. Towers everywhere. I kept saying I'd build proper shelves. Always said 'next weekend.'" His voice wavered. "She asked twice this week. I didn't listen."

The bottle felt slick in her hand, sweating. She stared out the window. The city glowed with laughter and light while her mother lay cold in their garage, books without shelves, her father bleeding guilt into the phone line.

"I'll sort flights in the morning," he said. "Try to get some rest."

The line went dead.

The hush was unbearable. It pressed against the walls, thickened the air. Iris sat for a second, glass limp in her hand, then she drank what was left in a single swallow. Her stomach buckled, but she forced it down. Forced the burn to numb the pain. It didn't work. Nothing worked.

Her body lurched into motion. She staggered to the desk, tipped the last of the bottle into her glass, then lifted the bottle itself, tilted her head, drained it like water. The clunk as she set it down echoed like a gunshot in the quiet room. Empty. Empty, like her.

She stood swaying, nails digging into the desk edge. The laptop glowed, rota letters swimming. Zurich, Heathrow, tomorrow, next week, endless strings of flights that felt grotesque. Her mother was dead and she was supposed to report for duty in twelve hours to smile at strangers and offer them juice. The thought made her laugh, a thin, sound that hurt her throat.

The uniform jacket lay on the bed. She reached for it, pulled it tight to her, clutched it like it was protection, comfort. The polyester smelled of recycled air, of safety demonstrations, of pretending. She pressed her face into it, desperate for some trace of her mother, but all it gave back was static and sweat. She threw it aside. It landed half off the bed, limp, useless.

Her legs folded. She slid down the side of the mattress onto the carpet. The fibres scratched her cheek. She sobbed then, full-throated, animal. No control left, no mask, just raw sound tearing out of her. She buried her face in her sleeve, tried to muffle it, but the sobs came anyway. Ugly. Shaking. Heaving. Her body convulsed around grief that refused to fit inside her skin. She curled on the floor like a child, jacket bunched beneath her, forehead pressed to polyester, begging for breath.

She wanted more drink. Needed it. The minibar. She scrambled across the carpet on hands and knees, yanked the fridge door open. Tiny bottles lined up in perfect rows, soldiers ready for deployment. She grabbed vodka, twisted the cap, swallowed. Fire spread through her, bile-hot in her throat. She coughed, wiped her mouth with the back of her hand, reached for another. Downed it. The glass clinked against the tile as she threw it aside. She didn't taste the third, only felt the warm flood, the spreading numbness that wasn't numb enough.

The bathroom mirror caught her on the way up. She froze, horrified. Her face was swollen, mascara smeared into raccoon shadows, lipstick bleeding at the edges. Her eyes were pits. She looked like someone beaten, someone discarded. Not a professional, not even a person. Just a ruin. She slammed her fist against the glass, once, twice. Pain bloomed in her knuckles. The mirror held. She turned away, retched into the sink, wine and vodka spilling back in bitter streaks. She rinsed, spat, rinsed again, but the taste clung.

She stumbled back to bed, stripped down to tights and blouse, collapsed sideways onto the duvet. The cardigan was still on the floor. She reached for it weakly, dragged it up, pulled it over her like a shield. It smelled faintly of perfume counters and duty-free sugar. She buried her face in it and wept until her throat grew raw.

Time fractured. Minutes, hours, she couldn't tell. She drifted in and out, sweat-soaked and shivering, punctuated by ragged sobs that came in waves. When she surfaced, the lamp was still on, light too harsh. She turned it off. Darkness collapsed over her. For a moment it was mercy. Then her brain filled it with the garage – her mother sprawled, blood pooling, saw buzzing. A picture she'd never seen but now couldn't unsee. She groaned, pulled the duvet over her head, tried to smother the images. They came anyway.

Her stomach heaved. She rolled off the bed, crawled to the bathroom, vomited until her throat was raw. Sour wine and bile bit her nose, tears streaking her cheeks. She clung to the toilet bowl, forehead pressed to cold porcelain, hair sticking damp against her face. She rocked there until the spasms stopped, until only shudders remained. Then she dragged herself back to bed, stinking of vomit and sweat, too weak to care.

Sleep came in violent fragments. She dreamed her mother's voice calling her name, not gently but urgently, angry, pleading. She dreamed of shelves falling, cookbooks crashing, blood spreading across tiles. She woke gasping, screaming into her pillow, or fists shoved into her mouth. Drifted off again. More nightmares. More waking. The night an endless loop of grief and sickness; her body trapped in its own cycle of torment.

When dawn bled grey through the curtains, Iris surfaced into something worse than nightmare: reality. Her skull throbbed, every pulse a hammer strike. Everything tasted metallic. Her stomach cramped with emptiness and acid. She sat up too fast, the room lurching sideways, spots exploding across her vision. She clutched the duvet until the world steadied, then dragged herself upright, legs trembling.

The desk was a wreck. The empty bottle lay on its side, last drops of wine dried into sticky rings. The minibar bottles scattered across the carpet; caps tossed like confetti. Her glass was chipped, a smudge of lipstick across its rim. She stared at the mess, then at her phone blinking with notifications. Her father. Missed calls. Texts. Funeral arrangements already beginning. The words swam in her vision.

Her body screamed for a drink. Her hands shook as she opened the minibar again, grabbed another tiny bottle, twisted, swallowed. The sting was instant, the relief as fleeting as a breath. She tipped another back before she'd even finished the first. Hair of the dog. Smooth the edges. Pretend she was capable of standing.

By checkout she had three empty minis rattling in her handbag. The receptionist gave her a smile, neutral, sufficient. Didn't comment on her red eyes, didn't ask about her trembling hands. Iris muttered something about travel disruption, signed the receipt, and stumbled out into the pale autumn morning.

Budapest glared at her. Too bright, too loud, too alive. Trams rattled past, cafés buzzed with chatter, tourists pointed at maps. Her sunglasses barely dimmed the assault. She carried her suitcase like an anchor, found a taxi, muttered "airport." The driver nodded. No questions. She was grateful. She had no answers.

The airport was a blur. Security, passport, gate, her body moving without thought. She floated through queues, nodded at staff, handed over documents without meeting anyone's eye. The terminal smelled of coffee and pastries, but her stomach recoiled at both. She bought water anyway, forced herself to sip, then caved and bought another miniature wine. Drank it in the corner, quick and furtive, the paper bag crumpled between her knees. Shame hit hot across her cheeks, but the liquid dulled her hands enough to stop them shaking.

On the plane, she buckled into a window seat, cardigan wrapped tight around her. The safety demo blurred, the flight attendants' voices tinny and distant. When the engines roared and the plane tilted up, she tensed. She clutched the armrest until her knuckles stiffened, the wine sloshing sour in her stomach. Zurich came and went in fog. She barely noticed the Alps below. She followed the crowd, boarded again, sank back into a seat for Heathrow.

As the plane's wheels hit the tarmac, Iris' body felt brittle, each bone rattling loose in its socket. Her head pounded, eyes gritty, breathing a challenge. Heathrow looked like every other airport – grey, sprawling, endless corridors – but the thought of her father waiting at arrivals sent fear screaming down her spine. She wanted to vanish in the crowd, hide in a bathroom stall, buy another drink. But the doors slid open, and she saw him.

He looked smaller than she remembered, shoulders stooped, his face hollowed out in a few days. His hair was thinner, his eyes bloodshot, his jaw unshaven. For a second, Iris almost didn't recognise him. Then he opened his arms, and her legs carried her forward before her brain caught up. She stepped into the hug stiffly, then collapsed against him, feeling sawdust and aftershave and grief clinging to his coat. He clung back, his body shaking silently against hers. A stranger who had once been her father.

Nobody spoke. Outside the windows, the motorway unfurled, a ribbon of asphalt against a backdrop of fence posts and hedges that were little more than a green streak. Her father gripped the steering wheel like it was the only thing anchoring him. Iris watched him sideways, the lines of his face deeper, jaw muscles twitching. She wanted to tell him to turn around, to take her anywhere else, anywhere that wasn't home, wasn't grief. Instead, she stared out the window.

The house was smaller than she remembered. Paint flaking from lintels, drainpipe leaning at an angle, curtains half-drawn though it was only afternoon. Inside, the air was thick with wrongness. Too calm, too stale, as though grief had its own scent. Iris moved quickly through the hall, suitcase wheels bumping against the skirting, and stopped dead at the door to the garage.

Sawdust littered the floor. Planks leant against the wall; the shelves never built. Seeing her mother's final destination for the first time, she felt an urge to enter. To sit, take some kind of communion and attempt to sense whatever spirit of connection might exist inside. She couldn't bring herself to enter. She tried anyway – gripped the frame, tried to force herself through – but her body refused. For once, it won.

In the kitchen, cookbooks were stacked in unsteady towers on the counter, precarious and heavy as tombstones. Her stomach turned over. She couldn't breathe in that room, couldn't look at the spectre of unfinished promises. She escaped upstairs, dropped her suitcase in her old bedroom, collapsing onto the dented mattress that carried the shape of her teenage self.

The funeral came too quickly. Her father moved like a machine through arrangements: the vicar, the florist, the service order. Iris went through the motions, her smile a pale imitation of enthusiasm. She let her drink be her escape, a way to numb the awkward gaps between polite conversation. Gin in the evening, wine with lunch, vodka from the bottle hidden in her handbag. She learned how to survive meetings with neighbours she half-remembered, how to let the alcohol smooth the edges of her shaking voice. She bought a black dress at Marks & Spencer in a blur of fluorescent light, the fabric too loose across her waist because she'd stopped eating anything that wasn't liquid.

On the day itself, rain fell steadily, unrelenting. The cemetery was a sea of umbrellas, mourners pressed together, raindrops pooling on black coats. Iris stood beside her father, his hand clamped around her arm like a lifeline, his face stoic. She felt the mud seep through her shoes, tights clinging wet against her legs. She didn't cry. Couldn't. She stared as the coffin lowered, oak wood slick with rain, ropes squeaking in damp hands.

All she could think was that her mother had hated damp cellars, had complained endlessly about mildew in the bathroom. Now she was left to rot underground. The thought was obscene, but it stuck, looping like a broken record in Iris' head until her stomach clenched and bile rose. She swallowed hard and forced her face still, despite the temptation to laugh at the irony.

Afterwards, the house was cluttered with people and food – sandwiches lined up on trays, sponge cakes wrapped in cling film, tea brewed in batches so strong the tannins coated her tongue. Voices in every room, condolences wrapped in platitudes. Her father stood stiff among them, nodding, thanking. Iris slipped away, found her suitcase upstairs, uncapped a hidden bottle, drank half of it in the bathroom with the extractor fan running. When she returned, her smile was loose enough to pass for grief.

The days blurred together after that. Flowers drooped in vases, sympathy cards piled on the mantel, the water in their vases turning brown. Her father spent evenings in the living room, the television on but silent. At his elbow sat a glass of dark liquid – a tumbler of what she assumed was his usual whisky. It remained untouched as he stared at the flickering screen. Iris drank alone in her childhood bedroom, curtains drawn tight, bottles lined behind books. She told herself it was temporary. Just to get through. But the bottles emptied, and the weight stayed. The only movement she could muster was the search for refills.

Once, he tried – just once – to reach her. It was late, the air heavy. She'd just uncapped a bottle in the kitchen when he lingered in the doorway, his hands twisting together. He held a mug in one hand, its ceramic worn smooth from years of use. "Iris… maybe you should cut back," he said, his voice a low plea. "For your health."

His words cut sharper than any accusation. She spun on him, eyes red, mouth bitter.

"Don't you dare tell me how to cope," she snapped, cruel in her defence. "You killed her with your laziness, with your bloody beer and football. Don't you dare."

His face crumpled, colour draining, and he turned away without a word. The silence after his retreat was worse than any argument. Iris drained the bottle in jagged gulps. She never apologised.

Her body began to betray her. Tremors that made pouring orange juice dangerous, hands shaking so violently liquid sloshed onto the tray. Nosebleeds left tissues soaked red; headaches split her skull like lightning. She carried plasters for the cuts on her knuckles where she'd slammed fists against mirrors or walls in rage at herself. Even when she forced food down, her stomach rejected it, twisting with nausea. Only drink stayed down.

The nightmares were constant. She saw her mother on the floor, head twisted at an impossible angle, calling for help that never came. Worse, she dreamed of her mother alive, sitting at the kitchen table with tea, smiling and saying: *Why didn't you ever call me back?* Those dreams shattered her more than the death did. She woke screaming, gagging herself with an old teddy bear so her father wouldn't hear.

Six weeks after the funeral, she tried to return to work. She stood in front of the mirror in her uniform, hair scraped back, tights already laddered, lipstick trembling at the corners of her mouth. Her reflection looked drained; her skin too grey to pass for health. She picked up the phone and called in sick, voice falsely bright, claiming flu. No pushback. She celebrated with gin until the room blurred.

By the second month, the spiral tightened. She lost track of mornings, afternoons, nights. She measured time only by bottles, hiding them around the house: under the bed, behind stacks of cookbooks, in the airing cupboard, everywhere except that damned garage that she could never again muster the strength to enter.

Her father didn't comment. Or maybe he noticed and ignored it. They moved through the house like strangers bound by grief, circling one another without touching.

One night she wandered into the garage. The shelves leant unfinished against the wall; sawdust unmoved in the corners like an accusation. The sight knocked her to her knees. She pressed her forehead to the cold concrete and sobbed until her voice broke, words spilling in slurred apologies: *I'm sorry, I'm sorry, I should have been there*. She whispered it over and over, her tears soaking into the dust, but no voice answered.

The next morning, she woke with a bruise on her temple where she'd struck the floor. Her stomach churned with acid, throat raw. She poured vodka into a glass before noon, her hands trembling until the alcohol steadied them. Her father passed her in the hall without a glance, a wall she couldn't breach.

Two months after her mother's death, Iris' body refused to carry her any further.

It happened in Madrid. She remembered boarding the plane, smile painted too brightly, hair dragged into something approximating neatness. She remembered forcing herself through the safety demo, her voice clipped, almost cheerful. And then, somewhere over the Bay of Biscay, the world narrowed to a tunnel. Her ears filled with rushing blood, her vision collapsed, and she woke on the galley floor with colleagues crouched around her, passengers craning to see.

"Exhaustion," someone murmured. "Low blood sugar."

She let them believe it. She even smiled, shaking it off with the brittle ease of someone too used to putting on a happy face. But inside she knew. Her body was screaming what she refused to say aloud.

She should have quit. Should have sought help. Instead, she doubled down, hiding better. Miniature gins decanted into water bottles; vodka tucked into make-up pouches. Drinking in airport toilets between boarding calls. She told herself she was still functioning, still competent, still passing. But the truth was obvious in her trembling hands, her raw throat, the black circles beneath her eyes that foundation couldn't mask.

As much as she tried to march confidently from airport to airport, flight to flight, her stumbling and fumbling were becoming impossible to hide.

And then came Warsaw.

An ordinary hotel room in an ordinary city – thin curtains, a minibar humming faintly, carpet rough against her knees. She had finished another bottle, vodka rolling empty against her thigh, stomach cramping, bile scorching her throat. She sat slumped against the bed, cardigan bunched under her cheek, in a pose that could have been mistaken for sleep.

The curtains didn't quite close, and her reflection hovered in the window. Hollow-eyed, hair tangled, makeup smeared. She stared at herself for a long time, long enough that her own gaze became a stranger's.

And then she whispered, hoarse, to no one but the glass: "This isn't coping. This is dying."

The words came out broken, a confession more than a revelation. She couldn't take them back once spoken. They settled in the stale air of the room, undeniable.

It wasn't a cinematic moment. There was no lightning bolt of resolution, no prescribed formula for recovery. Even as she said it, her mouth ached for another drink, her hands twitched with the instinct to reach for the minibar. But something had shifted. The lie was broken. She could no longer pretend alcohol was the solution. She knew now – clear as the bruise on her temple, the rawness of her throat – that it was the problem.

She lay back on the carpet, body heavy, tears leaking sideways into her hair. She let herself feel her mother's absence without pouring something down her throat to drown it. The pain was unbearable. It was also honest.

And honesty, however small, was the first step toward survival.

Chapter 35 – Ebb and Flood

The paperback lay face down on the striped hotel towel beside her, its spine bent in a way that would have made book-lovers wince. *The Waves*. She'd chosen it deliberately, a test of endurance disguised as literature. If she could sit long enough to make sense of Woolf's sentences, then perhaps she could prove to herself that serenity was possible. But the sea breeze had already caught the pages, ruffling them like wings, as though even the book was restless. She'd read three paragraphs – maybe four – before the words dissolved into something too close to thought. She read the first line – "The sun had not yet risen. The sea was indistinguishable from the sky, except that the sea was slightly creased as if a cloth had wrinkles in it." – and felt it land like a diagnosis. The same sky, the same sea, the same creased cloth. No difference between her internal turbulence and the external world. Reading it was like staring into a mirror that refused to hold a steady image.

She snapped the book shut, its sound barely louder than the shuffle of pebbles beneath her towel. Daisy. Daisy. Daisy. The name surfaced in her thoughts, a tidal current of its own. A name the Mediterranean itself seemed to whisper every time it broke against the shore.

She lay back on the towel and closed her eyes, hearing Woolf's cadences mix with the rhythms around her. The hiss of waves collapsing onto pebbles. The squeals of children making last, desperate sandcastles before their parents packed them away. The rattle of a cyclist's chain as he wove a path across the promenade behind her. It all blurred into a single sound: presence, life, motion. The very thing Iris had been trying to escape for six months.

Six months. She felt every one of them stacked in her bones, layered like geological strata. Six months of departures stamped across her passport, six months of hotel minibars and rota changes, six months of never staying anywhere long enough for the bed to lose its starch. She'd told herself it was healing – keep moving, keep working, keep collecting kilometres until distance transformed into clarity. But it hadn't transformed. Nice was another city in a long sequence of cities: beautiful, yes, but empty in its own way. The Promenade des Anglais curved out of sight like a promise she had no intention of keeping; the light so aggressively blue it seemed to mock her.

The students nearby noticed. There were six of them, spread across three towels, their bodies at ease in a way that made Iris ache. They were young enough that nothing seemed permanent – gestures loose, laughter easy, bottles of Orangina shared with absent-minded generosity. She couldn't follow their French quickly enough, but the tone was unmistakable: philosophy dressed in passion, big declarations about truth and love and freedom, arguments that ended in laughter rather than wounds. She envied their conviction, their ability to believe that ideas could shift the world. Once, she might have joined a circle like that, argued late into the night about the nature of reality. Now she barely trusted herself to finish a novel without circling back to the same two or three unbearable thoughts.

The sun slid lower, turning the surface of the Mediterranean to beaten gold. Boats skimmed the horizon – fishing trawlers making for port, a yacht heading toward the harbour with its sails cut sharp against the light. She watched them without envy.

Movement had lost its meaning when every departure led only to another anonymous arrival.

She'd become someone who collected pretty moments the way children collect shells – admiring their shape but never really possessing them. And like shells, they crumbled when she tried to carry them too long.

Her phone buzzed against her hip, breaking the fragile trance. She didn't check the screen. Work, probably. Another rotation offer, another chance to stretch her exile a few more weeks. Or Mary. Or her father. The uncertainty itself was unbearable. She pressed the phone deeper into the towel and let it vibrate itself silent. But the spell was broken. The students' laughter grated now, their freedom a rebuke. The sunlight that had seemed golden turned sharp, too bright. Even the waves sounded insistent, like they were trying to push her back toward the promenade, toward motion she hadn't asked for.

She sat up, brushing sand from her arms, and gathered her things with a neatness that surprised her. The book, the towel, the empty bottle of water. She slipped her sandals on and followed the crowd trickling off the beach. The promenade opened in front of her: wide, white, endless. Tourists strolled with gelato in paper cups, couples leant against the railings to watch the sun set into the sea. Rollerbladers wove between them with skill, headphones clamped over ears that shut out the world. It was all designed for leisure, for people with someone to share it with. Iris walked alone, clutching her towel like a shield, and felt the separation sharpen with every step.

The Negresco rose ahead, faintly absurd in its pink dome and Belle Époque flourishes, a hotel that seemed to belong more to fantasy than reality. She passed its doormen, immaculate in their white uniforms, and imagined what they saw: another woman in sandals and sunglasses, indistinguishable from the thousand other transient women who passed their steps each day. The thought didn't sting. Anonymity had become her chosen camouflage. Blending in was easier; nobody expected much from wallpaper.

As she reached the curve where the promenade bent toward the harbour, the old town called to her. Vieux

Nice. Its alleys promised something different from the staged perfection of the beachfront: shadows, smells, disorder. She turned into its narrow mouth and let herself be swallowed.

The transition was instant, like stepping through a membrane. Light narrowed, sounds thickened, air cooled. Here the city had no interest in performing. Laundry hung from balconies in mismatched colours, cats lounged on windowsills with territorial indifference, shutters opened onto interiors that smelled of garlic and thyme. Market stalls were closing, their pyramids of aubergines and tomatoes dismantled, lavender tied into bundles for tomorrow. The calls of vendors echoed from walls worn smooth by centuries of passing bodies. Iris drifted with the tide of pedestrians – families heading home, tourists chasing dinner reservations, locals carrying groceries – and felt again like a spirit passing through someone else's life.

She wanted height. Perspective. A vantage point from which the city would spread like a map she could read. Her feet found the path toward the Colline du Château almost involuntarily, the hill that promised panoramic understanding. She climbed stone steps worn concave by generations, her breath uneven though the incline was gentle. The gardens were half-lit, palm trees casting long shadows, tourists pausing for photographs while dogs trotted beside their owners. Iris kept moving, refusing to stop until she reached the top.

The view struck like a reprimand. Nice lay at her feet in impossible harmony: terracotta roofs clustered around the cathedral, boulevards stretching straight as an idea toward the airport, the curve of the bay glittering under a sky turning lavender. The promenade traced its elegant arc, dotted with figures strolling as if painted into a composition. It was too beautiful, almost hostile in its perfection. She stood at the rail and felt nothing but estrangement. A ghost surveying a city of the living.

She turned back to the book in her bag. *The Waves.* She hadn't meant to bring it up the hill, but there it was, its weight impossible to ignore. She opened it at random. Words drifted: *"I see a ring. It quivers and hangs in a loop of light."* Even light demanded permanence, coherence. For Iris, nothing held still long enough to be grasped. She closed the book and stared at the city again. If there was a ring of light here, it belonged to someone else's life.

The descent was easier, though she barely registered her own steps. The hill released her back into the old town, the alleys narrowing as the evening settled in. Light spilled differently now – gold softening to amber, shadows thickening into violet. A group of children ran past her, their football scuffing against cobblestones, their laughter reverberating off stone walls. She was invisible in their game, a passing figure who meant nothing.

She drifted without aim, guided more by sound and smell than by map. Restaurants were coming alive, their kitchens spilling garlic and rosemary into the street, their waiters carrying chalkboards out to announce the day's specials in looping handwriting. She paused outside one doorway and watched through a window as a chef bent over his pans, flames leaping at his wrists. His movements were exact, almost balletic – choreography performed for no one, though the rewards would be consumed by strangers. She thought of Daisy, briefly; of how effort could be invisible until someone paid attention. And then she pushed the thought away, because it always led to the same cliff edge.

A square opened before her. Tables filled its centre, metal chairs clattering as people claimed their places. Strings of lights zigzagged overhead, not yet lit but already hinting at transformation once the sun dropped below the horizon. Couples leant toward each other across bottles of rosé, groups of friends spread plates between them, conversations rising and falling like waves against the shore. Iris moved around the edge of the square, careful not to brush too close. She became a voyeur again, stealing glimpses of connection she no longer knew how to create. Every laugh sounded too sharp, every kiss too loud, every toast too cheerful. She couldn't imagine being a part of it, not now, maybe not ever.

The streets narrowed again. She passed a window where an old woman sat reading to a child perched on her lap. The child's hair glowed in the lamplight; her small body curled like a comma against her grandmother's chest. Iris slowed, then forced herself forward before she became the stranger staring too long. But the image clung. A body curled in trust. Time given freely. She could almost smell the must of the books her mother had once read aloud, hear the scrape of her father's chair when he returned late, everything she had once thought normal until she'd decided she wanted to be anywhere else.

Her hotel appeared almost by accident, tucked into a side street where cobblestones glistened with the day's heat. Its facade was pale cream, shutters throwing long blue shadows. The lobby swallowed her in cool dimness, the air thick with polish and faint lavender. She climbed the stairs without thinking, her body running on a GPS built from hundreds of similar staircases in hundreds of similar hotels.

The room was small but clean. French doors opened onto a narrow balcony, curtains lifting in the evening breeze. She dropped her bag on the chair and crossed to the window. Below, life unfolded without her: a woman pegging laundry across a line, the shirts snapping like flags of surrender; two boys chasing each other between scooters parked at odd angles; a man with a glass of pastis, folding his newspaper precisely between sips. All of them anchored. All of them known to one another in ways that required no effort, no explanation.

She touched the book again – *The Waves* – then let it fall onto the bedspread. Woolf's voices had been circling her all day, but what they offered was too dangerous: consciousness moving toward other consciousness, voices trying to meet. Iris had perfected the opposite art. Solitude disguised as motion. Avoidance dressed up as career.

Iris stared at the phone cautiously before picking it up. The small room was too quiet, her thoughts looping in circles she couldn't escape. She almost put it back down – another rota change, another chance to choose exile – but instead she scrolled to "Home" and pressed call. The word itself was enough to soften her shoulders as the line began to ring.

"Iris! Darling, how wonderful to hear your voice." Mary.

Warmth transmitted across miles, an eagerness that slid past defences whether invited or not. Iris closed her eyes, feeling the sting behind them.

"Hi," she said. "I'm… in Nice."

"Nice! How marvellous. Your dad went there once, years ago. Said it was like living inside a painting. Is it as beautiful as he described?"

"It is." Iris glanced out at the orange glow sinking over terracotta rooftops, the lines of laundry catching last light. "Almost aggressively beautiful, if that makes sense."

Mary laughed, that familiar laugh that turned judgement into camaraderie. "It does. Sometimes beauty can feel like pressure, can't it? As though you're meant to rise to it. Are you there for work?"

"Layover. Twenty-four hours." She sank onto the edge of the bed, grateful for the cool press of the quilt beneath her palms. "Just thinking, really."

"Oh, sweetheart." There was no reproach in Mary's tone, only relief at being trusted with something even half-honest. "Your dad will be so glad you called. He misses you terribly, though of course he won't say so. He's at his Wednesday meeting just now. He's been worried, though he tries not to show it. And… there's this woman at the meetings, Daisy—"

The name detonated quietly. Daisy. Her Daisy. The syllables thudded in her ears like the bells she'd heard on the promenade. She forced her voice level, summoning the training that had taught her to keep steady no matter the turbulence.

"Yes," she said, attentively.

"She was doing so well for a while. Opening up, really making progress. But something happened about six months back – she won't say what – and it knocked her sideways. She's been absent, missing meetings, and when she does come, she sits at the back and leaves straight after. Your dad thinks she's protecting herself from something, but he can't see what."

Six months.

The words folded over again, suffocating. Right after Iris had kissed her and then fled across borders, mistaking running for protection. Daisy had been left with the ruins.

"She's in pain," Iris whispered.

"She is. And she's so bright, Iris. So sharp. But she doesn't trust the good things. Your dad says she reminds him of someone, though he can't place who. He says she looks like someone waiting for bad news."

Waiting. Always waiting. For Iris, maybe. For explanation. For amends.

Mary's voice softened. "When you do come home, you should meet Daisy properly. I think you'd understand each other. You've both got that way of seeing through nonsense, though she's gentler about it than you were at her age."

After the call ended, Iris sat in silence, the phone heavy in her hand. Outside, the evening gathered itself into rituals: shutters thrown open, lamps switched on, voices rising over dinner tables. Life moving forward while she remained paralyzed, caught in a loop of avoidance. Daisy had been there all along, showing up even when it hurt, sitting in the very room where their disaster had begun. And Iris had been here, running from city to city, mistaking beautiful places for safety.

She thought of the wedding, of the petals scattered like surrender, of Daisy sitting at the back of the meeting hall like a shadow. She thought of her father's steady presence, of Mary's quiet compassion. She thought of all the places she had run to, and of the one place she had avoided.

The bells tolled again, fainter now, marking the late hour. She rose, crossed to the balcony, and looked out at the city. The square below had emptied. A waiter cleared tables, stacking chairs casually. Somewhere distant, wedding guests sang as they walked to a reception, their voices carrying across the stone like promises.

Iris leant against the railing; the air cool against her skin. She knew, with a clarity that cut through everything: tomorrow she would fly to London, and this time she wouldn't run again.

She was going home.

Chapter 36 – The Green Wedding, 2022

Lilies and cleaning fluid, musty dust. The smells of a church were nothing new, but the anticipation of a wedding was. Iris hadn't attended one since she was a kid; she'd run away from home as soon as she was able, first to university, then onto the airline.

Now, she felt obligated to be here.

Mary had asked her to be a bridesmaid, the maid of honour, but she'd said no. Not through a lack of love for Mary – she loved Mary – but because saying yes felt somehow disloyal to her own mother.

She watched the flower girl practice her walk, a friend's daughter chosen for the role. Iris tried not to take it as a damning indictment that she and her soon-to-be-stepsisters had yet to provide a suitable person for the job.

She spotted her dad nervously chatting with her Uncle Mick, his chosen best man. "My job is to put on a suit, show up, and not embarrass her," her dad had said, wisely.

She left them to it, not wanting to get involved in that conversation, and moved towards Sophie, who looked stunning, as always.

"Sophie!" she shouted, gleefully, wrapping her in a warm hug. "And you must be Sarah," she said, holding out her hand to Sophie's new girlfriend. "I've heard so much about you."

"Good things?" she responded.

"Too many," said Iris. "We're still teaching Sophie about boundaries."

Sophie slapped her on the arm. "Your dad looks good. I didn't even know he owned a suit."

"Oh, come on, you know he rented it," Iris replied, then mimicked him, "I'm not spending a thousand bloody pounds on a suit I'll only wear once!"

"Pete is legendarily tight," Sophie explained to Sarah, "if he'd had his way, we'd be doing this in his back garden with Iris ordained off the internet and an Iceland party platter for afters."

There was a quick murmur of hurry as news spread that Mary's car had arrived, and everyone found their seats. Iris and Sophie were, of course, in the front row on the groom's side, with them both being very wary to place themselves between Sarah and Uncle Derek who was – to be frank – a problem they expected to be managing all day.

As the processional music began, everyone rose to their feet, eyes turned to the door to see the bride in her dress. Iris, of course, had already seen it, having been dragged to the fitting alongside the bridesmaids; it was suitably elegant and classy.

She looked at her dad, steadfastly staring ahead at the altar. If anyone asked, he'd say he was being a stickler for tradition. She knew he was probably getting emotional and trying to hide it, but she let him have his pride.

She watched the bridesmaids trail Mary in; Molly, Holly and Polly – Mary was kind, not creative – all dressed in the same green dress, the same one Mary had insisted Iris wear, even though she'd declined the invitation to formally be a bridesmaid. A small concession to make to her new stepmother. Besides, it was expensive and pretty, even if she was sick of wearing green by now.

Thankfully, being not necessarily religious, Mary and her father had decided to keep the wedding itself short. From the "We have come together in the presence of God, to witness the marriage of Pete and Mary…" to the "…blessings of eternal life" as fast as possible. Perfect. Well, almost. The vicar probably could've left out the bit about kids being born. Unless he really believed in miracles.

Her eyes scanned the church as they were doing the registration paperwork – paperwork, she assumed, that she wouldn't be completing any time soon – and saw happy faces exchanging glances nervously. Everyone clearly sharing her own sense of lack of purpose.

The ceremony complete, they gathered outside the church whilst everyone was forced to rotate in and out of poses for pictures by the overly-eager photographer. She found herself next to Sophie in the wider family photo.

"You're next," she whispered to her cousin.

"No pressure," Sophie replied sarcastically.

"Well," she responded, "it's either me or you." She gestured to Sarah, "and you're winning."

"We'll see," said Sophie.

When they left – she'd chosen to drive with Sophie, rather than ride with the wedding party – she'd learned that Sarah was a doctor and they'd met at a festival. Good for Sophie; she deserved someone who could take care of her. She was usually the one taking care of everyone else.

They'd paused for what Sophie termed a "pit stop" on the short journey between the church and the hotel. It was an excuse to grab a pint and fortify before any of them had to force smiles and make small talk with vague distant relatives and old family friends that they'd rarely seen since they were children.

The country pub was nice. Quiet. Logs in the fireplace, old men with dogs, everyone minding their own business. A good place to bridge the gap between celebrations.

As they arrived at the reception, things were starting to get in full swing. Various clumps of family members and social groups were making quiet conversation; children who'd already found the sweet table ran around furiously.

A lone girl with auburn hair in a scarlet dress stood quietly in the corner, her gaze distant, as if she were a million miles away. She held a cigarette, twisting it with a slow, precise motion before she took a drag. The smoke, a perfect, unwavering stream, was the only movement she made. There was something about her quietude, the way she was so contained, that broadcast a quiet defiance to Iris.

Iris already knew she'd be seated at the table; she didn't know if the demotion was Mary's kindly revenge for refusing to be a bridesmaid or an act of hopeful geniality in the hope that she, too, might find herself a special someone.

Iris found herself at one end of the long singles table, flanked on either side by two young, handsome men.

On one side was Steve, an accountant from Bristol that Mary had met through the rooms. He launched into a detailed analysis of the "perfect" width of a road bike tyre and the appropriate terrain for a mountain bike in a city. He was a nice guy, but Iris wasn't going to be swept off her feet by a detailed analysis of the pros and cons of different brands of cycle shoes.

On the other side sat Will, a cheerful estate agent who spoke rapidly, like he was trying to negotiate a deal. He was impressed by her "potential," her "good bones," and how well she was "situated" in her career. He was nice, but transactional relationships with men weren't Iris's thing anymore.

The sound of laughter from the other end of the table gave some indication that Mary's matchmaking was working for somebody, at least.

The food arrived at a time when Iris most hoped for a break in conversation. Some kind of asparagus-based starter. Small, like the hotel chef was trying for prestige, but lacking the inspiration or flavour. It gave her a short break from having to feign interest in Steve's two-wheeled adventures or Will's lamentations about a lovely three-bedroom cottage in the Cotswolds that he was trying to shift, if only the owners would budge on price.

The main course was a creamy chicken pasta affair. The sauce was thick enough to not spill, and bland enough to match the magnolia walls of the hotel. She remembered the many men she'd conversed with on her misadventures, and how horrified they'd be by this offering. They dined in places that had Michelin stars, not places that served the same meals for occasions as they did for room service.

All of them better company of an evening than Steve or Will, as nice as they seemed to be.

The speeches, as per tradition, arrived between the main course and dessert.

The father of the bride wasn't there. Not dead, as Iris had assumed, but not invited. Mary had gone non-contact with him years ago, telling Iris he was an incurable drunk who found joy in making others miserable. Iris hadn't pushed for details.

In his absence, Mary gave her own speech. She spoke of her last marriage, which had ended so badly, and how happy she was to have found a man who didn't run when things were hard. Iris let the comment pass.

The youngest, Iris noted, was in her mid-20s, and the oldest was closer to Iris' age – mid-30s – and recently married herself. Iris hadn't been able to attend that wedding, though she'd been asked. Rotation she couldn't get out of, *"you know how it is."* She probably could've gotten out of it if she'd cared enough to ask, but the idea of attending the wedding of a future stepsister that she barely knew seemed less exciting than the London-Paris-Copenhagen triangle.

Her dad spoke fondly of her mother, and shared his own story of how lucky he was to find Mary. How all he had to do to get a second chance as a husband was "cut the bullshit" – his catchphrase, which made Iris cringe whenever she heard it – and how happy he was to blend their two families together. He was always a good public speaker. It was a shame he chose to speak in cliches.

Uncle Mick gave his speech, mostly bad adult jokes and little digs at her father's expense. She caught a couple of strays for not being at the head table, but nothing ill-natured. Something about being proud of his little brother for trying again, how happy their parents would've been to meet Mary – they were actually dead – and all that good stuff.

Then Molly. Or Polly. She could never remember which one the oldest was. Holly was the youngest one, for sure. Mary described her as her "Christmas surprise" every time she talked about her, that was the only reason she remembered.

Mary's eldest talked about how kind Pete was, how different he was to her own father, how happy her sisters were to have him in their lives. Didn't mention Iris, so presumably she still wasn't happy that she'd chosen the Little Mermaid over the big occasion.

And then dessert. Presented by the waiter as a "chocolate roulade with pistache royale velouté and a toffee-orange coulis." In English, that was a yule log with pistachio ice cream and a toffee-orange sauce. She knew that, because at the planning stage her dad had asked "what the fuck is that?" and she could tell from watching his face as he tried it that it wasn't to his taste. Nor hers, it turned out, as once again the chef's ambition had far outstripped his ability.

Once dinner was over, the DJ started playing in the function room. This was the one small victory that her dad had achieved in the wedding planning – a band was too expensive, he said – and the celebrants slowly filed onto the dancefloor after the happy couple had finished their first dance.

People looked genuinely happy. Sophie and Sarah were sparing no energetic expense on the dancefloor. Truly in-sync, which was a beautiful thing to see.

She spotted Scarlet Dress sitting alone at the singles table – ironically by herself again, more testament to Mary's excellent matchmaking – and considered making conversation with her until she saw she was being approached by Uncle Derek.

Ugh. Creepy Uncle Derek.

She considered saving her, but as she went to make her move, James – Mary's nephew or something? – swooped in chivalrously to make the rescue. Good for him.

She caught Mary looking over to the scene and smiling wryly, as if her master plan was working, but Iris was pretty sure James was gay. Maybe not. Who knew? Who cared? Chivalry wasn't dead, at least. Lucky escape for Scarlet Dress, that's for sure. He led her off to the dance floor, and let Derek continue his mission to leave with someone drunk enough or a restraining order. It was a coin toss.

At that moment, Mary came walking over. "How are you doing, love?"

"Good. Everyone seems happy. You look lovely."

"Thanks," she replied, "and honest answer?"

"That was an honest answer. I'm genuinely happy for you." Iris smiled.

"How were Steve and Will?"

"Nice."

"So?" She probed.

"Not going to happen," she sighed. "Nice guys, but not for me."

"I guess we'll keep looking then."

Please don't. "I guess."

As the night wore on, she found her dad regaling anyone who'd listen with tales of his policing career. She knew it was more shoplifters than serial killers, but it was probably more interesting than his current life of paint and plaster.

She spotted Sophie, worn out from dancing and drinking, making her way over to her.

"You look lost," Sophie observed.

"I feel lost," Iris confirmed. "It's strange, isn't it? I can feel at home in any city on the continent, but the second you bring the family together, I don't know where I fit."

"Life," Sophie slurred, "isn't about fitting in with people. It's about making people fit into you."

Iris laughed at the unintentional double-entendre. "I'm pretty sure that's Mary's job."

Sophie took a second to process it, then laughed. "Singles table was a bust, huh?"

"They should let Mary run one in Guantanamo Bay. Somebody would talk."

"You know, you'll—"

"—find someone." Iris interrupted. "I've heard. But, here's the thing: what if I'm not looking?"

"In my experience," Sophie looked over at Sarah, making her way over to them with more drinks. "That's when they find you."

As Iris slipped into her hotel room at the end of the night, she thought about Sophie's words. She had chosen a life of solitude, of exploring and making her own fun. Yet every night, like this one, she ended up in the same place: a tedious hotel room.

Perhaps she was losing her sense of home.

Chapter 37 – This Too Shall Pass

Iris had expected her homecoming to be greeted by more... fuss.

Instead, she was greeted at Heathrow by her father and Mary with hugs as warm and questions as non-existent as a weekend business trip. The car ride home was a quiet, comfortable space filled with nothing but the soft sound of the engine, the serenity of it a foreign pressure against her chest.

Arriving at their house – mercifully not the one where she had grown up – she was greeted by the warm, savoury smell of a stew in the slow-cooker, the friendly thump of a cockapoo's tail (a new addition in her absence), and a feeling of peace that made her shoulders drop as if to finally rest.

She'd been given her space as she settled into the spare room and unpacked; the conversation in the car had remained casual and friendly. Mary's daughters – her stepsisters, she supposed – were doing well, as was her young nephew, and everyone had missed her.

After she'd taken a long, hot shower and changed, Mary was keen to summon her for dinner. Excited, even.

As she arrived at the table, Mary was ready with her "I need a favour" face.

"So, I noticed from our calendar that someone has a birthday today."

Iris was confused. *A birthday? Had she forgotten something?* She glanced at the calendar, and there it was; in neat handwriting *"Iris (16)"*

Her sobriety birthday. She'd been so wrapped up in work, the travelling, her escape, that she'd not been keeping track of the date. At least, not to the extent where it had occurred to her.

"I was thinking it might be nice if we marked the occasion by having you give the main share tonight. How does that sound?"

It sounded horrendous, if Iris was being honest, but she got the feeling that Mary wasn't making a request: this was a recommendation.

"Sure," she said, trying to sound as casual as possible. She hadn't been asked to give a main share in so long that she didn't really know what she was going to say, but she'd figure something out.

"It might be really helpful if you did," Mary added. "There are definitely people who could do with hearing your story."

"Come on, Mary," she replied, "I'm a drunk, not a prophet."

"I think Daisy—" the name cut through Iris like a knife.

"I don't want to talk about Daisy."

"Oh," said Mary, "I didn't think you knew her that well?"

At that moment that her father walked into the room. "What's happening? Did she say yes?"

"Did you know Iris knew Daisy?"

"I mean, I didn't think it was out of the realms of possibility. They've both been in the rooms long enough."

"What's wrong with Daisy, love?" Mary asked, looking directly at Iris.

What wasn't wrong with Daisy? Iris thought. But then the honesty that was harder to confess. "Umm… I am."

Her father and Mary fell silent, their faces a mixture of confusion and shock. The sound of cutlery on plates and the low hiss of the slow-cooker were the only sounds in the room.

"How can you be what's wrong with Daisy?" her father asked, seeming genuinely confused.

"She hasn't talked about me?" Iris had assumed that she might have shared something. Hoped, maybe.

"No, love," said Mary. "She's never been my most forthcoming sponsee, but she's not mentioned anything about you."

"Oh." Disappointment.

"She's really only given the occasional hint of whatever is going on," Mary continued, "something about 'misjudging a relationship,' I think."

"Oh." Guilt.

"Do you know something about that?" Mary asked, betraying her surprise.

"I… might." She admitted, cautiously.

"How could you know something about it?" her dad asked. "You haven't spoken to anyone in six months."

His tone was steady, his eyes full of patience.

"Exactly, love," Mary said, reassuring. "And whatever started her problems happened—"

"Six months ago," Iris interrupted. "Six months ago."

She took a deep breath.

"The thing that happened six months ago… was me." She braced for impact. "I was the thing that happened to Daisy. I broke her."

"Broke her?" Mary asked.

"How could you have broken her?" Her dad asked almost simultaneously.

"I might have, uh," she hesitated, "broken her heart."

Her dad, a look of discomfort etched across his face, joined them in sitting at the table.

Iris told the whole story; how they'd met. Twice. The thirteen-year hatred that turned quickly from hatred to help to friendship to... flirtationship?

"And then she kissed me."

"Oh, love," Mary said, "And I guess you had some kind of falling out because you're, you know, not like that?"

"No." She took another deep breath. "No. I ran."

"Well, that's only natural. I'd have run." Mary agreed.

"No, I didn't just leave the flat. I *ran*. I left the country."

"Well, that's a bit of an overreaction," her dad added.

"I know that now. It took me six months of wandering through European cities to figure it out."

"To figure what out?" Mary wondered.

"To figure out," one more deep breath, "that I didn't run because I'm 'not like that', I ran because I am. I just hadn't figured it out yet."

There was a silence in the room that lingered heavily in the air.

"That makes sense," her father broke the quiet. "You've always struggled with emotions. You ran from me and your mum when we were having issues. You ran when she died. Of course you ran from this."

"I don't want to run anymore, dad."

"Then don't," he responded. "And you've come back."

"So, what do I do now?"

"You take stock," he replied. "In the past, whenever you've run, you've come back drunk. You've escaped the problems physically; you've tried to escape the emotions with alcohol. This time, you've escaped physically, but carried the emotions with you. Lived with them. Learned from them. You didn't drink."

"That's progress, Iris," said Mary.

Nothing followed, as if all three were sat with their feelings.

"Can you give us a minute, love?" her dad said to Mary.

"Of course," she said, rising and gently brushing Iris' arm reassuringly as she left the room.

"You know," her dad began, "the relationship I had with your mother was far from perfect. We put you through some things that we shouldn't have done, and I'm sorry for that."

"Dad—"

"No, listen," his voice was kind, not firm. "When she died, I think we both blamed ourselves, and maybe even each other, for what happened."

Iris nodded. She was used to hearing her dad's version of honesty in meetings, but this was more personal.

"But then, life moved on. We moved on. We both looked for help, we both got sober. Our lives got better. Our relationship got better. And you stopped running."

She nodded again, wondering where this was heading.

"When you ran," he said, solemnly, "I wondered if it was something I'd done—"

"Dad, no—"

"But then I thought about it," he continued. "Alcoholics, Iris, are creatures of habit. You run when you're overwhelmed by emotional things. And Daisy… she withdraws from the programme. Stops coming to meetings regularly."

He put his hand on top of hers, reassuringly.

"I don't pretend to be the smartest man in the world, nor the most emotionally intelligent," he continued, "but I'm not stupid. It didn't take long to connect the dots."

"You knew?" she asked, almost incredulous.

"Of course I knew," he laughed, "I'm your bloody dad."

She smiled. She didn't even consider the comfort that having his support would bring.

"When I met Mary," he went on, "it wasn't easy. It was complicated, and we tried to hide it from everyone because we were worried about what they thought."

"Everyone knew, dad," she laughed again, "the cat hair gave you away."

He laughed with her. "Well, be that as it may, eventually it reached a point where we couldn't hide it anymore. Or didn't want to. We had to accept it, and share it with everyone we knew. We couldn't let others define our happiness."

"So, what are you saying?"

"What I'm saying," he leant in conspiratorially, "and if you ever tell her this, I'll kill you — but Mary is the best thing that ever happened to me. That sometimes you have to embrace the change, to be willing to let someone in. To be open to loving someone, and being loved. To feel worthy."

"I—"

"Iris," he said, his voice firmed, "You're worthy. And I've been hoping that you'd find someone who'd make you feel that you're worthy. If that person is Daisy, fantastic. If it isn't, great. But you've got to stop shutting yourself off to possibility and running from the difficult feelings. Otherwise, you'll learn to stop feeling anything at all."

Mary came rushing into the room, apologising for interrupting. "I forgot the bloody stew! It'll be mush by now!"

After dinner, Iris retreated to her room to prepare. It wasn't an "outfitty" occasion, but she wanted to look presentable. She thought about what she was going to say, about her journey – journeys, she supposed – and what she could pass on to others.

The truth was, Iris was used to preparing, but – for some reason – preparing felt alien to her in this situation. Preparation for Iris was packing, schedules, travelling. Sharing was unpacking. It was about looking back, trying to catalogue a life she'd mostly left to chance and apply lessons she'd learned mostly through happenstance.

She was surprised to find her hand shaking as she got ready, a flicker of nervous energy she hadn't felt in a while.

She tried to calm herself by focusing on the familiar rituals of setting up the room. When they arrived at the hall for the meeting that evening – with its beige walls and plastic green chairs – she chose to focus on the things she could control. She set out the chairs, the literature, the candles. Greeted, welcomed and made small talk with people as they came in. Waited for her moment to come, trying to keep her mind busy to avoid letting any nerves creep in.

When the clock struck nine, the secretary opened the meeting, going through the usual routines and rituals until it was primed for Iris' big moment.

"My name is Iris," she said, speaking steadily, "and I'm an alcoholic."

She took a deep breath and continued.

"Sixteen years ago today, I walked through those doors for the first time—"

The familiar creak of the door broke the serenity. Iris's eyes, fixed on a point in the back of the room, held their focus. Her voice didn't waver.

"—and I'm not sure I ever stopped running until today."

And, right on cue, the door opened fully.

Chapter 38 – The Beginning

As always, Daisy was running late.

She'd had a busy day at work, followed by an intense therapy session where her therapist had insisted on digging into her past life – with Faye, with Marisol, with the kids, in the ring. It had, as her therapist was proving incredibly capable of doing, busted her wide open, leaving her emotionally raw. She needed a meeting.

She'd barely made it home for long enough to take a shower and eat a Pot Noodle before heading out to catch the bus – and, predictably, it was late. Unusually, she actually half-prepared what she might share. For the first time in six months, she felt a need to release herself: from Iris, from the kiss, from everything.

She needed a fresh start, a clean slate, and she had to accept that she might face a small amount of criticism and judgement from those in the meeting for letting a relationship in the rooms knock her off track.

But 12-step judgement was different from the judgement she faced on the street, or in the job market, or on the internet. Safe judgement. A kind of accepting judgement that meant, in a room full of fuck-ups, you had fucked up the most. A necessary bridge to cross, maybe even obliterate, for her own sake.

When the bus pulled up at the stop nearest to the meeting, the smart thing to do would've been to run to minimize her lateness, but… not in these heels. She lit a cigarette and smoked it slowly, procrastinating. If she was going to bare her soul, she was going to need to steady herself as much as possible beforehand.

She arrived at the hall, straightened her outfit – appearances mattered, even to herself – and took a deep breath before she opened the door and slipped into an empty seat in the back row, avoiding eye contact with everyone.

She took off her scarf and coat, and settled in to listen. The speaker was already in motion.

Iris.

"—and embraced a new life. A life of sobriety."

Holy shit.

"I figured out that I was an alcoholic long before I admitted it to myself on an overnight in Warsaw. I had been drinking constantly for months, years even. I'd been responsible for the safety of tens of thousands of people whilst barely able to see straight, and when I wasn't responsible for others, I was working hotel bars like a prostitute, selling my company to businessmen for alcohol."

A few scattered laughs rippled across the room. Laughs of recognition. Daisy recognised herself in that.

"Not for sex – I almost gave my dad a heart attack then—"

Pete reacted – looked relieved. *Wait.*

"—but just an honest exchange of conversation for alcohol. Because that's what this addiction costs. I'd already spent all my own money on the drink, and now I was giving away myself to fund the addiction."

Giving away herself. Not for sex, but for conversation? *Jesus, she's a much classier whore than I ever would've been*, thought Daisy.

Iris stopped and took a breath. A dramatic pause, maybe?

"After my mum died, shortly before Warsaw," she continued, "I saw my dad – you know him as Pete – struggling. Now, I'm not going to retell his story, God knows we've all heard that enough—"

Laughter around the room. *Everyone* knew Pete's story, but he'd kept the Iris part secret.

"—and we'd argued and fought about her death but the truth is, I'd judged him too harshly. You see, I ran from my parents—"

Because they were too nice? Daisy thought.

"—because all they did was drink and fight, ran as far as I could, travelled the world… but what I didn't see when I came home for the funeral was the progress they'd made."

Oh. Iris stopped to smile at Pete.

"Not that I took the time to ask, or even paid enough attention to notice, but they'd stopped drinking long before I'd come home. And after I made the decision to get sober, he helped me to get sober. He became my higher power, I guess."

Daisy was still reeling from the revelation.

"And so, I came home. Initially just for a while – long enough to get clean, sober, stable – before going back on the rotation and back out to travelling. And I got to see the world. Really see the world. The people, the beauty, the culture. I got to know myself."

She paused again, to take a sip of her coffee.

"And I had to come to terms with what I'd done. The trail of destruction I'd left across Europe. I spoke to my bosses, told them what was happening, and they were understanding but, understandably, grounded me until I could prove I was sober. And dad helped me to do that."

Daisy found herself nodding. She knew about leaving trails of destruction.

"And then I went back on the road. Not to run, but to return to normality. Or, as close to my normality as I could get. Eventually, I started to make that amends list – the easy ones, like my dad – I could handle. The harder ones, like my mum, weren't so easy."

Iris made eye contact with Daisy for the first time.

"But, as we all know, the work doesn't stop with the apologies. I had to keep taking stock of my life, working out who I was and what I wanted to be. I mean, dad has moved on, found Mary, built a lovely life for himself with her. I—"

Another sip of coffee.

"I wanted some of that. So, I talked to the airline just over a year ago and I came home. Took a desk job, a training role. Grounded myself. I decided that I was done running. I wanted to be around to build a life and be around my family. Maybe find one of my own."

Build a life of her own, Daisy thought, *not rebuild mine.*

"And this programme, it teaches us to build our lives through carrying the message to other alcoholics. And I found one. I had to listen to my dad's advice, and cut the bullshit."

She looked at Daisy again. Deeper, more intense.

"I found someone in the programme that I thought needed me but, in reality, I ended up needing her. I thought I could make her life better in the practical sense, by helping her to organise her life but I also found that she made my life better in the spiritual sense."

Florence bloody Nightingale, Jesus. Daisy thought.

"She gave me that sense of serenity, of happiness of… family."

Iris was starting to tear up.

"So, because an alcoholic can never have too much, too soon, I went to her, ready to turn whatever we were into something. Something real. And she kissed me. And I ran.

She just said it. Out loud. In front of all these people.

She was softly sobbing at this point.

"I ran. Again."

Mary offered her a tissue and put an arm around her to help her steady herself.

Eventually, she continued. "I ran, because for all the talk about how I'd wanted to settle down and make a life for myself, I hadn't figured out what that looked like. Hadn't prepared myself for what that might mean for me, what that might mean that people thought of me."

She ran because of me. Not because of me, of who I am, of my fucked-up life. The thought was a quiet epiphany: Iris didn't fear Daisy, but what Daisy represented – the end of a life on the run. Enough knowledge to end six months of confusion and frustration with a fragile peace.

Another deep breath. Another dab with the tissue.

"A few weeks ago, I was in Amsterdam. I had a long layover, and I did all the tourist things. Really engaging with the city, learning about myself through it. And, incredibly, I was able to name everything that I felt. And then—"

She shot another look at Daisy.

"I was in Nice this past week, and I saw a glimpse of the life that I really want. And I knew where I'd find it. So, I came home. I stopped running. And I hoped that maybe, just maybe, after six months of running, the thing I was missing would be right where I left it. It's selfish, I know, but that's what alcoholism is – a selfish disease."

One more deep breath, like she was building to something.

"One thing we learn in these programmes is that we don't just work the steps and stop. We keep working them. We always have a problem, and we always have to face them. I realised that I had a problem, a person I'd harmed and an amends to make."

A person she harmed. Not a problem to solve, not a project. Just a person.

"And once I've done that – whatever the outcome – I'll start again from step one with the next problem and the next problem and the next one."

She turned to look at the secretary.

"But I haven't had a drink today."

Daisy found herself letting out a short laugh, which she quickly stifled.

"Thank you."

The room erupted in thanks as Iris took her seat.

Everyone took their turn sharing back to Iris, telling her how much they'd enjoyed it and their own stories of working through the steps and relationship mistakes and overseas epiphanies and work drama.

Everyone except Daisy. Daisy's rigidly-planned share was meaningless now. She'd prepared to burn bridges, but she couldn't burn the bridge when it was right in front of her.

As the meeting drew to a conclusion, she slipped out, quietly.

Iris saw the lights come on and scanned the room for Daisy. She was gone. She panicked, weaving her way through the people hurriedly gathering and stacking chairs. Maybe she'd gone to the toilet? No sign of her in the bathroom, and she wasn't talking to Dad or Mary.

Iris rushed outside, into the night, scanning the darkness for any sign of life. Nothing.

And then it came. A small red light in the corner of the yard, where the picnic tables were.

"Daisy?"

A cloud of smoke soundlessly lit up the night.

"Nice speech."

"Thanks."

The red light lit again, followed by more smoke.

"Is she worth it?" Daisy asked. "The effort?"

Iris sat next to her on the table. She let the question hang in the air, a final cloud of smoke on a night of revelations. Daisy took another drag, and in the small silence, a single thought echoed in her mind: *Am I?*

Iris gently took the cigarette from her hand, her touch surprisingly soft, and watched it glow for a moment. Then, with a flicker of defiance, she threw the half-finished cigarette into the night. She rested her hand gently on Daisy's leg, her voice low but firm.

"Well," she said, "she fucking better be."

Acknowledgements

First of all, I'd like to thank my family for always being there to support and guide me; I can't thank you all individually, because there are too many of you, but I love you all.

Particular thanks go to my mother. This book wouldn't exist without her – her love of literature is probably the reason I love storytelling.

To Chloe, my incredible daughter: I told you not to read this, but you've got your mother's stubborn streak, so you probably did. I hope you didn't get scarred too badly.

To Nick: Thank you for the hours of amazing conversation, your support, your guidance, and for keeping me sober. You've helped me "cut the bullshit" for over a decade now. I'll get good at it one day.

I also want to thank my Sixth Form English teacher, Fiona Little. I have no idea where you are in the world these days, although I've tried to reach out to thank you personally. You were the first person (outside of my family) to acknowledge and encourage my writing ability. You were also the best English teacher I ever had – and not just because everybody in our class had a massive crush on you!

I'd also like to take a moment to thank some fellow writers. It's gauche to thank people for inspiration, but I think my influences are probably name-checked as pop culture references in the book, but I want to thank some of the writers I've been privileged to know personally.

I've been very privileged to have some excellent chats about life and writing with Allison Burnett, Annie Murray and the late Sir Terry Pratchett, and I'm grateful to all of you for your kindness, time and guidance. Terry, I promise I'll finally finish reading the *Discworld* books before we meet again.

Also, to Stewart Garden, for allowing me to keep my typing skills sharp by contributing to his Oxfordshire Music Scene magazine on and off for far longer than either of us wants to admit.

Finally, to you, the reader. Thank you for being you.

Resources and Support: The Map for Your Afterlife

If the "disaster" is currently happening, or if the "afterlife" feels too heavy to navigate alone, these people can help. No judgment, no flowery nonsense—just support.

On Gender Identity and Transition

Mermaids (UK): For when the world feels too small or too hostile. They've been on the front lines for trans and non-binary people for a long time. [mermaidsuk.org.uk]

Gendered Intelligence: A trans-led crew who actually get it. They work on the ground to make life for trans people more than just "surviving." [genderedintelligence.co.uk]

The Trevor Project (Global): Specifically for the younger ones. If you're under 25 and in crisis, they are awake 24/7. [thetrevorproject.org]

On Sobriety and Recovery

SMART Recovery: If the "higher power" talk of AA isn't for you, this is the science-based, self-empowered alternative. It's very much in the spirit of Daisy's "roadmap." [smartrecovery.org]

Alcoholics Anonymous (LGBTQ+ Meetings): If you need the rooms but want to make sure you're with people who understand *all* of your identity, look for "Pink Chip" or LGBTQ+ specific meetings.

We Are With You (UK): Free, confidential, and they won't lecture you. They deal with the messy overlap of alcohol, drugs, and mental health. [wearewithyou.org.uk]

On Mental Health and Crisis

Samaritans (UK): The gold standard for when you just need a voice in the dark. Call 116 123 anytime.

Shout: If you can't face speaking out loud, text 'SHOUT' to 85258. It's 24/7, silent, and vital.

On Bereavement and Loss

Cruse Bereavement Support: The big one. They offer the space and the helpline to help you make sense of the pain when it feels senseless. [cruse.org.uk | 0808 808 1677]

The Good Grief Trust: An "umbrella" network that stops you from having to search a dozen different sites.

They'll point you exactly where you need to go for your specific loss. [thegoodgrieftrust.org]

AtaLoss: A straightforward search engine for support. Filter by your age, location, and the type of disaster you're navigating. [ataloss.org]

Specialist Support for LGBTQ+ Grieving

Switchboard (The Grief Project): Based in Brighton but a beacon for the whole community. They understand that our grief often comes with "extra" baggage like family estrangement. [switchboard.org.uk]

The New Normal: Peer-to-peer support. No experts, just people who have been through the blast radius and stayed to help others through it. [tnn.org.uk]

On the Loss of a Partner

WAY (Widowed and Young): If you've lost a partner before your 51st birthday, these are your people. They have a brilliant, "glittery" LGBTQ+ subgroup. [widowedandyoung.org.uk]

Sue Ryder: Beyond their shops, they offer serious online counselling and a forum specifically for LGBTQ+ grief. [sueryder.org]

A Letter from the Author

Dear reader,

First and foremost, I'd like to thank you for reading my debut novel, *The Afterlife of a Disaster*. Chances are that you parted with your ever-more-precious hard-earned cash to buy this, in whichever form you chose, which means the world to me in these trying times.

I'd also like to thank you for spending time with *me*. Or, a version of me, I suppose. In the publishing industry, they call this genre "autofiction", which I can't decide if I consider the most pretentious thing I've ever heard or like an unnecessarily clinical name for the note one leaves before going to a noose.

Autofiction is supposed to be a heavily-fictionalised autobiography, where all the events are true but attributed to fictional characters to keep those involved out of court. This, technically, isn't that.

Daisy, in her various phases of life, is based on me. On the many personalities I've held as I've grown through adulthood. Many of the events are based on real events; many of the people on real people.

But the first rule of fiction is "write what you know." This book is probably 60-70% fiction. Even the things that are based in truth are things that I couldn't have recreated 100% faithfully even had I wanted to – memory is fallible (especially when you've been hit in the head with steel chairs as many times as I have), and real life is often more boring than romantic. And literature is supposed to be romantic.

In fact, the reason this book exists at all is that my mother has been saying, for years, that I should write a book. An autobiography, maybe, because I've lived an interesting life. But autobiographies are for old people. People reaching the end of their lives, who have achieved great things and want to leave the full story for their fans, friends and families.

I am, in the grand scheme of things, a nobody. More importantly, I'm not old. I'm 40, with 41 on the horizon. Aria, as a lived experience, isn't even a teenager yet.

With that in mind, I wanted to take a little time to share a few insights with you into the correlation between this book and real life. Obviously, most people won't read this letter – and if you prefer not to have your head canon shattered, I recommend you stop now – besides, you've already read 90,000+ words that I wrote – but for those who have questions, I hope this helps.

Daisy's parents appear as peripheral characters in the book, mentioned in passing, and I think it'd be easy to draw the conclusion that if Daisy is based on me, her parents must be based on mine.

It gives the impression that Daisy is somewhat detached from her parents – this is honestly dramatic licence in a lot of ways (although the coming out stories are true). I have a very good relationship with my mother, and I've been blessed to have two fathers, both of whom have repartnered (is that a word?) since. I have a good relationship with both of them. They appear in the book as peripheral characters purely for time and relative distance to the core story. And, to be honest, Daisy's mum is nothing like my mum – Daisy's mum is very much a typical British mum archetype on purpose.

Even had I wanted to, I hadn't the room to include analogues to all of my family – I am blessed to have a dozen step- and half-siblings and their assorted partners and children. Maybe they'll get a spotlight in a future book.

As for the other characters, and their level of reality, I'll just checklist them. There was a Faye, there is a Marisol. And, yes, many of the references to them in the story are very much based on events that truly happened.

Most of the Faye arc is real – although I didn't sit on the beach for an hour after the scattering of her ashes. This, in many ways, is the conversation that I wish I'd had with her. Better late than never.

As for Marisol… yes, I actually did that to her. I was an idiot. But her life is pretty happy now, as far as I can tell. We don't talk very often, and her life isn't exactly as described in the book, but the fact that we talk at all is a sign that she's a better person than I deserve to know. Honestly, our relationship actually sounds a lot more mature and functional than it really was in this book, but that "Sliding Doors" moment I mentioned? I do still think about that, regularly. The one that got away isn't necessarily "The One," and I feel like "got away" is doing more work in that idiom than people give it credit for.

Olivia is a real person; obviously, I'm not going to give much more information than that. I have a daughter, she's wonderful (when she gets out of bed) and I don't get to see her enough.

Other side characters, Shane, Sophie, Martin, Jason, etc. are either based on real people or amalgams of people. Some are entirely fictional. I don't know a Neil.

I have an Uncle Derek. Actually, if you include Great-Uncles, I think I have three of them. I don't know any of them well enough to assert that they'd behave in that way at a wedding – "Derek" is just the most generic uncle name I had in mind. Probably because I've got multiples.

Everyone else at the wedding is fictional – actually, they're characters that were protagonists in other book, film or sketch ideas I've parked. So, if you happen to stumble across a book I've written that features a gay tree surgeon, a renewable energy expert, a cycling accountant or an overly-cheerful estate agent, you'll know them already. They're that person you met at a wedding years ago and promptly forgot after promising you'd "keep in touch."

Pete and Mary are based very much a collage of some of the very kinds of people I have encountered in twelve-step meetings. I've not reproduced anyone's actual story in those scenes, any stories shared were deliberately as generic as possible. Every addict has a story to share, but it's theirs to share. I just tried to cover a few of the common genres.

The therapist is based on some of the many therapists I've had over the years, and will continue to have, I suspect. Likewise, Daisy's boss and colleagues are based on several bosses and colleagues I've had over the years.

Now, the elephant in the room.

I'm sorry, there is no Iris. Iris is a complete work of fiction. I tried to keep her from being a classic "Manic Pixie Dream Girl", but I have no idea if I succeeded. I am, in real life, single – almost painfully so. There hasn't, in fact, been anyone since Faye. But a girl is allowed a romantic fantasy from time to time, even if they know better than to expect them to come true.

If it makes you feel better, the cowboy bar audition scene? That actually happened to me. In fact, I wrote that scene less than a week after it happened in real life, and it's much less fictional than a lot of things in the book.

Now that I've shattered some illusions, I just want to talk about my relationship with some of the issues that Daisy encountered. It's very easy to include a list of resources, but that isn't necessarily as helpful as lived experience shared.

I am creeping up on 14 years of sobriety as you read this. I hope that I get there. All the stories I told in the book about drinking to cope with the things I'd seen and done, or to keep Aria quiet are true, or based in truth. So is the story about walking into a meeting, deciding I wasn't old enough to be an alcoholic, and leaving to go to the pub.

At my worst, I was drinking 20 pints a night and chasing it with a bottle of spirits (alcohol was affordable in those days), and putting everyone I know through hell. I was isolated, depressed and emotionally unavailable, and I did it for years. If this sounds you, please find and attend your local meeting. I promise you, it gets better on the other side. And whilst I say I've been sober for nearly 14 years, the greatest wisdom I ever heard in a room was that "the world record for sobriety is twenty-four hours." We count years for vanity, and days for survival.

Now, I know that, by law of averages, some of my readers – if not a large percentage as time moves on – will be trans, or questioning their own transness.

Chances are you got to this point because you either searched "transgender literature" (or similar) on Amazon or because that well-meaning friend who over-enthusiastically shows allyship by buying you everything with a rainbow on it stumbled across it and gifted it to you. If this was the one book of the 50 they've given you that you actually read, I'm grateful.

Everyone's journey is different. I knew I was trans from a very early age, I just didn't know the word for it. I grew up in the wrong time for it. You know the main beats, because Daisy lived them.

Now, I could throw out empty platitudes about how you are valid, and you are loved – and you are, but those mantras are losing meaning – but times are trying as I write this. We live in a world where fascistic billionaires have chosen us as their target to distract the masses from their contribution to the horrors of late-stage capitalism or, in many cases, their commission of the actual crimes that they persistently accuse us of.

Like Daisy, I am actually a law graduate. My specialism is Equalities Law, and the crimes that the LGBTQIA+ community are persistently accused of in rotation through the decades are my speciality. If you've ever looked at the statistics that the TERF community likes to pass around to condemn us and wondered about them or, worse, taken them as truth without question, I want you to know the facts.

Trans people – men, women and enbies – account for less than 0.01% of all crimes committed worldwide. When it comes to sexual offences, we are responsible for a microscopic number as a community. When I wrote my master's dissertation in 2021, I tried to cover as many of these alleged crimes as I could find. I found less than twenty instances of any note, and I searched back as far as records would allow – well over a century.

There are people who accuse us of being dangerous criminals who, given their history, may have committed 20 crimes in the time it has taken you to read this letter. And almost certainly have in the time you took to read the book.

There is, categorically, no correlation between transness and criminality. Or, at least, perpetration of criminality. Sadly, we're rapidly rising the charts when it comes to victimhood of criminality – and all at the say so of corrupt billionaires, powerful convicted sex offenders and writers who are so terminally incapable of accepting valid criticism that they've chosen to take it out on our community.

Chances are that, if you're trans and reading this, you've been the victim of at least one hate crime and, more than likely, a sexual assault. I know I have. I'm sorry that you've been through that, and I wish I could make both the past event and the remaining trauma go away. Sadly, at this time in the history, it has become more important than any time in my life to protect the dolls, and for the dolls to protect themselves.

If reading this has triggered any feelings around bereavement, I actually do recommend the resources in this book. I haven't used them, but writing this made me realise that I'm in no place to give anyone any sage advice about dealing with loss. Although, it turns out, writing a book helped. It was the most cathartic experience of my life.

Finally, I'd like to address the idea of poverty expressed in this novel.

As I said, Daisy is based on me. Heavily. Daisy's poverty very closely mirrors my own, real life, state of poverty. It's reasonably likely that I'll be bankrupt and homeless within a year of writing this letter. And whilst I could make another joke about the horrors of late-stage capitalism here, the truth of the matter is this: poverty isn't caused by a lack of desire to work. I'd love to work, and writing this book was an attempt to fill the void that work has left. As, I suspect, will the next one be. And the one after that.

Poverty is caused by a lack of opportunity. In my case, I tick the boxes that employers are supposed to value: I'm highly educated (not a brag, I just assume that having two degrees makes me "highly educated"), I have a wealth of work experience, and I'm both competent and personable. Unfortunately – and this is not an accusation of any particular employer, before you try and get litigious (although you know who you are) – I *have* lost jobs because I'm trans.

And I've heard how very, very quickly recruiters' demeanour changes when they realise that Aria Sky isn't a perky 22-year-old cis girl. Yes, we see that. You don't hide it well at all. Just be very grateful that it's almost impossible to prove a "look or tone of disgust" at an employment tribunal.

Here in the UK, at least, the government is actively legislating to remove trans people from public life. Never in obvious ways, but the more creeping, insidious ones. By removing our access to healthcare, they hope they can stop us existing. And, when we rebel and go DIY – which is unsafe, but unfortunately necessary – they legislate to stop us using bathrooms based on the falsehoods previously discussed.

This is where they get clever: if you can't use the bathroom – either because of government or company policy, or just because you'd rather not be sexually assaulted by a cisgender man (they only commit over 96% of sexual assaults, but trans girls are the problem, allegedly) – you can't work. I don't care how determined you are, it is neither healthy, plausible nor, indeed, possible to hold your bladder for an entire 40-hour work week.

If you can't pee, you can't work. If you can't work, you can't afford to eat, rent a home, pay bills, buy meds, or exist socially in society.

Never let anyone fool you: a bathroom bill is never *just* a bathroom bill.

People want to believe that trans people aren't being discriminated against, to bury their heads in the sand. The reason this book is self-published isn't due to a lack of quality (I believe). I've had some very candid conversations with agents over the past few months who have told me, outright, that most publishers simply are not considering trans authors right now. It's too big a risk, allagedly.

Torrey Peters – as much as I love her work, because her work is truly phenomenal – cannot be our only voice in the literary mainstream. Not because her voice is wrong, but because she cannot live all of our lives for us. We, like 40 year old women, are not a monolith.

I realise this letter went from being gracious, to helpful, to political, factual, and depressing very quickly. As I said, you've just read 90,000 words that I wrote, and now, you've read 2,500 more.

If you got this far, I probably did something right.

If you'd like to ask any questions, discuss things further, offer me a job, movie deal, money or advice, I can be emailed at chasinglamely@gmail.com. I thought about setting up a website, but that felt like a lot of work for one book.

If you'd like to hang out with me more often, I create YouTube content under the names "ChasingLamely" and "ChasingLamely: Queer Law and Life." I also stream regularly (almost every night, as I write this) at www.twitch.tv/chasinglamely. It's mostly me playing video games where I manage, build or kill things, but you can literally ask me anything on stream, and I'll answer it unless it puts myself or someone else in danger.

I also have a Patreon if you'd like to support my work and call yourself a patron of the arts.

That's at www.patreon.com/chasinglamely.

Once again, thank you for reading my book. If I'm lucky, it changed someone's life – either their perspective or their mood. If I'm really lucky, it changed mine, and I'm no longer worried about homelessness a year from now!

Thank you for reading, and for being you. The world really is a better place for you being in it.

Aria Sky, January 18th 2026.

About The Author

Aria Sky is a forty-year-old trans woman, writer, and former paralegal living in Swindon, though she still considers herself in exile from Oxford. She has two law degrees and was runner-up in the 2017 *Legal Week* Legal Talent competition, but her path to law was far from ordinary: before returning to university at thirty, she worked as a bartender, professional wrestler, stand-up comic, actor, and journalist.

She has been writing since childhood – starting with a *Frasier* spec script at twelve – and her work now spans comedy, legal commentary, and journalism in music and sports. She also runs two YouTube channels: one dedicated to sports video games, and another providing legal advice for the queer community and practical guidance for aspiring law students.

The Afterlife of a Disaster, her debut novel, draws from lived experience but transforms it into fiction, asking what it means to rebuild when the world seems determined not to let you.

Printed in Dunstable, United Kingdom